Watchman

Watchman

D. G. Finlay

C

CENTURY PUBLISHING
LONDON

First published in Great Britain in 1984 by
Century Publishing Co. Ltd
Portland House, 12–13 Greek Street, London WIV 5LE

ISBN 0 7126 0238 0

Photoset in Great Britain by
Rowland Phototypesetting Ltd, Bury St Edmunds, Suffolk
and printed by St Edmundsbury Press
Bury St Edmunds, Suffolk

For Rosie
Without whose expert editorship this book
would have appeared sooner
but much paler.

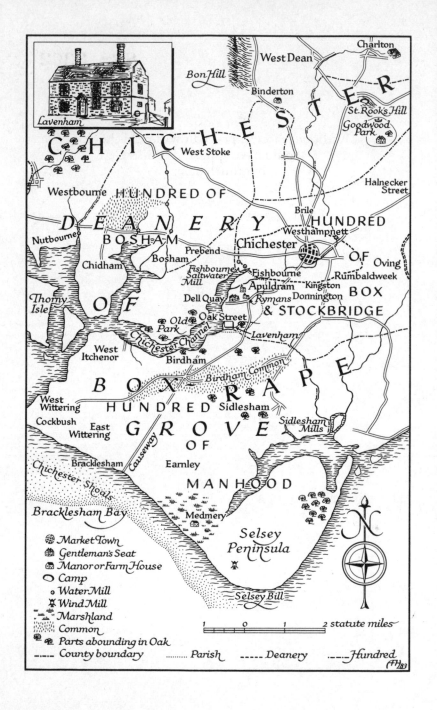

Charlton

West Dean

Bon Hill

Binderton

St. Rook's Hill

Goodwood Park

Lavenham

West Stoke

West Stoke

Westbourne HUNDRED OF

Halnecker Street

Brile

DEANERY HUNDRED

Nutbourne

BOSHAM

Westhampnett

Chichester

Chidham

Bosham

Prebend

OF Oving

Fishbourne Saltwater Mill

Fishbourne

Rumbaldweek

Thorny Isle

OF

Apuldram

Kingston Donnington

BOX

Dell Quay

Rymans

& STOCKBRIDGE

Old Park

Oak Street

Lavenham

Chichester Channel

West Itchenor

Birdham

Birdham Common

BOX RAPE

West Wittering

HUNDRED

Sidlesham

Cockbush

East Wittering

GROVE

Sidlesham Mills

Bracklesham

Causeway

OF

Earnley

MANHOOD

Chichester Shoals

Bracklesham Bay

Medmery

Selsey Peninsula

Selsey Bill

N

⊕ Market Town
🏰 Gentleman's Seat
🏠 Manor or Farm House
◯ Camp
○ Water Mill
🏯 Wind Mill
-·- Marshland
∴∴ Common
🌳 Parts abounding in Oak
-··- County boundary ·········· Parish ----- Deanery -··-·· Hundred

1   0   1   2 statute miles

(FH)33

Author's Note

When I embarked upon this series, I had little idea of the quantity of fine historical detail that was going to have to be accurately dove-tailed into the fictional plot. Having chosen a part of Sussex which is seldom written about but is rich in history and action, I soon discovered how difficult it is to superimpose a fictional family upon recorded events, mixing them with the forebears of families who are very much in evidence today.

May I therefore apologise to anyone reading this book – and those which are to follow in the series – if their own kith and kin are mentioned and there is any inaccuracy involved. I have spent a great deal of time researching the area and the lives of those who are mentioned here. With the exception of the Bayless Family and Lavinia Freeland, virtually all other characters in this book actually lived in the period covered, in the places mentioned and occupied themselves in the way that I infer. The Freelands are buried at Apuldram and Chatfields, Ayles, Beers and Cobbys may be found in churchyards all round the Chichester and Manhood parishes.

May I thank the Vicar of Apuldram, the Reverend Richard Ratcliffe, most warmly for his abiding interest and help and also the Phillimores at Rymans and the Sawdays at Manor Farm for their various contributions and co-operation. My thanks also to Alison and Peter McCann at the West Sussex Records Office and Rosemary Gilmour at the County Museum, Chichester and a dozen other occasional specialists. Last, but certainly not least, special thanks to Mrs Jean Willis, without whose constant and tireless perusals of almost every reference book published about West Sussex I would certainly have missed most of the juicy bits.

D. G. Finlay.
Chidham, 1983

Prologue

Jess Bayless was just past his fifth year when he was deemed fit
to join his cousin Fedor in the daily scouring of the woodland
for hedgehog or rabbit or even the chance of a fine fat bird. It
was the first time that he had been given the grub sack and was
dragging it happily after him as he worked through a tangle of
brambles and stinging nettles in that part of the wood which
surrounded the old Roman brick kiln. He could hear Fedor
some distance to his left, combing the shore where there were
plenty of holly bushes, a favorite hiding place for the crafty
hotchiwichi. Jess butted through tangles of ground ivy and
troughs of last year's fallen leaves, sharp eyes straining into
every shadowed place, alert for movement.

Something stirred nervously in the paper dry leaves ahead of
him and he stood quite still, hardly daring to breathe. All was
quiet and then there was another small shifting. It was a baby
hedgehog, too young still to have been separated from its
mother. Jess stood like a rock as his father had taught him,
trying to control the slight tremor of excitement in his stocky
legs. The little creature seemed suddenly aware of danger and
scuttled away through a patch of warm sunlight and shifting
grass. Jess, crouching low, legs scratched and sap-stained,
followed as quietly as his inexperience permitted, feeling a
twig snapping beneath his bare feet. His whole attention was
focused on his prey as he thrust his head through a curtain of
whippy hazel wands into a small dell – and it was as though he
had stepped over a cliff into space. He spun, falling like a stone,
his heart huge and thunderous in his chest. Then he realized

that he was sitting in a pool of warm light which seemed to come from around him rather than from the thick interlace of tree branches above his head. His chest was filled with a wild pounding and he stared about him in panic, badly frightened by the warning clamour of his instincts. He was in a slight hollow in a glade surrounded by dense undergrowth and ancient, twisted trees. They leant towards him like aged sentinels, the tangle of their woven branches spreading from gnarled and scabious grey trunks. Everything was bathed in a strangely bland golden light.

The glade seemed to hold its breath as he turned his head, taking in his surroundings. Nothing moved. There was no soft whisper of sea breeze through the tree branches; no comforting bird song, no small creepings underfoot from the tiny creatures that dwelt at surface level. The little hedgehog had vanished.

Jess leaned back on his elbows, giving way to a warm languor that had begun to sweep over his small body. The blood, singing in his ears, still sounded like thunder but he no longer felt afraid – only concerned with the dizziness that made his vision swim and brought a sick tightness to his stomach. He stayed very still and slowly the feeling drained away and was replaced by another, a strange . . . heady sensation. He waited, feeling it seep into him, filling him from the top of his dark curly head to the soles of his bare feet . . . coursing through him in a warm, smooth tidal wave of elation and strength – and POWER.

He was too young at that moment to know what that word meant, but he was well able to recognize the bursting sensation of pure strength and – unaccountably – he seemed to have the sheer muscle and knowledge of ten men. There was sound after that – and a kind of fear and anger grew in him and voices spoke in a tongue that he could not understand for there was a veil over the surface of this new awareness and behind it was movement and great heat and a young voice calling . . .

His eyelids were heavy and he sank into a dreaming state and watched Jasper, his father, planning the first of their owling expeditions with Master Tovey and Farmer Diggens in the Manor Farm kitchen.

He saw the first shadows of disease in his mother's body and knew that it would consume her. He saw little Amy and knew her to be as close a part of him as his own arm.

He saw a small girl with the corn and apple blossom colouring of the gorgio gentry and knew that his life would have the greatest significance in hers.

There was a period of floating during which he saw and felt nothing but the growing of his own body. It was as though he had been borrowed and then returned to himself.

He opened his eyes. The bright light had left the glade and it was just a pretty little dell with a moss-covered floor and for company some old grey stone boulders, mottled with dried lichen, half submerged in the undergrowth. He stood up uncertainly and pushed his way out through the leafy curtain. The hazel and nettles sprang back into place behind him. He notched a couple of tree trunks with his gutting knife to mark the entrance.

PART ONE

Amy and Jess

Chapter One

How long does it take a child to register abnormality in others? Certainly Amy Bayless was aware of her deformed foot by the time she had learned to walk, for she quickly discovered that she was not able to skip and run like Jess and her elder sisters. Frustration was soothed by the presence of Jess, who appeared to have decided from babyhood that he would be her protector against the rest of the world. They were rarely out of each other's company and the rest of the Bayless Clan quickly came to think of them as a single unit . . . Jess'n Amy. Amy and Jess.

It was Jess' 'differentness' which took its time to register in Amy's head – and she was three years old before it became conscious fact to her. She was not surprised of course, for, in her eyes, Jess was everything perfect rolled up in one small six year old. He was a gentle boy, loving and considerate towards his family and everyone else who earned his respect, and was already handsome enough to turn the heads of passers-by in the fairs and markets.

He was Jess and, like Amy, he was different. They closed ranks and were content. All the same, the way in which Jess differed from other people often worried Amy. There was no single way of putting a finger on it – but sometimes he would become abstracted in mid-conversation and a certain look washed across his face, making the warm grey eyes glaze over. When this happened, he became preoccupied with his inner thoughts and the whole of him seemed almost to lose focus so that the very contours of his body blurred over.

Since no one else appeared to have noticed this occasional

phenomenon, Amy accepted it as her own special vision of him.

There was no doubt about the first occasion that she had seen his 'differentness' used in the positive sense. It was the time that the Revenue men set up an ambush on Copperas Point. Jess had been quiet all day, working hard with the other boys on the wheels of cousin Naffie's wedding waggon. When the light began to go, they put aside the pots of fish glue and whippy felleys of seasoned oak and gathered round their fires, ravenous for the bread and soup whose fragrance had been teasing their nostrils for hours past.

Jess slumped down beside Amy who was sorting hazel rods beside the fire. He took his knife from his belt and began stripping the young rods, ready for the girls to cut up into clothes pegs to sell in the Thursday market.

The summer dusk was heavy with an oddly sharp brilliance; a backdrop of violet light, vivid within its own dying radiance. It threw an uneven pink tint over everything for a brief spell, so that trees and houses and all the contours of the landscape became etched in an eerie clarity. The moment faded, its lilac light sinking into blue dusk and the Evening Star was suddenly on display – a drop of white fire against black infinity.

'Pictures in the fire, Love? . . . They do say you can see your whole life in them flames if'n you look hard enough – an' if'n you can tell what you're seein' there.' Jess raised his chin from his knees and looked up into his mother's face. She stood beside him washed in shadow and rumpled his tousle of hair, combing the jet black curls upwards with her fingers. 'Your Puri Dai (grandmother) was one of those, Jess. She could tell.'

He caught the sigh in her voice and smiled up at her before turning back to the fire – feeling it there in his own eyes too; the drum of that other pulse beating in his temples. He needed to be alone with it, to get used to its strangeness for he could not share it with anyone yet – not even his mother.

He spread his hands out in front of him, palms up. The fire glow turned them the colour of new brick. They were steady. There was no tremor, although he could feel it coursing through his veins like a heartbeat – in his fingers and toes and inside his elbows and under his arms. He picked up his knife again, automatically testing its blade with the ball of his thumb, and continued stripping hazel rods which Amy took from him and piled up on the ground beside her. He watched her careful movements, wondering how long Romani folk had been doing these same things that he and she were now about. He knew all about their history, of course, for it was always learned at the Puri Dai's knee – and she had been proud of the pure Akbar blood in her veins and so the fireside stories had been wondrous tales, full of colour and excitement.

The Romani Wandering had begun over four hundred years before, in the north-west of India when a tribe of Harijans (untouchables) by the name of Akbar was driven out of their State and fled westwards through Persia and Turkey. They tried to settle in many places and succeeded for a time in Greece. What made them move on again was not known but by the beginning of the fifteenth century they were on the road once more, travelling north and always westward, through Germany and then France – until they reached the Channel. By this time they had learned to protect themselves against the pale-skinned Europeans and considered themselves an infinitely superior race. They were vigorous discoursers by nature, humorous and greatly given to mimicry. It was in France that they established the first recorded 'hoax' on the rest of the world – and which had clung firmly to them ever since. They had solemnly explained their presence by announcing that they were Egyptian pilgrims on a journey of expiation. From this colourful fantasy sprang the name of 'Gypsy' – and they would never lose it thereafter.

They were gifted storytellers and metal workers, mystics and minstrels and by the time they saw the English Channel they had traversed half the Earth, leaving behind them a litter of superstition and a growing reputation for dishonesty and thievery. Naturally, wherever they went they left a family or two behind them, for that was the way they lived – but the wandering ended when they landed on the shores of England for there was nowhere else for them to range except for Ireland.

The English were a very different race from the Akbars, cold and insular with their hearts fixed in the traditional past. They were deeply suspicious of the dark-skinned 'pilgrims' who had travelled so far, picking up the sophistication of many cultures as they went. The Akbars were not made welcome and so it was necessary for their survival to take what they needed wherever they could find it.

They had brought with them only two enduring things from the far away continent that had once been their home. The Sanskrit language which they came to call the Romani tongue – and their strong Indian culture, by now well-padded out with a dozen others. They had one other attribute – an overpowering will to survive as a People. That survival meant the consolidation of the group and rejection of all others. For a time they succeeded in keeping the strain relatively pure but with no further travelling ahead of them, it became impossible to control the natural mating urges of their young and there were many marriages outside the tribe.

The Akbars had changed their name to Hator during their wanderings, for it was realized that Akbar sounded too Mohammedan. When they reached the English shores and gradually began to scatter through the land, the name was changed again and again until there were Lockes, Boswells, Woods, Smiths and a score of others. Even so, the main Tribe retained its name of Hator. The Baylesses were descended from this line through Saiforella Hator, who had run away with a gorgio, Joshua Bayless. She had been a formidable woman who had never taken her husband's name although it seemed that Joshua must have insisted that his sons be called Bayless. They were Jasper and Piramis, Abram and Vasher.

A cackle of laughter floated across from Piramis' fireside and as usual it was Naffie struggling out of the trees with a cumbersome load for the wood pile. Naffie was a clown, always teasing and laughing – and usually somewhere else when the heavy tasks were handed out. You couldn't help having a fondness for Naffie all the same, for he was an incurable optimist and never a dull companion. Jess was glad that his cousin Naffie was to 'jump the broomstick' with his oldest sister Saiforella after the last lickerin' of the year. They would make a good couple for Naffie's tall colourful buffoonery was a perfect foil for Saiforella's more solemn beauty. She was the one who most resembled their mother with the gorgio blood coming out in the nut brown richness of her hair and a soft rounding to her features. The rest of them were all Romani Bayless through and through; lean and wiry with prominent cheekbones and hair as black as the crows that cawed over the salt pans.

As the last of the light drained out of the day, Jess and Amy paused in their tasks to watch the setting sun's red rim dip into the trees to be strained through the woodland lace like a great rosy plum. He held his knife firmly against his knee as he had been taught, blade upturned so that he could draw a hazel rod back and forth against it, skinning the bark cleanly from the wood. A carpet of bark lay in long curling ringlets about his bare feet, their soft white linings tinged pink in the fire glow.

Amy collected a last bunch of stripped rods and sat watching him solemnly, thumb in mouth. He gave her a wink and she dimpled at him.

She was so small that he could easily lift and carry her although she was five years old now, three years younger than he. The other sisters teased her, calling Jess her sweetheart, but there was no real malice in their words. He concentrated on the blade of his knife and went on turning hazel rods against it, trying not to think about the pulsing that was slowly building up within him. Unbidden, a thought took shape in his mind, forming so gradually and softly that it was some time before he registered it. Then he became aware and the feeling of growing conviction grew and deepened until its sudden urgency forced him into movement. He put his knife down among the bark curls and scrambled up. Amy laid aside the rods and pushed herself up onto her feet expectantly.

With Amy dogging his steps, Jess dodged between the benders, skirting Piramis' hearth and headed for the long Lickering sheds.

Jasper Bayless was clearing up at the end of the day with Piramis and Abram. The children could hear their voices echoing hollowly against the clash and thump of the dippers as they skimmed the last of the brine. An acrid stench hung in the air, waiting for a night breeze to lift it from the pans and filter it off through the woods and fields all the way to Chichester and the downlands beyond.

The two children peered down the gathering gloom of the Lickering shed. Their father and two uncles were hauling the last of the sludge from shallow wooden troughs through whose perforated bottoms the salt liquor dripped into stone jars. Watching them, Jess was suddenly afraid and called out to Jasper. The tallest figure raised his head and peered down the length of the shed. It was almost dark now and they had lit rush lights where they were working. A great well of darkness yawned between.

'Dada . . .' The boy's urgent voice made all three heads turn.

'Come down here, Chavi. Don't hide in the darkness . . . What's up with you?'

Jess hung back close to the door and the last of the evening light, Amy's hand gripped fiercely in his. After a moment his father strode down the shed, his shadow huge on the wall behind him, threading his way between the troughs and cooling pans. Jess' certainty had become tinged with a feeling of dread. It loosened the shyness that gripped him whenever he spoke with his father.

'Them Law men, Dadrus . . . They're to be in the woods just under the bank where the Point has a shale spread. Don't let me uncles go there, Dadrus . . . There's trouble in store for them. I feel it so strong.'

They stood in the shadows, close together. He felt a tremor in Amy's thin little body pressed against his side. Jasper Bayless' hand gripped his shoulder, digging hard fingers into Jess' tender flesh.

'What are you sayen' to me, Bor? How do you know this?' His voice was low and rough. Alarm bounced off him.

Jess shrugged, anxiously searching the pale blob of his father's face to discover whether he was believed. 'I don't know, Dada . . . but I feel it so strongly.' He tugged at the rough cloth of his father's jacket sleeve. 'You've not to let 'em go there. It feels real bad for them . . . I know it.'

They stood together in silence, locked in the probings of their minds. Then Jasper loosened his grip and gave the small

20

shoulder a pat. 'I'll tell 'em what you just said, Bor . . . can't do better than that. Tonight's a large load and Master Tovey'll be over to the store to see it delivered for once, so we can't disappoint him, can we?'

There was no more that he could do. He nodded and turned away, pulling Amy behind him. They left the long shed and retraced their steps slowly, hopping over the soggy ground and along the bank towards the glowing fires and the black humped silhouettes of the waggons.

He wondered whether Jasper would question him again for it was the second time in a week that Jess had warned him of impending trouble. The first time was while they were in the sheep market in East Street three mornings before. Jess had pulled his father away from the pens, moments before a large ram had gone berserk and broken from its tethering ring to run amok among the crowd. There had been plenty of cuts and bruises before he was recaptured and taken away.

It was not until later that Jasper had remembered the boy's words. 'Come away from there quick, Dada . . . It has the scent of you. It's going to bolt. Come away now.'

He had responded to the urgency of his son pulling him round the corner into North Street without thinking – but as they walked back to Apuldram he had stared down at his son's curly head thoughtfully. Jess realized that the incident would be discussed with his mother and the other adults in the Clan. Maybe that first warning would make them take this one seriously.

They returned to their own hearth and settled down again among their sisters and reached for their soup bowls. There was an air of departure round the firesides. Two more suns would be enough for the work ahead and then Abram and blind Vasher and their families would be away, for it was time to let the wind blow through the wheels of their waggons. It was the end of October.

Jasper returned to where his brothers worked in the flickering rush light, his hawkish face stern. They didn't question him but continued to haul the salt paddles out of the troughs, sluicing them down and scrubbing them with straw before stacking them against the far wall. When they had finished and were closing and bolting the heavy double doors at the end of

21

the shed Jasper said, 'Stay by your fires till I get back. I have to see Master Diggens before we tackle this night's work.'

The brothers nodded, knowing that Jasper would tell them all they needed to know when the time was right. He probably had word of a patrol. Better to be sitting in comfort and innocence round their fires, swapping gossip when the militia came snooping, than for them to come upon the Camp and find it full of women and children and not an able-bodied man in sight. The authorities knew the ways of the Romanies well enough to know that they never left the camp without one adult male to keep guard – unless they were up to some private business.

Jasper took one of the cobs and made off into the darkness, cutting across the newly-cleared fifty acre field and up over the Dell Quay waggon road into Manor Farm Meadow. Light edged the shuttered kitchen windows as he clattered into the cobbled yard. He hammered on the back door and waited in the rioting night as the bolts were drawn back. Light washed over him as the door was opened and he stood blinking away his night vision and touching his forehead as he recognized Mistress Diggens' stocky figure. Her husband was lounging comfortably in the high-backed settle beside a blazing hearth, long-stemmed pipe in hand and a dish of meat and pickled vegetables beside him. When he saw who it was at the door, Diggens rose and beckoned with no more than a perfunctory greeting and the two men clattered down the stone passage and into the parlour.

They stood in the darkened doorway, heads close together.

'Sorry to trouble you, Sir,' Jasper said. 'I've had wind of some trouble planned for tonight. Thought I'd better let you know right away in case you want to change the arrangements.'

He saw the sudden alarm on the farmer's weathered pink face. He was a good soul, Henry Diggens, but beginning to feel his years. Hard times had left their mark and he seemed older than he really was. His faded blue eyes searched Jasper's gaunt face, waiting to hear the rest of it. The hand that still held his pipe trembled slightly.

'I've heard that they plan to hide up in the woods below where we're landen' the goods and then jump us. I dunno if'n this be just a rumour, you understand. In any case, it's too late to warn the "Lady Jean" now for she'll already be on her station. What say you if we was to creep in and nab 'em in good time before the galley arrives?'

Diggens ran a hand through his sparse hair. 'Bless me, Bayless. That's all I need this evening. I've lost two swine since yesterday and one of the cows is in fever. Now you tell me the Revenue are on to us. How do I know whether you should jump 'em or not? How many are there waiting there? How many are there of you? We don't want bloodshed round here, you know that, Bayless. We've always managed to steer clear of trouble before . . .'

Jasper interrupted and his voice was gentle, as though he was soothing a child out of a bad dream. 'Don't you worry, Master – there'll be no trouble. They'll never know who hit 'em an' by the time they wake from a nice little nap, we'll have done what has to be done and be long gone, I promise.'

Henry Diggens looked suddenly old in the half light – a stocky, gaitered gnome with the weight of the world on his shoulders. There had never been any violence in their operations, but they had been lucky – and careful. There had always been one part of his mind that had acknowledged the possibility of discovery, ever since he and Geoffrey Tovey had begun night running. He was not a violent man and certainly had no wish to injure any official simply for the sake of his own purse. He listened to Jasper's quiet reasoning and was once again grateful for the man's good common sense. There would be no point in asking how he had come across such vital information. It was enough that they had been warned in good time. He gripped Jasper's arm and nodded till his jowls shook.

'There's Samuel Kirby and young Bray can lend a bit of muscle,' he said. 'If we don't know how many to look for, I dare say you could do with as many strong men as you can get.'

Jasper left him and looked into the long barn where the two labourers slept up in the hay loft. By the time the three of them were on their way back to the salt pans, the rain had begun to fall.

★   ★   ★

The men left the Lickering sheds like shadows in a dark sea, a quiet flitting of movement that was lost in the lashing rain. Jasper led with Abram at his side, Abram who matched Jasper in height but had a twisted left shoulder which gave him a gnarled appearance of suffering that he didn't feel. He was meaner in a brawl than the other three put together and twice as swift to take offence.

At their back Piramis followed with his two elder sons, Naffie and Tover and Abram's son, Jenk. Kirby and young Bray from Manor Farm followed as best they could for the Baylesses were used to the night and moved swiftly with scarcely the crack of a twig to betray their passing.

Blind Vasher, with his son Manfri, was already long gone to Oving, unaware of the danger into which he would be heading his dray in a short while. If Jasper could not flush out the patrol in time, Vasher would drive straight into an ambush out of which he might not emerge. He was strong as an ox and twice as willing but blindness is no help against such odds.

The wood had been whipped into such ferment by the wind and rain that it was unlikely that their progress would be heard by any watchers on the shore. Although there were only eight in the party, surprise was their main weapon and advantage. Surprise and their undoubted skills of tracking and field work.

The column halted and Kirby and Bray cannoned into the figures in front of them.

'Jenk . . .' The word was soft in Jasper's mouth, lifted up and carried away by the rattling branches around them. The boy was pushed forward from shadow to shadow until he crouched against Jasper, head close to his uncle's face to catch the murmured instructions. Then he was gone – away into the heaving darkness. He was just past his fifteenth birthday but already the finest tracker among them. The Law would never know when he found them for he moved with the waving shadows, as much a creature of the night as the wild things that dwelt in the shrubberies.

Time stood still and they waited, motionless, for Jenk to reappear. Then suddenly he was beside Jasper once more and the men leaned close, trying to hear what was said.

There *was* an ambush party on the shore. He had not had much trouble discovering them for they must have been there for some time already and were wet and disgruntled and becoming casual about their cover. There were five of them. Three militiamen and two Customs officers, both of whom he thought he recognized. If that were so it meant that the Baylesses would be recognized. The soldiers were armed with flintlocks, the others with cudgels. They were crouched in a shallow dip just above the bank over the shale beach. The tide was in because he had seen the luminous creaming of waves as the wind whipped it against the pebbles.

Jasper divided the group into two parties. There was little need for words for this had been their practice for some time past. He sent Piramis off with Naffie, Jenk with young Bray and closed his own group round him before striking out through the trees towards the north-west of the wood.

The Baylesses had good night vision made sharper by years of nocturnal activities. Jasper heard their quarry first and crouched, rock still, with a warning hand held out behind him. Somewhere ahead, no more than a few yards away, a man coughed. The sound was whipped away by a gust of wind, through the dripping trees. Jasper leaned forward and moved a bramble with one finger. A few yards away he could pick out the dim shapes of two men huddled together against the bulbous bowl of a tree. Metal clinked against metal and a voice muttered angrily. Somewhere just south of them an owl hooted. Piramis was also in sight of the prey.

A voice suddenly broke the silence of the teeming night.

'I saw a light on the water. Look . . . there it is again, Master Coombe.'

That was good, Jasper thought. It meant that the attention of the whole party would be focused out over the Channel. There was no time better than now.

The stick in Jasper's belt was swiftly transferred to his hand and he dived through the thicket with a roar that shook the saturated air. He had ordered that every man cover his face with his 'kerchief so that only the eyes were visible. Anonymous shadows – faceless ghosts.

The assault was so sudden and, at that precise moment, so totally unexpected that there was no time for any sort of defence. Crouching miserably in the sodden grass with all their attention directed at the yellow blinking eye out in the

Channel, they were felled from all sides. The man with the cough felt a mighty blow to his head which sent him sprawling – senseless – across the bank and down into the evil smelling mud. The armed soldiers were jumped from a different angle and the damp muskets wrested from their grasp as they were cudgelled to the ground beside the Customs men.

The whole operation was over in minutes. As Jasper lit the signal lantern swinging from his belt, its fleeting light stole over the figures of his brothers as they bent over the fallen Patrol, strapping their hands and feet together with their own belts.

'Not much satisfaction in that tussle,' Abram said with regret. 'I'd have had a better fight bussen' Parson Kelway's missus outside church gate.'

Chapter Two

It was a long time before Jess decided to share the Place with Amy. Even then it was not really sharing, except the secret of its locality, for he forbade her ever to go there on her own. It was the only thing in all his life that he felt he owned completely and it was just not possible to share its mysteries, even with one as deeply loved as Amy. She readily agreed with any promise he wished of her. In her heart, she wondered what all the fuss was about for it seemed a pleasant enough spot in a small dell, wedged deep within the tangle of thicket in the northern corner of Salterns Wood. It was just a quiet place with a few worn grey boulders, speckled with moss and dried lichen for company. Try as she would, she could feel nothing of the excitement and disorientation that it seemed to generate in Jess. Anxious to feel what he felt – to be what he was – she finally disobeyed him and ventured there when he was gone to market with their father. The only feeling she experienced was the guilt of going against Jess' wishes for the first time in her life. That – and maybe a little something else as well.

She had sat down in the middle of the glade as Jess did, back against one of the stones. She sat there for a long time with her eyes closed and her hands folded loosely in her lap.

It was summer and the air was warm and sweet and filled with the scent of trees and bruised grasses. She drowsed, waiting for the enlightenment that always came to Jess and feeling only a soft lassitude and the distant sound of voices. Lovers walking in the wood . . . children hunting for berries. They called and shouted a long way away, on the very edge of

27

her consciousness. The great power that made Jess feel things and see things, that made him able to flame a hedgehog at twenty feet without even lifting his hand to it, that filled him with such deep serenity; all evaded her.

As she opened her eyes on the empty place, she realized that the voices had been calling in some strange language that she had never heard before. They suddenly frightened her – and in the same instant that she scrambled to her feet she realized that they were gone and that the wood sighed quietly, only disturbed by the lightest of breezes rattling the tree branches over her head. The air was heavy in the little glade and no birds sang in the thickets. She put a hand on the old stone, seeking the comfort of its sun-washed warmth. It was cold under the small brown starfish of her outstretched fingers. Cold as the sea in winter. Cold as the grave. She backed away from the boulder, feeling a sudden animosity building up about her and fled through the crowded undergrowth, knowing she had disobeyed Jess and suddenly terrified of the force of his anger for it was there in the Place, accusing her . . . threatening her.

She had never been able to admit to Jess that she had disobeyed him, nor had she ever returned to the Place alone, but the depth of that unease remained with her and even acquired a certain sweetness in her memory.

Had it not been for Jess and his protective instincts, life would have been almost unbearable in those early years of life, camping beside the saltpans with the other members of the Bayless Clan. It was difficult enough to be a daughter of Jasper Bayless without also being his seventh girl. Jasper's brothers all had sons as well as daughters, but Jess was the only male child that Grace Bayless brought into the world, other than two sickly boys who died within days of their birth.

By the time Amy was born, Grace had had fourteen children of whom Amy was the eighth to survive. Maybe it would have been kinder had she not, for her left foot was turned inward at a misshapen angle and the leg that supported it was wasted. As an infant she had lived in a box under the waggon and from the first it was Jess who took her to their mother when she was hungry and Jess who slapped his sisters to get them to remember to change her and clean her small sore behind. No one noticed the little boy's anxiety about the delicate new baby.

A long time later she realised that had he not made himself responsible for her right at the beginning, she would probably have died within her first few months – unnoticed and certainly unmourned. As it was, she struggled with life and achieved an element of success for which Jess was largely responsible. It took her a long time to learn to walk on the stick-like leg and twisted foot, but Jess' grim determination became her own and between them they scorned the crutch that Naffie Bayless made for her. Jess was all the crutch she needed and slowly she discovered a crazy balance with a hand on his arm and the weight of his teasing and cajoling to boost her spirits. By the time she was three she could walk on even ground but depended upon the hand that always held hers for spiritual, rather than material support. It had been noticed that she was beginning to blossom into a wide-eyed and attractive toddler which earned her more attention and kindliness.

Grace Bayless became very sick and died during the winter wandering of 1714–15. Amy was not quite nine years old at the time. She studied Jess' grief at the passing of his mother with interest for she had never felt any emotion at all towards the calm gaunt woman who quietly governed the lives of Jasper and all his brood. Saiforella was married to her cousin Naffie the following June and May ran off with a sheep shearer in Hungerford during the next winter wandering. Nell, Mary and Jemma went into service in Chichester and all of a sudden the overcrowded tent held only Jasper and Jess, little Amy and Shoshi, who was a year older than Jess.

It was during the summer of 1716 that Jess met John Freeland. Amy afterwards decided that he had begun to change his outlook as a result of that meeting. Jess smiled at her and shook his head when she broached the subject.

'No – I was already looking ahead by then,' he said. 'Don't you remember our spying games? Shinning up the chestnut that grew beside Church Path so that we could peek into Rymans garden and watch the gorgios taking tea and the children playing on the lawn?'

She had remembered well enough, for it had been the first

time that she had seen the look on her brother's face that was usually reserved for her directed towards another. She had watched his unblinking study of the boy and his baby sister, playing beneath them, unaware of the audience over their heads. The boy was about Jess' age, a noisy tubby boy with a tousle of sandy hair and a good natured face well dusted with freckles. But it was the little girl who seemed to rivet Jess' attention. She could not have been more than two years old, a beautiful golden moppet with enormous cornflower blue eyes and hair the colour of ripening corn. She laughed with delightful abandon, as though the joy was being squeezed out of every inch of her. Seeing the rapt attention to her on Jess' face, Amy hated her at once.

They often climbed the tree to watch and observe the Freelands after that. They learned that the boy was John and the girl Lavinia, children of Master Thomas Freeland, Chichester Attorney and Steward of the Smyth Estates.

Jess and John finally met out fishing the River Lavant when they were still short of their teens.

Jess always took Amy with him on these expeditions for it involved little walking once a suitable location had been selected. On this occasion they had come up onto Apuldram Common through the fields, skirting Manor Farm and following the river inland to a marshy patch where the wild life was plentiful. They settled down to wait for fowl. The day was muggy and overcast with a hint of rain in the air.

Amy curled herself up small, content to watch Jess. Flaming his quarry required complete concentration and she had learned very early to meld with the bushes and remain perfectly still until he came back to her.

A family of ringed plover splashed and hunted among the reeds over to their right.

Jess squatted in the muddy water, watching . . . selecting. His face assumed a waxy pallor, his body a rigidity in which only his eyes moved, following a fat young male bird through the water. There was a period of total suspension. Amy held her breath as she sensed the enormous gathering together that was being manifested in Jess' head. Then there was a distinct flash – as though the sunlight winked sharply for a moment on a ripple of water. The plover dropped like a stone and the others flew upward with a thunder of frightened wings and swooped away, rising and dipping over the common to sink back to the springy turf round a bend in the stream. Jess stood up among the reeds and sloshed through the water to where the bird lay. It was warm, unblemished – and very dead. He stuffed it into his satchel with the rabbit they had downed on the edge of Hempstettle field and waded back towards Amy.

Then he noticed John Freeland. He was sitting further upstream among the bulrushes, fishing with a cane rod and a length of cord. Jess grinned as the boy fidgeted, constantly raising his line to examine the bait on its hook. He beckoned to Amy with his finger to his lips and they crept forward until they stood behind him, watching cast after cast.

'You'll never catch nothen' with that.'

The boy looked up and seeing the two ragged children smiled, unoffended and put on the forlorn face of a clown.

'Perrott from the Quay said they'll rise to hard cheese . . . but I've been here for hours and haven't seen a ripple.'

They surveyed each other, taking in the contrasts between them in speech and dress. John Freeland hesitated, unsure of himself.

The boy on the bank above him seemed like an apparition; tall, even graceful in spite of the raggedness of his clothing, and his face had such dark beauty that he could do little but stare up at him, mesmerized. The little girl beside him hung back shyly, the tangle of wiry black hair almost hiding her face.

Jess slid down the bank, removed the satchel from his back and sat himself beside the boy as he attempted to cast once again. The cheese went into the water with a determined plop, leaving a pattern of concentric circles on its oily surface.

'I'm John Freeland,' the boy said politely. He was square shouldered and almost as tall as Jess. His hair fell in light brown ringlets over a round friendly face, so that he was obliged to brush it out of his eyes every few minutes. He looked with regret at the undisturbed water and slack line curving idly against a lazy current.

'I know who you are,' Jess said shortly. 'Seen you often enough.'

They sat in companionable silence, gazing across the Lavant to the moorhens swimming in and out of the reeds on the opposite bank. Amy crouched uncertainly up the bank behind them, her stunted foot tucked out of the way beneath her homespun skirt.

'Want I should show you?'

John turned and nodded, making no effort to keep the relief out of his eyes. He hauled in his line.

'We don't use no line, Bor . . . You never seen a romani guddlen' for 'is supper, then?'

He saw the puzzled look on the boy's face.

'Guddlen's what we call catchen' fish with the hands, see? No good tryen' it here though. I caught a fine perch up through Burnt House meadows last week. Want to try there?'

They collected satchel, rod and creel and crossed the common, fording the Lavant where the lane from the old village of Apuldram crossed into New Fishbourne parish. They said little as they walked for Jess had a shut away look about him. Amy kept her eyes down and stayed close to his side and John, feeling unsure of these new friends, was content to enjoy some unexpected – if speechless – companionship.

'Do you do much fishing?' he asked eventually when the silence began to pall.

Cool grey eyes flicked over him and turned away towards the approaching curve in the river. 'Sometimes we fish when the rain comes – makes the fish rise, see . . . but mostly we traps in the woods, like. From now till Sloe Fair I'll be with me Dadrus and the others in the pans or the lickeren' shed. Then in October we go jallen' the drom.'

'Are you from Holland?' John had no idea what the strange boy was talking about. He could tell that they were foreign in some way for their skins were tanned, hairs a tangle of uncombed black curls and the high cheekbones had a southern look to them. He found the boy's thickly lashed eyes oddly disturbing. There was a deceptive gentleness about them that seemed almost like a caress but he knew, without knowing why, that they could chill to steel when they wished.

'I'm – I'm sorry. I didn't mean to sound offensive. I haven't heard words like those before, that's all. I thought you might be from Holland or Spain . . .'

The boy grinned broadly at him. 'Jess Bayless . . . an' this is Amy. We works the Salterns, south of Copperas Point. You

32

could say we was foreigners if'n you wanted. We're romanies – or at least me Puri Dai was pure blooded. My Mam was a gorgio, so I s'pose you'd say we're a mixture. We follow the creed though.'

John was intrigued. The boy seemed about his own age. On closer examination, he was not the ruffian that he had seemed at first sight, for there was a restraint about him that had nothing to do with the fact that he knew he was in company with Apuldram's most affluent son. He probably didn't even regard John in that light. There was a lack of affectation about him that had no familiarity or disrespect in it. He decided that he was going to enjoy the company of Jess Bayless.

They paused on the edge of the river bank by an old ruined cottage and Jess squatted on the balls of his bare feet, staring down into the stream among the reeds. After a while, he stripped off his shirt, lay flat on his stomach and plunged his arms into the slow-running water. There was no breeze in the overcast day, but now and then a drop of warm rain pitted the stream's glassy surface.

John crouched beside Jess, watching him intently. Nothing happened for what seemed a long time. Then – 'Ther'm three . . . maybe four fishes out there, d'you see? Over by that floaten' branch.' Jess' voice was little more than a murmur. 'Fish are funny, see. They like to lie among the weeds, under the banks or in the shallows an' let them tickle along their sides . . . Makes 'em all drowsy, like they was in a trance. Next – they see these long things that are my fingers, waven' around and they think, "here are some nice ticklen' plants for a good scratch" . . . and along they come and slip up against my fingers . . . an' I go on waven' and ticklen' until I feel that they've just about gone right off to sleep, see? Then I close both hands round 'em, real gentle . . . then up I comes with both me hands tight round 'em and flick 'im over onto the grass, neat as can be.'

He chuckled over his shoulder at John's rapt expression. 'Come on down here by me or you won't see how to do it, Bor.'

It had been a magical afternoon. They had caught three fish and one had even been John's own triumph. They lay on the bank, oblivious of the soft grey mist of rain that stole over them. Twice fish came to John's hands and twice he was too quick and they slithered away. When, at last he got a grip and brought the fish up out of the water and over his shoulder, he let out a whoop of joy.

'I've never done anything like that in my life. Just you wait till I . . .'

'No, you don't, young sir,' Jess said sharply, though his eyes still sparkled. 'D'you want me put in the stocks? Come on . . . No good tryen' any more after that ruckus. All the fish in this part of the stream will have heard you and hightailed it up to Chichester as quick as they can go.'

'Will you give me another lesson tomorrow?' John asked before they parted. Guddling was much more fun than sitting on the end of a cane rod.

And there was Jess. He didn't want to lose this intriguing new companion.

Jess nodded and put out his hand, palm up. Puzzled, John lifted his own hand and Jess pressed them together with a faint slap.

'That's how we shake hands, Bor,' he said softly. 'Don't forget it . . . It means friendship.'

Childhood proved to be an uneasy battleground for Amy's loyalties. There were so many contenders for Jess' affection and there were a few for whom Jess cared almost as much as he cared for her. Top of the list was Yoshi. Yoshi had been their waggon nag ever since Jasper had picked her up as a yearling at Tavistock Goosey Fair nine years before. She was a stocky, rough-coated little cob standing no higher than fourteen hands, short bodied on ample rounded quarters. She was placid and affectionate with an apparently limitless supply of energy. She had produced half a dozen tough little foals and only dropped two, which was something of a record. Proud of the health and strength of the little horse, Jess loved her absolutely and gave more attention to her daily welfare than the rest of the Bayless Clan gave to the whole string of their horses put together.

Jess' attentions to Yoshi constituted no great threat to Amy. She had no personal feeling for animals, her own survival occupying the greater part of her attention but, because Jess loved Yoshi, Amy was prepared to be nice to her also. Even Jess' friendship with John Freeland was not too difficult to accept, for he was a cheerful and uncomplicated companion and always treated her with a courtesy that she had never received from her own people. But the way Jess' eyes lit up whenever there was mention of little Lavinia Freeland somehow turned her stomach. It mattered not at all that Jess had never met Lavinia – or that the child was still in her baby frocks. Instinct put Amy's hackles up at the mention of her name and she would inch closer to Jess and slide her hand into his for reassurance. He, amused at her anxieties, was nevertheless touched, for he was all too aware of their father's disregard of this small cripple.

Amy was with him, as usual, when chance played into the hands of the Baylesses and they spied the Arab stallion.

They were on their way back to Sussex from the West coast near Barnstable and had camped overnight by a stream in the gracious parkland of some nobleman not far from Salisbury. Naturally they had availed themselves of the produce in His Lordship's woods, finding them well-stocked – and no keeper lurking in the vicinity. It did not take them long to discover that they were looking at a very fine deer park and were sorely tempted to poach themselves a young deer. They resisted this temptation for it would have meant that they'd have had to move on straight away and this was not convenient for they needed to gather good quality hazel for tent rods and clothing pegs. They contented themselves with cutting hazel, washing their clothes in the fast running stream and doing a little surreptitious snaring with gratifying results.

It was while Jess and Amy were crouched on the edge of the wood that he saw the stallion. It was grazing only yards away from him in a fenced-off paddock which sloped downhill through a scatter of gorse bushes to the stream. The horse was the most beautiful creature that Jess had ever seen and he squatted with his hand gripping Amy's arm, watching the fluid dignity of his movements and the perfect column of his neck and head as he cropped languidly from tuft to tuft. Proud and stately with perfectly-fashioned quarters, his glowing chestnut coat shone in the February air as though it had been buffed with a polishing leather. Unbelievably, the mane and tail were the colour of bleached silk. Their contrasting colours were riveting.

Even as they watched, the stallion seemed to sense their presence and his head came up, ears pricked forward as he moved up to rummage in the thicket, sniffing and blowing – a bare yard from where they crouched. Jess stared through dead brambles at the magical creature, longing to stand and run his hands over its withers and fondle those sensitive ears which even now sought to identify the two children. A wild and impertinent thought came to him, quickening his pulse and he nudged Amy, signing her to follow him as he backed quietly away from his magnificent 'find'. Grinning with the simplicity of his idea, he took Amy's hand and threaded his way back through the bare wood.

'Dada,' he said to Jasper. 'There is a fine stallion in a field on the other side of this wood. Coat the colour of chestnuts and, you wouldn't believe it – golden mane and tail. I never saw a horse the like of that one. He's only a little way off from here . . . Not far for Yoshi.'

It was a moment before comprehension dawned on Jasper's gaunt face. He looked across the grass to where Yoshi was tethered to a tree in case her urges drew her elsewhere. Most certainly she was ready, for she had been mokada (in season) for over a week. Looking at the usually complaisant Yoshi's impatient stamping and rolling eyes he nodded, a rare smile softening the hard lines round his mouth. Yoshi was very ripe indeed for mating. 'Show me,' he said.

The rest of the operation had not been difficult despite a few anxious moments. A study of the paddock revealed that the stallion was alone and that he was taken in each night. The perfect moment came soon after dawn when a groom brought the horse to the field.

Jess had been waiting in the wood for most of the night and, as soon as he spied the dim shape of the stallion cantering down the field from the distant gate, he doubled back through the wood and, with Jasper, Shoshi and Amy circling, watching out for keepers, brought Yoshi through the stream and into the trees. He had not wasted the time spent waiting for the stallion. With infinite care he had removed two fence palings and now he led Yoshi through the gap. They were well below the crest of the slope at that point and the whole spread of the lower paddock was broken by gorse bushes. It would not be possible to see what was going on from the gate at the top of the field.

Yoshi and the stallion took to each other at once with little encouragement and surprisingly few displays. It was almost as though they realized that this was a clandestine mating for they circled each other with rolling eyes and soft whinnies and Yoshi was quickly submissive. Jess and Jasper prowled round the paddock perimeter, alert for the first suggestion of movement as the dark grey dawn lightened into day. The only life they saw was a solitary rabbit loping away from them between the mole hummocks.

It was over quite swiftly without damage to either horse except for a small cut on Yoshi's brown woolly shoulder. Jasper held the now anxious stallion while Jess looped a rope halter over Yoshi's head and led her away through the gap in the fence. Jasper followed after them to repair the breech in the railings.

For three successive mornings the same routine was followed – and then the weather broke. There was no point in staying on the site any longer and so, by the time the early morning rain had cleared, the Baylesses and their waggon were two miles down the road with their faces turned towards distant Apuldram. They had stolen nothing – nothing, that is, that the beautiful stallion had not been eager to give . . . On the other hand, they had possibly gained a rare treasure.

They continued back towards Sussex, rolling the days away at the leisurely pace of the waggon wheels.

Yoshi foaled at Apuldram after Jasper had delayed taking to the road to ensure the best possible conditions for her and the prime new blood in her. She had had no trouble during the eleven months of her gestation and there was considerable interest in the Clan as to the quality of the foal she was to drop. When it was clear that her time was imminent, Jasper allowed Jess and the two girls to be present and Amy was told to keep well clear as she might not be able to move out of the way quickly enough. It took two days for Yoshi to decide that the right moment had come and then she became restless and

37

tetchy, swishing her tail and snorting deep in her throat as she nosed about the salterns shore. Finally she permitted Jasper to settle her in the lee of the waggon, out of the wind and sheltered by the woods, by which time it was clear from the milk pearls on her teats and the sag of her hind quarters that labour was under way. It was her fourth pregnancy and she seemed quite calm in spite of her constant peerings round at her flanks.

Jess slept close to her for two nights, worried that she might foal fast without the attention she undoubtedly deserved. As expected, she came to term during the third night and dropped her foal without any assistance, in spite of the size of the little creature. Jasper had been concerned that the Arab stallion might cause too large a foal for Yoshi to deliver safely and he was indeed larger than any of her previous young. As he was born, Jess drew in his breath, entranced – for even before the exhausted little creature was cleaned of its membrane bag, he could see the pale gold of its sticky mane and tail and the promise of burnished beauty in its wet coat.

It had been a magical event for the children, in spite of the fact that they had seen several of the waggon horses foaling over the years. Yoshi was such a calm little cob. Motherhood came easily to her and she was proud of the long-legged and graceful foal of unusual size and colour, inspecting him as she cleaned the membrane and secretions from his nose and eyes and coat. She was on her feet within half an hour and in no time she had nuzzled and nudged the little colt onto his wobbly feet.

'Oh, look at him, Dada,' Jess had said to his father. 'He has just one white sock. May we call him Olivas?'

And Olivas he became, as surely as he was also Jess' own horse from the very first moment.

The mating of Yoshi with the Arab stallion had been a most fortunate union, for Olivas developed the strength and health of his sturdy little mother. Combined with the grace and fine proportions of his sire was the promise of speed and endurance in his fine shoulders and quarters and, within months of his birth, it was clear that, in Olivas, the Baylesses possessed a horse that was beyond their wildest dreams. It introduced a new kind of problem for if they took him on the road with them, the chances were that they would be accused of stealing him and find themselves up before the magistrate in some distant court, too far away from Sussex for proof of their ownership to be possible. If that were avoided, it might be even harder to prevent him being stolen along the road. They wisely left him in the Home meadow at Manor Farm and Jess keened and fidgeted to be back with him during two winter wanderings. Then the pattern of their lives was changed by Jasper's death.

Chapter Three

1721 was a difficult year for Amy. Just after her fourteenth birthday, Jasper Bayless collapsed in the lickering shed and was dead before his brother Piramis could get him back to his tent. Such an unexpected tragedy decimated the Clan for Jasper's wisdom and confident leadership had permitted them to make a steady living from the contraband runs with the minimum of risk. It was quickly realized that neither Piramis nor Abram had the same strength and ruthlessness to carry on the work without supervision. Within the month they had fallen foul of the law and cousin Jack Bayless had been caught and deported to the colonies for ten years. A week later, Abram had his left ear blown off by a close shave with a musket ball and Naffie broke a rib tackling the Riding Officer who had fired the shot. Neither Diggens nor Master Tovey were determined enough to continue risking their capital without a properly organized gang and decided to cease their activities for a period.

Piramis and Sarey Bayless discussed the futures of Shoshi and Amy at length and eventually found work for both girls – Shoshi over at Donnington House where she became nursery maid and Amy up the road in the Manor Farm kitchens assisting Mistress Diggens.

It was a traumatic separation for Amy. She had never been outside the family in her life, never been without the constant comfort of Jess' support and affection. It was strange and frightening to find herself in a house built of bricks and mortar for the first time, separated from the sounds of the countryside and the comforting wind in the trees. Houses, she discovered, were cold places filled with unpleasant smells and dust and bad humours. Mistress Diggens was a kindly enough person who understood the girl's timidity and slowness and made no effort to hasten her about her work. It was a new experience to be in the company of a woman who spoke gently to her. After the inevitable misery of the first few weeks, she discovered that her natural cleanliness was much appreciated and that her mistress actually approved of her. It did much to settle her in the Manor Farm kitchens.

Henry Diggens suffered two strokes when Amy had been with them for just under three months. He needed constant nursing and the kitchen became Amy's own kingdom since her mistress spent the greater part of each day upstairs with her husband. She came to depend on Amy a little more each day. Henry Diggens died of a third stroke shortly before Christmas. The months of waiting for this moment had not been wasted for Master Freeland, the Estate Steward, had tactfully made preparations for this sad but inevitable conclusion. Mistress Diggens and her young daughter had been moved into a tithe cottage on the Selsey road and a young farmer from Felpham called Thomas Chatfield had moved into the Farm with his bride of a few months. They had been very glad to employ Amy for the house was large and rambling and Mistress Chatfield was four months pregnant. For the first time in her young life Amy found that she was being depended upon and that the responsibility pleased her. She was able to visit Jess each week on her free day and she was growing tall and straight so that the game leg was scarcely noticed until she moved.

The cowman began to take an interest in the Manor Farm kitchen maid and it was noticed that John Blunden from Rymans was over delivering messages a great deal more often than he had before. Amy ignored both her suitors and kept her eyes down on her cooking and cleaning. They simply didn't exist for her, however often Blunden appeared with posies from the Rymans garden and Sam Kirby dawdled over his quickfare and tried to engage her in conversation. Her eyes were on her work and her mind was away in the woods with Jess.

After Jasper's death, when he had been buried beneath an

oak tree and his waggon and all possessions burned according to their custom, the family had broken up. Naffie and Saiforella left Apuldram and settled in the New Forest. Piramis and blind Vasher Bayless felt that they had had enough excitement and were content to work the saltpans in summer and help with the harvest before taking to the road for the winter roving. It had seemed a natural move for Jess to build his own bender in the woods for he had always preferred his own company – Amy hardly counting as a separate entity. The only thing that caused comment was Jess' choice of location for his new home. The glade at the northern end of the wood was full of unseen spirits who seemed to disturb his uncles and cousins for instinct told them it was a place filled with ancient death. Jess was unconcerned at their distrust. It would ensure that he was seldom disturbed by the Clan unless there was a good reason.

With the establishment of his home in the Place, Jess began a period of adjustment which became one of the happiest times he had ever known. The excitement the Place stirred in him gave him renewed confidence in himself and strengthened his resolve to build with bricks and mortar a proper home on that very spot so that he could protect his invisible Spring from . . .

It was odd but he could never decide just what it was that might endanger the Force in him. Its strange pattern of soundless voices had been the same in his head for so many years that he knew each inflection by heart. The uncomfortable surging in him during his moments of recharging no longer worried him as they had done as a child. The only worry he did have – and it grew with every passing day now – was that the strength of his instincts was gradually lessening. For the first time, he began thinking of life without the Power. It was this realization that time was no longer his ally that finally decided him to form his own smuggling gang.

It had taken time to put together a new group of men who were reliable and who would respect and obey one so young. The first volunteer had been John Blunden who was the son of the Rymans cook and Thomas Freeland's man servant. He worked in the garden at Rymans and was a solid, reliable giant, some twelve years older than Jess.

John Freeland, of course, had volunteered as soon as Jess had spoken to him of his aims. His affection and respect for Jess amounted to a kind of shy worship and this feeling spread to most of the others as they were approached and brought into the group.

Richard Farrington, whose father was one of the Chichester judges and his mother – a wealthy and difficult person who had little time for her only child, was small and quick-witted and made up for his lack of inches by possessing the slithering swiftness of a pick pocket.

Anthony Fowler, herdsman at Manor Farm; James Hunt, the Manor Farm carter; Andrew Lawrence, ploughman from Rymans. All were approached with caution and all were equally impressed by young Bayless' grasp of organisation and determination to avoid all risks of discovery.

Finally there was Nicholas Smyth; love child of Hannah Smyth, disputed heir to all the Smyth Estates since the death of her uncle Thomas. Jess had taken him on after Nick had come to him, begging to be allowed to prove himself. He was an unfortunate mixture of complexes. Proud and arrogant at one instant and pathetically vulnerable the next. The others were divided in their welcome of Nick Smyth but he had been as good as his word and had not lacked courage or obedience. He had also been useful in finding many a client prepared to pay handsomely for French brandy and Indian tea.

It had not been easy for Jess to convince Master Tovey that he was as competent to organize a night run as his father had been. Jess was only just eighteen at the time and although he was already a commanding figure over six feet in height, broad in the shoulder and undoubtedly strong as an ox, the cautious merchant was loath to trust an investment of several hundred pounds to an untried boy. At the same time he was feeling the absence of regular capital increase since the old gang had broken up. Against his better judgement, he gave Jess permission to do a trial pickup the following week. After they had parted he sat in the dark cubbyhole of his counting house behind the shop in East Street, and wondered what had made him give in so easily. It had been something to do with the way the lad had looked at him, he would swear. Those amazing grey eyes had looked deep into his very soul and he had been caught and his mind bent to an invisible will and he had heard his voice agreeing with young Bayless, even as he had tried to protest and shake off the strange mesmeric languor that had gripped him. He shook his head and told himself not to start imagining things. Those gypsies were odd folk, he knew. Some of them seemed to have the reputation for some pretty ungodly practices but he'd never imagined that Jess Bayless was one of those. It had been a mighty odd sensation, all the same. He waited for the results of his foolishness and was gloomily prepared to accept the loss of the whole consignment of French brandy.

The drop had gone without a hitch. The group, grinning at each other from soot-blackened faces, christened themselves the Apuldram Blacks and were delighted to accept the guinea and half anker of spirits that was their night's fee. It was the beginning of a brotherhood that would continue for a decade.

The empty marsh stirred and sighed, ruffled by the squall that drove across it. The silent straggle of men pushed forward, heads down into the wind and rain, their sacking hoods running with water as they sloshed through the darkness behind Cobby, their guide. Muddy water swilled about their ankles and the men leading the four horses muttered to their animals comfortingly, through the kerchiefs bound round their faces.

It was little more than a mile from Ham Farm across to Earnley Thicket, but already they had been on the move for over an hour, creeping at a snail's pace through the angry darkness, eyes straining to keep sight of the shadowy form of the man ahead. Four well-loaded pack horses and ten men, including Cobby.

There had been one bad moment already as they passed Ham Farm. Two sheep dogs had come streaking out of the yard to snap and worry their ankles and the farmer had not been far behind. It was necessary to pay him off with a tub of French brandy before he would call the snarling dogs away. The moment of danger had not been great for what is one man against ten . . . but it was enough to set every man's nerves jumping as they inched their way through the turbulent night.

44

Jess shivered beneath his sacking cloak as a gust of wind blasted across him, stinging his forehead with a whiplash of rain. 'No moon on a night like this', one part of his mind said comfortingly. The other half thought of the thirty acre field behind Rymans and prayed that the same rain would not be washing out the new seedlings that had taken him and seven other men, women and children three days to dib in. He felt the tension in the men behind him. None of them liked an untried rendezvous, especially as they were being guided by a stranger as shifty as John Cobby.

Jess strained red-rimmed eyes into the darkness ahead of him and saw the guide turn, and the quick pale flash of his face as he made sure that the Blacks were following him.

'Earnley Thicket's right ahead, Master,' he said in a hoarse whisper, cupping his hand and leaning close. His breath smelt sour and Jess turned his face aside. 'We go through the ditch here and the woods are twenty yards off with Coney Mill just over on the right. I doubt they'll see a thing on a night like this.'

Coney Mill. Something stirred in Jess' mind and he gripped the man by the front of his streaming jacket as he turned to move off again.

'You told me there were no buildings, no tracks even, between the Beach and Earnley Thicket, save for Ham Farm,' he said, jerking Cobby up against his chest. The man's stolid face loomed in front of him, bovine and without comprehension.

'B'ain't nothen' here just like I said, Master. The Mill be quarter mile away from 'ere. Won't be nobody round these parts on a night like this.' He turned away, jerked his jacket free and moved off.

Something thundered in Jess' head, warning . . . warning. He sloshed forward and caught up with Cobby.

'If you've said a word to a soul, Cobby . . . Just one person. If you've blown us to anyone, I'll see you hung, drawn and quartered.' His voice was low but carried clearly through the thunder of the night's torment. 'Don't you ever forget that, Cobby . . . One word of tonight's doings – just one – and you'll swing right here on the Bill . . .'

Cobby hunched his shoulders as though to rid himself of

45

something unpleasant. He quickened his pace. 'Come on . . .
It's all right, I tell 'e.'

He was to remember the impact of Jess' words many
years later when, as the last member of the infamous Hawk-
hurst Gang to be sentenced, he stood below the gibbet on
Selsey Bill and felt the rough noose being tightened about his
neck.

Trees marched out of the rain, scattered and then closing
ranks, became woodland. The column hurried in under invisible bare boughs, the horses blowing with the weight of their
heavy loads.

'I wish we weren't a prey to such dirty weather always,'
John Freeland said mournfully, coming up to Jess with hat and
cloak dripping and saturated. He sneezed and wiped his nose
on the wet sleeve of his coat. 'Who needs snuff when you can
clear the tubes with a dose of pneumonia for free if you run
with the Apuldram Blacks.'

Jess hardly heard him. He was listening to himself.

There was something about Cobby that put him instantly
on his guard, something about the man's stony indifference
that didn't ring true. It had not been there at the beginning of
the operation. He had been friendly and respectful, impressed
by the size of the reward Jess had offered him in return for
showing the Blacks through the wide stretch of marshy land
that made the coast between Selsey Bill and East Head such a
treacherous place. There were hardly any paths or buildings
and the sea shore was almost unreachable in places.

It had been quite a new idea to send a shallop in from the
Lady Jean as she rode out in Bracklesham Bay. It was a
precarious experiment for there were any amount of dangerous rocks just below the surface of the sea waiting, like
Houngate rocks, to rip the bottom out of a boat. They had
made a good land fall however, and the prize had been well
worth the risks. Brandy and Indian silk by the bale and
precious Eastern ornaments in jade and exquisite inlays.

This kind of drop had to be handled with particular care. No
rough stowing onto a dray and then away through the night as
fast as the load would permit. This time, each package was
tenderly placed in panniers on either side of the saddles of four
of the waggon horses. The tubs were loaded onto special sleds

that trailed out behind the horses and each horse was attended and guided by two men. The rest of the gang kept the sleds running straight and upright behind. With such an incriminating load, it was imperative to avoid the remotest possibility of discovery.

The night was perfect for their purpose and they had started off in high spirits, for the profits were to be greater for this night's work than they had ever received before. The awfulness of the January weather had quickly wiped the smiles from their faces. That and the fact that Jess was abstracted and moody.

When Jess was in that frame of mind, it meant trouble. None of them knew or cared how Jess seemed to smell danger from afar, but there was no getting away from the fact that, when he sensed trouble, trouble was what they got. Seeing the hunch of his shoulders and the way he kept turning his head and stopping to listen, they recognized the signs – and their own uneasiness increased.

The party passed through Earnley Thicket without incident and crossed Bracklesham Causeway, an old Roman road. The ground was firm now and soon they were moving freely over open ground, past Summerly Green and on to Birdham Common. At the crossroads they moved the horses into the protection of a small copse while they settled with Cobby and, after watching him disappear into the buffeting storm clutching his tub and a pouch of gold sovereigns, pressed on towards Birdham windmill. The tubs were to be unloaded there and the special cargo taken to Mistress Mcready at Allhallows Cottage, on the Siddlesham road.

Halfway across the Common, Jess stopped suddenly, his head cocked to one side, smelling the saturated air. John came up to him from the end of the column.

'What's up, Jess? You've been edgy the whole night.'

Jess pulled the red kerchief down from his nose. He stood swaying against the wind, sniffing the air like an animal, with the rain streaming off his skin in runnels.

'I don't know . . . I think we have company.'

They stared at each other and in the moment between his words and the impact of what he had said, night opened like a flower into blinding light and shattering sound. They flung

47

themselves flat. The world caught fire over their heads.

Lifting his face from the mud John saw Jess scuttling crablike to dive at one of the horses as it reared in terror and flung away from the melee of movement and noise erupting among them. The crash of musket, screams of terrified animals, the thud and cough of cudgel striking home . . . Abram's enraged and delighted battle cry. Figures had burst up out of the undergrowth on either side of the Common path, springing from under the hooves of the horses, arms swinging, heads lowered. John rolled over, away from a well-aimed boot and jack-knifed up onto his feet. He drove his shoulder into a figure as it swung a stick over its head to thump down across Richard Farrington's back. Something exploded close to him and the smell of cordite soured his nostrils. He gasped as a hobnailed boot drove into his stomach and curled over, retching as the air jerked and hiccoughed out of his lungs. Boots cannoned into his curled-up body, tripped and tore at his head. Men grappled and swore over him and he was dealt a blinding blow to the head and went swirling away into a black pit of infinite nothing.

Someone was singing a monotonous chanting wail close beside him. He lay and listened to it before realizing that it was the blood singing in his ears. He opened his eyes. 'I was beginning to think you had settled into my bed for keeps.'

He turned his head and looked up at Jess sitting, knees steepled, beside him. A lantern flickered and popped on the tamped earth floor by his side, throwing a comfortable, friendly light round the inside of the bender. He tried to raise himself up on an elbow and the throbbing in his head became jagged shafts of pain. With a groan he lay back again and closed his eyes.

'What happened, for God's sake?' he asked, feeling the rest of his body and discovering agony in a rib and blood in his mouth from a broken lip.

'They were waiting for us out on the Common, Bor. That bugger, Cobby, must have shopped us. Just as well I thought to tell him that we would be just the four horses and four men as a precaution, else there would have been half an army out there waiten' for us. As it was, we counted two Revenue and four of the militia.'

John opened his eyes again. Jess hadn't moved. He had a long cut across his forehead but it had been cleaned and glistened with an oily balm. There was a sharp odour of mint and garlic in the air.

'Go on then . . . What happened? I don't remember anything much after seeing you go after one of the horses and then someone started kicking hell out of me. Are the others all right? Did we inflict any casualties? I heard old Abram howling like a demon.'

'They got Edward Beer. He's done for. The others are all right, apart from a few bumps and bruises. We felled the lot of them. Don't know what their injuries are, but they were all out cold and we didn't wait for them to wake up, I can tell you. We rounded up the horses, put you and young Farrington over a couple of saddles and legged it over that Common before there was any more trouble.'

It had been a bad night. He had felt the warnings as soon as they began the slow journey back from the beach. The aspect that worried him most was that his gift seemed to be losing its strength where instinct was concerned. There had been no weakening in the strength of the Force as he had flamed two of the attackers, though. He had not meant to kill them but as he went to help Edward Beer who was grappling with a burly riding officer, to judge by his coat, one of the men had fired at Edward from almost point blank range. He could not even recall hearing the report of the musket but Edward's face was suddenly etched in the flash of the explosion, his candid blue eyes wide with surprise as the ball hit him in the jaw. For an instant teeth and white bone hazed his exploded face and then drowned in a mist of bright blood. He pitched backwards into the darkness and Jess had spun round on the man, and the Power had burst from him, felling the Officer and the other who ran forward with raised sword. He had been flung to the ground by the sheer strength of the Power's eruption from him. When he picked himself up, the two men were dead, sprawled like rag dolls across the path.

Edward Beer. Long after he had taken a partially recovered

49

John Freeland back to his home and the ministrations of his family, the name kept sliding into Jess' mind.

You could work yourself into a stupor for every daylight hour, until exhaustion provided a state of weariness so complete that any exercise of the mind was impossible. Feed Olivas and comb him down. Pull the burrs from his golden tail and the knots from his mane. Murmur softly into those sensitive ears to show him that he was still as well loved as ever. Then roll into the straw bed and wait for oblivion. It simply didn't work.

Edward Beer. The name began to toll in him like a bell ringing out the cost of a Country's greed; the greed of them all. It burned into his mind during the quieter reaches of the following nights. Edward Beer – husband and father, was dead with the word 'criminal' on his tombstone because Jess Bayless had made him one.

Well, it was no longer that way for him personally but Andrew Lawrence and Tover certainly sought excitement before gold and so did Richard Farrington – and maybe even John as well. Nick Smyth was motivated by something deeper and similar to Jess' own ambitions, for he sought the foundations of a fortune upon which to create his own security. His father had never been named and on her death the whole of his mother's estate would go to her sisters. Bastards had no legal rights. James Hunt, Anthony Fowler, John Blunden . . . Money was what they were after. Money and the prestige that it brought them in the Parish. They were prepared to put their companions' lives against the weight of their own ambitions. Where was it all meant to end?

On this latest and most complicated of night runs, they had brought in two new men; Tover Bayless and Edward Beer.

Tover was Piramis' second son. He was easy going and quiet and had been eager to join the Blacks for some time.

Edward was different. He was not really the right material for the job but Jess was concerned for him. He operated the Toll on the Dell Quay road and made such a small pittance from the job that Sarey Beer had admitted that they were close to starving. Edward himself would never have mentioned his problems in the Parish. He was grateful enough to have the toll cottage to live in, rent free. Sarey, however, had three step children to feed and clothe and was four months pregnant herself. She had only been married to Edward for a year and was twenty years his junior. Jess was fond of both of them and, knowing that Edward would not accept charity, had finally suggested that he might like to accompany them on their next trip.

Edward had accepted with gratitude. How could they have known that his first trip would also be his last?

Oh yes, they were all looking after Sarey, of course. She was better off than she had ever been when Edward was alive, but she had loved him with a young girl's lusty passion and all the assistance and food and comfort in the world would not bring him back to her. It struck Jess suddenly that she might not be the last wife that he made widow. The thought was like a hard blow to the stomach. Dawn found him still without sleep, staring up at the roof of the bender with smarting, red-rimmed eyes.

Chapter Four

Jess felt unusually diffident as he rode over to Rymans. He had taken a great deal of trouble to wash himself from head to foot and was clothed in new breeches, shirt and cutaway coat. He had combed his wiry black hair until the tears started from his eyes and now it was fastened into the nape of his neck in a neat cue. His face was freshly shaved and he smelt of wood smoke. Olivas had been given the same treatment and gleamed like burnished copper as he picked his way over the pot-holed road, lifting his elegant hooves with proud grace.

Horse and rider made a fine pair, Thomas Freeland thought, watching their arrival in the yard through an open casement. Young Bayless might be a gypsy and something of an opportunist but there was considerable panache in the way he sat his horse – and the energetic and precise way he went about any work that he took on called forth a grudging respect – even from his superiors.

Freeland watched Jess, liking what he saw. He sensed in the young man a deep well of humanity that was rare in one so youthful. He knew also that it would have been difficult to find a more stubborn one. All the same, he considered that his own son, John, had been influenced for the better by Jess over the years, for he now emulated Jess' strict code of ethics and was far steadier than he had been as a young boy. True, there was that owling business which was a dangerous as well as an unsavoury occupation but young men must be allowed to work the wildness out of their systems before settling down to the serious business of living. It appeared that Jess had his gang under such strong discipline that they had had very little trouble until this last regrettable affair. Of course there was not a shred of evidence to lay the blame of those two dead men at the Blacks' door. Jess had been wise enough to leave poor Edward Beer out there on the Common where he had fallen, so there was nothing to connect him with them, especially as it was known that Beer had not done any running with the Apuldram Blacks.

He strode through the house to his office and was still considering the subject when Blunden ushered Jess into the room. 'Come in, come in,' he said waving Jess forward as he settled himself behind his huge mahogany desk. 'Sit you down then and make yourself comfortable.'

He surveyed Jess through pince nez that were perched on the end of a long and angular nose. A twinkle softened his bucolic stare. 'By George, Jess – you're looking prosperous. Not thinking of getting wed yet, are you?'

Jess' long face puckered into an expression of acute alarm.

'God forbid, Sir. There can't be a maiden in the parish that could be doing with my habits. I did come to see you about a woman though, in a matter of speaken'. I came to put in a word with you for Sarey Beer, Master Freeland. To ask whether you could see your way to letten' her stay on in the Toll cottage and take the dues in Edward's place. She's young and strong, Sarey is – and won't stand any nonsense from the carters. Well, she don't stand any now, for she's ben doen' the job for two weeks already – ever since he was laid to rest.'

Freeland leant back in his chair, pursing thin lips and staring at Jess, deep in thought. He always thought deeply before making decisions and woe betide anyone who interrupted him before he was ready. His keen gaze was returned by eyes the calm colour of pigeons' wings. 'My word,' the old man thought with grudging admiration. 'The fellow becomes more striking and personable every time I see him.'

'We-ell . . .' he wavered, more for effect than for any real hesitation. 'I had been thinking of putting old Jack Knott and his family in there. Jack's no good for Customs Boatman now, after that bad fall of his, but he knows the ropes and most of the carters using the road. I certainly wasn't contemplating leaving Sarey in the cot.'

'Would you let her stay on for a limited period then, Sir? Just long enough for her to sort herself out and allow me to be better placed to help her get settled elsewhere? She's got a child on the way, you know – as well as Edward's three nippers by Lizzie that died. I shall be in a much better position to help her in another twelve months. If you can't see your way to letten' her stay on at the Toll cot for a spell, she'll have to go on the Parish . . . and you may end up haven' to pay out more to the Poor House in Chichester than you would if you let her be where she is.'

Freeland nodded. 'That's fair comment, I grant you that. Let me think on it. Was there anything else?'

Jess grinned across at his host. 'Well, Sir . . . the other item isn't a problem in the sense you mean . . . or I hope it isn't.'

He slid deeper into the leather chair and took a deep breath. 'Sir, you know all about my family. We come from mixed Romani stock but we've worked the pans for two generations now and hope we might go on doing it for two more. Although we're travellen' folks by nature, there's enough Gorgio blood in our veins for some of us to want to abandon that practice and settle in Apuldram in proper homes. I'm one of those, Master Freeland – and Amy's another. I've always had a powerful urge to better myself, Sir . . . to own a house of bricks and mortar and go into business. I can read and write pretty fair now and so can Amy, for Mistress Chatfield gives her lessons each afternoon and she's as quick as a clerk with her numbers. Well Sir, the long and the short of it is this. There's more ways to make money besides worken' the fields and the salt pans, as you know . . .'

Freeland flashed him a quick look from under bushy eyebrows. They were both well aware of the activities upon which Jess' interests were founded. While Freeland took no active part in the business, he did not condemn the practice and even occasionally passed on to his son some small snippet of information that might be useful to the Blacks. His well-stocked cellar and his wife's elegant French window hangings were evidence of their appreciation.

He nodded and dug into his yellow waistcoat pocket for his snuff box.

'Well, I've ben thinken' along these lines, Sir. I've more than enough money to invest now in the builden' of a house. Not a cottage . . . a real decent house about the size of your own. Apuldram has been the only home I've ever had and I'd not be happy to put my roots down in any other place. Would you be good enough to ask Mistress Smyth's trustees whether they'd consider leasen' Salterns woods to me, Sir? I'd want to clear a few acres north of Copperas Point and west of New Barn field and build me a fine house there, with access along the west boundary and into Salterns Lane. I plan to put Olivas to stud and breed a strain off him and some of the New Forest and Devon cobs that my people use. Then I'd put the rest of the woodland to grazen' swine. That would soon clear the under-growth there and give the oaks a better chance of growen' . . .'

He stopped. It had been a very long speech for him and he found that he was perspiring freely beneath his shirt. He sat forward on the edge of the ladder-backed chair, his stomach muscles suddenly knotting with tension.

Freeland took a clay pipe from his desk rack in silence. He lifted the lid of the tobacco humidor and carefully selected one leaf after another with apparent concentration. He pressed them into the bowl and tamped them down. Jess watched the long tapering fingers preparing the pipe with unhurried skill. 'Tell me, what sort of acreage are we discussing?'

Jess rubbed his smooth jaw, frowning. 'Forty . . . maybe forty-five acres, I'd guess.'

Suddenly it sounded like a lot of land and Jess clenched his hands together between his knees. He'd asked for too much. The whole Parish only amounted to about twelve hundred acres. Master Freeland might be persuaded into agreeing to such a lease but the Trustees would never contemplate it . . .

Freeland struck tinder to steel and applied the flaming taper to the bowl of his pipe. He sucked and puffed and sucked again, knot-veined hands cupping the bowl. The tobacco caught and he leaned back, pulling the aromatic fumes into his lungs with deep contentment.

'And are you going to tell me next that you are then considering taking Sarey Beer and her family into your em-ployment once you are living in this fine mansion of yours?'

Jess grinned across at him, hearing the touch of banter in the old man's voice.

'Why not, Sir . . . and others too, for I aim to raise fine pigs and finer horses so that the name of Apuldram will be on many a breeder's tongue before long. I've made plenty of useful friends in the last three years, Sir. It's my serious hope to raise enough money to buy myself into partnership with a man who's Master of his own ship. And one day, Sir, I want ships of my own, you see.'

'Bought with your ill gotten gains, no doubt.' Freeland chuckled, well pleased in spite of a natural scepticism, with the breadth of the boy's ambition.

Jess agreed with a shrug. 'That may be where the first cash comes from but the whole business of free trading is too chancy to rely upon totally. It is my intention to invest the money wisely and to stop night runnen' entirely, before I settle down to a business partnership.'

Freeland took the pipe from his mouth and banged his fist on the desk top. His enthusiasm for this young man grew with every word.

'Wisely said, my boy – very wisely said, although men with far more experience than you have been caught out with those same sentiments. The Investment Market is still in the doldrums after the disaster of the South Sea Bubble, y' know.'

He spoke ruefully, from the blow to his own pocket after the collapse of the great South Sea Company in 1720. Almost every man with a few guineas in his pocket had invested in that dream. King George himself, together with the Government, had sponsored the project. It did so well that in 1720 it was even in a position to offer to pay off the National Debt – provided it had the exclusive handling of the consolidated fund.

For a few short months a heady atmosphere swept across the land as the get-rich-quick fever spread. Then, in the sudden way that catastrophe so often strikes, share prices began to drop. A few wise speculators sold swiftly and made huge fortunes out of their foresight – but the main block of shareholders were small investors, interested in a steady annual income.

The Bubble burst and many thousands of investors were

ruined. The tragedies in countless lives would have been even more disastrous had it not been for the quick thinking of Robert Walpole, Chancellor of the Exchequer. He managed to juggle with the now worthless stock between the Bank of England and the East India Company and was finally able to pay the creditors about a third of their investment. The Freelands had been dealt a body blow which more than halved their capital. Thomas Freeland considered himself fortunate that his losses were not even greater.

Jess looked at the old man with understanding, well aware of these events. Their financial pressures had been one of the reasons that John had allowed himself to be drawn into the Apuldram Blacks.

'My sights are set on legitimate trading with my own country, Sir . . . not the wholesale shipping of blacks into bondage. I'm thinking of the East Indies and all the fine wares that are manufactured there, just waiting for English merchants to come buying.'

Freeland puffed and a small wreath of smoke trailed from his pipe and rose, spreading. 'How much money have you got?'

Jess was ready for the question. 'Seven thousand pounds and three hundred silver crowns, Sir. I would like to spend five thousand pounds on the house and land and invest the rest in a Marine partnership.'

Freeland blew fine blue smoke out through his nostrils.

'I can't argue with that, Jess. Countless numbers of our Peers enjoy the comfort of large Estates and fortunes today simply because of the irregular practices of their forebears.'

He sank back into another of his pondering silences and Jess held his tongue and curbed the impatience that suddenly welled up in him. He watched as the old man mused, tapping steepled fingers together. Jess sat rigidly, longing to rise and pace the floor in his anxiety.

Just as he began to feel that movement was imperative, Freeland raised his eyes and leaned forward across the green leather top of the desk. 'Now, I'll tell you what I am proposing to do. I shall recommend that the Trustees of the Estate lease you thirty-five acres of the untended woodland north of the salt pans; the condition being that you agree to clear a percentage of oak wood, the felled trees remaining the property of the

Estate. Further, that you build a dwelling house of a design and size to be agreed with the Estate – the whole messuage to be on a renewable lease of twenty-five years. I can't agree to you having the entire tract of the south woodlands because other uses are already planned for the land that runs westward from the highway.'

Jess jumped up, his face red with relief, thanks pouring out of him, but the old man waved them away and fixed him with a suddenly stern look.

'Wait a minute before you go running off to start planning a mansion to equal Goodwood. I would prefer to think that you and those who come after you may wish to be regarded with respect in these parts. With that in mind, Jess, I'd like an unwritten promise from you that there will be no further night running from Copperas Point during your tenancy.'

Jess stared at him in astonishment, consternation drawing down the corners of his mouth.

'For God's sake, man – if you're going to live there, you won't want to sully your own nest. Go and make your fortune by any means you please – further along the coast, if you must – but don't do it so close to home. You've been mighty lucky up to now but your good fortune is not necessarily going to last for ever, is it? When you've built that house of yours – and good luck to you with it, I say – you're going to go out and find yourself a wife so that you can father a brood of sons to carry on where you leave off. If your ideals are as fine and honourable as you imply, you would not wish to risk involving innocent women and children in the violence and danger of that work, would you?'

The craggy hardness of his face relaxed. He stood up slowly, rubbing the ache from the small of his back and then stretched out his hand across the desk top.

'Give me your word and your hand on it, Jess – and I'll be glad to speak to the Trustees for you at the earliest opportunity.'

Jess let his breath go with a deep sigh. He pressed his lips together so tightly that the dimple in his chin deepened into a sharp Y. Smiling, he held out his hand and grasped Thomas Freeland's in a vice-like grip that made the older man wince. 'You drive a hard bargain, Sir, but – yes, I can see the wisdom in it. I agree then . . . No night runs from Copperas Point once the lease has been signed and the land is mine.'

Thomas Freeland sat pondering for a long time after Jess had left him. It appeared that Jess Bayless had a great deal more to him than he had thought possible. He was clearly going to make his mark in the area before they planted him in the ground. Abigail would smile when he related the conversation. She had been a great advocate of Jess' worth for a long time, seeing with her woman's eyes all the strength of the boy's character, and little of his waywardness. Now he had to admit that quite possibly she had been right. It would be interesting to observe the progress of this ambitious young shooting star in the Apuldram firmament.

Jess rode home, listening to the clop clop of Olivas' hooves on the road. Bricks and Mortar . . . Bricks and Mortar . . .

It was a slow and tortuous road to get within reach of his goal . . . but today he had taken a great stride forward so that he was almost in sight of it. Sign his name to the land – build his house – establish an acceptable sum in a respectable business and then . . . then he could begin to plan the finer details which were still a confusion in his mind. The remainder of the morning he spent dreaming in the little glade, trying to keep his bounding thoughts within the realms of reality.

It was impossible not to dwell on Lavinia and after a while he gave in and feasted his mind upon her – John's sister . . . still only a child of ten but golden and delicate and surely the most perfect specimen of young girlhood that nature had ever created. She was only just aware of him but already she would pick up her skirts and fling herself at him whenever he appeared with John at Rymans. He accepted her admiration with secret pleasure but was careful not to encourage it openly in case it caused offence to Master Freeland. Thinking of her, he groomed Olivas, working on the gleaming coat as though his very life depended upon it.

Chapter Five

By the time Sarey Beer came to term and gave birth to a daughter, Tover Bayless had become a regular visitor to the Toll Cottage. At first it had simply been his intention to offer his help in any way he could but the visits became more frequent as the months passed. Nothing was missed in the Parish and note was made of the fact that Tover was usually to be found in the vicinity of the young Widow Beer. There was no surprise for Sarey was a cheerful, big-boned girl with a good sensible head on strong shoulders and fine brown eyes to roll in his direction. By the time Piramis and the rest of Tover's family returned from their travels the following spring, he had moved in with Sarey and had even permitted himself to be taken to church and wed in proper Christian fashion.

The Toll cottage was bare in the extreme for Edward had never been very successful as a bread winner and their possessions were few. Before Tover moved in there had been concern in the Parish for Sarey and her family since there was no work available and only the Poor House in Chichester, if her cottage was given to another Toll keeper. There was general relief when it became known that Thomas Freeland had accepted her as the official Toll Keeper, and once Tover became responsible for them all, the problem seemed to be resolved completely. All the same, whenever Amy went to visit Jess, she always paused at Sarey's to hand over a meat pie from Mistress Chatfield or a loaf of freshly baked bread.

Amy lightened her basket as usual with Sarey, and hastened on down the track towards the distant line of trees, placing her patten-shod feet with care to avoid the muddy ridges made by the waggon wheels. She moved as fast as she could, for she had not seen Jess for seven whole days. The weekly visits were in their sixth year now and still she badly missed having him close by. Great changes had been wrought in both of them, she knew. She was not as shy in company as she had been when first she had gone to Manor Farm. And she had grown – so tall, so willow thin that Piramis and Sarah wondered what it was that the gorgios were feeding her.

And Jess – just look at him now. He had shot up and filled out and looked like a king. She liked nothing better than to hear the way Mistress Chatfield spoke of him, for he was certainly the handsomest man in the Parish and there wasn't a woman, young or old, who didn't have a soft spot for him.

She limped into the wood, keeping to the well-worn path, humming under her breath as she went.

Jess was polishing Olivas' leathers as she came into the clearing. His eyes lit up and he sprang to his feet and strode across the short grass to greet her, thinking how well she wore the Bayless colouring these days. Nearly as tall as Jess himself and slim as a hazel rod; and then that distinctive identity of bright blue eyes with a ring of darkness round the pupils and rich black hair that frizzed in damp air and had to be tied back under her cambric cap with a bright coloured ribbon.

'Sar shan,' he said.

He took her basket and put both his arms round her and kissed her on her upturned mouth. He was unshaven and the stubble grazed her cheek.

'You taste of plum cake,' he said softly. 'You've stopped in at Sarey's on the way.' Her pale face flushed and she clung to him until he put her gently aside and began to delve into the covered basket.

'Let's see what your kind mistress has sent over this time for the poor gypsy.'

Amy sat down on a log and clicked her tongue at him, dimpling at his half serious tone.

'Poor Gypsy . . . Dordi dordi, Jess. There can't be many gypsies less "poor" than you . . .'

She couldn't wait. She had to ask him. 'What's this we're all

61

hearing from Rymans that you are going to build a fine big kenner (house) down here, then?'

He stood with the basket at his feet and a large pink smoked ham in one hand. A wide grin set the grey eyes sparkling.

'Aha . . . so the tongues are beginning to wag already, are they?' he chuckled. 'What a fine joint this is, Pen. Please convey my thanks to Mistress Chatfield. Very kind of her . . . most generous.'

Amy clicked her tongue at him in exasperation.

'Why are you such a tease? Please tell me what's afoot. The gossips have been hard at it all week and I couldn't wait to discover what is really going on. Tover didn't seem to know any more than I do. What are you up to?'

He dropped the ham back in the basket and reached over to lift the cambric cap off her head. 'Let's see you looken' natural with the hair of you loose and free, the way it ought to be.' He looked down at her, soothing and soft, his expression almost a caress.

Obediently she raised her hands and pulled at the red ribbon and her hair sprang free, wiry and strong and quickly curling into corkscrews in the moist air.

He sat beside her on the log and put an arm round her shoulders. 'One day, when I was just a bitti raklo, I decided that it wasn't going to be enough growing up just to be Jess Bayless of the Saltings. I decided that somehow, I was going to learn my letters and my numbers and I was going to be someone to reckon with. I was going to make a fortune and build a kenner of my own with plenty of land so that I could breed fine horses and have servants to do my bidding.'

Amy smiled. This was a familiar theme. She had been listening to Jess' dreams for all the years that she could remember.

'Then the Power came to me, Amy. At first I was frightened by it for I was too small to understand what was happening to me. I still don't understand but I've realized that it can be used to help me. It's a funny thing about the Power, you know. It seems to be a negative influence in some way because I can sense things from a distance but never close to – and the worst of it is that it definitely has a gift of death rather than of life. That side of it worried me very much when I was a nipper but now I can, to some extent, control its volume . . . and I don't think it likes that. Lately I have felt the strength of it growing less than it was when I was younger. So it is all the more important for me to make the best of it now – before it leaves me altogether.'

She sat leaning against him, feeling the heart ticking strongly in his chest against her body. She was scarcely listening to his words. It was enough to be in the shelter of his arm, afloat in the closeness, the masculinity of him.

'Anyway . . . I have enough money now to start thinking about that house. I have been to see Master Freeland and have his promise that he will recommend to the Estate Trustees that I be offered a lease on the Salterns woods along here. Piramis has agreed to stay over the winter months and help with the clearing of the woodland and there won't be a shortage of labour at that time of year.'

His arm tightened round Amy and he buried his face in her hair for a moment.

'We'll build us a house, Amy – and when it is ready, I want you to come and care for me there . . . Would you do that?'

She twisted round and gaped at him, mouth open. She saw the light dancing at the back of his eyes and the words stuck in her throat and she nodded, feeling tears welling up into her eyes. He watched her happiness grow and was content.

She had become a striking maid with her cloud of dark wayward hair framing a pale and piquant little face with the features of a suffering saint. She was far too withdrawn with most people but when they were together she became animated and natural and a soft colour came into her cheeks, giving her sudden life and beauty.

'Why do you turn down all the swains who come courten'?' he said.

She dropped her eyes and twisted a fold of worsted skirt in her fingers and shrugged. 'Never found one that moved me, I suppose. I've been content at Manor Farm and once I'm back with you . . . There's nothing more I want in life. What would I want with wedden' and haven' a litter, one every year until I'm spent and like to die young. I want to live, Jess. I want to live to be old and care for you. That's what I really want.'

63

He was satisfied. She would come to him when he was ready for her.

They had their heads together, talking quietly over chunks of ham and rye bread when Nick Smyth strolled into the clearing out of the gathering dusk.

'Thought I'd pay you a call and pick your brains about a new horse for my good mother to ride to My Lord of Richmond's hounds.'

He dropped to the ground beside them, and banged a stone jar of portuguese sherry on the grass at Amy's feet. His eyes flicked over her in much the same way as Jess' had done earlier but she was looking down and so missed the sudden flare of interest in them. It was clear that he had been attacking the sherry on his way down the path, having left his carriage at the Dell Quay landing stage.

It was not the first time that Nick had made an unsolicited visit to Jess' fireside. There had been several previous occasions when he had felt restless and dissatisfied and had made his way from Binderton to Salterns woods in search of the comfort of Jess' company. Life at Binderton was a constant strain for the natural heir to the Estate, as the son of Hannah Smyth, the eldest of three sisters who claimed inheritance from their uncle, Thomas Smyth, who had died in 1721. There had already been three years of litigation in the Court of Chancery over who had the right to inherit and the odds were now heavily with his mother.

The fact that Nick was illegitimate and that Hannah was unmarried – and likely to remain so – made his position almost unendurable at times. He knew who his father was and the knowledge gave him constant satisfaction for his blood was infinitely superior to that of the Smyths. He deserved Binderton. He had lived there all his life for Uncle Tom had been kindness itself to Hannah when the rest of the family had chosen to disapprove of her misfortune. It seemed, though, that Chancery would not recognize his claims for Aunts Mary and Barbara were both married with legitimate sons and daughters ready to carve up the Estate. He despised them all.

In view of his superiority, it was odd that he should go to a gypsy for comfort and encouragement, but there was something about Jess Bayless which had attracted him from the very first time he had clapped eyes on him in one of the Chichester taverns. There was an air of such calm and attractive dignity about the tall gypsy that it drew men to him and Nick, searching desperately for the assurance and presence his existence merited, found an element of peace and pleasure in his company, denied him by others.

It was quiet in the wood and companionable round the hearth as the shadows broadened and slowly drowned the trees beyond the fire glow. Nick had also heard the rumours and was curious to hear what Jess was up to. He sat with his elbows resting on his knees, his arrogant face turning like a metronome between Jess and Amy, noting her rare animation with an increasingly glassy stare. He continued to help himself from the jar, wiping it with his sleeve before passing it on to Jess.

It was very late by the time Amy rose to leave. The hours had fled for there was so much to discuss. The strong sweet sherry made her feel lightheaded and Jess gripped her arm to steady her as she stood up. Both men pulled themselves to their feet as she picked up her empty basket and tucked her hair back into her cap.

She smiled at the two of them, pleased at this show of respect to a servant girl – but then, here in this clearing, where Jess was master, Nick Smyth was no more than a companion and business associate for all his education and fine breeding. She held her head high as she had seen the gentry do and bowed slightly to the two young men.

'I think it would be wise if I were to walk you up the track,' Nick suggested. 'You have no lantern and who knows who may be skulking out there in the dark.'

She was grateful for his thoughtfulness, even though he had always been a person she neither understood nor cared for. The tension and anger in him was an uncomfortable companion. All the same, she was glad to accept the offer. It showed that her climb to gentility had begun.

The night was very still. All air movement had ceased at sunset and now the darkness seemed to hold its breath as they felt their way round the scored potholes of the pathway. They could see well enough, in spite of the moonless night, by the time they passed the dark mass of Andrew Lawrence's cottage

65

at New Barn. A window gleamed faintly after them and Nick put a hand out to steady Amy's elbow as her pattens slithered in mud.

'Forgive my presumption, Miss Amy, but my large feet are better suited to supporting us than yours.'

She felt the warmth of his hand through the wool of her coat. He pressed close to her. They walked slowly and she realized that he was leaning more heavily upon her than she was on him. She caught a whiff of soured sherry as he belched loudly. Oh God, he was drunk as a Lord.

Jess stretched his feet out and raised his arms high above his head with a deep, contented sigh. His whole body ached with delightful languor for they had worked with few breaks from before dawn until early dusk, heaving stooks up onto the waggons until the whole of Fifty Acre was finally cleared. It was the last field to be harvested. Now all five were neat carpets of pale gold stubble that would lie fallow until winter ploughing began. His shoulders were stiff from the monotonous swinging action, from hooking the stook onto his fork – then turning and flinging each one upwards to be caught and stowed by the waggoner. He massaged his shoulder muscles, thinking of Amy and the delight that he had lit in her funny little heart. He recalled the jolt of relief he had felt at her touching declaration of loyalty to him. Amy had been a part of him for as long as he could remember that there were times, watching her grow to graceful womanhood, when jealousy had eaten into him at the thought of some other man assuming the care of her. For what other man would know of those things that hurt her – like reference to her deformity. She would never mention such sensitive subjects and would suffer as a result. What other man would know that when she had a bout of hiccups it was because something had frightened or angered her – and the hiccups would continue until Jess had wormed the cause out of her. There were so many very private parts of Amy for she was too shy to speak her mind or to share her doubts with others.

It was a great relief to know that she had no intention of permitting anyone else into her life. She was his little bird and he knew how to quieten the occasional tantrums she suffered; how to bring smiles and dimples to her solemn little face and the light dancing into her eyes.

It came to him quite suddenly, as it always did; no gradual warning – just the sudden conviction that out beyond the trees to the north of the clearing, something was generating the first flickers of alarm.

He stood up, sniffing the night – probing with every sharpened sense and trying to analyse those small flickers of someone else's fear. He tasted the air, turning his head from side to side like a hound getting the scent of the fox, the soreness in his shoulders forgotten.

Nick Smyth stumbled and would have fallen had Amy not grabbed his coat and held him up. He teetered, regained his balance and cursed under his breath. 'Sorry,' he muttered. 'Sherry's gone to m'head a trifle, m'dear.'

He draped a leaden arm round her shoulder and seemed to have forgotten who he was with, for he let his hand brush against the soft curve of her breast. She walked stiffly and slowly, eyes straining into the total night, silently cursing him for his disgusting condition and familiarity. It would have been much better for her to have gone home unattended. She would have been there by now, instead of having this drunken gorgio slobbering all over her. His fingers closed with fumbling deliberation round her right breast and she jerked away from him in shock.

'Don' run off like that.' His voice was in her ear and the arm was back. 'Nice little handful . . . don't be unkind to a fellow . . .' The words slurred together as she tried to twist out of his grasp. His arm locked round her shoulder and neck and he stood still and pulled her towards him.

'Stop that . . . don't you touch me, Nick Smyth . . . don't touch me like that . . .'

But he was strong and the other arm came across her chest and she was squashed up against the rich brocade of his french waistcoat. He began to push her backwards towards the grass verge and the sherry breath filled her nostrils as his lips slid down her face and fastened like a leech on her mouth.

*   *   *

The urgency in Jess suddenly leapt into screaming ululation in his head and he ran, tearing across the glade and onto the path as it twisted out of the woods, skirting the shorn fields. AMY . . . AMY . . .

He could feel her horror, feel terror laced with revulsion. The Power simmered and flared in his head and he pounded up the path, trying to keep his breathing regulated to the beat of his thudding feet; trying not to think . . . trying to let her know that he was coming. He heard her as he panted past New Barn Cottage. A ragged cry that was cut off sharply. His eyes glared through the darkness, gouging across lines of shadows where the path merged with the thin hedgerow.

The Force was building in him wildly, ballooning up like a huge, terrible flower. It was too much for him to keep down . . . AMY . . . he didn't want to keep it down.

Movement – sharp and violent, threshing movement of pale shapes that riveted his attention – and he fixed his fury upon it, fixed upon the unseen image of Nick Smyth's pouting, insolent face. He staggered as the white hot explosion erupted outwards from him, saw the flash and smudge of a body flung up and back, arms outstretched; a lifeless thing that was etched for a split second in blue lightning.

Then he was beside it, reaching across the legs to Amy's huddled shape flattened against the dewy grass.

'It's all right now, Pen . . . it's all right, my darling . . . It's over.'

Chapter Six

Nick Smyth's death shocked the whole of Apuldram for he was young and apparently healthy and it seemed inconceivable that he should have suffered a fatal heart attack at twenty-two years of age. Jess' grim silence was taken to be masking the grief he must be feeling.

The funeral was at Binderton and of the Blacks, only John Freeland and Richard Farrington attended.

Jess' mood was still subdued after the next two runs – even though one of them was a consignment of record proportions which involved fifteen men and the whole night to distribute the shipment amongst waggons and light carts. The night's work was undisturbed and earned each man the sum of ten guineas. For Jess it meant nearly four thousand pounds to add to his assets.

A lease was arranged for the Salterns woods and one December morning Jess signed his name to the parchment document in Thomas Freeland's Chichester office and exchanged it for a pouch of two hundred guineas. It was an oddly moving moment for him and afterwards he paced his new boundaries, from Copperas Point along the rim of the Saltings to the footpath that led from the pans to the Chichester highway; left and northeast, skirting New Barn Field on two sides and then northwest once more through uncultivated scrub land to the marshy banks of the Chichester Channel.

Thirty-five acres of oak and beech wood . . . just asking to be set in order. He strode into a biting wind, noticing nothing of the frost laden day. A flight of geese scythed the crisp blue air over his head and wheeled in tight formation out over the Bosham farm lands before circling in to land against the Chidham shore beyond. Jess saw only his trees and the choked tangle of undergrowth that must be cleared and uprooted with the help of Tom Chatfield's punches during the remaining winter months. Piramis was already alerted to oversee the clearance of the first five acres and work would begin immediately.

The site he had chosen had its farthest boundary against New Barn Field and stretched across to the Channel shore. The little glade that housed his bender was at its centre. The house was to be built with the Place at its heart.

The clearing operation progressed through the winter months and well into spring. It would not have taken so long had it not been for the rate at which the casual labour abandoned the work. The brooding watchfulness in the atmosphere was certainly so strong that it even had Piramis looking over his shoulder so that he breathed a sigh of relief when the last tree had been uprooted and the site was ready for the masons.

It was no real surprise when the masons, digging foundations for the new house, came upon evidence of other, infinitely older ones on the site of the Place. Jess insisted that they were not disturbed, the feeling strong all about them that nothing must be changed, that the old stones must remain as they were. The masons crossed themselves and murmured together that the gypsy was building on unhallowed ground and that no good would come of it – or of him. Their mood deteriorated even further after an incident which occurred soon after the trenchwork began.

There were eight labourers and the youngest of them, Will Tregus, was a simple lad, a trifle touched – so his mother said – but hard working enough once he got going. He was always the first on the site each morning, well before dawn, and was hard at work by the light of one of Jess' lanterns by the time the others arrived. Jess was up and preparing himself a parcel of food for his midday meal. He could hear the boy moving about in the half-dug trench across the glade. As he hung his night blanket over the wood pile to air, an odd scuffling made him pause. It sounded as though Will was in conflict with one of the woodland pigs who were at their most aggressive at this time of the year.

'What's amiss with ye, Will?' he called, ducking out of the tent to see for himself.

Dawn was still an hour away but the density of the night had thinned into milky greyness. By the lantern's light he could just make out Will's head bobbing up and down from his place in the foundation trench. He went across to investigate, alarmed by the muffled grunts the boy was making. By the time he stood over Will Tregus, the boy was on his knees with his arms clasped tightly round his head, as if to defend himself from a vicious attack. There was nothing in the trench with him – and no sign of the muddy earth being trampled by anything other than Will's own large feet.

'What's up with ye, Bor?' Jess asked again.

The boy curled himself up into a tight ball and his only movement was the trembling of his whole frame. Jess jumped down into the trench and spoke gently to the boy, seeing that something had frightened him so deeply that he was almost paralysed. He was still trying to get some sense out of Will when the other men arrived for work. It was no good. Will was struck dumb, unable to do anything other than slobber and mouth unintelligibly. Two of the men took him away for there was no work to be made out of him in that state.

It was much later that same day, after the sullen men had finished work and thankfully left the site, that Jess noticed the marks on one of the old boulders. They had been cut deep into the stone so that they stood out clearly like a branding mark. There was a crude heart flanked by two sets of initials. W.T. on the left side and P.L. to the right. The blade of the knife had slipped on the L leaving a deep scar running away from it down the boulder.

Jess stood looking at the stone thoughtfully for a long time and then he understood. Will Tregus had desecrated the sacred stones and had been struck dumb as punishment.

Strange tensions hung over the clearing after that and the men went about their tasks silently with many a glance thrown over their shoulders. Tempers were short and the strain that each man felt was reflected in the increasing numbers of arguments and fights that broke out among them almost daily.

71

A brooding presence stood over them, daring them to make a mistake, an unseen threat over their heads. The moment the foundations had been dug and laid the men collected their money and withdrew in haste. Young Will Tregus was unable to relate what had befallen him for he never recovered his speech or his senses.

'Why did you have to choose this particular place?' Piramis asked Jess in exasperation, when he had difficulty in finding bricklayers to put the walls up.

'You've bought yourself nearly forty acres – and you go and choose a spot that's inhabited by Mullos (ghosts). Can't you feel 'em, Bor? The place is awash in 'em . . . an' those voices – haven't you heard the voices? We've all heard 'em . . . and felt the pressure in our heads. Terrible. Dordi Dordi . . . you wouldn't catch me liven' in a kenner on such a spot.'

Jess let them mutter and complain, for it released some of the tension, so that they laughed a little sheepishly at each other and tried to make a joke of their fears. When the walls were up to the eaves, he stood in the gap which would one day be his main entrance and stared across the shallow slope of the cleared ground to where the water of the narrow channel winked and sparkled on its way to the open sea.

Lavenham. The name sprang up from the spongy earth and filled his head.

Lavenham . . .

The bricks and mortar of this house should be named for just one woman who was already becoming the corner stone of his whole ambition.

Woman? He smiled at the thought, the whole of his face softening at the bold assumption that such a precious and eternal child would ever become woman.

Lavenham . . . A house of grace and beauty as becoming to its mistress as she would most certainly be the jewel at the heart of the house itself.

Lavenham . . . for Lavinia.

The house squatted in its ancient foundations, pulsing as the soft opaque moonlight flowed over its unfinished walls and jutting roof timbers like warm milk. The woodland and cruelly-scoured clearing stood out sharply in the white un-compromising glare in harsh jutting slashes of black against the silver water. The sour brine smell of the saltpans hung about its skeletal rooms and paneless windows, like the rotting admission of death in the ruins of centuries of forgotten lives.

The Watcher was confused, feeling the house's menace but seeing ruination and destruction where he knew he was witnessing the beginnings of his whole past.

There was nothing to see save the unfinished walls and churned earth where the dray carts had dug deep furrows in the oily clay. The place was empty – and yet it teemed with the imprints of a thousand desecrations. Shadows yawned and threatened in languid agony as though scourged by forgotten tempests. He heard the silent screaming of long obliterated curses, felt the bitter horror of unendurable shame. They were the same voices as the ones in his nightmare – but a little louder . . . a little nearer. Gagging in the depth of his fear he withdrew.

When John Freeland was home in Apuldram on his rare visits from London, it became natural to ride over to Birdham and, on his way homeward, to detour down the Saltings path and turn right into Jess' newly-gravelled drive to study the progress of the house.

Work was slow in the summer months as all the auxiliary helpers were fully employed in the fields. It delayed, but did not stop, the progress on the house because Jess had three well-paid masons hard at work and the structure was already emerging, the walls built from Donnington bricks and local grey flint.

The finished house would not be large. The ground floor consisted of a spacious hall with a parlour to the right and kitchen quarters to the left. On the upper floor there would be three sleeping chambers and a linen closet. On the northern side of the house, various outbuildings were planned. Brewhouse, dairy, still room and a 'dutch' barn. Terraces were being laid round the house, already prepared with foundations, to become additional wings in later years. To the many curious visitors the house had unexpected style and

73

simplicity and was neither ostentatious nor out of keeping with its surroundings. Even before the roof timbers were complete, it sat in the untidy clutter of builders' and carpenters' paraphernalia as though it had always been there and was simply undergoing improvements.

As soon as the ground floor was completed and the roof sufficiently advanced to give protection from the weather, Jess struck his bender and moved into the kitchen quarters.

It was the first time in his twenty-two years that he had lived and slept within brick walls. At first he found it difficult to get used to being cut off from the comforting sounds of the wood but he adjusted quickly to his new environment and gained quiet satisfaction from the very vibrations which daily frightened his workmen so deeply. He made himself comfortable in the small room which would one day be the servants' chamber.

The following February, Amy stopped working for the Chatfields and joined Jess at Lavenham. Her excitement was so out of keeping with her usually shy demeanour that Misstress Chatfield was startled and even a little shocked, for it simply was not done to express such almost carnal longings to be at the side of an unmarried brother. Amy didn't even notice her disapproval but continued to dream of Jess and the quality of the new house. She had always been a quiet girl but in recent months, since the death of her brother's friend, she had been even more silent and such poor company that Mistress Chatfield was almost relieved when the waggon, bearing Amy and the chattels she had accumulated in her six years at Manor Farm, rattled away down the lane to the distant highway.

By that time, the roof was complete and the chimneys built, and Amy was quite content to sleep on a pile of straw near the kitchen hearth until the upstairs chambers were ready for occupation. She and Jess were back together once more by their own fireside and the look in his eye promised that she need never leave him again.

The chimneys standing sentinel over the house were a constant pleasure to Jess, for they were the only elaborate indulgence he had permitted himself. They were tall and fashioned in spiralled brick in the Elizabethan style. Long ago there had been a grand house that he had admired greatly, set among hills in the far west of Devon. It was possible to see the beautiful barley sugar chimneys long before the rest of the building came into view. To possess his own version of those majestic stacks was another milestone towards the ultimate goal.

The house sat serenely amid a jumble of brickwork that would one day be its outhouses and stabling. The soft pink brick was offset by dove grey window mullions of Bembridge stone and the windows themselves were of leaded glass, reflecting the blue opaqueness of the sky.

'Sar shan, Bor.' The quiet voice at his elbow jerked Jess from his contemplation and he turned to the speaker, a smile broadening as he recognised Manfri Bayless, Vasher's elder son.

They stood together in companionable silence, taking in the disorder surrounding them all the way down to the fast-moving waters of the Channel.

'Builden's comen' on a fair treat,' Manfri observed after a pause. Jess grinned at him.

'Bricks and mortar, Bor,' he said, eyes twinkling. 'They're no bad way to build, after all, are they?'

Manfri's long pinched face crumpled into smiles. 'Good for some of us, maybe . . .'

He was small and wiry, the top of his unruly head little higher than Jess' shoulder. He was older than Jess by four years and looked more, for the flesh of his gaunt face seemed already folding into lines and creases. The fine blue Bayless eyes topped high cheek bones over which the olive skin was tightly stretched, giving him a foxy look but for the humour in him and the relaxed upturning corners of his strong mouth.

He was a quiet one, Manfri. Content to attend to blind Vasher's needs and care for the sick among the Clan's horses.

Knowing that his visit would not be a social one, Jess waited quietly for enlightenment.

'How's that boil healen' on Olivas' hind quarter?'

Jess clapped his cousin on the shoulder.

'You're a real choviar (magician) . . . come and see for
yourself. The swelling is down and the wound as clean as
lambs in clover. He's as right as rain now, Bor.'

They made for the north meadow where Olivas cropped
contentedly, close to the wattle hut that was his stable. He
lifted his head as they approached and whinnied his welcome.

'Thinken' of putten' him to a good mare yet?' Manfri said
casually after examining the fast-healing wound.

It had been in Jess' mind since the beginning of the barn
foundations had commenced. Olivas was eight years of age.
He had sired half a dozen fine foals on the Bayless nags and
only lost a couple, but the sheer quality of him cried out for
union with a dam of similar worth. It had been in his mind to
ask John Freeland whether he could locate a suitable mare but
the building of the house and outbuildings had occupied most
of his attention during the past months.

'I can get you a real little beauty for three goldies.'

He laughed at the surprise on Jess' face.

'Et's no great mystery, Bor. Young Edmund Gibbons –
over to Runcton – he won this pretty little mare at the gaming
tables off of that little bleeder, me Lord Sherwood. Next night
'e lost all 'is ready cash the same way he won it . . . Now 'e's
offeren' it to me for three guineas. She's a fine little thing, Jess,
just three years old and in good health. Thought you might be
interested in haven' her . . . and maybe I should pitch me
bender here and make sure the two of 'em thrive and give you a
fine stable?'

Jess stared down at the wizened little face lifted to his in
such guileless innocence. The crafty beng (devil). He must
know just how swiftly Jess would jump at such an offer – and
to offer himself with a fine breeder for Olivas thrown into the
bargain – there could be no question of refusal.

He pursed his lips and shook his head.

'My great aunt Shatmah,' he said in wonderment. 'I thought
I was the best businessman among us Baylesses but that's
about as neat a piece of inducement as I can remember. You
know the answer, Manfri my old son. Yes – and yes to both
questions. I'll have the mare as soon as you can arrange it – and
I'll gladly welcome you here to take over the stables. No
benders though. This place is for houses of bricks and mortar

and when the barn's complete, you'd live there. Could you bear with that, d'you reckon?'

Manfri's eyes flowed over Olivas with calm tenderness. He nodded.

'Reckon I kin get used to it if you can,' he said shortly. 'I'll fetch Glimmer over here within a next day or so. Then I'll settle it with me Dad and young Jack and bring me bag over.'

They pressed hands on it, the arrangement as tightly sealed as though their signatures had been laid on a document. Behind them the masons worked swiftly and quietly raising the walls of the long barn.

Within a month of Manfri's arrival, the roof timbers were being set and Manfri's little bender was established against the side of Olivas' wattle shelter. He and Glimmer grazed side by side, obviously much taken with each other. There had been no trouble from the young mare. She was high spirited and inclined to buck but there was nothing sly or ill-favoured in her temperament and Jess was delighted with her. By the time she came into season, Manfri was ready for her. He had spent days watching her with Olivas and as soon as it was clear that Olivas was becoming interested, he moved her into the small fenced yard he had been busy erecting.

'She'm a kicker,' he observed to Jess. 'We'll have to hobble 'er back legs till Olivas be mounted.'

The separation made Olivas anxious and, hearing his whinnies and calls, Glimmer quickly responded. On the second day of her isolation she was ready for him. While Manfri and his brother Jack held Glimmer in a twitch, Jess brought Olivas to her and waited as they greeted each other with snorts and high-pitched whickers and a great show of nuzzling and barging. He had never been difficult to control, coming to erection without haste so that Jess had always been able to handle him without help. Now the pattern unfolded naturally. Olivas quickened and grew and Jess led him to Glimmer and walked him in a circle, bringing the snorting, sweating horse up behind the hobbled mare with practised good timing. Olivas squealed shrilly, jerking his head upwards and then down as he mounted her. She shrilled and shivered and tried to crouch but Manfri and Jack brought her up in the twitch, her leg hobbles controlling her unshod hooves. It was over within

77

a couple of minutes and Olivas dropped his fore feet to the ground as the brothers deftly manoeuvered Glimmer's hind quarters out of harm's way.

Jess grinned at his cousins across Olivas' sweating back.

'Made for each other, I reckon,' he said happily. 'Did you ever see better manners in a courting couple, Bors?'

'Better'n I see'd you a few year back with that bint from Birdham, Sukie Lukis. Humpen' 'er in full daylight, back 'o' Heyworths lumber stack you was – and no more'n fifteen you was then.'

Jess laughed as he walked Olivas back to his field. Sukie had been only too happy to initiate him into the delights of her private places, he recalled. Sukie had been a continuing source of pleasure to them both until a sailor from Holland had proved even more attractive and he had been obliged to look elsewhere for a tumble. He hitched a piece of sacking from Olivas' groom box and rubbed the sweat from the horse's steaming coat with strong strokes.

'There y'are, my fine fellow,' he said softly to Olivas. 'A good performance, Bor . . . A few more like today's and I reckon you'll have made a fine little 'un for us. What say you, hmm?' Olivas was still breathing as though he had run a race but he turned his head into Jess' chest and snorted against his coat. He knew all about the threads of his master's dreams.

Chapter Seven

Jess stood on his wide stone terrace, rocking back and forth on the balls of his feet, surveying the building work with critical complacency.

The geese were doing a fine job of keeping the grass short between the gravel forecourt and the slope down to the creek. It was a constant relief to find that building the house had not affected the habits of the wild things, for the place still teemed with life – from coot and widgeon, mallard and oyster catcher through to the larger birds like the family of swans that nested among the reeds and the wild geese in winter and the herons that bred each year further up the creek in old Park Wood. Light airs sang through the summer-clad oaks and stirred the rushes at the water's edge. Away to the right, beyond the new dutch barn, Olivas cropped stiffly in white-spatted dignity and he could just see Glimmer and her foal sauntering across the second paddock beyond. Her movements were slow for she was again heavy with foal.

Behind Jess the house lay, its rosy brickwork and grey stone blending with the first tints of early autumn.

Contentment was his companion; achievement his balm. In the preceding twelve months the Blacks had made over sixty successful deliveries, with only one confrontation with the Law. The profits had been so handsome that he now held promissory notes from twenty-three borrowers and a comfortable income from the interest of each loan.

Warren Chaldecott, the Chichester Silversmith, had first suggested that Jess should make loans. It was a great deal more profitable than simply storing coinage in his chest in Tovey's strong room.

'Plant your sovereigns 'n watch them grow,' he'd said – and judging by the growth of his own fortune, Jess could see the wisdom of such advice.

Now, just one year later there was enough money, and more, for him to think of the next step.

Amy, coming from the kitchen door at the side of the house, saw the look on his face and knew from the unfocused softness there that he was thinking of Lavinia again. She stamped off towards the trees, a basket of washing under her arm.

'Why that one?' she thought for the umpteenth time, ramming a clothes peg savagely into a shirt cuff on the sisal line. 'She's only a gawky girl with her white face and silly simpering. Why should such a pale, bloodless creature like that occupy his thoughts so constantly?' But she knew the answer. The Freelands were gentry – part of his beloved Apuldram. From his way of thinking they were all part of his great plan for living and if he wished to wed a Freeland, who would stop him?

She snorted with a peg in her mouth as she hung a blanket by its corners.

It wouldn't be as easy as he seemed to think. She knew what the gorgios thought of gypsies, even if Jess chose to think of himself as one better. *He* might think himself a man of growing wealth and a potential catch in the neighbourhood – but they would laugh at him and slap him down for his impertinent presumption. She wondered, with a small malicious smile, just how Jess would take that humiliation. He had never known what it was to be denied anything. Returning to the house with her empty basket, she stared up at its sightless windows.

'Just you watch,' she said to it. 'Just you keep 'em out.'

Jess heard the sound of hooves and watched as a horseman rode round the dutch barn and into the forecourt. He started forward with hands outstretched.

John Freeland raised his crop in greeting and slid down from his horse. 'Sar shan, Bor.'

80

He clasped Jess' hands and hid his surprise at the change in the man since his last visit, eight months before. Jess looked older – far more than his twenty-five years. He had filled out and was simply but expensively dressed in strong cord breeches and a well-tailored brown leather jacket over fine lawn shirting. His unruly curls had been cued neatly into the nape of his neck and the grey eyes danced with pleasure as he pumped John's hand. It was Jess' face that had startled him, for he had always known it as the bright, open arena for all his friend's moods. It was still as handsome – possibly even more so, but new lines made a stranger of him, deep creases round his mouth and below his eyes. John wondered, as they turned towards the house, what strictures the place was laying upon one who was so essentially elemental.

'Amy . . . come and see who's here,' Jess bellowed as they crossed the hall towards the parlour. There was a light, dragging patter of feet behind them and Amy came through the kitchen door, wiping her hands on her apron. She had a dusting of flour on her nose. 'Master John – how good to see you. You've not been home for such a long time. You will stay and eat with us, won't you? There must be such a lot for you and Jess to talk about.'

He was swift to accept, looking from sister to brother and thinking how fine they both were. Tall and straight-backed and with a dignity about them that he found most endearing.

Amy was still willow slim, her hair bushed out from under her cap, down the back of her dress like charred gorse. Her sleeves were rolled up to the elbows showing a creamy expanse of olive skin.

Something stirred in him and contemplated her. She was startlingly handsome with the piercing blue eyes of all the Baylesses with the exception of Jess. No coquetry about her, though. She simply didn't try to project her womanliness so that there was a lack of animation about her that cooled any ardour her looks inspired. He returned his attention to Jess.

The parlour had changed dramatically since he had last seen it as a bare place being panelled and shuttered by an army of carpenters, a place without life but for the rasp and crash of the workmen's industry. Now it had become a delightful room, the pale panelling gleaming with polish and heavy yellow damask curtain hangings to draw across the shuttered windows on cold nights. There were bookshelves lining one wall and even some leather bound ledgers piled up on the two lower shelves. A pair of large highbacked fireside chairs, upholstered in flowered gros point, stood sentinel on either side of the hearth, a polished mahogany torchere beside each chair.

Jess' desk dominated one end of the room. It was a magnificent piece of carved and polished mahogany, its leather top cluttered with a mess of papers and scrolled documents.

Jess smiled broadly, following John's glance. 'Your Mother gave me that,' he said. 'It was the first piece of furniture that I ever owned – apart from the kitchen table and my bedstead.'

He glanced round the room.

'Now I mention it, there's a gift in here from each of the Freelands . . . Do you see yours?'

Their eyes rose to the picture that hung in the centre of the longest wall. It was a painting in oils, a seascape filled with winter grey water and a single sailing ship bent low as she drove through a curtain of spume before the wind.

John smiled at it and massaged his chin as he remembered the reason for its purchase. Sloe Fair in October last year.

Milling crowds and the warm meaty smell of a thousand perspiring bodies. He and Lavinia had always enjoyed Sloe Fair more than any of the lesser seasonal gatherings. It was by far the largest Fair that Chichester saw in the year, with dozens of brightly decorated stalls and tents erected on the Broyle and all the way down into North Street as far as the Cross. People converged upon the town from as far away as Horsham and Fareham, arriving in a steady dribble of humanity all through the night before the Mayor of Chichester declared the festivities to begin.

Boxers and tumblers, fortune tellers, physicians and wandering players; all came to entertain at Chichester Sloe Fair and, with the sweetmeat, ribbon, whitesmiths and haberdashery stalls, there was enough to intrigue the dullest browser for all the daylight hours. When they were children, Mistress Freeland had taken them each year, accompanied by two servants for their protection against pick pockets and drunken rogues, but as John was eleven years older than his sister, by the time she was thirteen, he was permitted to escort her with John Blunden's powerful presence at their backs.

Sloe Fair last October had been unusually crowded with strangers. Clusters of guttural voiced seamen blocked every street corner and it seemed that gangs of warring smugglers were pouring in from Kent and the Hampshire forests. Where the day had dawned on hundreds of happy people gathered together for their mutual enjoyment, by late afternoon it was clear that Chichester was about to be torn apart. John and Blunden had been hurrying a protesting Lavinia as far as Richard Farrington's house in South Street when they were attacked by half a dozen drunken ruffians within yards of the Farrington's gate. They had pressed Lavinia against the brick wall surrounding the house and tackled the gang as best they could. There had been one moment when John had felt that they must be overpowered – and then quite suddenly the pressure had fallen away and Jess had been there with them. He seemed to do very little fist work but in a moment had the iron gate open and had picked Lavinia up as though she was no heavier than a kitten. Then they were all through and Blunden crashed the gate shut behind them and the gibbering old watchman, who had done nothing to assist them, was locking and bolting it against the press of the crowd.

Jess had never quite explained how he happened to be passing. It was usual, at that time of day, for him to be exercising the three mares that he had bought for Olivas to breed with. His visits to the Chichester fairs were always made in the mornings. He had carried the frightened Lavinia right into the house and had set her gently down and wiped her tears before giving her into Lady Farrington's care.

The sea scape had been John's personal thanks for Jess' timely appearance. His parents had also been warmly grateful and had made Jess more welcome at Rymans since the incident. Lavinia had chosen to dramatise the whole thing and turn Jess into a knight in shining armour.

'Really,' he had protested more than once. 'You make too much of a simple act. I would have gone to anyone's help in the same circumstances . . . and so, John Bor, would you – so please forget the whole thing. I'm glad that Mistress Lavinia was only shaken by the experience. Now, come and let me

83

show you the new fencing I've put up in the north paddock . . .'

Now, as both their minds probed the memory once more,
John quickly slid onwards to the subject of the painting and the
dream which most occupied his friend's mind these days.

'Are you any closer to achieving that particular desire yet?'

Jess nodded. 'Next time you visit these parts I should have
my own vessel in commission. She's being built in the Birdham yard now and Master Ferris reckons that, if the work on
her continues to progress at the present rate, she should be
down the slip and into the water by the spring.'

'Ha then,' John said, seating himself in one of the chairs and
hunting in his pockets for his snuff. 'I shall be here in that case,
to wish her God's speed – for I take my Articles in September
and back I come to Chichester in time for Christmas to take up
an appointment with Joshua Daley, the West Street lawyer.'

Jess sat himself opposite John, legs splayed out in front of
him. 'Will you represent me then – or am I too great a risk for
your expensively acquired new reputation?'

'I'd be honoured to act for you. I shall be starting with no
reputation at all, Jess – until I can show my paces – and your
business is liable to be as complicated and laced with litigation
as any freshman could wish for.'

Jess' eyes twinkled. 'There's the gravest danger of my
becoming a respectable citizen in the very near future, you
know. I have met with a man of extraordinary vision, not to
mention an impeccable background. His name is Thomas
Weston. He seems to have more contacts in France and Spain
and even as far as the Orient and India, than any other man of
my acquaintance. He hails from Barnstable way . . . a far cry
from here, I grant you, but that may be no bad thing when I
tell you that the Law seems only to have been created for the
express purpose of trying his wits against it. I think he gets
more enjoyment from cheating the very government he represents in Parliament than anyone I've ever met. I'm thinking of
using him as my contractor until I have made my own
reputation with the foreign agents . . .'

He peered at John, the grey eyes suddenly sharp and cold.

'D'you want to come with us next week on a run? You
haven't been with the Blacks for a long spell.'

John shook his head. 'I doubt whether I shall ever earn a dishonest guinea more enjoyably ever again,' he said ruefully. 'I've got to watch myself from now on for I must be seen to be upholding the Law that I'm presently to represent. T'won't prevent me from making a regular order with you, all the same, Bor . . . That reminds me. Do you have cellarage here? My father regrets the lack of proper dry storage at Rymans and has been making much of late, of removing into Chichester.'

'Well, I have – and again, I haven't.'

John waited. He had long ago learned not to try and question Jess when he was being deliberately evasive.

'I considered building this place up from large cellars at first, for they afford any building a drier ground floor and I could easily have used all the space beneath this place. However, when we were clearing the undergrowth to begin building, we came across some old foundations that I don't want disturbed. They seem to have some sort of significance for me, Bor – I can't explain why. But I dare not touch them. So I made no cellar after all, but instead have a fine capacious brewhouse with a cellar that is not known to the authorities since it was made by my own uncles and cousins.'

John smiled before such inventiveness. The man really was an entertaining companion. 'God . . . London's a dung heap,' he said, stretching hugely for sheer pleasure in his surroundings. 'It's marvellous to be home in clean-smelling air again.'

London was full of activities, from the theatre to the gaieties of the Court in winter. All the same, he was a countryman at heart and much preferred the gentle pace of Chichester's social life. To ride out by Selhurst Forest or fish with Jess in springtime; that was what he hankered for now.

'May I bring Lavinia to call tomorrow?' he said.

He watched the quick flare in the grave grey eyes, as swiftly quenched. 'That would be a welcome pleasure for Amy – and for me,' Jess said lightly, his tone almost impersonal. 'She embroidered the cushion behind you – and gave it to me for Christmas. I treasure it greatly.'

John remembered the canvas that had seldom been out of Lavinia's hands. For months she pored over the design and had worked a pattern of oak leaves and acorns and then sprinkled

85

her charming woodland with mice and rabbits and birds, oversewn in gleaming silk thread. It had taken her a long time, unusual for her for she was deft and quick with her needle.

'Well, she has been belabouring me ever since I came home – begging me to bring her over to see you – and also the new foal that everyone is so excited about. She says that the foal is the main attraction but I suspect that her gallant rescuer has the greater pull.'

Jess laughed, groaning in mock exasperation. 'She's not still pulling that one, surely? I thought we had brought her back to earth when Magistrate Egon named me as the organizer of practically all the illegal traffic between Chichester and Romney Marsh.'

He jumped up, pulling his watch from his waistcoat pocket. He flicked open the cover and took his time counting his numbers before tucking it back out of sight.

'Come on, Bor,' he said. 'I nearly forgot until you mentioned him. Olivas' dam, Glimmer, has produced the finest little foal we've bred so far. He's four months old now. Come and take a look at him before Amy starts complaining that we're spoiling her hot food.'

The paddock had been fenced round with stout iron palings to prevent the horses from eating acorns and other undesirable berries. It was a large field, divided into two sections connected by a five-bar gate. The sections were grazed alternately throughout the year until winter came and the frosts drove the whole string into the barn, under cover.

Olivas and one of his sons served only carefully selected mares and the resulting quality of most of the foals had already begun to draw interested breeders to the Bayless stables. Even the Duke of Richmond had been pleased with the two visits he had made and had sent one of his own mares to Olivas with highly satisfactory results.

Jess and John leaned on the barred fence, watching the horses grazing in companionable silence. The grass in the field was lush and John counted nine animals. Olivas lifted his head, saw his visitors and moved towards them, swishing his pale silken tail and shaking the flies from about his head. He was unquestionably Monarch of the field, magnificent in carriage and quality, even though he was now no longer young. He

86

approached, whickering a welcome in the back of his throat. He nudged Jess and blew in his ears, knowing that his Master never came to him empty handed.

Jess fondled the stately head. 'Oh, yes, my fine fellow. You think I've brought some choice little morsel for you, don't you? Well then, let's see . . .' He patted his pockets and looked worried. 'Where could I have put it, Poori Bor?'

Olivas gave him a melting look and joined in the search, nosing Jess from neck to hip until two small oat cakes were discovered in an inside pocket.

The three mares hung back, giving Olivas precedence with the visitors and then curiosity drew them slowly towards the little group by the fence, trailing their young as they approached. They were shades of brown, from bay through chestnut to sorrel. All but two of the colts were golden of mane and tail and all were leggy and well formed. They were russet shades of autumn – except one.

'Look at him,' Jess said quietly, pointing.

The foal had been too small to catch John's eye at first, but now he came timidly towards the jostling horses at the fence, peeping at them from behind his mother. He was a spindly little creature, delicate as a fawn, but with the promise of such grace and balance about him that John drew in his breath as the foal stood shyly on the edge of the throng. He was a completely golden animal, his coat the colour of wet sand and the still stubby mane and tail like liquid cream.

'Isn't that the most perfect sight you ever saw?'

Jess' voice was husky, as though the air was knocked out of him afresh each time he looked at the little creature. They watched it quietly as it stood against its dam staring at them with huge black eyes. Then, tired of the lack of action, it backed away and gambolled off across the paddock, bucking its tiny hooves as it went.

'Phew.' John realized that he had been holding his breath as he watched the foal's perfect movements – and let it out in a rush. 'Beautiful, Jess. He's surely the most handsome little creature on four legs that I ever saw.' His eyes continued to follow the gyrations of the small distant figure circling and leaping in the sunshine.

Something distracted his attention and made him turn away

87

from the horses. He swung round and leaned his back against the rails and looked at Jess, to find himself staring into grey pools filled with an intensity that quickened his pulse. He stared back, unable to tear his attention away, hardly aware of Jess' quiet voice.

'Midas is his name, Bor . . . after the king who turned everything to gold. And John . . . I'd like to give him to Mistress Lavinia for he is the most perfect possession I have. Do you think I might safely ask your father's permission to do this? I . . . don't want to offend them so that they feel bound to refuse me. Will you mention it to them and see how they feel about it?'

The eyes held him. He felt weighted down so that neither his limbs nor his brain would respond. The deep grey pools swam round him like eddies of smoke in a fathomless black cavern.

Jess blinked – and the moment passed and might never have been.

'What do you think, Bor?' His voice sounded eager – anxious, tentative. No more, nor less than any other young suitor on the verge of committing himself to a declaration.

He must be mad – he knew that the answer would be in the negative. Jess was a good and valued friend but Thomas Freeland would never permit his only daughter to marry a gypsy.

Even as that thought was created he heard himself say, 'S'truth, Jess – that animal will be worth a king's ransom in a year or two. Is it Lavinia you're after?'

'You know I am, Bor.' The deep voice was gentle, patient with even a hint of humour in it. 'You know me . . . I hate to be refused anything that I've worked so hard to win. There's never been anyone else for me. Sure, you and I have been wenchen' in our time but that was just boys' games. Now I'm a man, John – and I've plenty to lay at her feet. I've watched her grow from a little child into the perfect young woman she is today. There never was anyone else, Bor – and there never will be.'

John's silence seemed to reach out to him and he hurried on as though afraid to hear his reply.

'After this year, I will not be going on any more trips,

John . . . Richard Farrington will be ready to take my place and the men are so familiar with our system that they will remain disciplined enough to carry on under his leadership. I shall set up the contacts and then concentrate on legitimate trade with the "Grace". My fortune is in safe hands, John, and well able to bear the responsibility of supporting Lavinia. She would not be wedding a gypsy, you know. I would have a good house for her to come to – and a man whose love for her will always be strong and abiding.'

John put his arm round Jess' shoulder and they strolled back towards the house. 'You know that I'll do all I can on your behalf,' he said. 'We've been brothers for so long – sister swapping seems a natural progression. Amy would chase me right out of the Parish if I were to try to court her, but at least I can enjoy her excellent cooking when I come here.'

'I'll speak to Father as soon as the right moment presents itself,' he said before he left.

'Thank you, Bor,' Jess said simply.

Amy watched him go. There was an element of worry in the cheery farewell he gave them. She hoped devoutly that his concern was justified.

Chapter Eight

Jess waited for word from Rymans.

Each day saw him in a different place, feverishly negotiating the sale of timber here, collecting interests on his loans there. He kept up a furious pace as though the need to add to his already considerable capital would ensure that his reception at Rymans was cordial.

Amy missed nothing – but then the surveillance of her brother had always been her main occupation. She had been pleased to see John Freeland when he called for he was a pleasant enough companion and never stepped outside the bounds of his excellent manners. Long gone was the noisy, cheerful boy of their youth – the tease who put frogs in little maids' pockets. Now the boy who liked guddling with Jess had become a sharp and intelligent weapon with which to defend his clients, with a mind well capable of interpreting the labyrinth of the Law to their best advantage. Her approval was in no way personal, for he meant nothing to her although his presence did not give her the dreadful fits of trembling that most other male company instigated. He would, however, be an invaluable advisor to Jess in the years to come.

Her feelings towards his sister were honed into a much sharper focus. The girl was growing into a contriving woman. She was always polite to Amy but the feeling remained that there was nothing between them; no warmth nor liking and only the discipline of strict good manners to separate them from open dislike. That Jess should want Lavinia with the dogged determination she knew he felt, was a constant pain to her. Her eyes followed his departing figure, willing his mounting anxiety to drain away; calling on the house with its mysteries to help her to rid him of his fever so that these charmed months together could continue for always without the necessity of intrusion.

The whole pattern of her life had changed since her arrival in Jess' house. They had fallen back into the easy and affectionate companionship of their childhood and it was as though there had been no parting. He was delighted and impressed with all that she had learned at Manor Farm for she was not only an accomplished cook now but was also able to read and write and even to keep the household accounts in commendable order. As each room emerged from the carpenters and painters hands, they had worked side by side to turn the emptiness into comfortable living quarters and now – now the house reflected Jess' fine taste for good furniture and Amy's way with colour. Every chair and table, every oak window sill shone with the depth of her love and gratitude. The lead lights were never dusty or rain stained, the floors were becoming a shining hazard to her own uncertain balance. She drank in the deep warning that hung over the whole house, luxuriating in the fear it induced in others for it would surely keep the men away from her and the women away from Jess.

Amy turned back into the house and cleared the mess of dinner dishes from the refectory table. Her leg hurt her this evening and a deep sigh escaped her as she loaded her tray with the clutter of plates and bowls.

'Tired, Pen?' Jess put an arm round her shoulders and gave her a quick hug. 'You work too hard, you know. I've been thinking about that for some time and was going to talk to you about it. How about having a girl in the kitchen to give you a hand?'

She looked up at him in alarm. 'I'm not having a stranger in this house,' she said sharply, hunching her shoulders under his hand.

He laughed and smacked her bottom. 'Don't worry, you jealous hussy. She won't be a lass who'll catch my eye. You can choose her yourself.'

She shook her head and turned away from him with her loaded tray. 'I manage very well, thank you . . . I enjoy the work here, Jess. It's *our* house, isn't it? There's nothing difficult about polishing fine furniture – or in feeding you and Manfri, for that matter.'

The subject was not raised again then. He settled himself in the parlour among his ledgers while she tidied up and put away the platters and cutlery and stoked the kitchen fire. When she came through to the parlour and closed the door behind her, she had her sewing with her.

'Oh good,' he said, looking up. 'Let me pour us a drink and then you can tell me what's been ailing you today. You look quite peaky.'

It was her favourite time of the day when they closed the doors and the curtains and shut out the rest of the world. She settled down in one of the comfortable fireside chairs with her sewing in her lap and her painful foot on a small stool. He brought her a glass filled with amber liquid from a crystal decanter and placed it carefully on a salver on the torchere beside her.

Then, with a ledger still in his hand, he sat down on the rug at her feet and leaned his head back against her leg.

'Now, tell me how you are and why you look troubled today.'

'I'm all right,' she said lightly but he could feel the tremble in her body and the black rage flared in him as it always did when he saw the poor girl wracked this way. The severity of Nick Smyth's attack on her had been intense and because it was Amy, she had thrust her shock into the deepest recesses of her mind so that she need not think of it. To all intents and purposes, the terror of that night might never have happened, for she never referred to it. At the same time, fits of uncontrollable shivering had begun.

Within weeks they had become attacks of fainting during which time she shook violently, a fleck of white spittle sliding across her cheek. The turns lasted no longer than a few minutes but afterwards she would be limp and dazed and best off resting for an hour or two. It seemed to Jess that they were getting more severe, more frequent. He sat quietly against her leg, gauging the tremor in them and talking quietly to her as though neither of them knew of her struggle.

It was no good. Within minutes, her efforts to hide the

trembling had given way to teeth chattering shivers and she dropped the glass of sherry and watched with impotent fury as the sticky liquid splashed down the front of her flowered gown and the long stemmed glass shattered into a hundred pieces in the hearth. Her eyes filled with tears as she sat, hugging herself in her effort to stop the movements of her body. Jess jumped up and put his arms round her.

'Gently there, Chiriklo . . . Don't worry. It will soon pass.' His voice was soft and crooning and she buried her face in his neck and gave way to the terrible movements.

It was a bad one – the worst she had had. It seemed to go on and on and in Jess' arms she felt like a wooden puppet in the hands of a mad master. Through it all, Jess held her and when it was over he lifted her and carried her up the stairs to her chamber.

She was weak and perspiring from the ordeal and he helped her out of her gown and slipped a shawl round her shoulders as he tucked her into the high bed. Then he sat beside her, holding her hand. 'I think this illustrates what we were discussing earlier,' he said gently. 'These "turns" are not getting any less, Pen, and I shall have to talk to Doctor Sanden about them. But first of all, you must have help in the house. What happens if you have a "turn" one day when you are alone?'

'I've had several,' she said, instantly on the defensive.

'Not as severe as the one you've just had, I'll warrant.'

They both knew the truth of that and he went on quickly, 'I shall go and visit Mistress Ayles in the morning, Amy. Young Polly is needing work and I'm sure that you don't find her displeasing. She'd jump at the chance of service in this house, wouldn't she?'

Amy nodded, too tired to argue that the intrusion of anyone was offensive to her – whether she liked the individual personally or not. She closed her eyes and relaxed under Jess' stroking hand. The house would send her packing almost certainly. She would have to rely on that.

He brought Polly Ayles back with him the following morning, complete with carpet bag and plain smiling gratitude.

*   *   *

93

When, after a week, there was still no word from John, Jess' restless mood deepened. He prowled about the fields and woods, examining fences, checking the horses' legs and hooves, striding among the swine in Salterns woods without noticing them run squealing and grunting from under his feet.

The money-lending business seemed suddenly to demand the establishment of a town office and he had no difficulty in finding suitable premises after announcing his needs in the merchants bar in the Swan. With feverish energy he bought two desks, chairs and ceiling-high bookcases, moved most of his clutter of documents and rate books from Lavenham and, within three days had established himself as a mortgage and fire assurance broker in two rooms on the first floor of 16 East Street, above Cardman Smith the Tailor. Although such an advance was greatly to his benefit, such was his mood that he found himself quite unable to remain cooped up in the two small rooms. He engaged a clerk to attend to the considerable ledger work and returned to Manfri and the horses who were less than appreciative of his short temper and restlessness.

'You'm maken' Glimmer jumpy, Bor,' Manfri complained, watching the swollen mare recoil from Jess' outstretched hand and lumber away across the field streaming her gangling bay foal behind her. 'Rubbish,' Jess snapped, kicking an overturned bucket out of his way as they surveyed the state of the dwindling bedding straw.

'S'truth, Manfri. You keep this place like a pigsty. For pity's sake, get it into your woolly head that we can't up sticks and leave this place once the mess gets too great. This barn is permanent. It must be kept clean and sweet – you know that.' He picked up a hay fork and poked at the thick mass of bedding straw in one of the stalls. The surface looked damp and the whole barn gave off an odour of sour horse urine.

Manfri humped his shoulders. 'Year, Bor – I know. Just haven't seemed to find the time this week to muck out.'

'Well, do it now. I'm not having the foal put in here on wet bedding. The two new mares arrive tomorrow and look, man . . . you haven't done a thing about setting up their stalls yet.'

'I know – I know. Ben all took up with getten' their tack from the saddler today. Just let me be, Jess, an' I'll have it all as neat and fresh as yer own chamber before the mares arrive.'

Jess stamped away towards the house. What in tarnation was the matter with Manfri, he thought. His whole life centred round the horses and their welfare and yet he was untidy and disorganised and clearly having problems about settling in permanent quarters. Well, if he couldn't do better, he'd have to go back to Vasher and a trained stableman would replace him.

Jess stood in the drive between the barn and the house, watching the empty drive for a messenger from Rymans.

Manfri stood where Jess had left him, watching the rigid figure of his cousin until he turned the corner of the barn. Fair bothered he was, these days. It must be all the booti (work) he was taking on in Chichester. Not like young Jess to be rough with people. Mind you, he had a point. The health of the horses was the most important item if they were to breed seriously and successfully from Olivas. He must work out some daily routine and maybe ask Jess for a lad in the stables to assist. By the end of the month they would have four horses and two foals and this time next year . . .

Jess strode into the kitchen. 'Bring me a pot of Amy's cider,' he said to Polly and went through to the parlour where he dropped into his swivel chair behind the desk and drew paper and quill pen towards him. He wrote feverishly and was sanding the note when Polly came in with the brimming tankard. He folded the note, sealed it with red wax and held it up to her.

'Take it over to Rymans right away,' he said. 'It's to be placed into Master John's hands only. I know that he is there this morning so don't give it to anyone else.'

Polly bobbed and fled with the note, encouraged by the stony unhappiness in her master's face.

The hasty scribble that she brought back only increased his anguish.

Dear Jess

I'm sorry about the lack of communication but the problems are legion and mother and father are in constant strife so that, so far, nothing is resolved. You will have to be patient because your appearance at this time would only exacerbate the situation.

Lavinia is quite unaware of the cause of our parents' discord and is naturally most concerned about it. I fear that my father's increasing ill health makes him unreasonable but I think you have a right to know that Lavinia acquired a suitor during her stay in London. I understand that my father considers him an appropriate match.

The letter tore away the last of Jess' peace of mind. He went about his business in a state of thunderous anger, snarling at his cousins and even shouting at Amy. She bowed her head before his misery but only to hide the satisfaction she felt at the way things were turning out.

Nine days after Jess had spoken with John, a note was delivered, asking him to call at Rymans the following morning. He donned fresh linen, groomed Olivas until they both glowed, and tried to control the swooping changes of mood that the command had created in him. One moment he was convinced that he was about to be refused – and his spirits plummeted . . . but then, reason protested that, had that been so, a polite letter would have sufficed.

'Wish me luck,' he said to Amy as he swung up onto Olivas' comfortable back. She looked up at him with such fervent worship that he tickled her ear with his crop as he moved off.

She stood looking after him until the image blurred and two large tears spilled over and down her cheeks.

Rymans was a hive of activity. Jess was obliged to make his way with care across the yard and round the new seed drill that had just been acquired for Tom Chatfield to use on his three hundred acres. At any other time Jess would have been intrigued to know more about this astonishing invention. As it was, his eyes slid over the ungainly machinery without comment and he went across to the Hall door and knocked, hat in hand. John Blunden let him in and took him straight to Freeland's office on the far side of the house. He put his head round the narrow door and announced Jess' arrival.

Thomas Freeland rose with difficulty as Jess advanced to grip his hand and then help him back into his chair. The room was dark in spite of the sunlight streaming through the three small windows. A sullen fire smoked palely in the grate.

Jess said nothing, remembering the last time he had been in the room. He had rehearsed the things he wanted to put to Master Freeland until they were engraved upon his memory, but now that he was standing beside the sick man's chair, waiting to be invited to sit down, all he could think of was that this man was dying.

Freeland's colour was unnaturally high, his faded eyes glowed with an inner fever and his formerly robust frame appeared in a few weeks to have shrunk so that he sat huddled beneath a knitted shawl like a bundle of discarded clothing.

There was nothing at all the matter with his voice. 'I'm obliged to ye for calling, Jess. I'd have come and seen you myself but for this damnable pain in m' guts.'

He waved aside Jess' sympathy.

'We won't waste words on regrets. Talking makes it worse and there are one or two things that you and I have to straighten out.'

He waved blue veined hands impatiently as Jess tried to speak. 'Let me do the talking, Damn it. You can have your say afterwards. Sit down, can't you . . . hovering about confuses me. Sit down and don't keep hopping from one foot to the other.'

His voice became thin and troubled and brooked no interruption. 'Jess, I must tell you that your hopes have not met with our blessing. The main reason is that Lavinia is considering another young man whom she met while visiting her aunt in Kensington. He has also pressed his suit and her mother and I are favourably impressed by him. What do you say to that, hmm?' He peered up at Jess through beetling brows and drew his shawl round his shoulders more closely.

The old man's words came as a profound shock to Jess. He flushed to the roots of his hair but said nothing. A nerve ticked jumpily in his right cheek. Thomas Freeland went on talking. He had not really expected any outburst from Jess, knowing the extent of his self control. His voice softened.

'Now , I've always had the warmest regard for you, as you must know, Jess. You are John's most valued friend here in Sussex and I'm sure that you will continue to be so, long after I am gone and he is administering the Smyth Estates. My wife is also fond of you. You have used your natural assets to better your situation in a most spectacular fashion and I have no doubt that you will go on to even greater heights of achievement. You have my full respect – my admiration – in all that you achieve. On the other hand, the fortune that you are amassing with such determination has largely been acquired through unlawful practices – and every day that you continue to make money at the expense of the Treasury, you shorten the odds on coming to a most undesirable end. That is not the kind of life I would permit my daughter to be party to. Where Lavinia's future is concerned, I look for a man of complete stability from a good family background, a son-in-law who will be a credit to myself as well as to her and her children.'

'How do you compete against such pomposity?' Jess thought in exasperation.

'Sir,' he said, bringing all his charm to bear. 'Please consider one point. Mistress Lavinia's future is in your hands, naturally, and I respect what you say but would you let her wed someone like – say Viscount Pendred? You might have been describing him when you spoke of old and noble families, for his pedigree is unassailable . . . but would you want him for your son-in-law?'

Freeland banged the arm of his chair.

'That's not what I mean and you know it, Bayless. That dissipated popinjay is not representative of his station . . .'

'Then surely I prove my point, Sir – that there are good and bad examples to be found in every walk of life. I know that I have no background with which to impress you – but surely, Master Freeland, my own efforts speak for themselves and are worth some sort of respect. My whole life has been planned round Mistress Lavinia, Sir. It might have been a presumption to have felt that way at one time but now – now I am able to offer her as great a security as her own family has. My house is hers and everything I own and it would be my intention to settle a sum upon her that would ensure her comfort and security, whatever my fate. I have always vowed that my smuggling activities would cease altogether when I married. You must know that I offer her a husband whose sole aim in life is to please her and be worthy of her.'

98

'Oh, heaven preserve me from poets and plunderers. Speak plainly or leave me be, boy.'

'No, Sir – I am no longer a boy,' Jess said quietly. 'This has all come about far too quickly and before time too, out of my request to be allowed to present Mistress Lavinia with Olivas' new foal. I realized that a gift of this kind would require some explanation and so I told John of the way I have always felt about her. I am not pressing for her hand now, Sir. She is young and will want to stretch her wings yet. But I earnestly beg you to consider my suit in the future – and to permit me to present Midas to Lavinia in the meantime.'

The old man slumped deep in his chair. He looked exhausted. When he spoke his voice was little more than a croak.

'I can't talk to you any more, Jess. Keep your foal. My daughter may not accept it. And rid yourself of these dreams, man. She is not the one for you. I'm sorry, lad . . .'

He closed his eyes. His voice was like dried leaves in a breeze. 'When you stare at me like that I find my resolve weakening in the strangest way, so forgive me if I shut my eyes. This way I can tell you more firmly that my mind is quite made up. I'm sorry to hurt you, Jess, but you may not call upon my daughter. I trust that we will continue to retain the respect for each other that we have always enjoyed. Good day to you . . .'

Jess stared down at the shrunken figure, forcing himself not to will him to open his eyes; forcing the adrenalin to cease its wild thumping; forcing himself to control the violence that swept through him.

Finally he bowed to Freeland's drooping head and turned on his heel. He closed the door firmly and strode across the hall into the Great Chamber. The rooms were empty and his ears ignored the hasty rustle of swirling skirts as he went out into the sunny autumn day.

Jess drove Olivas across the stubbled fields to the Manhood Highway, using the speed and the drumming hooves to catch up with himself and slow his rage down.

The Power was fading.

It was the first time that it had been successfully resisted – and that it should have been on the subject of Lavinia brought his blood back to the boil as he thought of it.

He had broached the subject too soon, he saw that now and cursed himself for the foolishness of his timing. Another few weeks even, and the resistance would have been diminished. Thomas Freeland was a mortally sick man with fast failing strength – and after this next Nutbourne Run, he would be having no further direct involvement with the Blacks – apart from making the arrangements and financing the operations.

In a month or two he could have presented himself, not only as Jess Bayless of Lavenham but also as owner of the "Grace" – a combination that should have impressed the most reticent of fathers.

Reason gradually quieted the fury and bitter self blame, and he brought Olivas down to a gentle canter and then a trot, stroking the shining neck and feeling the horse's laboured lungs heaving between his knees.

'I'm sorry, Bor,' he said, leaning along the long, damp neck. Olivas wiggled his ears and kept moving. No one understood better than he did, the mercurial hills and valleys of Jess' moods and he had always responded to them as though they were his own. They cut across the empty fields, back onto the Highway, towards the straggle of cottages that separated Birdham Mill from the boatyards.

'Leave me alone, Amy. I'm in no mood for company.'

She stared at him in surprise, in the act of settling herself in the chair opposite him as she did each evening. She sat down slowly.

'I won't disturb you,' she said stiffly. 'We don't have to talk, do we?'

He glowered up at her from his place on the sheepskin rug. 'Are you deaf, Girl? I said I want to be alone.'

The colour flared up into her cheeks and she stood up quickly so that her precarious balance slipped and she stumbled heavily against her chair.

Contrite, he put up a hand and took hold of her russet skirt. 'I'm sorry, Pen. I'm a rude, evil tempered bastard and I can't think why you put up with me so patiently. Come back and sit down here on the rug and cheer me up.'

She put her sewing on the chair seat and settled down beside him, the two spots of high colour still bright on her cheeks. She could feel the torment in him and, knowing the source of it, gloried in his pain. Let him suffer . . . His hurt will turn to indifference one day.

The look was in his eyes and, recognizing it she said nothing, but sat quietly gazing into the embers of the fire in the basket grate. He took her hand and smoothed it across his knee and she let it lie there, comforted by the gentle stroking motion.

He stared into the red coals, concentrating once more upon searching within himself for the Power, calling to it and feeling only the emptiness of total loss. It was there in the house; he could feel it as surely as he could sense someone standing behind him – but it was outside him . . . Not within any more. The influence was different and filling him with compulsions of such sensuality that he groaned aloud, stirred by erotic fantasies of Lavinia which would never be fulfilled.

'Why torture me with these images if you won't have Lavinia here . . . I won't have another woman in the place if I can't have her . . .' He saw her delicate face in the glowing embers, staring back at him with parted lips and a reflection of his own longing in the huge blue eyes. He saw her mouth upturned in laughter, the pink movement of her tongue moistening her lower lip, gleaming . . . full.

He felt Amy's soft hand under his and began tracing the contours of each finger with the tips of his own. Thin hands; long and strong and the nails as smooth as glass. Warm glass.

Warm hand lying across his thigh like a small waiting bird . . . caught in the shadow of the hovering hawk; knowing . . . submissive . . . almost entranced by the knowledge of its danger.

Lavinia . . . hear me . . . need me – want me . . .

The pent up feelings of years seemed suddenly to flow outward from him as a swollen river bursts its banks; flooding through him without warning and he groaned aloud again, knowing that it controlled him; staring into Amy's comprehension as her arms went round him, drawing him against her.

Soft warm skin with the clean woman smell, the scent of excitement – of wanting him. He wept with the vastness of his need, of her fast, shallow breath beneath his hands, of her urgency, the overwhelming response of her. He drowned in the smooth length of her body – olive skin against the olive of his own, blue Bayless eyes submerging in the hard cold steel of grey rage. He hurt her and the very infliction of the pain was sweet pleasure and her pleasure roused him further until images blurred and the fury drained from him.

They sat beside the dying fire and Amy stretched out and gathered their crumpled clothing into her lap. Jess stood up and held his hand out to her and she got slowly to her feet and followed him out of the room. Around them the house relaxed, the crescendo of its pleasure spent. The voices were little more than a rustle of shadows in the murky darkness, the soundless pulse beat an imperceptible flutter of the senses.

The Watcher sighed and prepared for the death of life newly sown.

PART TWO

Lavinia and Jess

Chapter One

From the day that Lavenham became his property Jess had managed the estate meticulously, having learned long ago from old Henry Diggens that where there was dirt and confusion lay waste and disease. His new boundary hedges grew well and he saw to it that one of the Baylesses trimmed and layered them in February each year, before the new growth began to sprout. The barn and stables, though, were Manfri's preserve. Jess – forever the perfectionist, relied daily more firmly upon Manfri to attend the better fairs and horse sales, for he knew just what Jess sought in a breeding mare by this time. It was a constant pleasure for Jess to see him watching the animals being put through their paces; chewing the inside of his cheek and missing nothing through half closed eyes. He studied the way a horse turned, showing the muscle movement of its shoulders, the way it carried its head, watched the stifle action in its hind quarters.

It was this acute awareness of Manfri's which recognized something special in Minta when he spied her at Horsham Spring Fair. She was penned with five other mares of varying shapes and sizes so that he walked past the little group several times before something made him pause by the wattle rail and caste his eye over them. Minta drew his attention immediately. She was a hand higher than the others, with a sturdiness in leg and shoulder which suggested reliability in the field. As if aware of Manfri's scrutiny, the light chestnut lifted her head and peered across the restless backs of her companions towards him. She had a long narrow head with a dirty white blaze from forehead to muzzle. She and Manfri surveyed each other and she watched as the little man turned and approached her owner. She was led out of the pen on a rope halter and Manfri lounged with deceptive casualness as she was walked up and down before him. The darting blue eyes missed nothing. Minta was a mature mare, six years old and had, he was assured, only lost one foal in five. She was a strong working cob, fifteen hands in height and sound in wind and limb. He said nothing to the stream of Minta's virtues but felt her legs with light hands, running his fingers over her body, checking her teeth and gums, teats and the angle of her tail. He discovered a crop of boils inside her thigh and extensive heel cracking. One watchful rolling eye pleaded with him through a film of bluish mucous which gathered and crusted round the lower lid. She was breathing fairly fast.

The farmer, recognizing Manfri's attention to such blemishes, was happy to part with Minta for two sovereigns. It was the only time that Manfri brought a less than healthy mare back to Lavenham.

'What in tarnation did you pick this sickly nag for?' Jess objected when he came to inspect the new arrival. Whatever it was that ailed her had increased during the journey south from Horsham and now it was clear that she was well below par and a second cluster of boils had broken out on her leg. She stood in her stall with head lowered, nosing the oat straw of her bedding. Her coat was dull and scurfy and from the infected eye a dark glutinous tear seeped down her left cheek.

Manfri grinned at Jess and ran a boney hand lovingly over the mare's hot quarters.

'Just you wait an' see, Bor,' he said with complacency. 'Leave 'er to me awhile and I wager you won't recognise her. She's strong as an ox, is Minta . . . Look at that fine head there, Jess. Look to the thickness of those leg sinews. She'm got a wondrous high steppen' gait an' when I've rid her of all the poison in 'er blood and she's feelen' well again, I'll put her through her paces for you. Then you'll see quick enough what I spied in 'er.'

Jess looked at the sick mare doubtfully. She seemed like two gold pieces thrown to the birds to him. Still, there was no denying Manfri's talent for spotting good breeding mares.

'Keep her well out of the way of the others,' he said, shrugging as he moved away from the stall and went out into the yard. There were too many other subjects on his mind then and he thought little more of her except to note that Manfri worked long hours through the night, the light from the barn casting a faint yellow glow across the grass fronting the house.

Manfri delegated most of his daily duties to an uncomplaining Rueb and concentrated on Minta. He talked to her as he cleaned and dressed the open wounds where he had been obliged to cut out the suppurating mess with his whittling knife. The tender sound of his soft murmurings deep in his throat seemed to quieten the horse's fear and pain and she stood still as though mesmerised by his voice, content to let him do what had to be done. Ten days after Minta's arrival at Lavenham, Manfri brought the chestnut round to the kitchen door as Jess was eating his morning bread and pork.

'Time you had a look at yer new mare,' he said with a touch of satisfaction in his customary goblin's grin.

Jess pushed back his chair and came across to the door, bread hunked in his hand. Minta stood quietly beside Manfri and pawed the cobbles delicately with the tip of her newly-shod hoof. She nodded her head and stretched out to inspect the food in Jess' hand with pinkly enquiring muzzle.

She was straight legged and firm muscled. Gone was the droop and air of dejection. She stood against Manfri as though contact with him gave her the new gleam and zest for life which radiated from her. Her coat was richly burnished and the white blaze on her nose shone like a flash of light. There was still one poultice bandaged onto her hock but there was no longer any sign of lameness in her movement. Her eyes regarded Jess clearly with a sparkling watchfulness, not unlike Manfri's own.

'She'll make a fine dam,' Manfri said softly. 'Come out and watch me exercising her on the plunger when I take off the poultice tomorrow. She'll take the breath from you, Bor . . . I promise.'

He turned away and Minta followed of her own accord, clopping slowly behind her small mentor with her nose hovering close to his right shoulder. For all Manfri's lack of inches he had begun to carry himself with a certain dignity as became his position as head groom and trainer. It was part of his dedication to sleep in the harness room at the end of the barn although he ate in the kitchen of the main house with Polly and Rueb. It had taken him a matter of weeks to establish an efficient work routine after Jess' admonition, and he'd quickly adjusted to his cousin's insistance upon meticulous cleanliness in the barn and yards and paddocks. Now it went a great deal further than the twice daily mucking out and sluicing down of the cobbled yards. The harnesses and saddles were swabbed and soaped, the irons scrubbed clean and each horse was given a long daily grooming so that their coats shone and all signs of rot in their hooves had quite disappeared.

The arrival of Rueb had been fortuitous when Jess decided that nine horses was more than the tireless Manfri could cope with. When the house mares foaled there would be four more to care for. Rueb, Piramis' youngest son, was an obvious choice. He was, at fifteen, a big silent stripling with an admiration for Jess which knew no bounds. He had no special skills except for a limitless capacity to keep going in whatever he was doing. He took over all the occasional jobs in the stables and the main house, an occupation which kept him going from dawn until dusk. His industry ensured that Lavenham was run on oiled wheels and prospered daily.

Apart from Lavenham, there were only two houses of any importance in the Parish of Apuldram – Manor Farm and Rymans. The farm was a pleasant brick and quarry-stone building with a spread of barns and cattle sheds on one side and a large orchard on the other.

Rymans, on the other hand, was a unique structure of such unusual design that there had always been rumour and conjecture about its past. It was a stocky, almost square building on three floors with more than a suggestion of the fortified tower about it, for its grey stone walls were three feet thick and in one corner, encased in a miniature turret, a medieval stone newel staircase curled up to all three floors. There was a much grander carved oak stairway in the Great Hall but the children preferred to use the spiral steps for it was possible to slide round and round, down and down on wooden trays when no one was looking.

Lavinia loved Rymans. It was surrounded by fields and the path to the church ran along one of its boundaries, for Saint Mary's was only a hundred yards away, standing alone in Church Meadow with the grass growing high round its Saxon stonework. She could look out of any of the windows as far as the eye could see and the only other buildings were their own outhouses, the Church and Manor Farm. The rest of the village was gone, ravaged by plague and fire more than two centuries before, leaving only the Parson's cottage still standing, tucked in behind a decaying procession of windswept elms between the Church and the long abandoned Apuldram jetty. The path that wound past Parson's gate had once been a busy thoroughfare with the villagers' cottages lining one side and a fast-running stream on the other. Now it was abandoned, save for the nocturnal passings of furtive men about their unofficial business.

Loving hands had levelled the ground on the west and northern sides of Rymans and laid out lawns and flower beds and a well-stocked orchard. The children had a swing here among the trees and John Blunden's father had even made them a see-saw with little chairs on each end of the long plank. At the bottom of the orchard was a huddle of bee skeps, tended with devotion by a very old man whose real name no one could remember since he was always referred to as Beezer. Lavinia might have been a solitary child since John was eleven when she was born, had it not been for the various mysteries which occupied her attention for most of her early life. The mysteries of the countless nooks and crannies in the house, the secret cupboards and even the evil smelling but still fascinating medieval privy built into the solid thickness of the wall in her father's office; all combined to provide a lively mind with limitless opportunities for exploitation and adventure.

And there was Beezer and the strange and wonderful bees with their industry and almost human life style. Very early in her life, Beezer began to talk to Lavinia about his charges. From as far back as she could remember she had, on countless occasions, sat beside him outside the tumbledown shed he slept in, at the furthest extremity of the orchard, listening to his often unintelligible ramblings, wide eyed and attentive with complete faith in every word he uttered. It must have been that very trust which had started him talking to her, for he said very little to anyone else. She chose not to divulge the essence of their conversations for it would have been difficult to have pieced together the fragmentary sentences of his mutterings, in order to turn them into recognizable conversation. But she knew what he was talking about – and mostly it was about the bees.

They had their own philosophy, their own strict code of behaviour. 'Be good to the bees,' he would say. 'An' they will be good to you. Move carefully near their hives, with kindness in your heart and they will never sting you – even though you walk naked among them. But put a hand upon their house when there is hatred or skulduggery in your soul – and you'd best beware for they know . . . They know what is in you – and if it is bad they will go for you.'

She loved the bees. They were so industrious and clever and their honey so delicious on the end of a dipped finger.

By the time Lavinia graduated to the schoolroom, she was able to handle them on her own. She had only been stung once and that was when a bee became trapped in her clothing. The fact that she had killed a bee – albeit unintentionally, made her mourn for days. The pain from the angry sting was born stoically as an act of penance. The bees were forgiving and there were no other fatalities, although once, one of the gypsy children from the saltpans had tried to steal a plaited straw skep and had been badly stung for her trouble. It was this incident that first brought Jess Bayless into focus for Lavinia.

She and her mother were sitting, poring over a map of the Indies when a commotion down in the garden brought their heads up in alarm.

There was a bluster of shouting and sobbing and Lavinia recognized old Beezer's hoarse voice.

'What is going on?' Mistress Freeland said with some irritation for the lesson was not progressing as well as she would have liked and any new interruption was sure to increase Lavinia's inattention. She leaned across to the bell rope and gave it a sharp tug.

Mistress Blunden came puffing up the stairs to the solar. 'It's those ragamuffins from the Saltings, Ma'am,' she said in high indignation. 'There's two of them come stealen' in through the orchard hedge and tryen' to make off with one of the hives, cool as you please. Old Beezer, he spied them and gets 'is stick to one and they drops the skep, Ma'am. The bees went mad and went for 'em. I didn't see but Beezer just brought in one of them – the other ran off. She's stung from top to toe an' pretty bad with it too. Little tyke. I've got 'er down in the kitchen. You'd best come an' see, if you will, Ma'am. She looks quite poorly.'

The girl was on the kitchen settle and Lavinia was shocked to see the state she was in. She must have been about twelve years old, dark skinned with an unruly tangle of uncombed black hair. Her only clothing seemed to be a single skirt whose hem had long since worn into a tattered fringe, and a bodice made from a piece of rough sacking. At first glance she seemed fat but then Lavinia realized that the girl's flesh was swollen out of all proportion so that her eyes were mere slits and her mouth almost lipless. She stared in dismay at the tears that squeezed themselves out of the puffy lids.

'Oh, the poor child.'

Mistress Freeland knelt down beside the sagging girl and gently lifted a limp hand and examined the fingers. Only one was relatively unswollen. She stood up and went into action without further delay.

They laid the girl along the settle with a cushion to her head. The scullery maid was sent scuttling for the medicine chest while a reviving infusion of mint tea was set on the fire to warm. The girl's stings were cleaned and gently rubbed with a salve of comfrey, oil of turpentine and St John's Wort and the puffed eyes swabbed with rose water. Through it all she said nothing. She lay stiffly on the settle, shivering with fright and pain. Seeing the raggedness of her, Lavinia said shyly, 'Mama, should we give her something better to wear? She is bitten on her body too, so you will have to remove those sacks she is wearing, to get to the swellings on her middle. Shall I get a gown of mine for her?'

John Blunden was dispatched to the Saltings to fetch one of the Baylesses but had not gone far before he met Piramis and Jess already on their way to Rymans in a light cart. By the time they arrived at the back door with their caps in their hands, the girl was dressed in an old but still serviceable skirt and petticoat of Mistress Freeland's and a pretty blue bodice with wide sleeves that Lavinia had pulled from her own closet.

The interview had been brief. There were apologies and promises of greater discipline in future; there were thanks for the kindness with which the culprit had been attended. Rose Bayless, almost unable to walk, had been piled into the open cart with little ceremony and taken back to camp.

Lavinia's memory of the incident was always a clear one because of her indignation that anyone should disturb their bees – and because of the disturbing presence of the tall boy who had accompanied his uncle to collect Rose.

He had stood in the kitchen doorway as Mistress Freeland and Piramis Bayless examined the girl, taking in the room with its strings of hanging onions and smoked legs of pork, the disapproval of Mistress Blunden and the smirking scullery maid – and of the small girl squatting beside his cousin, crisply dressed in a flowered gown that highlit the pale golden fall of hair from under her cambric cap. She had done her best to ignore this riveting scrutiny but it was difficult, for he was equally worthy of her notice. For all the roughness of his grubby breeches and the greyness of his shirt, he was astonishingly handsome. There was an easy looseness in his movements and he stood straight-backed and leggy in the doorway, the darkness of his colouring in no way swarthy as his uncle was. His mouth was full and only just not smiling for there was a natural upturning about it which suggested a pleasing nature. But it was the eyes that finally arrested her, so that she stared back at him in open fascination. They were long and slightly almond shaped with thick black curling lashes. The irises were the strangest grey that she had ever seen for they were the colour of the sea in winter with the same impression of restless mobility – but they were not cold as the sea was cold. They exuded a compulsive warmth and charm that made the subject of their attention aware of her own femininity.

The boy had not opened his mouth on that occasion but later, when John returned from school, he admitted that that must have been Jess Bayless with whom he went fishing.

★   ★   ★

The image of the gypsy boy had remained in Lavinia's mind. She saw nothing of him but listened attentively whenever John mentioned his name. In this way she built up a picture of him – seen in the very biased light of John's growing hero worship. Remembering the easy grace and calm admiration in his eyes, it had not really surprised her to hear of the determined progress he was making to shake off the image of common 'gypsy'. Without knowing why, it seemed natural to her that he was ambitious, even if rumour was correct about the way he was going about making his money. All the same, it was a shock to her to discover the new Jess Bayless who had leased the lower lands of the Parish and was now building himself a fine house overlooking the Chichester Channel.

It was Mistress Freeland's own curiosity which finally brought them face to face, for the intriguing sight of his chimneys going up was more than she could resist. From Rymans, the sight of the twin pairs of spiralling chimneys stabbed the horizon above the tree line like rose-tinted sugar sticks. She let it be known, through John, that an invitation to inspect the house's progress might be graciously accepted.

Jess was delighted. He chose a fine day when the mud which still surrounded the house was fairly firm and the entrance was made negotiable by an approach of freshly laid gravel. The sun shone warmly on their heads and the woods were full of bird song.

John drove his mother and Lavinia from Rymans in an open trap, delighted that his friendship with Jess was finally being recognized and accepted by his family.

'You'll be pleasantly surprised,' he promised both the ladies. 'There is nothing left of the barefoot boy about Jess these days. He is a very fine fellow, mother. Just you wait and see.'

They saw. He was waiting for them by the front door; a tall, broad-shouldered figure, well dressed in fine quality breeches and a creamy silk shirt beneath his dark green jacket. His voice was deep and musical as he greeted them and handed them down from the trap. He watched as Mistress Freeland looked about her, surveying the outside of the house with surprised approval. She looked beyond at a jumble of brickwork that promised the future outhouses and stabling. The soft pink brick was offset by dove grey Bembridge stone window mullions and the leaded glass windows reflected the blue beauty of the day on the visitors. The sun shone blandly on the backdrop of neat estate fields and curving woodland with a sparkle of water amongst the reeds where the Channel flowed by to the Harbour and sea beyond.

Jess ushered his guests into the hall where carpenters from Hershall Kimber's yard were fitting pale limed oak panelling to the walls. The noise of saw and hammer was deafening and he hurried them through to the kitchen quarters and closed the door on the dust and industry.

'I do apologize for all the chaos and especially for having to entertain my first guests in the kitchen,' he said with a complacency which belied the apology. 'The parlour will be completed within the month and then I hope very much that you will honour me with another visit when Amy and I will be able to make you more formally welcome.'

It had been a pleasant morning and Mistress Freeland returned to her own home filled with praise for Jess Bayless. His sister, Amy, had been a quiet but gracious hostess, making them comfortable in the wide kitchen window seat so that they could look out over the newly levelled ground as it sloped away to the water's edge, and entertaining them with hot chocolate and delicious thins in a porcelain cake dish.

Jess had been amusing and delightful company without exceeding his place for one instant. Watching him surreptitiously, Lavinia could only admire his composure for he did his best to give Mistress Freeland his complete attention, when he must be remembering the last time they had been assembled in the Rymans kitchens. Who would have imagined in his wildest dreams that that ragged leggy youth would now be Master of his own Estate, entertaining the gentry with such easy courtesy?

He caught Lavinia's eyes on him and winked.

She coloured slightly and lowered her eyes but the corners of her mouth fought and lost control of the little smile that trembled there. Confused by her own shyness she turned her attention to Amy who hovered over them with the chocolate pot. It was a small shock to see the stony unfriendliness in her eyes as she poured the hot sweet liquid into Lavinia's upheld cup.

There had been several visits to the Bayless house after that and Jess had become a regular visitor to Rymans for he played a fine hand at cards and made a good partner with Thomas Freeland when Geoffrey Tovey was visiting.

It was about this time that Lavinia became aware of her father's failing health. Nothing had been said of it but when a family is as close and devoted as they were, it is not possible to hide the onset of illness. She observed a gradual loss of weight and shortness of temper in him which was unusual.

'Why is Papa so crabby these days?' she asked after a particularly uncharacteristic exchange with him over his wish to send her to London for the winter season.

'Don't cross swords with him, Linnie,' Abigail Freeland had said gently. 'He has not been feeling very well in the last few weeks and I don't want him upset. He has a wretched pain in his stomach which is very worrying and Doctor Sanden doesn't seem to know how to ease it. Be a good daughter and do as he asks. Spend this season with Aunt Julia. Please.'

And, of course, she did as they wished.

Three months in London was the dream of most country girls in Lavinia's position. There was very little for most young ladies to occupy them in the country, other than sewing and visiting each other and making pickles and sweetmeats when the kitchen was not too busy.

Lavinia had never been bored with her life. She rode her pony daily, cared for the bees and kept a well-stocked herb garden. She was an accomplished needle woman and enjoyed nothing better than designing complicated patterns for cushions and stool covers. She discovered boredom for the first time in London.

It was not that there was not enough to occupy her, quite the reverse, for the days were filled with calling upon Aunt Julia's friends and trips to theatre and opera, picture galleries and exhibitions. It was the pattern of life in London, and many of those who created that pattern that she found at best dull, and at worst truly objectionable. They were cynical and cruel to and about each other. Their wit was barbed and clever and entirely contrived in her eyes. Their preoccupation with self adornment and admiration was quite astounding for it was not only the women who were guilty of this. If anything, the men were even more pretentious. She was accustomed to the straightforward honesty of her father and brother and found it diffficult to cope with conversations that were loaded with innuendo and often indelicate suggestion.

She returned to Apuldram with perfect manners, an ability to converse with new assurance – and a firm determination not to repeat the previous three months. Unfortunately she left behind her, with some relief, a suitor who had refused to take her dismissal of him seriously.

Lord Rathfarnan was the son of one of Aunt Julia's cronies. He was ten or so years Lavinia's senior and epitomized all that she most disliked about her stay in Kensington. He was to be found lounging in the drawing rooms of his mother's friends' houses from eleven o'clock every day. He was limp and pale with a fine profile of which he was well aware. He was instantly attracted by Lavinia's classical beauty, or so he assured her – dwelling upon the shape of her cheeks and the perfection of her mouth and the clear untroubled blue of her eyes – until she could happily have gagged him. He was idle and self indulgent, constantly borrowing money for gaming and there was absolutely nothing about him that she was able to warm to. Her rejection of Toby Rathfarnan angered her aunt and heated letters to Rymans followed her departure from Kensington – and then the correspondence between Rathfarnan and her father began.

Because she was so shocked with the deterioration of his health in the three months that she had been away, she dared not be too forceful about her wishes where Rathfarnan was concerned. She began to feel that she was being thrust into a position which would only end in unhappy circumstances. Trying to comfort herself, she would turn to the image of Jess. The unavoidable comparisons between him and the odious Toby only made her more unhappy.

It was some time since she had seen Jess. Two weeks after her return to Rymans he still had not been to the house and his name was not on her parents' lips. She was therefore not prepared for the unexpected sight of him slamming out of the Great Hall one morning. She had spied his tall figure from the kitchen window where she was making jam. She saw only his rigid back and that his movements were almost violent and quite uncharacteristic of him, as he flung himself up onto his horse and wheeled out of the forecourt. Troubled at such anger, she put down her jam ladle and went in search of her mother to discover the reason for his mood.

She found her sitting quietly with Thomas Freeland in the garden, patting his hand and talking softly to him. They looked up with troubled faces as she approached. She stopped the question on the tip of her tongue, seeing the toll that something had taken of her father. She would question Mother later, when they were on their own.

Lavinia put down the pillow case she had been stitching. 'Mother, I just can't. Every day now, either you or Papa bring this up – and every day I make the same reply. I don't want to be wed yet . . . and I certainly don't ever want to wed some-one like Toby Rathfarnan.'

It had been a harrowing week for them all. The parents had wanted to send her away again to Aunt Julia, determined to encourage her interest in Rathfarnan but, most of all, not wanting her to see the increasing ravages that Thomas Free-land's illness was imposing upon him.

His condition worsened daily. It frightened her to see him crumbling away before her eyes, to smell the decay of his flesh and feel the dry wasting of his skeletal hands and hot skin. It was unthinkable to leave him for fear that she might never see him again. Her mother's undoubted anguish was being kept rigidly in check but Lavinia could feel the suffering all about her; the creepings about the house, the absence of laughter and singing which had always been an integral part of the essence of the house. There was a dreadful feeling of waiting upon Death. John had been obliged to return to his London firm at their mother's insistence but Blunden was ready to ride to the City to fetch him back the moment she felt that it was time.

In the middle of all her unspoken grief was a hurt and a

puzzlement that Jess Bayless was not in evidence as she knew he should be, quietly filling in for his friend at Mistress Freeland's elbow and being the pillar of strength to her that he had been to others in times of need.

Where was he?

When she mentioned the subject to her mother, she was distressed to see the blue eyes fill with tears.

'He would be here if father would permit it, I know,' she said, turning away and fumbling with her handkerchief. 'He would certainly be here, good soul that he is . . . but since their disagreement your father gets so upset if Jess' name is mentioned that I dare not send for him.'

She would not throw any further light upon the reason for their discord. She simply returned again and again to the subject of Toby Rathfarnan.

'Dearest girl – we only want you to enjoy the company of other young people. By this time next year, I'm afraid that our finances will be sadly diminished and the possibility of doing another Season may well be out of the question.'

Lavinia did her best to keep her voice gentle and the exasperation out of it.

'Mama . . . dearest Mama. I keep on telling you that I don't want to do another Season. I don't like most of the people I've met at Aunt Julia's. They are so empty and prattling. I enjoy the Soirees because of the quality of the music which is delightful – and I love the shops and rides in the Park. But truly, dear Mama – I don't at all care for the rest of it and Lord Rathfarnan in particular. I love it here at home with you and father and the friends I have known all of my life. The air is clean here. London smells like a vast midden. Everything smells bad there and so do many of Aunt Julia's friends. For that matter, so does Aunt Julia, even though she pours those hideously strong and sickly perfumes all over herself . . .'

She stopped as her mother's frown warned her that she had gone too far and nothing excused vulgar observations, especially concerning her own flesh and blood. She gave her mother a contrite hug.

'I'm sorry, Mama. I didn't intend to sound so ungrateful. I just hate having to repeat the same thing, day in and day out. I beg of you to accept that I just won't leave you and father now

– and that I would not receive Rathfarnan if he were the last man on earth. He disgusts me . . .'

Abigail Freeland smoothed the fine golden hair back from her daughter's pale face. Dropping her guard for a moment she looked at Lavinia with all the love of a woman for the last child in her life.

'One day it will come to you, my darling. One day you will be in such a hurry to get to the altar – just as I was when I was your age and father first came into my life. One day . . .' She stopped, seeing the sudden flush steal across Lavinia's face. She stared at the telltale colour and her daughter's downcast eyes – and turned away quickly, biting her lip.

'So . . . you reciprocate his feelings, do you?' she thought, suddenly knowing it all. Had he already spoken to her then? Had they perhaps been meeting all this time? She closed her mind to the tumble of questions, torn by feelings of instant betrayal to Thomas' wishes and a grudging spark of private approval. He was so handsome – so full of life and vigour and bounding ambition. She quashed such romantic notions and drew the mantle of her sadness about her for protection.

On 20 March 1729, Blunden was dispatched to London to bring John back to Apuldram.

Thomas Freeland died in his sleep at Abigail's side just before dawn on 24 March. He was sixty-nine years old.

Chapter Two

Thomas Freeland had asked to be buried in Chichester beside his brother which was a disappointment to Parson Kelway for the little church at Apuldram housed few gentlemen's tombs and the dignity of such a funeral would have been of great benefit to St Mary's.

The funeral attracted mourners from every walk of life for Freeland had administered several estates and had been a wise and respected steward. When the service was over and the coffin lowered into the earth, the family and closer friends returned to Rymans where refreshments were served in the Great Hall.

Jess had been surprised and touched to receive a note from Mistress Freeland inviting him to attend the funeral. It had done much to lift the heavy mood which had afflicted him since the day of his last meeting with Freeland.

'Look at this,' he had said to Amy, waving the letter in front of her, unable to keep the hope from his voice. Her eyes had widened as she read it but she made no comment. He noticed that she had delicate purple smudges under them and that her pallor was suddenly accentuated.

'Will you press my black coat and breeches, please. I've to meet John in Chichester at three after noon so I won't be back before dusk.'

He came round the kitchen table and scooped up a fingerful of sweet pickle from the ladle and popped it into his mouth with an expression of glazed pleasure, then gave her cheek a peck and swung out of the door, a jauntiness in his step that had not been there for months.

Her hands crept to the front of her apron and rested there for a moment, then she turned back to the bubbling pot and continued skimming off the froth, her face expressionless.

It had been an interesting funeral, Jess thought afterwards. The mourners had come from far and wide and he had rubbed shoulders with the great as well as the needy. Thomas Freeland had been a compassionate administrator as well as a shrewd one. The respect shown to his memory had clearly been a great comfort to his family.

Jess had not stayed long at Rymans afterwards. He went to pay his respects to Mistress Freeland and John and Lavinia and not to drink at their table. He took Abigail Freeland's hand and bent over it.

'How old she looks, all of a sudden,' he thought and leant across to kiss her cheek.

'I'm truly so very sorry for having been such a burden to him at the end,' he murmured against her black bonnet. She drew back from him, keeping his hand in both of hers and her face was gentle in private grief.

'I was afraid that you might not come, Jess,' she said. 'But I prayed that you would, for at the end he asked that you be invited here today. He was sorry too, you know, for he had quite an affection for you in his own way.'

He had paid his respects to John and Lavinia, spoken most courteously with Controller of Customs, John Carr – and left the house without dining. He could not bear to be under the same roof now with Lavinia without telling her how he felt. He had tried to keep his eyes averted from her but it was impossible not to feast his gaze upon the small graceful girl in her mourning black which only enhanced the milky beauty of her skin and the silver gilt lustre of carefully coiled hair.

He had turned away from John Carr and found himself staring straight into her eyes. For one frozen second the room had receded, the murmur of voices died in his ears and he felt as though all life had stopped in him. She had regarded him for an instant and he was aware of an appeal, a reaching out – and then she dropped her gaze and a rosy flush gave her sudden vulnerability.

He left Rymans then, taking Olivas and pounding through the lanes as he had done after his last visit.

It was well after dark when he had finally returned to his home, slamming the door behind him and shouting for Amy as he shrugged himself out of the uncomfortably formal black coat. He kicked the small fire in the parlour grate and piled on fresh logs from the fuel basket and presently there was a cheerful blaze going. There was no sign of Amy.

'Hey, Chika . . . where are you? Come and help me off with these confounded boots. They're stopping the blood in my legs.'

She came to the door, wiping her hands on her apron. She looked drawn and ill.

'What's the matter?' he asked sharply, suddenly aware of her mood. She shook her head and her face was the colour of parchment. 'Just a little off colour. Nothing to worry about.'

Her voice was like the murmur of distant waves on shingle and she came forward to kneel and take the foot of his uplifted boot. Jess watched her as she pulled and tugged, keeping her eyes on what she was doing. The boot came off and she put it behind her and turned to tackle the other.

'What's wrong, Amy?' he said quietly. 'Is it another "turn"?'

She looked up, squatting before him. Her blue fustian gown was the same colour as her eyes.

'I'm with child.' Her voice was the faintest whisper.

They stared at each other.

The fire popped and chuckled beside them but they heard nothing of its cheerful clamour. The room shimmered round Jess and he felt the beat of a pulse deep down in the heart of the house; a striving . . .

'Are you sure?'

She lurched to her feet as though jerked up by her collar. 'Of course I'm sure . . . How could it be anything else? I have not been mokada for three months now and I am tender and sometimes sick. Now I am beginning to swell. Of course I'm sure.'

They were both shocked by the vehemence in her voice. She

had never spoken to Jess that way – never in any way other than with love. Now suddenly her voice was harsh, ugly.

He put his hands on her shoulders and drew her against his chest. They stood very close together and she let him stroke her hair.

'I'm sorry, Amy,' he said and all the grief of the day and his own self condemnation was in his voice. 'I'm so sorry, Chiriklo. It should never have happened and I'll never forgive myself . . .'

'Why shouldn't it have happened?' she said fiercely into his shirt front. 'I'm glad it happened. I love you more than I can ever show you – so how else do I express myself? You know you have always been *God* to me, Jess. You know that you always will be. I feel like a woman with you, so it's only right that I have your child to express it. You could never have given me more . . .'

He held her away from him and stared down into the white, mutinous face with great tenderness and then gently put her from him.

He went into the kitchen and picked up his working boots from the yard door. 'I have to think about all this and then we'll talk about it later,' he said, pulling them on.

He yanked the kitchen door open and disappeared out into the dark barn yard.

'We don't need to talk about it,' she said to herself, stroking the front of her apron. 'It's there and it won't go away – now or ever, Jess.'

She felt the eyes upon her and her skin prickled. She looked about her but there was nothing there. There never was. Just the certainty that she was not alone in this place.

Lately, fear of the presence had come upon her, visiting her in sleep. It came in a torment of the soul – in voices that called out to her in a tongue that had no meaning, yet she knew that there was terror there and anger of a kind too vast for her to have experienced; and subjection and debasement of fragile innocence. She woke from these charged dreams in a sweat of fear that was mixed with the sweetness of the very pain that had been inflicted somewhere . . . sometime in the place where this house now stood. Analysis was difficult but she savoured a bitter sweetness in the carnality of that ancient anguish. The dreams were part of her submission to Jess, part of the cruelty that had surfaced in him. She began to pant as though she was running and the tremble started as she bent her head over the kitchen table and waited for the rest to come.

Chapter Three

Small parishes have few hiding places from prying eyes and the birth of a daughter to Amy Bayless spread like wildfire from one end of Apuldram to the other. She had not called on the Birdham midwife but had had the child as the rest of her Clan did – in the bender of Aunt Sarey Bayless, attended by Aunt Nannie and Saiforella.

The Apuldram Community was greatly dismayed at the news, for they had come to accept Amy as completely as they did her brother, Jess. She had served the Chatfields loyally during her six years at Manor Farm and had done more than her fair share of community work among the needy of the Parish. She had always appeared quiet and seemly and quite without the fire and coarseness associated with the Saltpans Baylesses. Heads were shaken in genuine regret, and the disapproval was compounded when Mistress Kelway reported that Amy had refused to name the father – or have the baby churched and baptised.

'Violet is her name,' she had said with uncharacteristic firmness to Mistress Kelway. 'Violet Bayless. What blessings can your church give her that she does not already possess?'

The gossips had a field day and the rumours concerning the identity of the baby's father spread among the cottages. Amy was quite unmoved by the commotion. She remained quietly at home and waited for the novelty to wear off and for another topic of scandal to draw the attention from her.

Mistress Freeland only mentioned the subject once to Jess. By that time, he had become a welcome visitor once more at

Rymans and had established the practice of meeting there each week in the Great Hall to play cards with John and his cousin, Joseph Freeland and sometimes Richard Farrington or one of the Chaldecott brothers. He liked to arrive at the house a little early so that he might go up to the solar to sit with the ladies for half an hour before the others arrived.

Violet was no more than a week old when Jess went over to take tea with Mistress Freeland at her invitation. She greeted him with less than her usual cordiality.

'Jess, how could you have permitted such a thing to happen? Now I hear from Jane Kelway of Amy's extraordinary refusal to have the poor little child churched . . . I really do think you should prevail upon her to take the baby to the Parson. Why, it's unfortunate enough to have produced a base child in the first place – but deliberately to deny her the benefit of Christian Sanctity is real wickedness.'

Jess watched the indignation puff her up like a laying hen. The strain of the last months of her husband's life was etched in her face and age had begun to erode her natural serenity.

'I do appreciate that your concern is meant most kindly, Ma'am,' he said carefully, anxious to avoid offending her. 'Amy's misfortune came upon her without warning – I can tell you no more than that because she has my promise that I will not discuss the subject with anyone – and to be honest, I agree with her entirely. It's enough of a tragedy that it happened at all, so I must rely on your knowledge of her as a person for you to realize that Amy is not a loose woman and certainly never consented to a casual consort.'

Abigail Freeland looked relieved.

'On the subject of churching, Ma'am . . . I think you must be forgetting that we come of Romani stock and have never embraced the Christian faith. It is my intention to take instruction one day with Parson – when the question of my own future is clearer. When that happens, no doubt Amy will do the same – but out of obedience to me, I assure you, rather than any wish of her own.'

Mistress Freeland's eyes had begun to twinkle. 'That's quite understandable, Jess. I know how difficult things have been recently for you both. It hurts me to hear damaging gossip being flung at your door. The business of not churching the baby has just added salt to the wound, you know. Could you not try and prevail upon Amy to have her churched? I am certain that if it were known that the poor girl was ravished, as you infer, the gossips would soon stop their prattling – as long as the baby is brought to Parson Kelway . . . and you also.'

Her words had an underlying sharpness to them and he sensed what it was that she was saying to him.

'Would it assist another situation if I were to become Christian?'

They regarded each other quietly with complete understanding.

'It might,' she said briefly and went on to talk of other things.

When, later on, he excused himself and went down to the hall where the two Freelands were already standing before the wide hearth, he found his mind straying from the game, stealing back to that one small clipped phrase.

He lost heavily that evening – unusual, for he was an excellent card player. He settled his debts with good grace and retired early, pleading a slight fever. Later he lay in his bed, listening to the wind combing the nearby woods and searching for a sign of that faint vibration in the bloodstream which betrayed the presence of the Power.

It was gone.

His body functioned with natural life, heart pumping quietly. The blood coursed peacefully through him – nerves responded to touch, senses waited upon his needs.

There was nothing extra in him any more.

He sighed and turned over with a deep sense of release. In the morning he would write a note to Mistress Freeland and once more ask whether he might present little Midas to Lavinia.

'Why so pleased with yourself?' Amy asked a few days later, eyeing Jess across the remains of the evening meal. He had come to the dining table in a mood of jaunty good humour and had just finished a huge plateful of meat and vegetables with great gusto. He smiled at her, wiping his mouth with a damask napkin.

'Two good reasons, my Pen. For a start I've decided on a name for the house at last. I've decided that it's to be called Lavenham. A good name, don't you agree? Lavenham . . . I like the way it rolls off the tongue, as though it has always belonged to the area.'

She wrinkled her nose, frowning as she tossed it about in her mind.

'Why Lavenham? Why not Salterns or Copperas House or something directly concerned with this piece of land? Why not just Bayless'? That's what it's known as at present by all the neighbours.'

He leaned back in his chair, unperturbed by her lack of enthusiasm. Amy usually took her time to get used to anything new. She'd soon be as delighted with the name as he was. 'I just like the sound of it. The Lavant river runs through to the creek north of here so there's a logical connection there – and the "ham" part of the name means "house" in the old Saxon tongue, I'm told. I've been thinking of this name for a long time, but I wanted to live with it for a while to see how well it would suit. It does, I've decided – so, Lavenham is how I shall have it written into the deeds.'

Amy said no more, knowing well that once Jess' mind was made up, nothing was going to change it.

'You said that there were two things that have pleased you today. What is the other?'

He drained the last of the wine from his mug, pushed his chair back from the table and stood up, dusting the crumbs from the front of his ruffled shirt.

'The other thing, Chiriklo, is that Mistress Freeland and Lavinia are taking tea with us tomorrow. They are as anxious to see how the house is shaping as I am to show them the foals.'

He strolled away into the parlour, humming quietly under his breath.

Amy stood staring after him, twisting the lace of her fichu through her fingers and feeling the fine silk tear. Lavenham . . . so close to Lavinia. It *was* to be offered to Lavinia then.

From over her head the baby's plaintive wail drew her eyes upward. She started for the stairs unbuttoning her bodice, the onset of her ague making her grip the bannisters tightly.

★   ★   ★

Lavinia looked at herself in her wall mirror, frowning over the image scowling back at her. He simply must notice her today. He had taken tea so often up in the solar here at Rymans and had never intimated that he saw her as anything other than John's young sister. She knew well that he admired her from the affectionate approval he sometimes showed her – but it was more of a brotherly offering than that of an interested suitor. She stared at herself critically. Was she still too young at sixteen to stir him? Surely not. She had not been too young at fifteen to have had the most unfortunate effect on Toby Rathfarnan – who still pestered her, after a year's absence from London.

There was nothing very wrong with the face that stared defiantly back at her. Without the lace cap, her hair shone like gold silk from all the brushing it had been subject to this day. The thick tresses had been bunched on either side of her face, curled into long ringlets with hot tongs and fastened together with silver hair clips. Her oval face was flushed from her efforts and the delphinium blue eyes gazed at her with a straight clear limpidity. She practiced a little pout and then decided that it wasn't in keeping and let the smile return to her mouth. Teeth good with no decay, skin creamy and unblemished, shoulders straight, waist small. The mint and cream travelling gown highlit her colouring most effectively, especially as it was such a contrast to the Bayless looks.

'Are you coming, Linnie?' Her mother's voice filtered up from far below. She picked up her bonnet, placed it carefully on her head and whirled out of the room, tying the ribbons under her chin as she went.

Jess stood in the middle of his drive, sniffing the autumn air. It smelt of sun warmed earth, tinged with the sharp pungence of charred stubble. Over his head, high in the sky, streamed trailing feathers of swiftly-moving clouds, riding the currents of the upper air like galloping horses' tails.

'Sloe Fair tomorrow,' he reminded himself, vainly trying to keep his mind off his guests. He smiled to himself, remembering the old camel that used to appear on that day, giving endless excitement to the throng and a ride to remember for the fortunate few who were able to stay on him. Sloe Fair, with its colourful stalls and tumblers and travelling players and minstrels. He would offer to accompany Lavinia this year – and her mother, of course.

They were coming. His sharp ears had picked up the distant clop of hooves in the lane. The phaeton clattered into view with Lavinia driving a smart little piebald. She waved her whip at him as they swept past, up to the front door.

He hurried across the pebbled sweep as Rueb ran from the saddle room to take the pony's bridle, and was beside them with outstretched hand before Mistress Freeland was ready to descend from the carriage.

'At last, at last,' she said gaily, giving Jess her neat black-gloved hand and leaning on him heavily as she stepped down.

'You have brought the sunshine with you, Ma'am,' he said with grave affection. He turned to Lavinia but she was already beside him.

'Good day to you too, Mistress Lavinia.'

She grinned at him, acknowledging the adult address he had awarded her. The sharp breeze whipped spots of bright colour into her cheeks.

Mistress Freeland was already exclaiming at the changes that had been wrought around her – the beauty of the long view across the harbour, the charm of the house with its warm brickwork and soft grey stone mullions. Lavinia hooked her arm through her mother's and all three strolled into the house, pausing on the threshold to admire the finished effect of the limed oak panelling in the hall.

The ladies were charmed and impressed with everything, for the house reflected unexpected taste in a man who so lacked background. It had been designed with obvious care and a fine attention to detail, and the position of the building looking downstream towards Birdham and Itchenor was as carefully thought out as Rymans itself had been. The windows all faced east and west so that there would be sunshine in the rooms from sunrise to sunset. The windows themselves were wide and set into stone mullions.

'Why have you not taken advantage of the new-styled sash windows?' Mistress Freeland asked, watching the sun glinting on the panes of leaded glass.

Jess led the way into the parlour. 'I don't like them here. That is to say – I like them well enough in a town house where the streets give protection from the elements and the maximum glazed area is needed to bring light into dark rooms . . . but here, Ma'am, we have plenty of light and we have to contend with savage gales in winter, so transom windows are better suited. In any case, I think they look more pleasant in this style of house, don't you?'

And once it had been pointed out, she had to agree.

They were settled in deep comfortable chairs with thickly padded arms and high backs. The room was indeed light without being cold. A cheerful fire blazed in the basket grate and the room glowed with colour and polish and flowers.

'Will you take tea now or after I have shown you round the garden and paddocks?' Jess was saying. Mistress Freeland noticed with an inward smile that he was looking at Lavinia with an expression that could only be described as heavily controlled joyous anticipation.

'Well, my dear, as you may have noticed, I'm not very good these days on uneven ground. I suggest you show Lavinia the paddock and let me rest here and chat with Amy, if she is at home.'

Jess rose, doing his best to keep the happiness out of his face. 'She is indeed here and will be with us directly. I believe she is attending to Violet who, no doubt, you will be obliged to inspect and admire. She is a good little scrap and minds her manners already. Just let me tell Amy that you are here. Excuse me for a moment.'

He left the room and Mistress Freeland said to Lavinia, 'Don't let him keep you out there long, my dear. The winds can be treacherous at this time of year and I notice they blow straight up the Channel and across the lawns. It must be a very cold house in winter.'

'I think it's lovely,' Lavinia said in a faraway voice. Before there was time to say more, Jess returned and she stood up eagerly.

'Amy apologizes for not being here to greet you,' he said. 'She will be down directly. I won't keep Miss Lavinia out for long, I promise.' His grey eyes danced at Mistress Freeland, the corners creasing into a web of fine lines and she dimpled, still woman enough to warm to the affection for her she saw in them.

She watched them through the window as they strolled across the freshly cut grass beyond the flagged terrace. Then they moved out of view, hidden by the dutch barn. The sun went behind a cloud and for some unaccountable reason she felt an icy chill course through her.

'Good day to you, Ma'am,' Amy said behind her.

He led the way down towards the water.

'How beautiful the creek is with all the leaves changing,' Lavinia said. He didn't seem to notice the shyness that had suddenly overtaken her.

'Look!' He pointed over the tops of the trees. Geese were coming in across the harbour, flying low in perfect formation. They stood and watched them out of sight, flying like a scythe towards the Bosham woods and fields.

'Is this where you bring in all the tea and brandy?' she asked innocently. It was common knowledge, though naturally only discussed in whispers, that this was how Jess Bayless was making his fortune.

He grinned at her. 'What do you mean, Miss? My time is entirely taken up with my loan interests and the administration of the "Grace" – not to mention the growing business of the breeding stables. It's been a long time since I went owling. I gave your father a promise which I have kept.'

They laughed at each other, knowing the lie of the words but savouring the pleasure of a small intimacy between them.

'All this is so delightful and peaceful, Jess. How do you manage to make the grass so smooth and green?'

He scuffed at it with a booted foot. 'It gets close scythed each week in the growing months and I have geese or swine over it in the winter. I started grazing the horses there but their hooves cut into the turf too deeply and made it uneven. The swine are the best grazers because they can crop all the way into the woods when the weather is bad. Acorns and hazel nuts, that's what they feed on – and there's plenty of both in these woods.'

They stood at the top of the bank above the water, watching

the marine traffic slide by on its way to and from Dell Quay and Fishbourne Mill. Lavinia's mint green bonnet was level with Jess' cheek. She was small and as neat as a doll, as tempting as a cream cake with her matching outdoor habit and cape fringed with white rabbit fur.

He resisted a growing urge to put out his arm and draw her close to him and instead put a hand under her elbow and guided her along the bank towards the paddocks. They leaned on the wooden fence and watched as Olivas raised his head among his mares and foals at the far end of the field. He tossed his mane and moved slowly towards them, nodding a sage welcome as he approached.

'I do love Apuldram,' Lavinia said wistfully.

Jess glanced away from the advancing herd and looked down at her upturned face.

'Mama feels that we should remove into Chichester, now that father is gone. John takes his articles any minute now, as you know – and then returns to practise here in the town. She feels that a house in Chichester would be more convenient for him than continuing to live out here in such a rambling place.'

'I'd hate to think of Rymans without Freelands in residence,' Jess said. 'Also, Chichester would not be very convenient for all sorts of reasons. I have waited so long for permission to call on you – I hope very much that your Mama takes her time before deciding on a move of any sort. Besides, I have a gift for you which might be difficult to accept if you were living in the town.'

Her eyes sparkled like blue stars. 'How lovely . . . what is it? Do tell me, Jess. Oh, I do love surprises. I can't guess what it could be.'

She was suddenly another Lavinia. All the carefully learned good manners of the schoolroom vanished and she was sixteen years old, the half of her who was all grave womanhood instantly submerged in the excited girl. She grasped both his hands and tugged impatiently at him. He felt old and infinitely protective – and shook his head in mock displeasure.

'Be patient, Miss, if you please. This is the first time that I have given such a gift to a lady, so I intend picking exactly the right moment.'

133

He laughed at her disappointment. 'How would it be if I gave it to you on your birthday?'

'Oh, Jess, how can you be so tantalizing? I would have to wait for another four months. Now that you have told me about a surprise, how could I possibly contain my curiosity for a third of a year?'

'True, Chiriklo . . . and I doubt whether my gift can wait much longer either. Maybe I should give it to you today, after all.'

'Ooh . . .' She gave his arm another shake and swung away from him in mock exasperation, just as Olivas came up to them on the other side of the fence. Behind him trailed the herd in a long straggle.

'How beautiful they are,' Lavinia said, stretching out her hands to them through the railings. They were golden and chestnut, the colours of autumn – fine legged and high flanked with proud arched necks and coats like well polished wood.

'Why do you call your horse Olivas?'

'It's Romani . . . means socks or stockings. He has the one white sock as you see.'

He told her the story of Olivas and she leaned towards him against the fence, fascinated by the tale – listening with half her mind and the other half studying the changes of expression in his dark, volatile face. Beside them Olivas cropped patiently, content to wait upon his master's pleasure before going through his pockets for the customary reward.

'. . . and so my father gave him to me and when we went travelling in winter, Farmer Diggens stabled him for us. He was far too precious, you see, to accompany us. He might have been stolen or else we might well have been accused of stealing him ourselves – which I suppose we did, in a way.'

She stroked Olivas' soft inquisitive nose.

'How special you are,' she said to him and he sniffed the faint steam of her breath on the chill air and whickered softly in his throat to her.

'He says that you are very special too, Linnie.'

She began to turn her head when something caught her eye among the converging horses.

'Oh . . . Jess . . . just look over there. Oh, have you ever seen anything so beautiful? Here, little thing – come here, here . . .'

She strained her arms through the fence rails, wiggling her fingers at a colt who stood pressed against Olivas' rump, peering at them with wide tawny eyes.

He was a yearling, slim and graceful and half grown – filled with apprehension at the sight of them and jerking his head from side to side. He was shades of golden sunlight like ripe corn with mane and tail the colour of bleached flax.

'That's Midas,' Jess said quietly. 'He is my gift to you.'

She drew in her breath sharply and stretched across the rail again, clicking her fingers at the colt. He stared back and then, after a moment's hesitation, moved timidly towards her.

'Here – give him this.'

She scarcely heard Jess' voice as he put a sweet biscuit into her outstretched hand. Without taking her eyes off the colt, she broke it into two pieces and offered him half. Jess held off the other inquisitive noses and watched as the two golden creatures came shyly together.

The biscuit disappeared and Midas permitted Lavinia to stroke the pink velvet of his nose with the tips of her fingers but veered away when she became bolder and tried to tickle the top of his head. He laid his ears flat and backed away from her, pressing through the crush of horses until he was clear of them. Then he was off, cantering across the empty paddock with a flick of pearly hooves and all the grace of a dancer.

Lavinia tore her attention from Midas and turned back to Jess. 'I couldn't possibly accept such a gift,' she said and suddenly there was no trace of the child about her.

'Linnie, just look at him. He is so like you . . . his shape, his colouring – even the way he moves. From the day he was born I have wanted you to have him. He is the most perfect foal that Olivas has sired and it is so important for me to give you something as perfect as you are.'

He had taken her hand without realizing and now he looked down at it, resting with such trust in his own large brown one. The sight was too much.

'Linnie, I've had the image of that perfect little girl in my heart ever since I first met you when I was just a barefoot boy. Baylesses were all simple gypsy folk in those days but the sight

135

of you – and the friendship with John – changed my whole life. I began to dream of better things than my own camp fire. You know what happened. John took it upon himself to begin my education and I have not wasted one chance to improve myself from that day to this. And I've done it, Linnie. I'm twenty-seven years old this month and you could say that I'm a well respected man in these parts today, couldn't you? I have a fine house and a newly built brigantine on which I owe nothing to anyone – and I have a healthy money lending business which, without even considering the marine side of things, brings me in enough income to support my family in comfort, even luxury.'

He stopped, realizing that he had been talking fast, gabbling out the rush of things he had to say to her before she stopped him; stopped him with her little flower face full of distress at having to hurt him – just as her father had done . . . for he was still a gypsy under all the finery, wasn't he?

He stared down at her in an agony of expectation. 'Please accept Midas, Lavinia. I want you to have him so that he can be with you always, nothing more, I promise. Only let me say that he represents all the devotion that this unworthy creature before you has to give.'

Her eyes were enormous, the blue irises flecked with tiny yellow speckles round the pupils.

'How can I possibly accept him?' Her voice was husky and so low that he had to bend his head to hear her words.

'Whatever you may say, Jess, you are making a declaration. My mother would never permit me to have Midas, knowing that you have declared yourself to me.'

'Yes, she would. I have been seeking your parents' permission ever since Midas was a foal – and was refused very smartly by your father. That was why we had that disagreement last year. When he died, your mother eventually intimated that I might resume my visits to Rymans and I finally persuaded her to agree to his presentation to you. There is no commitment, Linnie . . .'

'Well, Sir . . . it saddens me to hear you say that – for I should dearly have loved one.'

They gaped at each other, astonishment in both their faces. She put a hand up to her mouth at such presumption from her

136

own lips. Jess stood as though turned to stone, simply not believing what he thought he had heard.

'Do you realize what you said just then?' His voice grated harshly and she took a step backwards and realized she had been standing so close to him that they had almost been touching. She nodded slowly and the freshening wind snatched a golden curl from under her bonnet and sent it bobbing across her face. He smoothed it away from her forehead and tucked it out of sight, then took her hand and raised it to his lips.

'Mistress Lavinia . . . may I have the honour of calling on you tomorrow?'

Suddenly a puckish look of pure sparkling happiness filled her luminous face and she nodded with such eager pleasure that they both burst into laughter. The tension broken, he took her arm and they turned away from the paddock and, bathed in their own new intimacy, walked slowly back towards the house.

Chapter Four

Parson Kelway read the banns between Jess Bayless and Lavinia Freeland for three Sundays in May 1730. He was relieved to have this pleasant task as well as delighted in the participants, because his stipend was meagre and parish clergy were expected to rely upon the supplement of fees attached to baptisms, marriages and funerals for their living. As there were a maximum of forty-six souls living in Apuldram, of which more than a third were young children, the subsidies for the Kelways were few. It was hardly surprising that during the past three years, Thomas Kelway had been obliged to accept a regular fee from the Blacks in return for making available his cellar for the temporary storage of their contraband. He had long since ceased to struggle with his conscience and accepted any goods that Jess sent his way – and was more than grateful for the handsomeness of the fee he earned.

He regarded Jess Bayless with a certain reservation, in spite of finding him a young man of great personal attraction and gentle manners. He had been surprised – and then delighted, when the course of instruction that Jess took with him before his Baptism, quickly became a series of intelligent and mind searching discussions such as he had not enjoyed since his own theological education in Chichester. Jess' grasp of essentials and the depth of his arguments often kept them talking long into the night. Since Mistress Kelway had died suddenly only months before, these conversations were a great comfort to the Parson and the weekly lectures became a habit that continued long after the need for instruction was past.

*   *   *

The Parish watched the courtship of Jess and Lavinia with astonishment for, although he was now recognized as being by far the wealthiest and most evocative member of the community, he was still a gypsy. Educated and influential he might be, but heads were shaken in deep disapproval that he should aspire to pay his respects to a lady of Mistress Lavinia's gentle breeding.

Having once made her decision on the subject, Abigail Freeland countered the backwash of disapproving comment by mildly pointing out that three generations before, the Freelands of Aldingbourne had been simple peasant farmers – and that her own grandfather had been a peruke maker in Chichester. Jess, she insisted, was not only a most presentable suitor, but his ambition and reliability were only exceeded by his extraordinarily kindly nature. He was, she said firmly, an excellent match for Lavinia – and she looked forward exceedingly to having him for her son-in-law.

This kept further open comment in check and the gentlefolk and merchants of Chichester waited and watched to see whether this new star in their firmament would brighten further or burn itself out and drag down an honourable family with it.

It had not gone unobserved that Master Chaldecott, the Chichester Silversmith and Jess Bayless were doing a brisk trade in advancing money against property mortgages and that they had also recently become the town's agents for a new London company called The Royal Exchange Assurance. It was grudgingly admitted, therefore, that the match might not after all, be so ill-suited.

Thomas Freeland had not been able to set aside much of a bridepiece for his daughter before he died. Naturally, this restricted the Freeland's range when contemplating a suitable match. The gossips quickly discovered that Jess had made a large marriage settlement on Lavinia. The amount was so substantial that it emphasized Jess' own credibility in business circles and greatly enhanced the reputation that Chaldecott and Bayless were well on the way to establishing.

Both Rymans and Lavenham became hives of industry from the moment that Lavinia accepted a ruby and diamond betrothal ring from Jess. Three months was hardly sufficient time

139

for all the weaving and sewing, furniture making, brewing and cooking that preceded the wedding. Mistress Freeland brought in seamstresses from the town to make Lavinia's wardrobe but all her under linen and night robes were Lavinia's own responsibility and, in common with most girls, she had been stitching away at her clothing and household linen since she had been given her Bride's Chest on her twelfth birthday. She busied herself finishing off the lacework and fine pin tucks, but was never too busy for Jess' daily calls. She had been blissfully grateful for her mother's acceptance of Jess – and each day saw a deepening in the growth of her attachment to him. The only cloud on her horizon was the strange atmosphere she felt at Lavenham – and of Amy's attitude towards her. Confused by two such positive instincts about the Bayless house, she wondered whether they might be linked.

She had begun to notice the house's oddness the day she had gone over there with her mother to bring newly embroidered covers for the dining chair seats.

Jess was in the Chichester office, they knew.

'That won't matter,' Abigail Freeland said. 'Amy is there and it will be a good opportunity for you two to become better acquainted.'

They rode over in the phaeton with the seat covers in a box and a gift of honey for Amy. She received them coolly. The box of seat covers was not made welcome.

'I wonder what Jess was thinking of,' she said, very tall suddenly and remote. 'The covers we have on the dining seats were of his choosing and I am quite happy with them. Leather is more durable than tapestry work, don't you think?'

Lavinia flushed, embarrassed at her apparent intrusion upon the arrangements of Amy's home. She gave her mother a pleading look and Abigail said pleasantly. 'You are certainly right about that, my dear. They are durable but rather hot to sit on for long. Jess actually asked Lavinia to make these covers. How unfortunate that he didn't remember to put you in the picture about them. Now, dear, may we leave them here for now until you can mention them to Jess? While we are here, he did suggest that we might like to change the bed curtaining also and I have my measuring tape in my bag with me for that very purpose. Would you be good enough to accompany us upstairs?'

She began to move as she spoke and Amy was forced to follow her, a look of stony impotence on her face. Lavinia remained in the hall, watching them out of sight. It would be nice just to wander quietly round the house on her own without feeling that a resentful Amy was right beside her.

The hall was a beautiful place, long and remarkably light, in spite of having only two windows. The fireplace was large enough to have a small seat let into the brickwork on either side of the recess. She stood and drank in the limed panelling on the walls and the grace of the polished oak staircase. The two women were up in the main bedroom, the low buzz of their voices wafting clearly down to Lavinia's ears.

There was someone watching her. She looked round quickly, feeling the hard stare acutely, but there was no one there, no one in the open parlour doorway. The kitchen door was closed and from the movements beyond it, she knew that Polly Ayles was busy scrubbing. The feeling persisted – and Lavinia moved across to the parlour and looked in. The room was empty. A carriage clock ticked on the mantlepiece and the fire popped comfortably in the grate. She took a step inside the room and looked behind the door, feeling a little foolish. Suppose she came upon someone . . . what would she do? There was no one there – only the feeling of eyes drilling into her, raising the short hairs at the nape of her neck. The shadows in the corners of the room seemed almost to billow at her, like sails in a high wind.

She blinked. Behind her the door slammed shut making her whirl round in alarm. She could hear the strangest drumming somewhere in the house. Like a heart beat, it thudded against her ear drums, building up a tight pressure in her head.

She reached for the door handle, suddenly frightened of the room and almost tore it open – colliding with Amy and Mistress Freeland as she stumbled out.

'What on earth is the matter, child?' her mother said in alarm, catching her arm to stay her headlong flight.

Lavinia opened her mouth – and then closed it again, seeing the look on Amy's face.

'Nothing,' she said in a small voice. 'I just thought I could hear some very strange noises in there but I must have been imagining things.'

Mistress Freeland laughed and patted her daughter's cheek. 'Young ladies soon to be married often have odd flights of fancy,' she said comfortingly. 'It's the anticipation, I expect. There's nothing so worrying as considering embarking upon a new life, my dear.'

'Especially when you're wedden' a gypsy,' Amy said. 'They do say 's we have strange bed fellows when the moon is in the right quarter.'

Mistress Freeland looked at her sternly. 'Now, really Amy, I think it's very tactless of you to tease Lavinia with all that poppycock. Jess is the most loving of men and would never permit anything unchristian to exist near Lavinia. He is quite devoted to her.' She looked from Amy to Lavinia and back.

'I hope very much that the two of you will be company for each other once Lavinia is living here.'

Amy bowed her head. 'May I give you a pot of chocolate before you go?' she said flatly.

'Why is Amy so stiff with me?' Lavinia asked Jess the following day. 'Is it because she thinks me the wrong person to become your wife?'

'Amy is . . . Amy,' Jess had replied. 'She was never one for words and in the last year or so, she has become even more withdrawn than before. I'm sure that she has nothing personal against you, Chika. You see, she'll be much more friendly once you are here all the time and she has the opportunity and time to know you better.'

Amy seemed in no hurry to seek such a situation.

'Maybe,' Lavinia thought in despair, 'it's because Lavenham is, after all, the first proper home that she had ever had after years of living so degradingly in tents and caravans.'

She had to admit to herself that it did seem rather sad that this lovely new house must be handed over to another woman, after all the hard work Amy had devoted to making both house and garden as pleasing as they now were.

She determined to devote herself to winning Amy over into becoming her good friend.

Amy – and dear little Violet also. It would be delightful to have the house full of the sound of children . . .

On her next visit she took over a baby gown from her chest, one that she had made for her own future child. It was beautifully stitched with fine lace ruffles at neck and wrists and minute tucks across the chest and round the hem.

'I hope that you will accept this for Violet,' she said shyly to Amy, holding out the folded robe. They were standing in the hall. A long wedge of sharp yellow sunlight scythed between them from the open front door casting a sudden warmth across the front of Lavinia's chest.

Amy paused in the act of turning toward the stairs. She looked at Lavinia, making no attempt to take the proffered gift from the outstretched hands. Her eyes were long, the lids drooping, her thick curling black lashes veiling their expression. Her mouth pursed into a thin straight line. Behind her the shadows gathered into a purple density. Lavinia blinked for it was almost as though there was something behind the dark head that drew together and reared upward, waiting to . . .

'Please,' she said breathlessly, 'I made it myself and it is quite attractive – look.' She shook the little robe out of its folds and held it up between them.

'See the little tucks across the bodice? They are three thicknesses of the lawn and will protect her chest against ill humours without looking unsightly. See all the little leaves and curling ferns I embroidered down each of the tucks? They will keep them firm and neat under the iron, you see . . .' Her voice trailed away and she was left dangling in the full glare of contempt from Amy's hooded stare. She clenched her fists under the baby robe, fighting back the tears which suddenly threatened.

'Please take it, Amy.' She moved past the tall girl, almost throwing the little robe to her and hurried out onto the terrace.

Behind her she heard the stair boards creak as Amy continued up to her chamber. The child's robe lay on the bottom step where she had dropped it.

Lavenham began to glow with new colour as Lavinia's chosen materials were sewn into heavily lined curtains and covers for the chairs and beds. She and Jess did most of their shopping in Chichester where the quality of the craftsmen was the best in

143

the whole of the south. The greatest treasure in Lavinia's eyes was the large carpet from Arabia that Jess produced one day. It was laid in the parlour where its rich pattern of deep blues and crimsons gave the room an added warmth and elegance.

The days sped by. Each Sunday Jess accompanied Lavinia and her mother, and sometimes John, to morning service and appeared to listen to Parson Kelway's simple sermons with undivided attention. The offertory bag always yielded a larger harvest after the service. Jess again, the old man decided, because it had never contained more than a few pence before Jess began to worship at Saint Mary's. Now it never failed to contain a silver crown when he was there.

June is a busy time for Parish weddings. The weather is more inclined to be fair and the countryside is fresh dressed in its brightest finery for such happy occasions. The day before the Freeland–Bayless wedding found most of Apuldram involved in one way or another over its preparation.

Mistress Chatfield had organized Sarey Beer (now a Bayless herself) and five other parish women to decorate the little church. The Saltpans Baylesses had demurred from joining in this pleasant chore but had come to the door, bearing armfuls of pink and white apple blossom, yellow field gladioli and ragged robin; marsh orchids, moon daisies and bluebells. They were gladly accepted and heaped into the deep window recesses and arranged in copper milk cans along the communion step. The children gathered moss by the basket and lined the windows and font and pulpit. They tied posies of woodland flowers with grass and tucked them into place against the green moss. By nightfall the little Saxon church had been transformed into a place of bright and simple beauty.

Amy had been busy at Lavenham ever since Jess' betrothal had been announced. The house shone with polish and the air was pungent with the smells of her cooking and bottling. The brew house was in constant use for Polly Ayles was good at making fruit wines and it was a certainty that the whole Parish would turn out to drink the couple's health at the wedding – as well as half the gentry in Chichester.

The kitchens at Rymans were an even greater hive of

industry. Lavinia and her mother spent part of each morning making chutneys, puddings and sweetmeats while Mistress Blunden and the kitchen maids, Lizzie Beer and Annie Heberden, tackled the major business of preparing the meats. Suckling pigs had to be stuffed and roasted, lambs boned and cast upon the spits; cocks, ducks and hens by the dozen must be plucked and trussed ready for roasting the following day. Fresh bread was being baked in the Manor Farm ovens as well as at Rymans and Lavenham. The sun shone and there was much singing and laughter in the kitchens throughout Apuldram.

Jess rode into the barnyard in gathering dusk. He dismounted and threw the reins to Rueb.

'Give me a hand with the panniers,' he said to his young cousin. They lifted the two heavy bags off Olivas' saddle hooks and carried them across to the kitchen.

'Put them on the floor for now,' Jess said, seeing the table and every other available space already stacked with cooking pots and dishes piled high with pastries and meat pies.

Amy and Polly regarded them with exasperation.

'Not in here you don't,' Amy said. 'We're falling over those sacks of vegetables as it is.'

Jess obediently led the way into the hall. She stared after him and fired a parting salvo.

'And don't you go into the parlour at any price, see? It's all ready in there and I don't want to be up all night cleaning it through again.' She sounded tired and surly. The baby began to grizzle in her crib by the hearth.

Jess and Rueb humped the two panniers over to the long refectory table and laid them down with care, and Jess began to unpack them. He pulled out package after package wrapped in soft suede, and placed them side by side along the table. When the first bag was emptied, he kicked it aside and set about the second one. When he had all the packets lined up in front of him, he called through the open kitchen door to Amy.

'Hey, Pen. Can you spare a minute to come and look at what I've got here?'

Amy sighed. She raised her head from the dressing of a cold

suckling pig, wiped her hands on her apron and went through to the hall.

Jess was standing surveying his mysterious parcels with enormous satisfaction.

'I want you to be the first to see these,' he said to Amy. 'I ordered everything from Chaldecott's long before Lavinia agreed to wed me. We have the house now, you see . . . so it's only fitting that we have the chattels to go with it.'

He picked up a package at random and began unwrapping it. The soft beige leather fell back in his hands and he held up a shining silver spoon with a flourish.

Amy's mouth dropped open. Without a word, she picked up another package and unwrapped it. Three pronged forks.

It took them some time to unwrap everything. When they had finished and stood back silently looking at the table and its contents, even Jess, who had seen it all in Chaldecott's workshops, whistled at the sight. Silverware – gleaming rows of cutlery, coffee, tea and chocolate services; sweetmeat baskets, trays, bowls, goblets and candle sticks.

They stood side by side, picking up one piece after another, speechless before the richness of the hoard.

'Something for the future, eh?' Jess said. He took up the arms of a candelabra and began to assemble it. 'This one came from France. We brought in quite a lot of French and Italian silver last year and I bought a few pieces at the time – and Ned has been making the cutlery for me for over a year.'

Amy looked along the table to where he stood, fitting the finely turned arms of the candelabra into their elegant base.

'What do you want all that for, Bor?' Her voice was low and there was a harsh ring to it that made him look quickly at her. 'We've got enough here already. We've got the house and the land and the horses. What do you want with these . . . gaudy things?'

'When Lavinia becomes my wife I intend to ensure that she will not be taking a step down from Rymans,' he said. 'She will be able to entertain in the manner to which she is accustomed. We're not travelling light any more, Amy. These "Gaudy things" are roots that you are looking at. Roots to be handed down to the children, together with the house and the land as well as the blood of our forefathers.'

Her chin went up and he smiled to see it. He completed the candelabra and placed it in the centre of the table and stood back to admire its proportions.

'Yes . . . I mean what I said. I have made provision for you and Violet just as surely as I have for Lavinia and her children. Your futures are well taken care of – so that if anything were to happen to me, the two of you will never be in want.'

Her face was in shadow. 'What is to become of Violet and me, Jess?'

He looked surprised. 'Well, nothing, I hope. This is your home and will be for as long as you wish. Would you prefer other arrangements to be made?'

She shook her head and turned away. 'No, Pral (brother), I don't want to leave you. How could I? But don't ever think that I will accept gladly the situation you are creating here.'

Sympathetic understanding gave way to irritation. 'Now, that is ridiculous, Amy,' he snapped. 'I have offered you the choice of a home here with Lavinia and me or the privacy of a place of your own and you have chosen to stay here. Well, isn't that what you have, this minute, said? I am more than happy that such is your choice . . . but since it is, you will be inflicting any strain the situation provokes upon yourself. I am not putting you into an impossible position and nor is Lavinia. She is a friendly and warm young woman, little more than a child, and eager as a puppy for your friendship. If you are to remain here as we have always planned, Chika, you *must* cultivate a more kindly regard for her. I insist upon it.'

She left him without a word and returned to the kitchen, closing the door behind her with a sharp click.

The seamstress arrived at Rymans the afternoon before the wedding. She and her three needlewomen had the wedding gown with them. Lavinia was borne up the wide staircase to the solar for the fitting, jostled and teased by two young Freeland cousins and her aunt, Mistress Pay. They laughed and joked among themselves as they unbuttoned her from her working gown and petticoats and then stood back as the seamstress moved in with her small army of cutters and tuckers. Petticoat after petticoat of fine lawn and lace were slipped over Lavinia's head and patted and buttoned into place. Each layer had to have its final fitting, for the length of every hem must be exact so that she would not trip as she walked. The wedding gown was reverently lowered over her shoulders and there was a murmur of pleasure from all the onlookers.

The heavy Indian satin shimmered like polished ivory, a perfect complement to the golden lustre of her hair and the smoothness of her skin.

She stood very still, a quiet pool of contemplation among the chatter of her attendants, letting them turn her this way and that as every smallest detail of her appearance was checked.

'How shall I be able to take this off on my own? I'm sure Amy won't want to help . . . Jess said that the Baylesses are having their own wedding ceremony at Lavenham when we arrive. Should I wear this dress? Will they make me welcome? What will they do to us?'

Jess had laughed when she had anxiously tried to question him about Romani customs.

'Just wait and see,' he had said and put an arm round her and planted a kiss on the end of her nose. 'Don't worry, little one. They won't dance round you brandishing their knives. You'll enjoy it all just as much as you enjoy your Churching, I promise.' And she had had to be content with that.

It wasn't that she was frightened of the Baylesses. The presence of Jess was enough to ensure that she would be well treated by his relatives. It was Lavenham itself that was beginning to intrude upon her as a place to dread. When Jess was with her the atmosphere was bright and pleasant and welcoming as any new house might be. It was when he was not there that the whole mood of the place seemed to change. The sense of being watched was strong and sometimes the faint heartbeat would start and grow, beating upon her senses like a monstrous drum until she was forced to run from the house with her hands to her ears. Jess had laughed at her and tickled her under the chin when she had plucked up the courage to tell him about it.

'Dearest Linnie. This house is built around some very ancient foundations. Who knows what they once were? I don't feel any sense of danger or unpleasantness here and I think it's because I long ago acknowledged that this is some sort of hallowed ground. Once one accepts that and recognizes the existence of whatever was here in times past, then I don't think that you will be troubled any further. Next time you are in the house, try to commune with it. Sense it out with your inner instincts. Confront it and let whatever worries you see that you accept and respect its presence – that you even welcome it for, after all, it has been here for very much longer than you or I and has every right to dictate to those who disturb its peace.'

She did her best to obey him when he brought her deliberately to Lavenham for the purpose of exorcising her fears. He had put her into one of the comfortable parlour chairs and left her there on her own, closing the door behind him as he went out. She knew that he would go to the kitchen and take Amy off to the gardens on some pretext and that she would then be completely alone in the house.

Fighting down her nervousness she did as he instructed. She closed her eyes and leaned back in the chair, relaxing her body and doing her best to empty her mind of its images and tensions.

The clock ticked on the mantle, its comfortingly mundane pulse and an occasional hiss of popping resin in the burning apple wood, the only sounds that came to her. That and the far away voices which must be Jess and Amy. They must be in the paddock because she could hear the sound of the horses – even smell them – and there was one that seemed to be squealing, as though it had been hurt. Squealing . . .

She opened her eyes and sat up with a jerk, the sound turning the blood cold in her veins. The house lay quietly about her. Nothing broke its stillness. No squealing horse. No voices. Nothing with which to commune.

A pin pricked her and she started.

They were just in the act of raising the veil to drop it over her head.

'No, don't do that.'

She backed away from the upstretched arms of the sewing women.

'I don't want it on until tomorrow . . . Jess' sister, Saiforella, told me that it's bad luck to try on the veil and the wreath before the wedding day itself.'

'What nonsense, dear,' Mistress Freeland said with spirit. 'We have to try it on, just to check that it sits snugly beneath the wreath.'

She shook her head. 'No, Mama. There will be plenty of time for that in the morning. I've been standing here for so long, my knees are giving way. I beg you, that's enough for today. We can do the last little things in the morning. It all feels perfect, in any case.'

She felt close to tears and her audience – quick to sense her mood, tutted and soothed her, understanding the natural tensions that she must be feeling on the eve of the most important day in her life. In no time the gown was off, the petticoats unbuttoned and she was helped into her night robe and a comfortable chair with a hot posset, so liberally laced with good French brandy that it brought the colour rushing back into her cheeks. Then up came Lizzie Beer with a platter of sweet cakes and Bohea tea and Annie Heberdine after her, panting with the weight of the cider jug. Mistress Chatfield joined them and soon the solar was filled with chattering well wishers.

Lavinia sat quietly in the big chair, small within the padded folds of her dressing gown; lifting her face to be kissed again and again – and smiling her thanks as one gift after another was placed in her lap. The afternoon became a sequence of dreams and the laughter and chatter all round her no more than the fretting of birds in the evening trees.

'Yes, I certainly think we shall be catering for more than a hundred guests . . .'

A hundred men, women and children . . . all gathered to see the knot tied between Lavinia Abigail Freeland, spinster of this Parish and Jess Bayless, batchelor of the same . . . This time tomorrow she would be Mistress Bayless of Lavenham – and Jess . . . Jess with all his strength and vitality and the strangeness that came upon him, now and then – and all that heart-stopping Romani beauty . . . Jess would be there with her for the rest of their lives. She came up out of her reverie, pink cheeked and suddenly smiling.

Chapter Five

Rymans was astir well before dawn and by the time Lavinia woke to the crows caw-cawing in the elms, the fires had been lit, halls and kitchens scrubbed and preparations for the feasting well under way in both Halls and the big Barn. She sat up quietly, careful not to disturb Hettie and Sarah Pennicod, cousins who were to be maids of honour and who had shared her bed over night. The two small daughters of Rearden Lucas of Donnington were to be the petal strewers. They were fast asleep on straw palliases, cuddled up together under padded quilts like lambs in the fold. Lavinia wrapped her dressing gown round her and tiptoed out of the room. She knocked on her mother's chamber door.

They broke fast together, staying out of the way of Mistress Blunden and the busy kitchen maids and were later joined by their four visitors. There was no sense of urgency upstairs, although there were plenty of last minute jobs to be seen to and the boxes of Lavinia's personal effects to be checked before Blunden closed the lids and roped them securely. He would have them carried downstairs and hoisted into the two farm wains which were to accompany the newly weds over to Lavenham.

Halfway through the warm morning, John appeared looking puffy-eyed and woebegone. He and some of Jess' closer friends had given the groom rather too liquid a send off from bachelorhood the night before. There were now at least four sore heads this morning though Jess, he hastened to assure them, seemed to be suffering least of all. When Richard Farrington arrived, looking even more raddled, there was some consternation, for he was to be Jess' sponsor and John was giving his sister away. Both were sent down to the yard pump to wash away their ill humours.

The sun climbed up into a faultless sky and Lavinia stood at the solar window, watching its passage – and the fine white sand slipping through the hourglass on her mother's writing table. One more inversion of the glass and it would be time to go to church. She stared down into the garden where she had played each summer of her life until this day. Her eyes roamed the herb garden which had been her duty to tend, to stock and weed. She would have to set about the one that Amy had started at Lavenham, for it was not large enough for the household and contained an assortment of strange herbs and roots that might have some meaning to the gypsies but meant nothing at all to her.

'Jess, what are you doing now? Are you nursing a sore head like Richard and John – in spite of their assurances? Will you see me coming up the aisle to you through a haze of aching head and bilious stomach? Will you be regretting this day after all? And will I, before tomorrow comes?'

'Come now, Miss. You can't stand there dreaming today. Since you're all washed and your hair is combed, we'd better begin the business of putting you into your robes.' Abigail Freeland put an arm round her daughter's slim waist and drew her to a high stool as Lizzie Beer came into the room with a pan of hot coals for the curling tongs.

She allowed herself to be fussed over by the women, hair brushed for a fifth time and long ringlets made with the hot tongs until they fell sleek and controlled down her back and her head was ready for the veil. They lowered the heavy satin gown over her shoulders and she stood up for it to be buttoned and patted into place. Standing submissively, she realized that she would not sit down again until she was Mistress Bayless. Her cousins stood on foot stools on either side of her and placed the fine veil onto her head. Lucy Lucas brought over the wreath of orange blossom and tiny white rosebuds that Annie Heberden had just finished making, and it was settled reverently over the veil and pinned onto her head with ivory hair pins so that it would remain secure, however boisterous the wind outside.

She was ready. They stood back and surveyed her critically and clapped their hands and exclaimed at the beauty of this cream and gold young bride. Mistress Freeland pressed her own prayer book into Lavinia's cold hands with a little posy of ferns and orange blossom from the Goodwood vinery. She gave her daughter a kiss through the cobweb folds of the veil.

'You look very lovely, my darling,' she said softly, eyes bright with unshed tears. 'I am so proud of you.'

It was time to go. Suddenly Lavinia realized that she had been hearing the church bells pealing at the back of her mind for some time. The sound lifted her spirits and she straightened her back, twitched her skirts straight and gave her attendants a dazzling smile.

'Shall we go, Mama? The hour glass is empty. The sooner we get to church, the sooner these craven worms in my inside will cease their churning . . .'

She was late. He felt as though he had been standing at the chancel steps for half a life time. He stole a glance at Richard Farrington who was swaying beside him like a tree in a wind.

'He looks sick enough to be the groom,' he thought with a certain satisfaction. Richard's natural urbanity was clearly diminished for the moment by what must be the most blinding of headaches. His smoothly barbered face shone with the pallor of a dead fish and dark shadows underlay his heavily-lidded and protuberant eyes. Even the smallest sound seemed to give him pain and Jess noticed with grim amusement that he was doing his best not to turn his head.

'Suffer, you son of a shit shoveller,' he said to Richard out of the corner of his mouth. 'You'll be feeling even worse when this day comes for you, I promise.'

Richard moaned under his breath. 'Just don't speak to me, there's a good fellow. If I can live through the next few minutes I might be able to do my duty as your sponsor. Right now, I think the back of my head is about to explode. This damned peruke seems to have shrunk . . . It's gripping my skull like a leach.' He drew a long shuddering breath.

'We may well have to turn this ceremony into Farrington's funeral . . .'

The stalls were filling with whispering, rustling people, heads straining to see who was present and who was not; eyes swivelling to watch the door for the moment when the bride would appear on her brother's arm. The bells pealed out over their heads. Jess watched the two ringers moving with practised control, arms rising – waiting, pulling downwards into their bodies and then rising once more.

Ding dong – Ding dong . . .

'Why doesn't she come? Has she had second thoughts? Maybe she is afraid to give herself to a Romani. I will gentle you, my beautiful girl. I will be as tender with you as I would be with a new foal.'

There was movement outside the porch and a ragged cheer went up from the crowd that stood along the path and straddled the grave stones in the church yard.

Richard came out of his daze with difficulty. 'This sounds like your moment of truth, old friend,' he said, straightening his shoulders with another inward groan and putting shaking fingers into his waistcoat pocket to check that he still had the ring in safe keeping. Jess stood stiff and tense beside him, grey eyes fixed anxiously on the doorway, high over the heads of the congregation.

Outside in the sunshine the sounds of a flute mingled with the double clarion of the bells. Then Lavinia was there, at the end of the church, walking slowly up the aisle towards him.

Amy sat in the stubbly grass with Violet in her lap, watching a family of shelduck foraging among the reeds below the bank. They looked like prosperous merchants with their red beaks and green-sheened black necks, white waistcoats and brown, green and black wing feathers. Behind her back, her sister Saiforella and all the Baylesses still living in the area, worked over the huge fire and the spread of food and ceremonial drinks. The sound of their laughter and ribald banter echoed across the water. It was a long time since they had celebrated a wedding and this one was more special than those that had gone before. Jess had become a monument to them and his time for jumping the broomstick must have all the very best trappings that they could muster.

Violet crawled off Amy's lap and reached for a dragonfly which hovered, trembling its translucent wings as it drew nectar from a head of pink clover. Amy watched idly as the little girl sat back on chubby buttocks, staring in wonder at the dainty, quivering creature. Afternoon sunlight picked up flashes of green and turquoise on its sticklike body and her full mouth opened in amazement at the insect's strange beauty. A bright dribble swung from the pink fullness of her lower lip. Amy sat very still, suddenly reminded of something in the child's intense concentration. The round grey eyes stared, glazed, as the dragonfly drank until – replete – it suddenly swooped out and upwards, away from the empty flower and straight into Violet's face. There was a blinding flash like sunlight on glass. Amy instinctively scooped the child up into her arms as the dragonfly fell.

It lay in the grass like a curl of burnt bark, charred and robbed of its rich colours – and very dead. The little girl in her arms shivered, her baby's face a mask of shock out of which the huge grey eyes glared blankly. Amy hugged the little body tightly to her, rocking and murmuring small meaningless words of comfort until the rigidity drained away and she relaxed into her mother's neck.

Amy stood up and climbed the shallow slope towards the well-stacked fire in front of the house. She passed by the family, sitting, lounging and relaxed round the ceremonial fire, unnoticed with the child held tightly against her and disappeared into the house. She stood in the hall, listening to the light tick of the longcase clock that had been John Freeland's wedding gift. Its polished brass face gleamed in the shadows and the ornate hands showed that it was more than two hours past midday. They would be wed by now . . . How long would it be before they finished with the wining and the dining with the gentry from Chichester – before the clatter of hooves heralded the end of her sway in this kenner? She stood in the middle of the stone-flagged hall, feeling the anger of the house all round her. She rolled her shoulders inside her dress with the sheer pleasure the awareness gave her. It was always there, the soundless rage; a sensation far beyond her control. It hung in the air – a snarling accusation of guilt and the sensation excited her profoundly, stirring her as intensely as Jess himself stirred her. She stood in the dark cave of the empty hall, hugging the silent child to her and savouring the violence of her arousal from the ancient carnality all about her. The nipples hardened against her bodice and she tightened her buttock muscles, murmuring into the little girl's mop of dark curls as the heat washed down her body in exquisite languor.

Outside Vasher's fiddle ceased its lilting jig and the laughter and singing among the cousins sank to a soft murmur. Wiping the fine perspiration from her upper lip, Amy looked down at Violet and found that she was asleep. She took her through into the kitchen and laid her in her day cradle. The hall clock chimed, its sweet high notes like drops of liquid crystal.

They were inside the church door, pausing so that the attendants could drop her sweeping skirts and arrange the veil and marshall the two little red-haired strewers shoulder to shoulder in front of Lavinia and John. Daft Dicken lolled against the first pillar, spittle trailing down his chin. He was all of a tremble, his poor misshapen body jerking and quivering as it always did, but he held out a single beautiful white rose to her, shorn of all its thorns. She took the perfect flower from him, thanking him shyly. His lopsided face cracked into a hideous, stump-toothed grin and he gobbled and choked his admiration as she felt John move forward beside her. 'Poor Dicken – you can be no more shivery and shaky than I am . . .'

They moved slowly up the aisle, oblivious of the heads turning as they passed. The tableau at the chancel steps seemed so far away that it was difficult to identify them in the dim light. Parson wore his best surplice, freshly laundered but he had forgotten to comb through his overlong, receding white hair. Jess and Richard stood close together, like soldiers on palace duty.

The little red-haired girls threw the last of their rose petals to the floor as they reached the chancel steps and withdrew to stand with their parents in the Pennicod pew. Lavinia drew level with her mother and saw the sweet, lined face turned towards her, smiling encouragement.

Then she was beside Jess. She turned her head slightly and saw the look on his face and knew that everything – always – would be all right. She bit her lip to stop it from trembling in its relief and fixed her attention on Parson Kelway.

'Dearly Beloved, we are gathered together here in the sight of God . . .' She could feel Jess' closeness reaching out to her. We are like lost souls, huddling together in all this strangeness. She longed to look at him again – to search his face and discover there the same unknown terrors that filled her.

The old man's voice rose as he lifted his head, pausing between words to give the command greater weight. 'I require and charge you both, as ye will answer at the dreadful Day of Judgement . . .'

Lavinia stared up at him, standing on the step above them with his prayer book held in gnarled old hands that had been roughened by field work and swollen with rheumatism. Sunbeams shafted through the mullions behind him. She watched the air shimmering with dust, bright dots dancing up the golden rays. Why did dust always ascend sunbeams?

The sing song monotone thundered through the church as he lifted his head to survey the packed congregation.

'If any man do allege and declare any impediment . . .'

There was a rustle as weights were shifted from one foot to another and every man poised himself for a lone voice, raised in dissent. The pause was only long enough for the count of ten. No man came forward.

The most solemn moment had come. Jess turned to Richard who started guiltily as attention focused on him. He had been in a trance, trying to shake off the miasma which still threatened to send him scuttling out of the church to throw up among the tomb stones. He thrust his finger and thumb into his lorgnette pocket and retrieved the gold ring and passed it over to Parson Kelway with relief. The church became still. Not even a child whimpered in the porch.

It was done. They knelt side by side while the old man rustled the notes in the back of his prayer book. He cleared his throat and began the little sermon he had composed for them. She watched his mouth opening and closing, the craggy white eyebrows lifting and falling as he fixed them with faded blue eyes. One eye had a slight yellowish film across the pupil. Poor old man. If he should go blind now, how will he live? It was so unfair that he should spend the whole of his life in the service of the needy – and yet, when disability struck him down, he would likely end in the poor house amongst those he had done his best to help. She studied his tired face from beneath her veil and noticed the slight tremble in his hands. Maybe Jess will look after him. He took care of Sarey Beer before Tover wed her and he still gives them money, so Mistress Chatfield said.

The Address concluded and the register duly signed, the fiddler and drummer struck up a medley of hymns from the church porch. The procession began its slow jostling walk down the aisle and out into the warm sunshine and the ragged cheers of children and farm workers and tramps and passers by. Above them the bells clanged out their message of fulfilment across the Apuldram fields, and those who toiled there stopped for a moment, straightened their backs and leant on their hoes to dwell an instant on the memory of their own wedding day.

Across the corn and the Dell Quay road and the coppice of roman oaks and Olivas' paddock, the Baylesses heard the bells. They had been waiting for that moment and lost no time in filling their tankards with Polly's best ale and toasting the absent couple in the way they knew best. Soon the real fun would begin – but until the young couple were with them they were content to wait and swap long and flowery tales of past rummers (weddings) and drink the health of their host.

The way back to Rymans took all of ten minutes, even though the house was only a hundred yards from the church. There were so many well wishers to acknowledge, so many hands to shake. They walked round to the main entrance so that the crowd would not stream across the carefully tended grass. Lavinia, her arm in Jess', smiling her thanks to the well wishers and stealing a peep now and then at the tall, happy man beside her who was now so magically her husband. Suddenly she wanted all the festivities to be over, for the people to be gone and for them to be on their own to work out the newness of their situation. The fear of what was before her had become honed with sweet anticipation. After all, a small voice reasoned, mother had not died of it – nor even implied any disgust – and Amy had not either. Sarey Beer seemed positively to thrive on it – and so did Cousin Felicity Charter, who had seven children and grew jollier and more content with each one.

'Thank goodness for that,' Jess said under his breath as they passed through the arched doorway into the great hall.

The wedding luncheon was a drawn out affair for the food was excellent and the wines without equal. Speeches were made and toasts by the dozen slowed up the tempo of the occasion. While the tables were being cleared in the great hall so that dancing could commence, Jess and Lavinia went through to the barn where the village and local tradesmen and their families were making merry and waiting to toast the young couple. After that, it was all dancing and drinking and, by the time it was the right moment for them to leave, decorum had long been cast to the winds.

The family said their farewells in the comparative privacy of the solar. It was a painful moment for mother and daughter, for each realized with sudden clarity that something had come to an end and a certain intimacy between them was about to change.

'Oh Mama. Aren't farewells terrible? I'm only going a couple of fields distance away and yet I feel as though I shall be in another world.'

Abigail laughed, holding Lavinia tightly against her, sniffing foolish emotional tears away and loving this child whom she had just given to a gypsy.

'I shall come over to Lavenham the very moment that you send word,' she said softly. 'He will be a good husband – and if he's not – we'll have him hounded out of the Parish, d'you hear that, Jess?'

'I hear, Ma'am – and tremble,' Jess said solemnly.

It took time to make their way down to the waiting open carriage, for everyone wished to give them his own blessing.

Sarey and Annie stood with Mrs Blunden and blubbed un-ashamedly into their best Sunday aprons but eventually Lavinia and Jess settled themselves into the padded seat while the guests gathered round the carriage and the two wains that would follow them to Lavenham. Lavinia threw her wedding posy into the sea of expectant faces and then they were moving off down the drive with John Blunden up on the driver's seat and the crowd cheering and waving behind them. Children ran beside them for as long as they could, throwing rice into their laps to wish them luck, until the pair of Lavenham bays picked up speed and left behind even the fastest runners. Lavinia settled back into the cushions with a deep sigh of relief. The rice rattled and cracked beneath their feet.

'Mercy, what a day,' she said, rubbing her arms. 'Getting married seems to be a bruising experience.' Jess put his arm round her and drew her close to him.

'We'll have to ensure that I'm not responsible for giving you any more.' He looked down at her with such solemn happiness that the blood stirred in her and she rested against him, head on his coat front, savouring this new familiarity.

The sun travelled down the sky and hung in the tops of the trees as they turned left onto the highway and then right and bowled down the road between the apple orchards that stretched all the way over to Donnington. She traced the shape of his hand with a fore finger and sniffed the warm air contentedly. Somewhere nearby, applewood was being burned and its sweet scent was all part of the perfection of the day.

'Jess – you will guide me, won't you?'

He grinned down at her. 'Stop worrying about it, Chika. We have another marriage to go through before you need to discuss the intimate things.' He kissed her forehead, leaving his mouth against her smooth skin. 'I've waited so long for this day, Linnie. You may be sure that I'm not going to ruin your trust in me at this stage. We are man and wife in name now and we will take our time about the rest of it.'

They sat close together watching the orchards stream by. They waved to old Granfer' Jelley as they bowled past Pope's Cider Press. Jess looked over his shoulder to check that the two wains were following. It seemed little more than minutes before Salterns Lane came into view and Blunden slowed the slender bays before turning across the road into the narrow opening. Here the trees pressed in over their heads and the going was slower on the pitted track.

Then they were turning again into the Lavenham drive. They passed Lost Labour, rounded a corner thick with hazel and holly and Lavenham lay ahead, mellow pink and golden grey in the strong evening sunlight, the barley sugar chimneys poised expectantly and the long roof with its two attic windows like surprised eyebrows on the face of a wind-browned sailor.

Climbing roses were beginning to soften the contours of its newness and a fine magnolia from the Goodwood gardens was out in full waxy flower beside the front door.

They drove round to the terraced front, facing the Channel and pulled up before the entrance.

Across the pebbled drive the Baylesses rose from round the fire and streamed towards them, bronzed dark faces bright with welcome. Lavinia had never met the Clan en masse and was unprepared for the total contrast and foreignness of this new family. Now she found herself surrounded by a crowd of dark and swarthy men and women, with untidy children scuttling through their legs and climbing up into the carriage. She pressed closer to Jess and feeling her nervousness, he held her firmly.

'It's all right. Don't be frightened of them. They are as curious about you as you are of them. Come on down and enjoy a wedden' that's a little more informal than the church one.' He jumped from the carriage and handed her down among his cousins and sisters.

She was such a slip of a girl, still short of maturity but with a golden beauty and innocence that made the men suck in their breaths and the women smile. Her wedding gown glowed in the last rays of the sun and hands came out to touch the rich satin and stroke its shining smoothness. The women pressed round her, the children pushed in and out of resistant legs; a lurcher snapped as a bare foot kicked it away from the bride's torn hem.

'Come now – give us some room to move, there,' Jess bellowed good naturedly and they made way, laughing and calling to him while he led Lavinia by the hand towards the hearth where the seniors waited.

'First you must meet my Uncle Piramis and his wife, Sarey.' They approached the pair who stood side by side, waiting to greet them.

'Sar Shan.' Sarey's voice was deep and husky. She smiled into Lavinia's eyes and raised her right hand. Lavinia put out her hand to shake it and saw that it was not going to be taken for it was raised with the palm turned flatly towards her. Shyly she raised her own and, as the two palms came together, returned the woman's smile, liking the worn face and fine brown eyes. Piramis bobbed his head at her and turned back to the fire, awkward before such elegance. They moved on and all were named and Lavinia struggled to put each face and name in a corner of her memory so that she would not offend the next time they met. Blind Vasher was the easiest to recall. He was lean and wizened and merry, with more than a passing look of Jess. He alone touched her, taking her hands and running the tips of his fingers over them from wrist to nails.

'A bitti rawni, are you? They didn't tell me that. Small and nervous as a hare but there's good bone there . . . you'll grow more yet.'

He grinned so that his mobile face creased into a thousand wrinkles. The sightless eyes danced and twinkled at her. She liked Vasher too.

Rose and Saiforella and Naffie and Lovedy . . . Jenk and Sarah and Lena, Bori, Tod, Vashti and Jack . . . and a dozen tattered, grubby little children who bobbed and scattered at their approach or stood with a dirty finger in a sticky mouth. The Clan was ragged and unkempt, even in their best clothing for it was clear that the bright colours and beads and the flowers in the women's hair was the best that they possessed. Lavinia tried not to look down at her crumpled but beautiful gown. How different they must think her.

Jess brought her full circle round the fire and then sat her on a log with a sheepskin flung across it. As he settled himself beside her, Vasher took up his fiddle and began to play a strangely haunting melody.

They drank a toast from a shared cup and kept it beside them and, when Vasher had finished, Jess stood up and held out his hand to her. They went together and stood before Piramis and Sarey. Dusk was falling and bats wheeled and swooped silently against the vivid evening sky.

Piramis began to speak and his words meant nothing to Lavinia for they were in the Old Tongue. She contented herself with watching the two dark faces in front of her. Piramis was swarthy, not as tall as Jess but heavier. His thatch of dark hair was dusted with grey and hardship had etched deep lines between nose and chin. The dark blue eyes regarding her did so with remarkable shyness and she suddenly realized that, although Piramis was head of the family, he had little knowledge of gorgio women and none at all of ladies of gentle birth. Sarey was different. She stood beside her husband with great natural dignity, Matriarch of the Clan, surveying the two of them with penetrating hazel brown eyes that would brook no opposition. They missed nothing. Recognizing Lavinia's uncertainty, she allowed a twinkle to soften them.

Piramis stopped speaking and Jess said to her, 'That was the Elder's speech of welcome to you at our fireside. He does speak English, of course, but prefers the Romani tongue for these occasions.'

'I like it,' she said. 'It makes the ceremony more solemn, doesn't it?' And it did. They understood and there was an imperceptible easing in the atmosphere, as though she had compounded a fact that was clear to them but approved that she, too, had sensed it. There was total silence all round them so that the crackling fire was magnified within it.

Out of the gathering shadows, Amy came forward. The sight of her hobbling gait jolted Lavinia for she had forgotten about this other member of her new household. The tall figure with a scarlet shawl wrapped round her waist and hips and her thick hair brushed out in a dark bush, walked into the pool of firelight with two small loaves which she handed to Sarey and then stepped back among her sisters without a glance in Lavinia's direction. There was no time to think about the fact that she was the only Bayless who had not made Lavinia welcome, because Sarey had begun to sing in a strange, croaky voice and behind her the other women joined in softly. She raised her arms and held aloft the two little loaves and when the song was over, broke one in half and gave it to Jess. He, in turn, broke his bread into two and gave a piece to Lavinia.

'Eat it,' he said under his breath.

She put the bread into her mouth and chewed and found it so fresh that it crumbled and dissolved, leaving a faint flavour of something herbal on her tongue. Sarey watched and when they had finished, beckoned to Lavinia as she broke the other loaf in half. She held out a piece to Lavinia and nodded towards Jess and, understanding, she took the bread and broke it as she had seen Jess doing and gave him half. They ate and Jess crumbled the remaining piece between his fingers and motioned for her to do the same. Then he threw the crumbs up into the air over their heads so that the fine particles fell upon them with a soft patter. She did the same and felt the crumbs falling over her shoulders and into her hair. Sarey broke and crumbled the remaining bread and strewed it round the gathering and the men shouted and stamped their feet and the women and children crooned with queer warbling sounds deep in their throats. Piramis began to speak again, this time with a new passion and vigour, raising his hands above his head as Sarey had done. Behind his voice the Clan hummed, a low monotonous accompaniment. The night shadows leaned in against the firelight, drowning the last of the day.

Beside her Jess said quietly, 'He speaks of the blessed corn that grows in the fields around us. It is a wondrous thing, the corn – sent from the Gods for the benefit of all peoples, whether they be Romanichal or Gorgio. The sacred corn is the most powerful thing existing against evil and against death, for the corn grinds down into flour and the flour becomes bread – and the bread is the food that keeps us all from starvation. Piramis is saying that they wish bread upon our house always.'

Piramis came forward and lifted Jess' hand and laid it upon his own. Then he took Lavinia's and spread it across Jess'. Sandwiching the two in his own large hands, he raised his head and called up into the young night. The flat wall of oak trees covering Copperas Point caught his voice and threw it back in a hollow echo that brought the hairs up on Lavinia's neck. Behind them, the Clan rose to answer the call and the sound of their responses floated out like a lament across the still waters of the creek.

She stood rigidly, feeling the whole of her body imprisoned there between Piramis' hands and for an instant fear rose in her and she strained against the iron clasp. Then his eyes dropped to the two young faces in front of him and he released his hold and put an arm round both of them.

'You are bonded,' he said.

There was a shout behind them and the whole Clan yelled at the top of its voice and suddenly the fiddle had struck up and a flute joined in and Piramis and Sarey began to dance. They wove in and out of the crowd, hooking arms, clicking fingers. The tune was a lilting jig, a happy, catchy melody.

'Come on, Chiriklo, we do the same.' Jess took her arm and spun her round him. 'Just a simple jig . . . take this arm and round. Now this one and do it again. That's right.'

It didn't take long to get the rhythm and suddenly she was moving round him with all the grace of a practised dancer, oblivious of the others who whirled and stamped or sat and watched the small girl in her bridal finery with the roses falling out of her hair and the long golden ringlets whipping across her face as she pivoted by.

They danced for a long time, stopping to drink when Vasher and Naffie paused for their own refreshment and then whirling away again with a chicken leg in one hand and their arms round each other. Groaning tables of food appeared from nowhere but Lavinia was too excited and tired by now to eat. The moon rose over the trees and Vasher sang songs to the moon and the stars and the night and the men did a dance, a wild leaping dance, clashing their heels together in the air and whirling like tops. She watched their shadows gyrating in a dance of their own, looming hugely when the fire flared. Beyond them the house sat softly lit, crouched on the edge of darkness, watching her from its windowed eyes like a cat. Patient – waiting . . . Something moved behind the glass panes in an upper chamber. She shivered and dragged her eyes away.

'Are you cold?' Jess asked, feeling the tremble in her hand. She shook her head, comforted by his attention.

'Look,' he said, pointing. 'Amy is setting the chamber ready for us . . . It is time to jump the broomstick and then they will all leave us. What normally happens is that when the couple have jumped the broomstick, they climb into their nice new waggon and drive away from the camp and wander the land for as long as it takes them to settle to each other. We cannot ride away in our house – so when we jump, they will leave us right away.'

He stood up, pulling her after him. At once the music stopped and the Clan raised itself, none too steadily to its feet.

'It is time,' Jess said to them and added something in Romani that brought smiles to the men's faces and a softness to the women. He held Lavinia's hand and the children raced past them, eager to be the ones who laid the brooms across the threshold of the house. They clattered through the kitchen and came out in a noisy jostle, shouting among themselves and trying to wrest the two new besoms from each other. The brooms were laid on the doorstep and the children stood back in a huddle, suddenly shy and watchful.

There were no farewells. The Clan stood quietly in the dim glow of the dying fire, mute witnesses to the final ritual.

'Come on – we just jump over them.' Jess was pulling her across the grass now, breaking into a run. 'Pick up your skirts, Chika, so that they don't touch the besoms. It's bad luck for anything to touch them . . .'

She scooped up the full skirts and petticoats and trotted beside him across the gravel and up the steps.

'Jump.'

She was up and over and then they were standing in the dim hall laughing and breathless, arms round each other.

'Welcome to Lavenham, Mistress Bayless,' Jess said and suddenly the laughter was gone and she lifted her face to him. It took a long time for them to exchange their welcome. He had not kissed her with anything other than light affection before and now there was all the time in the world to savour his mouth and feel the first shafts of an excitement coursing through her that became almost a sweet pain.

There was a sound above their heads. Lavinia jerked away from Jess. She had thought that they would be alone in the house and the sound of a creaking board shocked her. There was a flicker of movement in the gallery above their heads as though something withdrew into shadow.

'Don't worry, my darling,' Jess said in her ear. 'It's only Amy.'

It was almost the best feeling of all to wake up and find that the curtains had been drawn back to let in the first light, and that Jess lay quietly at her side, reading from a small leather bound book. As soon as she opened her eyes he put the book on his bedside table. She lay and looked at him, taking in the breadth of his brown shoulders and clean unblemished body. He grinned at her with infinite tenderness, his face no longer guarded and sombre, but filled with a shining happiness which spilled over her.

'Hello,' she said shyly and put out a bare arm to touch him.

This time there was no trace of the tension and fear of the night before. In the early light it seemed exactly right to roam the contours of each other, discovering many mysteries and delighting in their revelations. It was a surprise to discover how quickly the sun traverses the sky when the attention is elsewhere.

They became ravenously hungry by midday and Jess rose and climbed into his everyday clothes, bent on bringing back to the bed chamber a feast of foods from yesterday's piled up platters. As he buttoned his breeches, he caught sight of a limp little posy lying on Lavinia's bedside table. He picked it up and stood with it in the palm of his hand, looking at it thoughtfully reading its message.

Lavinia smiled up at him. 'Amy must have left that on my pillow. Wasn't it a pretty gesture? I know that we'll become friends, once she is used to me being here.'

Jess looked at her, sitting up in the wide bed with her white robe demurely buttoned and the golden hair streaming over her shoulders. She looked so childlike, so eager and trusting. He cursed Amy for casting a blight upon his feeling of fulfilment and bent down to kiss that tender innocence.

'I shall get her to platter us a feast to eat up here,' he said. 'Then we can spend the day going round the house and I shall show you every bit of your new property – from the woods to the paddocks. Amy can take you over the domestic side another day. Today belongs to you and me.'

He went downstairs and she heard his feet clattering across the hall. She lay back among her pillows with a contented sigh and smoothed the embroidered quilt across her lap.

Jess strode into the kitchen where Amy and Polly Ayles were bent over the hearth pots. They looked up as he came in and Polly bobbed, her plain good-natured face wreathed in smiles.

'Mornen' Sur,' she said, wiping her hands on an already grubby apron. Amy put down her stew ladle and turned to the kitchen table.

'I hope we didn't disturb you too early with our tidying up after yesterday,' she said. Her eyes went to the little bunch of limp flowers in his hand and she flushed deeply.

'Polly,' Jess said, 'get us a jug of milk from the dairy and a tray of small foods, if you please.'

She scuttled away to do his bidding and as soon as she was out of earshot he said curtly to Amy, 'What do you mean by putting that on Lavinia's pillow last night?'

He flung the little bouquet onto the table between them and she shrugged, twisting her apron. 'I'm not going to have this sort of thing between you.' His voice was low and harsh. 'Yesterday I was wed and brought my wife back to my home. Now it is her home as well, Amy, and the sooner you come to realize that and acknowledge that she is Mistress of Lavenham, the easier it will be for all of us.'

His voice softened. 'Come now, Pen. It was always on the cards that I should wed. You and I are far too close to let that make a difference to us. Befriend Lavinia – please? She is little more than a child still and is eager for your affection. Don't go making cruel and vindictive gestures like this one. I might expect that from Polly or some such mouse brain – but not from you, Pen. Not you.'

She stared down at the mangled posy on the table. It had been so pretty when she had gathered the bright flowers and contrasting greenery in the woods the previous day.

Yellow tansies and pink foxgloves and speckled white dragonwort, mixed with a little spray of evergreen cypress and pale tender basil. Its aromatic scent still lingered.

Tansies for conflict and foxgloves for insincerity. Dragonwort for fear, the basil for hatred and cypress spelled – Death.

Chapter Six

'Everyone should marry in June,' Lavinia said, walking with Jess in the garden.

He glanced down at her and quickened at the sight of her upturned face, brimming over with happiness and excitement in this new ownership of her surroundings. She was having some difficulty in walking at his side, it seemed, for each rustle of her blue striped skirts suggested that she would rather be dancing ahead in a twirling jig of high spirits.

'Don't walk so quickly.' He tucked his arm into hers to anchor her beside him. 'You will lose me the pleasure of your company all too soon if you race round the property at such a pace.'

'Oh, I know, I know.' She snuggled closely against him and leaned her cheek on his arm for a moment. 'I just feel so marvellously happy today . . . and I simply must say good morning to Midas, Jess. I shall do that every morning for the rest of his life because he brought us together, didn't he?'

Jess laughed, moved by the innocence of her. She was such a child still. A lovely joyous creature, overflowing with the sheer exuberance of life. She was more like Midas than she realized, he thought for the hundredth time, listening with half an ear to the flow of her chatter.

They approached the paddock and leaned on the gate, waiting for the horses to acknowledge their presence.

'Come up, Midas – come up,' Lavinia called. Jess put his arm round her waist and kissed the top of her shining hair as they watched the colt lift his head and break from the grazing herd to trot, high stepping, down the field towards her outflung hands. There was something touchingly beautiful in the coming together of these two golden creatures, he thought. For all her elegant London manners, there was still a trace of coltish gawkiness in Lavinia's high spirits – the same innocent zest with which Midas was filled.

Midas broke into a canter and came streaking across the field, checking his pace at the very last moment with a little buck as he halted a yard from Lavinia's wriggling fingers. Jess watched. Horse and girl gazed at each other for a moment and then seemed to merge together as Midas moved forward and buried his soft pink nose in Lavinia's hair. She put her arms round his neck, kissed the side of his warm muzzle and let him blow softly against her neck. She scratched his ears, murmuring small private things into them and whatever the words were, Midas understood their message for his ears pricked and turned and signalled his response. His bright eyes seemed to glaze over in the fullness of love and he pressed against the gate, uttering small contented noises deep down in his throat.

'Hey, you two,' Jess said eventually, after their mutual admiration had apparently blocked out his existence. 'Come back to earth. I'm beginning to feel that I'm not wanted here.'

Lavinia turned to him and quickly reached up to plant a peck on his cheek. 'How could you think such a thing of either of us,' she pouted, wrinkling her nose at him. 'There was never a man more loved, nor a wife more doting. It's just that Midas understands every word I say. It is as though he reads me as well as you do, Jess – and I just can't wait for him to be broken in.'

'Well, that's just what Manfri and I were discussing a few days ago. He is about the right age now – and Manfri has had him on a lunger a couple of mornings. He will need you with him during training, of course – so, as soon as you wish, you may join him in the mornings. Your rapport with Midas is so strong that there is no reason why you should not be riding him in a very few weeks.'

He drew her away at last and they strolled back towards the house, skirting the barn and following the path along the bank of the creek.

'I want to discuss the household duties with you,' Jess

said, tucking her hand into his arm and covering it with his own.

'I feel so important,' she said breathlessly. 'I know that I have a great deal to learn, but Amy will help me, won't she?' The mention of Amy brought her thoughts back to a state of reality with a bump and she looked at Jess with uncertainty.

'Of course she will,' he said abruptly. 'She is not an easy person to understand and I hope that you will make allowances for her various misfortunes. She is subject to occasional fits which Doctor Sanden puts down to epilepsy. They are not pleasant to perceive, dearest . . . but Polly and I are quite used to them and there is a routine treatment which is carried out which we will teach you. Amy can be very surly at times but her heart is of the kindest, I assure you. Once the strangeness of your presence has worn off, I am sure that you two will become good friends. In the meantime, it will probably save the risk of poaching upon each other's preserves if certain duties are agreed between the two of you.'

Lavinia nodded. 'I do understand, Jess. This was Amy's home right from the beginning and I would hate her to feel that I am wresting her rightful place from her. Maybe I could start by being responsible for those things that I have always done at Rymans – like making jams and pickles and looking after the linens. I'm quite deft at my needle, if you recall . . . And then there are the bees, of course. I love my bees and Old Beezer has trained me well in the making of honey.'

She stared up at the brooding, watching windows of the house as they crossed the lawn towards it. In the sunshine it lay calm and beautiful, a home to be cherished and proud of. She had really been so silly to think it sinister. Now that the tensions of approaching marriage were being resolved so happily, her foolish fears of the house would certainly disappear also.

'Darling, you're not listening to a word I'm saying.' Jess' voice cut through her thoughts and she jerked back to him with a start.

'I'm sorry, Jess. I was just thinking how lovely the house looks . . . and how I'm sure that I shall find it much more friendly now that I am actually living here.'

He squeezed her arm and leaned down to plant a kiss on her

cheek. 'Take everything as it comes, my love. Do not try to tackle all the problems at once. The house most certainly has its own special mysteries but Amy and I have not found them unpleasant – and nor will you. You are beginning a new life and I shall do all I can to ensure that in marrying me you made the happiest decision of your life. In the meantime, will you take over the parlour and our bed chamber and whatever you feel you can manage in the garden?'

'Yes, that would be a very good idea at the beginning – as long as Amy doesn't want to arrange flowers or polish the furniture.'

Unaccountably, the smile left his face. 'Amy will leave *all* the flowers to you from now on,' he said shortly. 'I shall get you the linen cupboard keys right away. Then, when you are quite at home here, we can discuss your involvement with pickling and the kind of cooking that you have been used to.' He grinned at her again, the stern moment forgotten.

'Amy is a fine cook but that apple and tomato chutney I've had at Rymans is unbeatable and I'm not having her denying me little delicacies like that.'

They strolled round the side of the house just as a cart trundled into the barn yard and pulled up short of them.

'Why, Beezer,' said Lavinia, starting forward in surprise. The old man gave her a wide and toothless grin.

'Thought you might be lonely without you'm little friends, Ma'am,' he said. 'Brought over four skeps. Too late for swarmen' this month but I'll see ye away with 'em come September.'

All at once she felt very much more at home, knowing that her bees were near her once more. Rueb and Old Beezer set up the four skeps in the orchard of young apple and plum trees.

'Well, if that's where they're to be, you can pick the fruit yourself,' Amy said when Lavinia told her of their arrival. 'I can't be doing with the creatures,' she said, seeing Lavinia's surprise. 'Nasty tempered, they can be. A bee sting's a power-ful pain . . . to me, at any rate.'

'But I've been tending the bees for years,' Lavinia argued, 'and I've only had a couple of stings in all that time – and that was my fault because the poor things became tangled in my clothing. Really, Amy, you must try and commune with them. They are very intelligent creatures and quickly sense whether or not you are a friend.'

Amy sniffed and turned away. 'You can make friends with whoever you want,' she said shortly. 'They're no friends of mine.'

Luncheon was laid in the hall for two. 'Surely you will join us,' Lavinia looked from Jess' face to Amy's.

'I'm busy,' said Amy. As Lavinia lowered her eyes and sat down, Jess followed his sister into the kitchen.

'Pen, I am not going to make a scene now but I would like to see three places laid at the dining table in future and you will take your meals with us.' His voice was low so that he had to bend his head to speak to her. She crossed over to the fire and began ladling the mutton stew into a large tureen. 'Amy, do you hear what I am saying?'

She finished spooning the meat and gravy into the earthenware pot and turned to place it on the kitchen table. She looked at Jess in stony silence. His eyes held hers. For an instant they clashed and then she dropped her eyes with a shrug.

'Misto, Pral (all right, brother),' she muttered and turned her back on him again. He returned, frowning, to the dining table.

In the evening she ate with them but said nothing for the whole meal, sitting opposite Lavinia with a pale, withdrawn look on her face which discouraged friendly overtures. Lavinia breathed a sigh of relief when they rose from the table and made for the comfortable intimacy of the parlour on their own. Her troubled face smote at Jess.

'Don't take Amy's moods too seriously, Chiriklo,' he said. 'It will all sort itself out in time. It just needs our patience and your understanding.'

In the morning, Jess returned to the pattern of his daily work, asked Amy for the house keys and presented them to Lavinia with a gallant flourish.

'Amy, would you take Lavinia round the rooms and go through the household inventory and account books with her,' he said as he made for the stables. The two women stood either side of the kitchen table, watching him stride away from them. Upstairs the sounds of Polly sweeping in the chamber

173

over their heads were movements from another world. The baby Violet slept in her day cradle beside the settle. Now and then she made small mooes in her sleep. Lavinia bent down and watched her.

'How pretty she looks,' she said, smiling up at Amy, eyes pleading for a spark of response.

'They'm never pretty that young.'

Amy began taking jars down from the dresser, pushing past Lavinia and gradually easing her away from the cradle.

'Well – what shall I do first?' Lavinia said, doing her best to retain the happiness with which she had woken beside Jess that morning.

'You may do as you wish, Mistress,' Amy snapped. 'Just don't get in my way because I've eggs to pickle and the dumplings to get in the pot.'

'May I not help you? I can gather the eggs, at least.'

Amy flung her a look of contempt. 'I cleared the nests before you were out of my brother's bed this morning.'

The insolent implication brought a pink flush to Lavinia's cheeks. 'I *am* married to Jess, you know,' she said quietly.

She took a step forward and opened her mouth to speak further but Amy turned away and with a sigh Lavinia withdrew from the unfriendly kitchen and closed the door firmly behind her. She stood in the hall and watched Polly descending the shallow staircase, arms full of brooms and feather dusters and bed linen.

'Mornen' Mistress,' Polly called down cheerfully, seeing the forlorn figure standing uncertainly beside the bottom step. Poor little soul. That Amy would tear her to pieces if she had her way . . . Well, maybe Miss Lavinia would bring a little sunshine into the house and cast out its air of gloom. The place was more like a crypt with its dark corners and strong stable smells. She smiled broadly down into Lavinia's anxiety, seeing her friendliness wipe away the uncertainty hovering there, to be replaced by smiling relief.

'Good morning, Polly,' Lavinia said. 'May I help you?' She started forward and took the sheets from Polly's overburdened arms, opened the kitchen door and followed the girl through to the wash house without looking at Amy.

They filled the boiler with water, immersed the sheets and

made up a good fire under the cauldron. It was good to be working side by side with Polly. She was a cheerful, down to earth girl much given to laughter. It was something of a shock to realize that she had not enjoyed a morning's work so much since the day she had arrived at Lavenham.

'Polly taught me how to make soap this morning,' Lavinia said proudly to Jess that evening. 'She is such a pleasant, hard-working girl. I enjoyed myself very much and felt that I have actually been of use.'

'Has Amy done the inventory with you yet?' Jess asked. He watched a cloud lengthen her face and the animation fade from it.

She shook her head. 'She was busy.' She spread her hands out across her lap and stroked the rose coloured silk lightly. 'I . . . I didn't want to get in her way by asking her again.'

A nerve jumped in Jess' cheek and he stood up. 'Look, Chika,' he said grimly. 'I'm sorry that you are having this nonsense to cope with. I'm going to stop this thing here and now.'

He left her and she heard him crossing the hall and going into the kitchen. She sat very still. There was a pause and then he returned with Amy trailing behind him. He waved her into the room and closed the door with a sharp click.

'Now look here, Amy – and you too, sweetheart. I am a very busy man and when I say that the two women closest to my heart are to run my house and to make every effort towards the happiness of us all, I expect this to be carried out. Amy, I asked you to take Lavinia round the house today and go over the inventory of furnishings, silver and chattels with her. You have made no attempt to do that. Why?'

Amy looked at him, jutting her chin. 'I'm not her nurse-maid,' she snapped at him, ignoring Lavinia. 'I've got more than enough to do about the house without having to wet nurse your wife.'

She stood tall and close to him, her eyes only a little lower than his own. He saw the tremor in her body and the first flickers in her pupils and put his arms out as she swayed and began to crumble.

'Oh Jess,' Lavinia said, starting forward.

175

'Out of the way. Don't crowd her,' his voice was sharp and she jerked backwards as he lowered Amy to the ground and crouched over her, turning her head to one side, soothing the jerking, threshing body with gentle hands.

'There, there, Pen. It's all right, just relax, just try and relax.' The sing song voice spelt out a long familiarity with such situations and he talked and comforted without once looking up at Lavinia until the spasm passed and Amy lay damp and pale under his hands. He wiped the saliva from her mouth and pushed back the damp hair from her face. It was only then that he appeared to remember Lavinia for he raised his head with an apologetic grimace.

'This is the only way to help her at these times,' he said. His eyes were filled with an infinite sadness. 'Poor girl. You'd think that she had enough to contend with, what with her lameness and the trouble it affords her. These fits are not getting any better – worse, if anything.' A strange look crossed his face and was instantly gone. It was quite out of character for Jess to plead, Lavinia thought. 'It's because of these fits that I must have her here with us – where we can keep a close eye on her and make sure that her life is not too difficult.'

That was it. Amy in permanent residence was the price to be paid for Jess and Lavenham. She nodded, unable to find the right words to express her dismay – and her acceptance of his terms. He carried Amy up to her chamber and called Polly to disrobe her and settle her in her bed.

It was a small bonus to take Violet up and change her and set her in her night cradle still drowsy from her last feed, the feeling of the baby's warm dependence bringing her closer to Amy.

Lavinia woke from a sleep made all the deeper by contented exhaustion, disturbed by sounds which at first she could not identify. She lay on her back, feeling Jess' arm against her side. He was breathing deeply and regularly. She felt the light touch of his breath on her neck.

Then the odour reached her. The hot, acrid odour of horse. Horse that had been running. The smell swept over her so strongly that for a moment her confused, sleepy mind suggested that there were horses in the room.

Horses. She sat up in bed. There were sounds . . . Smell sharpened into stench. She slid out of bed without being sure why, seeking without knowing what she sought – aware of a dreamlike detachment.

The stench ballooned. It filled her nostrils so that she felt quite nauseated. Sounds . . . outside the chamber. Downstairs? She opened the bedroom door a crack. The darkness of the hall was total. Even the nightlight in Amy's room thrust no faint bar of light beneath her chamber door.

Sounds. Disturbance. She moved like a sleepwalker to the banisters and looked down from the gallery into the black well of the hall below.

Heavy laboured breathing just beneath her.

The hot reek of horse was overpowering now, making her gag and even as her eyes probed the black infinity she found movement down there. Something gleamed and shuffled and pawed . . .

Sudden cold terror flooded through her, bringing the hairs up on her arms and she backed away from the gallery rail into the bed chamber, slamming the door behind her.

'Who's that?' Jess' sleepy voice cut across the panic waves that rooted her, disorientated in the middle of the room.

'Lavinia, is that you? . . . Why are you out of bed, Chiriklo?' The blessed familiarity of his voice calmed her. She crept towards the comfort of the sound with outstretched hands, slid thankfully into bed and pressed herself against him.

'Can't you smell it?' she said against his shoulder.

He put his arms round her and cradled her against him. 'Can't smell anything except you, darling.'

It had gone. The terrible bitter stench of the creature's passion. The watcher. The sounds in the hall below them.

She must have been dreaming. A nightmare. What a terrible fantasy though. She shivered and put her arm across Jess' chest and pulled him even closer to her.

Violet celebrated her first birthday by producing her first tooth. Amy made no comment about it and it was some days

177

before Lavinia noticed. When she drew Amy's attention to the tiny blue-white chip emerging from the baby's lower gum, Amy continued shredding lavender heads.

'I know,' was her only comment. 'She's had it since her birthday.'

They sat with the kitchen table between them and the door into the yard open to let in the September sunshine. The little girl played round their feet, crawling happily between the aproned knees and table legs. She took hold of the flowered cloth of Lavinia's skirt and hauled herself up onto unsteady legs, bumping her head on the table supports.

'Oops there. What a bump,' Lavinia said sympathetically. She lifted the little girl onto her lap and cuddled her, rubbing the dark curls. Violet didn't cry, although her eyes filled with unshed tears. She sat and gazed up into Lavinia's face and, putting a fat finger into her mouth, settled herself comfortably in the crook of Lavinia's arm. Amy put down her lavender heads, rose and came round the table. She swept Violet up and limped over to the day cradle beside the settle. She settled her down among the covers and returned to her task.

'Why did you have to do that?' Lavinia asked. 'She was perfectly happy on my lap.'

'I'm not haven' her molly coddled,' Amy said curtly.

Lavinia stopped shelling peas. 'Come now, Amy. It's hardly molly coddling a little child to offer comfort when she hurts herself.'

'She wasn't hurt. She didn't cry, did she?'

'She was very brave . . . It was quite a big bump but it's hardly going to spoil a child to sit her on the knee and give her attention now and then,' Lavinia protested. 'All babies need love – they thrive on a kiss and a cuddle.'

'Is that your experience?' Amy looked at her with all the contempt of a mother for one who is childless.

'Romanies don't slobber over their young. They know they are loved. They have to learn independence at an early age. I was foraging for food by the time I was two.'

'That was because you were poor, Amy. Violet won't ever have to do that. Why can't she be allowed all the affection she can get? You don't let Polly near her, either. She should be having a perfect childhood here at Lavenham but if you don't permit anyone to love her, the poor child will grow up thinking the world is a dreadfully cold place.'

The little girl peered up at her from the depths of the oak cradle, her eyes like solemn grey orbs.

Lavinia's heart suddenly jolted as she recognized something. She was often regarded with the same concentration of veiled watchfulness by other large grey eyes. She studied Violet and noticed for the first time how the little girl's eyes were fringed with the same long thick black lashes and that her brows were the same straight, well-defined shape as Jess'. Her mind flicked over the Bayless Clan, searching for grey eyes among them and finding none. They were so very unusual, Jess' and Violet's eyes. She could not recall ever having seen truly smoke grey eyes before – a grey that could be soft and melting as wood smoke or hard as a storm-tossed sea.

She looked up to find Amy watching her; reading Lavinia's thoughts with taunting enjoyment of the disbelief and distress dawning in her sister-in-law's face.

'I – I was just thinking how like Jess' eyes Violet's are,' Lavinia stammered, feeling the flush of her shock pouring through her.

Amy stretched out and ruffled the little girl's dark curls. 'Fine eyes, they are,' she said with a smile that stopped short of her own blue eyes. 'Fine grey ones, just like Jess'. We never did know where he came by those for there b'ain't no other grey ones among the Baylesses, only his'n. And now Violet too. Makes her look more like him than ever, d'unt it?'

Lavinia clenched her fists. 'Children often resemble their uncles and aunts,' she said stiffly. 'Mother always says that John takes more after her Father Pay than after the Freelands.'

Insolent amusement turned Amy's melancholy face into a cruel angel.

'The blood in Violet's veins be closer than that,' she said with the contempt that Lavinia hated and dreaded coming into her voice. 'There only be Bayless blood in Violet so t'is to be expected that she be like him.'

She stared at Lavinia, watching the words sink in and find the tender spot to which they had been aimed. Tears pricked at the backs of Lavinia's eyes. She looked at Amy silently for a moment, the hurt giving her unexpected strength. 'You are despicable,' she said quietly.

She put aside her pea husks and left the kitchen, stumbling out over the yard cobbles towards the bank of the creek. Violet was Jess' child.

The impact of the statement smote her again and again, twisting the heart in her. Tears of mortification streamed down her face and she gasped as the pain of the words struck afresh. It was almost too much to contemplate . . . that Jess – the beautiful, tender man who was her husband and who clearly loved her more than life itself – Jess had lain with his own sister; lain with that gawky woman and found the same pleasure in her body that he found so constantly in Lavinia's. The bile lurched upward and she sank down into the long grass at the top of the bank and vomited.

'Heaven alone knows how I shall retain my sanity if those two continue bickering like fishwives,' Jess said bitterly to John Freeland in the private bar at the rear of the Swan. 'Hardly a day goes by that I don't return home to find either an altercation in progress or a blistering silence which is even worse.'

John's practical mind picked over the alternatives – as it had done with increasing frequency lately, for his mother had complained bitterly to him on many occasions that Lavinia was being most unfairly treated by her sister-in-law.

'Might it not ease the situation for all of you if you found a cottage for Amy?' he asked. He tilted his rocking chair gently back and forth and pulled at his pipe.

'No, that is just not practical.' Jess took a long gulp from his tankard. 'She is very incapacitated by the fits she experiences and has to be in company because of them. Besides,' he uttered the words with which he constantly placated his own increasing feelings of exasperation and concern, 'she's my flesh and blood and it would not be right to caste her and the child to one side on account of a domestic difficulty. Lavinia is young and resilient and she likes having Violet around, I know.'

John Freeland's neatly cued brown head nodded over the thin blue curl of smoke from his pipe. His face had long lost its youthful plumpness and, with the high-bridged nose fining down into maturity, was gradually assuming a mildly hawkish look, like a benevolent falcon.

'She is young, brother, I'll give you that . . . and she has a tender regard for all children and young animals but in time she will fill the house with children of her own. Would it not be kinder to her in her youth and inexperience, to permit her to run the home she shares with you – without having to concede most of it to her sister-in-law in order to avoid a clash of wills.'

'I . . .' Jess opened his mouth to answer sharply and was interrupted by a knock on the door.

'Message from me Lord of Richmond, Sir.' John Trew entered and hovered at his elbow, fidgeting to return to his desk. 'If'n it's convenient, Sir – he'd like to come over to Lavenham in the mornen' to have a look at the three colts you told him about.'

Domestic discord forgotten, Jess leapt up and thumped his empty tankard down on the table. 'Ha,' he said with immense satisfaction. 'The fish is nibbling at the bait. Thanks, John. Away with you then. I'll be at my desk in a few minutes and you may take the reply over right away. Is His Grace in his chambers or at home?' And, being told the former he gave the youth a friendly pat on the arm and sent him back to his ledgers.

'I've been trying to get the Duke to take a look at Olivas' foals for months,' he said to John. 'I'm anxious to sell him one, maybe that fine little filly that Glimmer produced this spring.' He rubbed his hands and paced the room, lost now in other, more productive thoughts.

John shook his head at Jess' back. Bickering women was a subject of small moment when the future of the herd came into focus. The sharpness of that scheming mind could turn most situations to his advantage, he thought with affectionate exasperation – except, it would seem, the problem looming in his own home. Walking back to his rooms along East Street he immersed himself in the recent legalities of Jess' new trading vessel. Jess would not be running true to character if there were not facilities provided for certain heavy duty cargoes to be imported past the noses of the authorities. It was an increasing struggle to perform his duties as Jess' attorney without smarting under the illegalities of one section of the Bayless business.

'S'truth, Amy, I will not tolerate this constant carping and anger.' Jess snatched the shirt she held out to him and threw it across the parlour. 'Have you never scorched a garment? Have you never had to learn the hard way? You and I both know the answer to that . . . so let us not forget that you are also less than perfect.'

'You would never have spoken in that way to me before you were wed,' she flashed back at him. 'You valued the quality of all that I had learned at Manor Farm then. Now you compare me with that simpering girl with such constance that I feel that I can no longer do anything to please you.'

Her anger became greater as tears threatened to overtake her. 'You tell me that I must teach Lavinia all I know. When I try to do just that, to train her to do her tasks properly instead of in the slapdash way she seems to prefer, I get whining complaints from her and then am admonished by you for obeying your instructions.'

Jess sighed. 'It is not the instruction that angers me, Amy. It is the harsh and unfriendly methods you use. Lavinia is doing her best – and is a swift and apt pupil – but if you insist on bullying her and submitting her to such constant disapproval, how can you expect her to do anything other than become despondent.'

'It's not me that makes her so jumpy,' Amy said with a small smile. 'She is frightened to death of the house. It's the house that is making her unhappy. She can't commune with what is here but permits it to dominate her fears and imagination.' She turned in a slow circle before him with her arms out, as though to embrace the air around her.

'I never had your gift, Jess, but I feel this place with every nerve in my body. I love whatever it is that dwells here. It gives me strength when my system is weakened. It fuels my anger . . . it quickens my need of you . . .'

'Stop speaking in that way,' he hissed under his breath. They stood staring at each other, knowing the depth of that wild lustful fury with which the place was impregnated. He looked at Amy and saw the glare of it shining in her whole body and for an instant was moved and exalted by it. The moment existed and passed.

He sighed and relaxed the taut muscles of his body. 'It was wrong, Pen, I know now. I should never have built the house here. It disturbed something that should have been left sleeping. I feel it so strongly sometimes that I am smote with fear for us all. At others, there is a feeling of such peace and contentment that I want only to abide in this one place for the rest of my days. I hoped that Lavinia would not have been affected by the situation but she is. I can only do my best to persuade her that what dwells here with us is not something to fear but to accept. Meanwhile, do you – for my sake – soothe your dislikes and live peacefully together. We have a long life ahead of us – and Violet to rear – and Lavinia's children also.'

She turned from him. 'Take note of your daughter,' she said limping towards the doorway. 'Observe her and you will be surprised with what you learn.'

By the time the harvest was in, Lavinia had been at Lavenham for four months. Thanksgiving came and went and she celebrated it with Jess and her brother John, at Fishbourne with Mistress Freeland. Lavinia spent more and more time with her mother as autumn drew the days in towards Christmas. She appeared to need her mother's counsel at every turn these days, Jess noted. There was constant reference to her advice on the subject of the linen room enlargement and over the surest way to gel her junket. Then the intriguing observation of John Freeland and his growing interest in Mary Blake kept their tongues busy for hours on end.

Watching Lavinia working at her lace pillow, he realized that she was looking brighter and happier than she had seemed for weeks.

'Rest your work and talk to me,' he said, patting his knee.

She looked up and smiled across the hearth at him, the dimple in her left cheek deepening. Obediently she laid the pillow with its gaily coloured clicking bobbins to one side and came across to him.

He perched her on his lap the better to admire her. She sat, happy and pink cheeked – everything about her sparkling and animated. It would seem that marriage to Jess Bayless was suiting her well, despite Amy's antagonism. He took her hands and rubbed them for they were unmittened and cold.

The days had suddenly sharpened into early frosts and the house was full of draughts. He saw that she was bursting with news, hugging it to herself with a little girl's secret glee, waiting to be persuaded.

'All right then, Chiriklo, let's be having it. You've been holding something back ever since I came home. What have you been up to?'

'Aren't you perceptive, my Jess. Well, I didn't wish to speak of it in front of Amy so I couldn't talk before, but . . .I'm with child, Jess . . . I have been hoping that I might be but now Mama tells me that I certainly am.'

She sat primly on his knee, very straight-backed and solemn, trying without success to keep the happiness out of her face. He gathered her up in a great bear hug and the evening chill was forgotten in the plans and dreams that a first child always generates.

In the kitchen, Amy sat beside the fire with Violet in her lap, knitting a shawl for the little one to wear during the coming months. She could hear Lavinia's voice and laugh and the rumble of Jess' replies. He lived in another world these days – a world where there was no place for his sister. Her place was here, in the kitchen – with Violet. As if the little girl sensed her name she sat up and smiled at her mother.

'Can you hear him talking, Russli (flower)? Can you hear him?'

The dark head nodded vigorously, curls bouncing. 'Who is it? Tell me who it is then.'

Violet considered, her attention sliding to the closed kitchen door before returning to her mother.

She beamed and clapped her hands, enlightenment dawning. 'Dada,' she said joyously. 'Dada . . . Dada.'

Amy nodded, satisfied and kissed the chubby hands. She put the child down and rose to build up the fire before they retired.

Chapter Seven

Occasionally the South of England finds itself in the grip of a winter so cold that the seasonal pattern is thrown off balance, putting farmers and merchants into confusion and the cycle of natural life into a battle for existence.

The winter of 1730–31 was the coldest for thirty-two years. The frosts came early, riming woods and hedgerows in icy sculpture that gleamed dully through blankets of mist, destroying the tender shoots which had already begun to sprout in fields and domestic vegetable gardens. On the Downs behind Chichester the sheep suffered, and in the oak forests even the wild pigs froze to death. The nights were suddenly so cold that even the snuggest homes took on a sepulchral chill and ice grew thick on the insides of the windows. Such heavy frosts brought immediate problems on many levels, for the earth was too hard for winter ploughing, water froze in domestic wells and even the Chichester Channel iced over from Copperas Point up to Fishbourne Mill so that the coal lighters were unable to offload at Dell Quay.

It was fortunate that Manfri, smelling the air, had decided to bring in the horses early that year and, when the weather broke, they were already stabled in the barn, safe and warm in their stalls with plenty of straw and fodder to see them through the coming months. The swine were not so fortunate for Salterns Woods were always raked by prevailing winds in winter.

Freezing mist penetrated the densest thickets, embroidering everything it touched with silver lace and freezing the swine to

185

death, even through their tough protective fat. In two nights the whole Lavenham swine herd was lost and every cottage in the parish was set to smoking joints of pork in their chimneys.

Abram Bayless' son Bori, was taken by the Militia at Siddlesham when his horse fell on the glassy ground and rolled on Bori, breaking his leg. The Blacks had been bringing brandy from their Siddlesham warehouse to Master Tovey's new wine shop just inside the South Gate and Richard and the gang had been forced to abandon him in order to make good their own escape. It had been the closest that they had been to arrest for some years and it made Richard Farrington aware of his position should they be less fortunate in the future. He resigned as leader of the Blacks and Jess put Tover in his place. Night running in the winter of 1730–31 was hard going.

Jess moved to more spacious premises in Little London, off East Street, just before the frosts began. In the town street directory he described himself as 'Jess Bayless. Banker and Importer.' The interests on his loans were now linked to the London Stock Market and interest rates were agreed with the other merchant bankers in the town. There were only three besides Jess, and Francis Diggens held more promissory notes than all the others put together. Diggens was an astute business man with a healthy respect for Jess' shrewd instincts and level head. He had been surprised when Jess had politely turned down his offer of a banking partnership, but took no offence. There was more than enough business in the town and surrounding districts to support half a dozen banking houses for, with the arrival in the south of three gifted architects and the enlargement of the Donnington and Hunston brickworks, a fever of building had begun, which promised to double the size of the town within a decade.

John Freeland was now establishing a fine reputation as a lawyer in the area. At twenty-nine, he was already an authority in maritime law as well as being a kindly and astute representative of all who sought his help. His chambers were conveniently near those of his brother-in-law so that time would not be lost in document bearing. He handled all the complicated legal side of Bayless', and the 'Grace' and her sister ship 'Golden Dawn' when she was finished, were to be handled from the Bayless offices also. It was a time of vigorous expansion and Jess took on Mark Woolgar as his shipping agent and John Trew was promoted to banking and general clerk. By the time Lavinia was brought to her confinement in the summer of 1731, the specially designed schooners with their 'extra accommodation' for all manner of foreign goods, were to be making large profits for the company.

The idea of building false compartments into the 'Grace' had been suggested by Builder Ferris after half a dozen ankers of Portuguese sherry had exchanged hands in the Birdham yard. They pored over the draughtsmen's plans and came to the conclusion that if false bulkheads were built to provide space of just one barrel depth (any greater loss of space might catch the eye of the Customs Searcher), there would still be sufficient storage area for sixty-eight barrels. The bilges might also be utilized and casks stored in the centre bilges with pig iron ballast fore and aft of them. Calculations showed that there was room there for another fifty half ankers. They tried it.

By not packing in too many barrels, the false bulkheads fitted perfectly into the hull design. Thereafter, every time the 'Grace' landed goods in Zealand, Dunkirque or Lisbon, she returned with an extra cargo which was not on the ship's manifests. Cargoes were all checked by the Customs officials at Cockbush as their vessels crossed the Chichester bar and anchored off Cobnor Point by Itchenor. After Customs inspection, the cargoes were offloaded into lighters and landed at Dell Quay. The emptying of the contraband however, was done by a picked team immediately after dark, and rowed into a variety of secluded spots from Itchenor itself to any of the reed-choked inlets that fringed the East Harbour basin. Tover and the Blacks made the pick-up and within an hour of landing, they were being stowed safely into lofts and cellars all over Selsey Manhood.

There was a sudden, but temporary thaw over Christmas. As the congregation streamed out of Saint Mary's after prayers on Christmas morning, a pale sun greeted them for the first time in weeks. There was a quiet cheer and the well-muffled families lingered in groups, happy to be able to enjoy its faint warmth on their faces. Jess and Lavinia strolled across to where Thomas Kelway exchanged courtesies with his parishioners. As the last family stamped away down the church path, Jess took the old man's arm and turned him gently towards Lavinia.

'Master Chatfield is closing the vestry,' he said. 'Let me guide you, Parson, for the sun is melting the mud along the path and already it's as slippery as a marling pond.'

'Oh . . . that is most kind, Sir. Yes, it does seem a little treacherous. Still, I must leave you here for Mother Heather will have the meat upon the table . . .'

Jess tightened his hold on Kelway's arm.

'Not today, she hasn't, Parson. Today you are dining at Lavenham, remember? And Mother Heather too. We've a very festive table waiting and Amy and Lavinia have been preparing their Christmas for days. Let us not stand long in the cold air – I will not let go of you.'

They moved off down the path to the waiting carriage, laughing off the old man's mild protests and thanks. He had been deeply grateful for the idea of having Mother Heather to come and keep house for him. It gave the two old people an added interest in life and they found each other fairly compatible. He was also most touched at the further increase in the offertory bag – knowing that this was Jess' way of ensuring that they had sufficient for their needs without feeling that they must bow to Charity.

He had become very fond of Jess Bayless and it was a pleasure to share Christmas with them and the Freelands.

Lavinia showed no sign of her condition and had not announced the coming event to anyone except her mother. All the same, she was looking unusually pale, Jess thought, watching her leaning forward to talk to the old people in the carriage.

'Are you feeling all right?' he murmured.

She smiled and nodded but he noticed faint worry lines along her forehead. She must be tired for he knew that she had been sleeping badly. She had complained of bad dreams recently and had woken from them, time after time, in great agitation. He put it down to her condition.

Lavenham lent itself to festivities for it was large enough to make many guests welcome at table, but not so large that all the hearth heat was lost. The huge recessed fireplace in the hall was roaring merrily as the church party came in from the bright winter sunshine. They closed the doors quickly lest any of its warmth escape, and removed their cloaks which Polly took and carried off to a bedchamber.

Amy had a potent cider punch already heated and she ladled the spicy brew into punch cups and handed them round.

Lavinia, Amy and Polly had taken great pains to make this first Christmas at Lavenham a special one. They had festooned the staircase and gallery banisters with branches of evergreen and swathes of red-berried holly. The dining table was also richly decorated so that when the platters of roasted and stuffed pig and sides of beef were brought in, they sat among sweet-smelling bouquets of herbs and winter berries, tied together with scarlet ribbon. It had been Polly, with her knowledge of the ways of the Baylesses, who suggested that they decorate the house. It was something the Freelands had never done, for it was said in Protestant circles that only Popish families decorated their homes at Christ Tide. Romanies, it seemed, had no such inhibitions. They enjoyed beautifying everything in their benders and waggons, whenever there was an excuse for celebration.

Lavinia had not been enthusiastic at first. 'I don't like the thought of the whole house filled with limp bunches of half-dead leaves,' she had said.

'Oh Ma'am, do let us have a go . . . just this year,' Polly pleaded. 'Last year Miss Amy had the hall looken' a fair picture and this year we could even decorate the parlour as well. I never saw it done so pretty as she done it, Ma'am.'

Lavinia clenched her fists. Anything that Amy did was instantly suspect and, raising her head to see what her sister-in-law's reaction was, she looked stonily into Amy's expressionless blue eyes. 'Take it or leave it,' the look said to her. 'I don't care what you do.'

Polly saw the exchange and the uncertainty in Lavinia and hurried on, anxious that her two mistresses should find something to bind them together in this season of generosity.

'Ma'am, the holly and mistletoe last for weeks and so do the evergreens. I'll take it all away on my own if'n you let us do it, just to show you, Ma'am.'

She looked so eager, so excited at the memory of the last decorating adventure that Lavinia nodded. 'Very well. We'll give it a try, though it all sounds much too churchy and Popish for my tastes.'

The green and red leaves and berries looked so attractive and the pine fronds from Halnaker smelt so clean and resinous that she quickly lost her disapproval once the work was under way. Now their decorations were admired by their guests and the scent of pine and applewood filtered through the rooms, mixing temptingly with the mouth-watering smells of roast meat and chestnut stuffing.

Halfway through luncheon, just as the sweetmeats were to be brought in with another jug of mulled wine, Lavinia left the table. The heavy food, heat of the fire and the stuffiness in the hall suddenly brought a wave of nausea flooding through her and she fled up the stairs and into her chamber before the sickness completely took over . . . She sank onto the bed with her stomach churning. Her body felt hot and cold and strange lights came and went round the edge of her vision. She closed her eyes and gave way to them.

There was a buzzing in her ears as though her head was swarming with bees and the strangest impression of voices all round her, projecting in and out of the waves of sickness – voices speaking one over the other as though she was surrounded by an angry arguing crowd. The voices ebbed and flowed and it seemed that each was repeating something again . . . and again . . . and again. Struggle against the pressure . . . What's that? What pressure? Struggle and get rid . . .

She was dreaming. She knew that she must be dreaming because all sense of reality had faded – her surroundings, her vision – and yet she knew with terrible certainty that she had surely offended Deivos the Sky Father in some way. Was he in conflict once more with Epona of the Horses and punishing the equine Goddess through her humble temple servant? Certainly the sword had come out of the heavens where Deivos dwelt, cleaving the little timber and stone sanctuary apart at the moment of her own dreadful travail. Was it a sign of his anger that she was doing the unthinkable and carrying a child of the horse to whom she had been submitted during the Samain Rituals to Epona?

The worthies had disbelieved her state of purity when her stomach began to swell, for it had never before been known for a priestess to conceive from an equine subjection. The Elders had come to the temple to revile and punish her and she had shrunk from their wrath and hidden herself within the inner sanctuary where none but the initiated may venture. When the churning pains began a full three moons before their time, they had quickly become such unspeakable agony that she had scarcely noticed the gathering storm over the temple and the south shore, for her own torment was infinitely more terrible than any wrath that the Sky Father might evoke over the land. When the rage within and without finally exploded with a livid blue flash which seered through her tightly closed eyelids and the building's roof tree had split, falling across her threshing body, it had almost been a relief – for death would put an end to the terror in her soul and the screaming agony of the creature's pounding struggle to be free of her . . . As rafters and stone columns collapsed in choking clouds of dust and destruction in the lightning's wake, she felt the heat of the fire bursting from the timbers. As oblivion took her, she heard the frightened voices of the villagers beyond the ruin that was her funeral pyre.

Too late for their sorrow . . . too late . . .

'Linnie, are you all right?'

Jess' voice . . . So far away, cutting through the roaring and the pain like a single clear bell in her ear.

'Linnie . . . Lavinia? Do you hear me?' Anxiety sharpening his voice now. Hands on her arm. Hands stroking her forehead. She opened her eyes.

'Chiriklo, are you ill?' His face swam through shadows and hung above her.

'It's all right now.' Her voice sounded as far away as his did . . . a whisper in another room. 'I felt a little faint. It's going away. I'll stay here for a while. Do, please, make my excuses.'

She closed her eyes again for the weakness persisted and for some reason there seemed to be moving shadows bunched behind Jess' head that were alarming, menacing. A tear. squeezed out from under her closed lids and slid across her temple into her hair. How terrible to think of Jess in terms of menace.

He sat on the side of the bed, watching her face and the trembling of her lower lip. He bent and kissed the snail trails left by the tears at her temples, then removed her slippers and pulled the quilt snugly round her.

'I'll get Polly to heat a warming pan for you, poor love.'

She made no answer and he tiptoed away and closed the door quietly behind him. 'Better that she rests now. Polly can help her out of her clothes later on if she still feels poorly.'

He went downstairs wondering why he had felt the oddest tension up there in the bed chamber, as though he had interrupted two protagonists in mortal combat.

Lavinia slept – and dreamed and, waking felt afraid to open her eyes. When she did, it was to find the crimson curtains drawn, the chamber fire burning cheerfully in the grate and Amy sitting in an upright chair beside the bed.

Lavinia lay quietly watching her sister-in-law as she read from a book in her lap. Her face in repose was most pleasing, for all the lines of that fortress she built up round herself were smoothed away and her sharply foreign features looked softer, younger. Amy felt Lavinia's gaze and looked up.

'Ah. You're awake at last. Do you feel better?' There was no animosity in her voice, nor warmth . . .

Lavinia nodded. 'I think so. I just felt very faint and churned up inside for a while. Now I feel as though I have walked all the way from London – but not sick any more.'

She raised herself on an elbow and realized that she was in her night robe and tucked properly into bed with a covered warming pan by her feet. She looked down at herself in surprise. 'How did I get into these? I don't remember getting undressed.'

'I changed you some time ago,' Amy said. 'You were in a

deep sleep. I don't think you would have woken if the house had fallen down about your ears.'

The words stirred something in her mind and she frowned over it, trying to reach into the clouded areas of her memory to identify it.

'How odd,' she said, sitting up. The dizziness had gone and might never have been. There was no sickness in the pit of her stomach either. She suddenly felt very well indeed.

'What you said just then . . . about the house falling down about my ears. I must have been dreaming of something like that . . . about things falling, I mean. I keep thinking of something falling across me. It's quite weird . . .'

Amy closed her book and stood up. 'I expect it's just because of your condition,' she said. 'Jess told us about it downstairs and caused quite a stir.'

'Oh, I must get up and go back to them.' Lavinia threw back the blankets and swung her feet over the side of the bed.

'It's too late for that now. The party was over long ago. Jess is downstairs playing with Violet but I'll send him up to you.' Amy's face was expressionless. 'It's Violet's bedtime in any case.'

Lavinia gaped at her. The afternoon had been young when she had retired. She put her feet back under the covers and slid down into her pillows as Amy went to the door.

'Amy . . . may I say good night to Violet?'

For a moment she thought that Amy would refuse. Then – 'If you wish. I'll bring her in, in a few minutes.'

She went, closing the door with a sharp click behind her.

'What a strange girl she is,' Lavinia thought. Silent and disciplined and so competent that sometimes she had been tempted to wonder why Jess needed a wife at all. But that was foolish because she knew exactly why he had married. Not for social advancement, as many had hinted. Not for physical relief – for, with his looks, he could cool his ardour anywhere he wished. No. The reason was simply that he had wanted Lavinia Freeland. And there had not been a single moment since their betrothal when she had regretted giving herself to him. He treated her with tender consideration and showed that she gave him the greatest pleasure in all things. Certainly he teased her and even scolded her when the need arose – but under everything ran the current of his devotion. It made her feel quite humble sometimes, for her own affection for him was not as intense but, rather, one of gratitude for his goodness and admiration for the magnificence of his ambition and his personal beauty.

She lay comfortably in her bed, hands gently massaging her stomach. What odd dreams she had had. The feeling of heat and being crushed was still sharp in her mind and the memory made her shiver, for it had been interwoven with such an alien feeling that something was trying to reach out to her . . . to harm her.

She shrugged off the memory impatiently. How fanciful this condition was making her. She must ask Mama about it – nine months was a very long time to be entertaining such frightening nightmares.

Amy returned, leading Violet by the hand. She brought the little girl across the carpet to the bedside and left them together. Lavinia reached down and lifted her into the crook of her arm.

'How heavy and strong you are growing,' she said to the little girl. Violet sat calmly in the curve of Lavinia's arm, her fat little legs stuck straight out in front of her, gazing up at her aunt with an unblinking concentration. Her cheeks were pink and clean for she had just been washed, the little rosebud mouth pouted and her tumble of dark curls trembled against Lavinia's white night robe. Jess' huge grey eyes – with the same dusting of dark specks around the pupil and fringed with his long curling lashes. It was still a small shock to see his eyes regarding her without their customary tenderness; without the humour that was so much a part of him. These grey eyes were identical materially – but utterly different spiritually. Neither were they the eyes of a baby of fifteen months, for she suddenly realized that they lacked – innocence. They were regarding her now with complete understanding.

Of what?

They looked at each other in silence until Lavinia laughed and planted an embarrassed peck on Violet's forehead.

'We could go on weighing each other up forever,' she said. 'I like what I see very much, Violet. What do you see?'

Amy returned and stood at the end of the bed as Violet put

her hand on the coverlet over Lavinia's flat stomach, the fingers spread out like a small starfish. She kept it there, her eyes never leaving Lavinia's face for an instant.

'Raklo,' she said clearly.

Lavinia looked puzzled. 'What did you say?'

'Raklo . . .'

The word hung between them, crisp and perfectly said. A small, clear assurance.

'I don't know what that means, Amy, but she certainly says it beautifully.'

Amy lifted Violet off the bed. 'It's time for her to sleep,' she said.

At the door she turned and the coldness of her dislike was back in her eyes. 'Raklo means Boy . . .'

Chapter Eight

Lavinia went into labour on a humid June night. They had been getting ready for bed when the waters broke and Jess lost no time in despatching Rueb with the light cart to collect Mistress Whittle, the Birdham midwife. Lavinia had wanted Sarey Bayless to attend her, liking Jess' aunt above all the Baylesses – but her mother had prevailed upon Jess to alert the midwife and allow her the run of the confinement. Jess had agreed readily enough, for Sarey had tended Amy in her own waggon and brought forth a healthy child, but Amy was Romani and so was the child. The circumstances were now quite different since this would be the first Bayless to be born in a house – his house. Rueb went off to fetch Mistress Whittle and then rode on to Chichester to alert Doctor Sanden.

Lavinia rested in a chair, loathe to retire to bed as her mother pleaded, for there was little likelihood of rest for any of them in the hours ahead. She felt very short of breath and the baby, lying low, was an uncomfortable weight that made movement awkward. Everything ached. Her muscles – her legs, her back. Jess massaged her, as he often did when she was weary but the rubbing no longer eased her tiredness.

The cradle stood ready beside the hearth, the first little gown aired and folded over its carved oak side. She had made many such garments, embroidering them with tiny leaves and curling vine fronds. Her mother had been busy too and produced a beautiful shawl knitted from the finest of South-down wools, light but warm to enwrap the newborn baby securely against the treacherous humours of the midsummer airs. The cradle sheets were lovingly stitched, a gift here – another there, and all the napkin linen was finished in drawn thread and hemstitch. Tiny frilled caps, lace slippers – all had been ready and waiting for weeks. Now that the time had come, Lavinia was undecided whether she welcomed or dreaded the unknown burden ahead . . . for the preceding months had been ordeal enough and she could only hope that the birth would put an end to her morbid fears.

She had begun to see and hear things regularly after her sickness on Christmas day. Reason told her that what she felt – and thought she sometimes saw – could only be caused by the heightened state of her imagination. Yet there was something grossly unnatural about the atmosphere at Lavenham. Amy revelled in referring to its 'soul' – and the disturbance of its peace by Lavinia and her Gorgio ways. Even Jess had gently admitted that he believed absolutely that the place was in some state of possession. Foolish Gypsy superstitions. That was how Mistress Freeland dismissed her tales . . . but how, in her present condition, could she resist being affected by their beliefs? Lately her fantasies were even beginning to focus on such total innocents as Midas and Violet. She had begun to feel the oddest sensation of fear whenever she visited the paddock or, latterly when Midas was brought to the terrace below her chamber window. His greeting of her and obvious delight seemed to have become overshadowed by aggressive excite-ment, as though the sight of her excited him . . . as though he were being brought to a mare for breeding. One day he had reared and screamed and kicked out at Rueb who had fallen, taken unawares by such unexpected aggression. Midas had veered away, trailing his halter and gyrated round and round in a tight dance, screaming and lashing out with his hooves, his eyes rolling upwards to where she sat in her window, watching, the colour draining from her face. He had done that twice and finally Jess had instructed that the visits should cease.

And Violet – whenever Lavinia entered a room or sat in a chair, Violet would appear at her side. Always, Lavinia was treated to the same unblinking scrutiny – until she felt she could scream.

'What are you looking at all the time?' she would ask, doing

197

her best to keep the edginess she was feeling out of her voice. 'Here is my brush, Violet. Would you like to do my hair?' She had discovered what a popular pastime this was with the little girl. It kept her happy for hours to brush and comb through the soft silken drop of golden hair. It also kept Violet behind her so that she didn't have to keep wilting beneath the unblinking glare of those intense grey eyes.

'Polly, close the casement, if you please. The smell from the stables is really quite overpowering today. Can you smell it?'

Violet's gravitation towards Lavinia did nothing to ease Amy's now open dislike of her sister-in-law. She did her very best to keep the two apart, a pursuit that she lost heavily in, to Lavinia's occasional regret. Violet found ways of doing as she wished by the simple expedient of keeping out of her mother's reach when necessary.

'You give Violet sweetmeats to attract her up to your room,' Amy ranted. 'I know – there is no point in denying it. I have seen you. Look.'

She lunged forward, whisking a blue painted tin box off the table beside Lavinia's chair. Inside were pieces of fudge, wrapped in twists of greased paper.

'Please give them back, Amy.' Lavinia held on to her rising anger. Keep calm, she told herself, she is just trying to upset you. She held her hand out for the little tin.

'Mother brought that for me yesterday when she came with Mistress Pay. I have given none of them to Violet because you told me that she was not to have sweets.'

'Oh, you think yourself so clever – so cultured. Never lose your temper with the lower orders – but don't you patronise me, Mistress.' There was something a little wild about Amy's baleful glower. She could see the thin strong hands bunching into convulsive fists and thought for one moment that she was going to strike her.

'Oh do, please, stop all these awful scenes,' she said wearily, arching the tiredness from her back. 'Can we not say one sentence to each other without each word being misunderstood and turned into some cruel slight? I don't patronise you. Why should I? If you imagine that I do, then the slight comes from your own mind. Now, please, Amy. I am doing my best to balance this month's accounts and I need peace and quiet in which to do it. I haven't given Violet anything, nor would I go against your wishes – so please leave me alone.'

It took Lavinia a long time to realize that the sour horse smells seemed to be more severe when Violet was with her. That and the occasional intensifying of shadows which would suddenly bunch up on the periphery of her vision, to assume fluid but almost finite shapes. They vanished as soon as she looked directly at them but she noticed them more when the little girl was with her.

At first she told Jess of her fears, hoping that she could share all things with him, but it seemed that he considered them simply to be an extension of her pregnancy for he could not see the looming things that pressed about her, nor hear the voices that came and went like the wind; angry frightened things that called to her till she thought that her sanity was threatened.

In fact, Jess was deeply concerned. He watched as the happy golden girl of his heart slowly paled into an anxious, delicate young woman who jumped at the slightest sound and was afraid to sleep at night. Doctor Sanden, having talked to her, had been reassuring about her youth and strong heart and general physical health. Her pallor was caused by too little rest, he assured them, and prescribed a sleeping draught at night until her body returned to its normal sleeping pattern. But the medicine only deepened the nightmares and she soon stopped taking it.

The dreams worried Jess most of all because there was an echo of familiarity about them, as though he, too, had experienced the same dreams long ago. To Lavinia, they followed the same pattern but became more violent as the weeks went by and her recovery from each experience took longer. There was such a feeling of weight on her always; as though her body were imprisoned, and fighting and clawing to escape. There was real pain, sometimes so bad that she would wake screaming and tearing at herself. And always there were the voices – a cacophony of voices – superimposed one upon the other as though there was no deliberate connection between them. Above all, there was a feeling that she was being watched . . . Watched in sleep as she dreamed. Watched when she woke and went about her daily duties. Watched as she lay awake beside Jess, trying to identify the watcher – or at least to understand why she should have such a strong feeling. It seemed to Jess that he too, had done that at some time very early in his life, before he had been old enough to retain memories. Somewhere, sometime in his infancy, he was sure that he had been aware and frightened by the same sensation of being watched. His recognition of that fact made Lavinia's delusions all the more worrying, for it had not failed to cross his mind that she might even be the victim of someone's malevolence.

He went to see Sarey Bayless as soon as she and Piramis arrived back at the saltings from their winter wandering.

It was good to sit by their fire, poking at the snapping logs with nostrils filled with the sweet aroma of wood smoke – listening to the tales that they had brought back with them. Piramis saw that Jess had something on his mind, and understood that it was Sarey who would hear him out and ease his trouble. He shooed the children away to Naffie's and Saiforella's fireside and went off after them without a word.

Jess took a deep breath and launched into the whole story of Lavinia's fears from the first instance. He told Sarey about his own half memory, about Amy's resentment of Lavinia, of his worry that her state might be caused by Amy's jealousy.

Sarey shook her head. 'No, Bor . . . it's not Amy. I sense her feelings whenever I see the two of them together and her jealousy comes straight from the fear that you do not need her now. Your eyes and your heart are filled with your rawni, for she is beautiful and tender and you thrive on the love between you. But Amy also dedicated her life to you from babyhood, for you were always her protector – and you are no less so today. The rawni is a small bird . . . the sweetest songbird of the king . . . but the king also prizes the cat who keeps his hall clear of vermin and purrs contentedly upon his lap in winter. There is plenty of room for the songbird and the cat in the king's mansions – as long as the cat preys not upon the songbird – for they are both beloved of the king and the destruction of one would result in the destruction of them both . . .'

Jess nodded, smiling at the beauty of the Romani tradition that dressed the advice of the seer in the language of fable and fantasy. It had been a long time since he had last listened to Sarey in one of her 'seeing' moods and now he recognized a similarity between the style of her narration and that of the psalms in the Bible.

Sarey took a knob of stale bread from the pouch that hung at her waist. She broke off a small piece and crumbled it in her strong man's hand, muttering to herself as she rolled the crumbs between finger and thumb. Then she tossed them upon the fire where they frizzled and burned in a moment, leaving a whiff of their scorching in the air.

She sat hunched on an upturned bucket, a torn grey shawl wrapped round her shoulders. Her hair was streaked with grey but still thick and curling down to her shoulders. Her lined brown face looked hawkish in the firelight.

'I see the tumult. I feel the pain,' she said suddenly. The breath rasped in her chest and sweat sprang up on her forehead. 'I see the tumult . . . I feel the pain . . . I smell the stallion.'

Jess stared at her, knowing that he must say nothing but watching the struggle in Sarey's face with anguish for he had seen it before in Lavinia's. She began to rock back and forth, hands clasped tightly in her lap, eyes fixed upon the red hot embers.

'Free me, lady . . . I beg of you . . . release me from the weight. Forgive my weakness . . .oh.'

She had been moaning the words in agony but suddenly she reeled backwards as though struck. Her eyes glared at Jess without recognition, and consternation and fear jostled for possession of her face.

'I am riven in two. There is conflict and I do not understand . . . for one seeks absolution and another thrives out of death – and over all, there is that which strives and strives to obliterate everything . . .'

She shook her head and her eyes cleared and she put her hands up to them for a moment.

'I don't know what is there, Bor – but it's a nest of snakes and I can't understand how you and your rawni have become involved . . . and it's not just the two of you either, Jess.' She lifted her head and there was in her face a look of such concern and pity and fear that the blood ran cold in him. 'Whatever it is, I see it streaming away from you and your seed – right down the road that you are treading and your sons and their sons after them.' She sat stiffly erect, kneading the remains of the crust of bread in her palm.

'You have begun something, Jess Bayless . . . and I cannot see the way to end it.'

Sarey's main help that night had been to make him realize that Lavinia was not imagining her dreams; that something had homed in on her pregnant state and was afflicting her. He said nothing more to Sarey but was suddenly sure that it must be connected with the Power that had come to him in childhood and had left him in young manhood.

Now, sitting beside Lavinia as she checked through the pile of infant clothing in her lap, he decided that she had a right to know at least a little of the circumstances that had led him into building Lavenham where he did. It might help her during her travail, to know that there were forces about the place that were not of her imagining.

He began the story of his discovery of the Place and slipped, without realizing it, into the sing song lilt of the Romani story teller. As she listened to him, astounded at his words but deeply comforted by them, the child within her began the first soft thrusting of its journey into life.

Jess talked Lavinia through the night. At one point, after Mistress Whittle arrived and examined her and found that all was as it should be, and then retired to the kitchen, he had put her to bed and had lain beside her in his clothing, holding her as he continued his story. Now and then she would interrupt with a question and he was obliged to break his train of thought. But it was an impossible task in any case, for how can a man explain how it was that he had possessed a power that was, in Christian circles, attributed to the Devil? How was it possible to describe the fading of that Power, so that, by the time he brought her to Lavenham it was gone from him completely? His words frightened her, although she had been comforted to know that he was no longer afflicted in that way. He said nothing about the flaming of Nick Smyth.

They dozed, heads together, until stronger contractions woke Lavinia and her movement brought Jess back to his vigil.

Sometime before dawn they both fell into a deep sleep and when daylight woke Lavinia again, it was to realize that the child had been making progress. She saw Jess' face on the pillow beside her, jowled with a day's growth of stubble, the lines of exhaustion giving him a vulnerability seldom seen in wakefulness. She moved to kiss him – and the dragging pain that had been gnawing at her back slewed round and gripped the base of her stomach and twisted hard.

She gasped, doubling up at the unexpectedness of it – and Jess woke with a jerk.

Doctor Sanden called during the day. He and Mistress Whittle conferred over Lavinia, probing, measuring and checking the length of her pains. The bed curtains were drawn together for by now the chamber was busy with visitors. Mistress Freeland arrived from Rymans and would not be persuaded to make herself more comfortable down in the parlour.

'Certainly not,' she said firmly when Jess begged her to leave the room and take some refreshment. 'A mother should always be close to her daughter during her confinement. After all, it is something that we share – our child bearing, and it was only seventeen years ago that I was going through this same ordeal to bring Lavinia into the world.'

Mistress Chatfield came to offer assistance and Sarah Beer also. And Amy and Polly were in and out of the room, bringing fresh coals for the fire and food when it was needed and water for the doctor – and Mistress Whittle came and went and once, just for a few minutes, Sarey Bayless came.

Sarey appeared at the door, not to offer assistance as Mistress Freeland feared, but with the good wishes and blessings of all the Clan – and with the Dannerin' Stone. Kneeling beside Lavinia, she patted her hand and folded her fingers round a smooth round pebble.

'When it gets so that you want to cry out, bite on the stone and it will help,' she said. She stayed only a little while for the pains were coming often now and Lavinia's eyes were getting a glazed, abstracted look. Not long after she had gone Lavinia began to lose touch with the familiar comfort of the bedchamber and the loving faces around her. An odd floating sensation began to fill the minutes between pains and then, as each contraction strengthened, the dream of the past months slid into focus.

The surge began; the violent thrusting that threatened to split her apart – and with it came another agony that had nothing at all to do with the child and its battle into life. Her body was imprisoned again and she cried out with the torture of the vast weight that held her down, crushing the life from her, mashing flesh and bone into bloody pulp . . . She could hear the wind as it moaned and lamented through the rubble all round her and she reached out, willing the other to hang on to that thread of life which still remained.

The pain receded and she found herself staring up at the pink and yellow roses of her bed curtains and beyond them the comforting glow of the fire – and Amy's pale face hovering near by. She said something but already she was fading again and then there was only the darkness and the terror in her, fighting her pain and confusion.

By late afternoon the leaden skies suddenly gave way to a storm that drove in across the harbour from the south west, obliterating the land in a blinding deluge. Huge waves were whipped up and thundered against the shore, uprooting trees and sweeping away a flotsam of wood, livestock and boats. The house shook as thunder rolled in across the Manhood, with thick yellow sulphur clouds so low that they were almost at tree level. The Birdham windmill was struck by lightning and burned to the ground; an abnormal tide smashed into the Itchenor boatyard and bore off the hulls of two nearly completed vessels.

In the middle of the storm it was decided that Rueb must ride into Chichester to fetch Doctor Sanden again, for Lavinia was in a high fever and the baby was no longer making progress. The striving continued but now there was bleeding and Mistress Whittle was unable to stem the flow. Rueb took off into the driving rain as though all the devils in hell were after him and Jess paced the bedchamber in an agony of anxiety, listening to Lavinia's torture and knowing that the nightmare was drowning her.

As Amy came into the room he gripped her wrist. 'Are you doing this to her?' he said in a low voice. She shook her head, looking hurt and full of resentment. 'What is it all about then, for pity's sake? What's possessing her? She is in some sort of desperate dream there, just as it has been for her these last months. I've shared it with her often enough to be able to recognize the signs, poor girl . . .'

'Hush Pral . . . it's only her fever talking,' Amy said with satisfaction for she too, had suffered from nightmares while she had been carrying Violet, but they had stopped as soon as she had gone over to the Bayless waggon at the salterns so that Sarey might attend her lying in. It was only now that she remembered them, and shivered recalling the violence they had underlined.

Lavinia cried out in the room behind them and Jess pushed past and went out and stood in the gallery, thumping the bannister rail with his fist.

It was nearly two hours before Doctor Sanden appeared, soaked to the skin, his clothing making great puddles on the hall floor. He shrugged off his overcape and gave it to Polly to dry, then hastened up the stairs and into the stifling heat of the bedchamber. Mistress Freeland met him in great agitation. She had never seen such violent delirium and had sat holding Lavinia's burning hand, stroking her forehead and murmuring soothing words to try and reach through the poor child's fever.

'I can't think why she should suddenly have taken a turn like this,' she said for the fifth time while the burly doctor turned back the bed clothes to examine Lavinia. She had been lying quietly but was suddenly seized by another contraction and moaned as the baby strove to free itself from her.

She was vaguely aware of her mother and had gained comfort from her presence, but the room was shaking with thunder as it hurtled itself against the lead lights of the windows – and there was thunder at another level and the voice repeating and repeating with dreadful monotony, 'Die now . . . die . . . die . . .' And she knew that it was her child the voice was commanding to die and a great surge swept through her, for her child was not supposed to die and all her strength and the love that she was going to feel for it flooded down her body into the burrowing baby.

The tempo of pain changed and tore her apart and in the midst of disorder she heard a voice screaming and the words had no meaning for her and she was carried along within the great wave. Her body worked of its own volition and there was singing in her ears and the voice was there with its high, shrill warble – calling to the Great One, begging to be admitted to the High Place.

She was empty. It was done . . . and yet not done for she struggled weakly to be free of her broken body.

She opened her eyes and watched the candles guttering in golden haloes round the bed and there was Mistress Whittle, bending over the crib and Doctor Sanden's rubicund face floating near her. A hand came down on hers and she smiled, knowing it was Jess for there was the familiar tenderness of his touch. She sighed, refreshed by the strength which seemed to stream from him into her. She closed her eyes, cradled in the comfort of his presence.

Jess breathed a deep sigh of relief. It had been touch and go and at one point, they had thought that she had gone, but then she suddenly seemed to rally and dragged a burst of energy from somewhere deep within her – and the baby had arrived in a rush. They had managed to stem the bleeding once the afterbirth had come away, and Mistress Whittle and Amy had cleaned her up and put cushions under her feet to tilt her blood flow back towards her heart. She had been too weak to know what was going on around her or even to ask about her baby but Jess watched with consummate pride as his son, Lawrence, was washed and the birth cord severed and knotted and he was wrapped in his swaddling clothes and the shawl that his grandmother had made him. He had taken the little bundle into his arms and looked down into the sleeping face of the baby. Such neat little features with a perfect mouth that was an amazing replica of his mother's. He had certainly taken his time in arriving, for another dawn was splitting the newly-washed sky. He gave the child to the midwife and went over to the window and drew aside the curtain. Funny, he'd not noticed that the storm had passed.

He gazed down into the drenched garden, savouring the peace in the quiet room behind him and knowing that Lavinia's voices had gone.

She slept deeply but felt a drowsy awareness come to her sometime during the night. The rain had stopped scouring the shore and the storm had rolled away leaving a freshness in the air that had a clean, good smell to it. She could go now, for the way was clear – but she waited for the other one, all the same, impatient to be gone from this needless carnage. It was a long wait, for the other struggled fiercely, striving to hold onto its brief and precious life. It was too long to wait. She had not been able to hold on, after all, and was already gone by the time the men returned.

The sun was the very best cure for Lavinia's weakness. Jess and Amy joined forces to oppose Doctor Sanden and threw open the windows to let the warm fresh air cleanse the ill humours from her lungs. She did not fall prey to chills and lung infections as he insisted she would. She breathed in the sweet smelling air with relief, feeling its purity healing her tiredness and bringing the colour back into her cheeks. After three weeks she was well enough to sit by the window in a comfortable armchair so that she might watch the boats passing and throw sweetmeats to a Midas who was suddenly calmed and obedient once more.

Little Lawrence was never far from her, tucked up in his crib by her side so that she could study his little fuzz of blond hair and one perfect pink shell of an ear. There had been no trouble with her milk and he had taken to her from the first so that already there were encouraging signs of robustness about both his appetite and his lungs. Mistress Whittle confided after the first week that, in her opinion, Mistress Bayless had been very fortunate indeed to survive what had appeared to be some kind of fit during the last stages of her labour.

Lavinia, free of all daemons and torments, knew only that a battle had been waged with the elemental evil in the house and that she had won.

★   ★   ★

Violet spent as much time as possible up in the big bedchamber, sitting on a footstool against Lavinia's legs and giving her undivided attention to the baby. His size fascinated her, for he was long and slender with a fine bone structure and a deceptively delicate appearance. He was very much a Freeland except for the suggestion of his father's high-bridged nose – and the huge grey eyes which already dominated the whole of his miniature face.

The eyes had given Violet a shock the first time she had seen him awake. He had been lying quietly on his back, staring up at the vague moving things that floated round the perimeter of his vision. As Violet peeped at him, his eyes had suddenly homed in and focused on her and there was in them a burning light that had hurt her in the head so that she recoiled from him, crying, and hid herself in the folds of Lavinia's peignoire. She kept her distance from the cradle for some time after that but by the time he was able to focus properly, curiosity overcame her fear. Lavinia watched one day as the little girl peeped cautiously over the side of the cradle and saw the baby's tiny hands reaching up to clutch at the air before his face. Slowly Violet put out her hand and waggled her own fingers in front of him. Lavinia smiled fondly as the little hands met and fingers entwined. The two children seemed to look at each other and understanding passed between them. She did not notice their recognition until Violet turned to her and the two pairs of eyes regarded her with solemn appraisal. Something caught at her throat and she drew in her breath, aware of a stirring at the back of their luminous greyness. Then Lawrence closed his eyes and slept and Violet climbed into her lap and asked for the piggy story on her fingers; once more a small cuddly moppet with long curling lashes that could charm a kiss from a hedgehog.

Chapter Nine

On a damp September evening, Jess visited Piramis and Sarey Bayless. He sat at their hearth, savouring the peace and watching the long shadows weaving languidly behind their heads. He took a deep breath, relishing the comforting reek of the saltpans and the blessed silence save for the rustling oakwoods at his back. Piramis smoked his clay pipe and whittled away at a knob of leather with his cobbling knife, humming under his breath and throwing Jess a pensive look now and then from under grey bushy brows. Sarey wheezed and puffed about them, stirring the pottage with a heavy wooden ladle. She had spread vastly with age but was still hard and durable as the leather in Piramis' gnarled brown hands.

They asked no questions. Jess leaned back and sighed with the rare pleasure of a repose free of the constant pressure of tension which pervaded the Lavenham atmosphere.

'How's that Pikie (expelled gypsy) shaping that wedded your Rose?' Sarey smiled across silken threads of blue wood smoke which rose between them.

'We've not seen them for two winters. Heard tell as 'ow he'd bin seen in Okehampton stocks this spring, though. Naffie see 'em a twelvemonth back. Says Rose had a mint pair o' boy kidder at 'er breast an' looked downright wearied.'

'I miss jalling the drom,' he said softly.

The two nodded their heads with complete understanding for their own life was far more pleasing, more rewarding and unfettered than the gorgio life that Jess had chosen.

'You'm happy with your rawni, though?'

There was an edge of concern in Sarey's voice and he grinned through the ember glow at her, nodding his head so that the thick curls bounced vigorously around his ears.

'She's a lovely chavi. Everything a man could wish for in a wife. She's young for her age in many ways but the innocence of her makes me feel almost humble at times. Sometimes I wish that she was not quite so inexperienced.'

'Here it comes now,' Sarey thought. 'This is the abscess which is eating into his soul.'

'I used to think that whatever it is that troubles my home would gradually settle when the happiness of those living there filtered through to it. It is not working out that way, though. Amy and Lavinia are constantly at each other, squabble, squabbling over the most trivial matters. What concerns me most, though, is that Violet has inherited the gifts I possessed as a child. I did my best not to abuse those talents – but I fear for her, Sarey, Piramis. She is a headstrong chavi with a large slice of her mother's stubborn nature in her. It makes me fear for the safety of our little Lawrence, too. Violet would never hurt him deliberately, I am certain, but Amy is becoming quite demented at times and might encourage Violet, baby as she is still, to harm him.'

Piramis sucked at his clay pipe. He spoke without removing it from his mouth. 'I seen you in your fine kenner (house), Bor. I seen you holden' court with yer rawni. I seen yer worken' out in they stables with yer fine grais. I seen yer in the town on market days, among yer rich friends an' off to Birdham where be yer great bero's (ships). I never seed yer with that chavi though . . . never seed yer take 'er through the woods as yer own Dadrus did with you – teachen' her the ways of the wood folk'n the plant life in the creek. That's the way to reach into the soul of a chavi, Bor, young as she is now. That's the way to fashion a discipline in 'er and learn 'er the reasons for liven'. The gorgio's don't do it our way, they never feel the throbben' of life under their feet the way we do.'

The old man's face was in shadow but his voice was gruff and soft with compassion, for here was the finest of the Clan – gone from them all and set headlong about his own destiny – but still hankering back to his roots when trouble brought him down.

'Don't lose the ways of our people, Bor. If'n yer do, I'd say you lose yer hold on yer family with it ˙ . . .'

It was true, every word the old man uttered and Jess bowed his head, knowing that it might already be too late to reach Violet.

Sarey sat down beside him, wheezing mightily. 'She won through this time, your rawni,' she rumbled at him, patting his arm. 'I seen it in the flames, Bor – the battle she had with the mullos (ghosts) in your kenner. She'll not do it like that the next time. They be gatheren' to take the issue of your body, Jess. Remember that for fear they take her too.'

He walked home through the wood where he had hunted the hotchiwichi, chasing it into a dell out of which he had never escaped until his manhood had released him.

Violet had the Power. He recognized it in the grey intensity of those wide black lashed eyes, had seen it happen already when she had flamed one of Lavinia's bees. The shock of her reaction had driven her, shaking, into a corner of the parlour where she had been playing beside the open window. He had looked away, numb with the shock of discovery – to find Amy smiling at him with the triumph of a striking snake in her eyes. 'Beware,' said her expression, 'for I can wield this Power through my control of Violet.'

He suddenly felt a desperate vulnerability for Lavinia and the baby Lawrence – and even for himself. She was telling him not to move them away from Lavenham and – with such a weapon to ensure her wishes, he would have to bow to that demand.

He had done his best to impose himself firmly in Violet's affections. He had made a point of seeing her each day as soon as he returned from Chichester. All too often, however, she had long been asleep in her cradle and was not aware of the nightly vigil that her father kept at her bedside, stroking the curve of her cheek with a finger and marvelling at every clear Bayless feature and the promise of such beauty in each baby line. As the months brought her up onto her feet, however, and less time was spent in the cradle in the kitchen, he kept her close to his side, so that Lavinia too might enjoy her company, for he was quickly made aware of Amy's jealous guard of Violet in the hours that he was out of the house. Violet permitted herself to be amused and indulged by Jess but he was wryly amused to observe that Lavinia – with her youth and golden looks – held far more fascination for his daughter than her father did.

Lavinia . . . With the whispering trees curving into a leafy roof over his head, a thought came to him in the depths of the woodland path and he stopped in his tracks to examine it, to explore its possibilities with a growing feeling of profound relief.

'Dearest, we just must not risk exposing you to such terrors ever again, as you had before Lawrence was born,' he said later to Lavinia after they had retired.

She turned her blue regard upon him and for a moment a cloud darkened the trusting eyes and the irises grew huge. She shivered – but then shrugged off the dread of that still fresh memory and smiled up at him, the dimples coming and going in her cheeks.

'It was only my condition,' she said lightly. 'I don't really mind whatever it is that dwells here, now that Lawrence is with us, safe and sound . . . and look, Jess. I have had no trouble since his birth, have I?'

'There will be other children, Linnie,' Jess said. He took her hand and stroked it thoughtfully. It was as small and thin as a child's and rested trustingly in his.

'I have been thinking that when you are with child once more, you should go to Fishbourne and have your confine-ment under your mother's roof.'

She looked up at him, searching his face and finding the depth of his anxiety for her in every new line that creased his brow and circled the corners of his mouth. At twenty-eight he looked ten years older, even if the new maturity suited him just as well as his youth had done. It was in her mind to protest that she must bear their children in their own home, but the intensity of his determination was too strong.

She tucked her arm into his and leaned against him among the pillows of the curtained bed.

'We have not reached that problem yet, my love,' she said, cuddling her body up against his side. 'I shall certainly do whatever you think best when the time comes. Fishbourne is only fifteen minutes drive in the carriage so the distance would be no hazard.'

They spoke no more on the subject but relief brought the youth back into Jess' heart and he gathered her up across his chest and buried his face in the warm lavender sweetness of her breasts.

Thanksgiving that year was a lean one. The summer had come and gone in a few scattered sunlit days, drowned in week after week of wind-driven cloud and chill rain squalls. Sheep perished on the downs, the pigs took fever and died by the score in the woods and the crops, which had shown so much promise of a lavish harvest in spring, withered under the lash of the weather and grew black with disease.

The immediate effect upon Lavenham was the high mortality among the foals. Of five born during July and August, only one survived. Since bedding straw was becoming a costly scarcity, the whole string was obliged to stay out in the paddocks, whatever the weather and when even the grass was cropped too quickly and showed signs of serious thinning, root crops were fed them until even they grew mouldy in the water-logged earth.

Polly Ayles watched the worry carve deep lines into Manfri's face as he struggled to keep the herd intact. Watching Manfri at any time was becoming a favorite occupation, especially as she was well aware of his admiration for her, as yet unspoken. It was pleasing to feel his eyes upon her across the kitchen table at meal times – even though such liberties were disapproved and often frustrated by Mistress Amy with her brusque orders to leave the table and see to the mistress' needs upstairs or to feed the fire in the parlour – or any other excuse that could be found to break the thread of their growing attachment. She sometimes slipped out to the barn when Manfri was too busy to come into the house for his food. As the grey, saturated days drove by towards a cheerless autumn, she watched Manfri fretting over his charges as first one and then another became sick. He sat up through the nights with them, often with Jess for company and Polly doggedly splashed through the puddles of the yard to bring them hot gruel to ease the stiffness in their tired, damp bodies.

Manfri's gratitude was drowned in a growing despair as one foal after another died, one from ringworm, another from fever – a third from pneumonia. When a young mare caught the coughing infection from her foal, Jess decided that immediate action was all that would prevent him from losing all his horses.

'We're going to have to build another stable for those who are sick,' he said to Manfri, pacing the aisle between the open stalls.

'There is no other way of keeping the sick horses apart from the healthy ones. The weather is too treacherous for them to be paddocked day and night for much longer – and in here they are breathing each other's bad air.'

A wooden stable was erected in less than two weeks and the sick horses moved in there. It seemed to work. With Manfri rubbing each healthy stallion, mare and foal down twice a day and applying embrocation of crushed mint and ginger root to their joints, there was no increase in ill health among the herd and only one more death. Yoshi.

Little fat Yoshi, stiff in the shoulders and uneven of gait; Yoshi who had appeared to have every intention of living forever.

Manfri was waiting for Jess when he arrived home from Chichester one evening in October.

'Come, take a dikker at old Yoshi,' he said briefly, before Jess was even out of the saddle. 'I've put 'er in the shelter,' he said, hurrying Jess across the cobbled yard.

She was in the stall nearest the door, lying on her side in a too thin bed of limp straw. Her woolly coat was dull and dusty looking and she rolled a tired eye at Jess and whickered in the back of her throat. He squatted down beside her head and put his face close to her muzzle and she smelt his breath and tried to raise her head to him. She did not appear to be in a fever but her ribs were showing and the flesh seemed to have shrivelled her strong sinewed neck so that the muscles stood out like half-spent ropes.

He stroked her and the touch of his hands comforted her and she closed her eyes and panted quietly under their gentle probing. 'Wasting and stiffness in the neck,' Jess said over his shoulder to Manfri who stood against the wall, watching the tender examination. He nodded.

'She were fit two days back,' he said rubbing his hand over his face. Dordi dordi, he was tired. He could sleep for a week and feel no hunger. 'I noticed her this mornen' all of a droop over in the far corner of the near paddock. Standen' with her head almost resten' on her feet, she was –'

'Poori grai,' Jess murmured to Yoshi. 'Poor old lady. What a brave little horse you are . . .'

He had been eight years old when Jasper had bought her at Tiverton Horse Fair.

He remembered her young and spunky, pulling the waggon with such gusto along the rough highways and tree lined paths that led west towards the Irish sea – or east as they headed back towards Apuldram through familiar villages and forests.

He remembered burying his face in Yoshi's warm coat and letting the tears come when his mother died. Yoshi had known the depth of that loving grief and had pressed herself against him, turning her head to look at him with bright young eyes filled with melting love and understanding. He remembered the discovery of the beautiful arab stallion in the Lord's parkland; the excitement of the idea that had come to him – the stealth with which their union had been achieved. He remembered the birth of Olivas and of Yoshi's complacent acceptance of her pale, long-legged, beautiful foal.

He looked at Yoshi, seeing the shivers that spasmed her rigid neck muscles and knowing that age was now the enemy.

She died in the night with Jess' arms cradling her tired head. In the pre-dawn silence of their bed chamber, he wept into Lavinia's shoulder – the only time it would ever happen – and she, in turn, feeling old and infinitely wise, gave him the same comfort in his grief that he and Yoshi had given each other over the years.

Yoshi was twenty-one years old.

★   ★   ★

The winter was mild and dank, setting the farmers' heads shaking even more dolefully than they had throughout the previous season. There was no frost to ginger up the soil and set the sap running in the dormant seedlings. There was no snow at all and very little to differentiate between the seasons since the previous spring.

Lawrence thrived and, growing fat and strong on his mother's milk, was much admired and visited by the matrons of the neighbourhood.

'You should bring in a wet nurse,' Jess said to Lavinia. 'Here you are, a fine strong girl, not yet eighteen years old and you're locked away in the house all the time, because you have the baby to nurse. If you were a Romani you'd be out selling your clothes pegs and riding the grai's again and dancing with your man when the music flowed.'

She turned and gave him a wicked little look, leaning back against the paddock railing and regarding him from half closed lashes.

'I'll dance with you whenever you feel like it,' she said. 'I long to ride Midas again each morning and attend the winter levees too, but I'm afraid that I would lose my milk if I were to do that and a wet nurse can't give Lawrence any better nourishment than I am doing, judging by the size of him now.'

He leaned away from her, taking in the slim waist, returned to its former neatness, the new rounded and eminently desirable contours of her breasts beneath their fichou'ed bodice and the luminous health of her clear creamy skin.

She suffered his scrutiny with calm detachment, enjoying the sensation it ignited in her. Just twenty-nine years of age . . . His dark and constant beauty still smote her like the heady scent of musky flowers, though youth had almost departed from him, leaving a deepening tracery of creases and lines about his face that was, maybe, even more attractive than his youth had been.

'I do love you so very much, Jess,' she said.

He put out a hand to her and stroked the soft down of her cheek with infinite tenderness. A sleepy bee droned across their path as they turned away from the constant pleasure of watching Olivas and Midas. It lumbered, heavily laden, in front of Jess' nose and veered away from him with alarm in the heightened pitch of its drone. Jess stopped and watched the hairy insect as it drifted on the light air current away from them into a patch of gorse.

'What ungainly creatures they are,' he said as it disappeared from view.

'They are not, really,' Lavinia defended them. 'They are fascinating when you get to know them. They have such a complicated and almost human pattern of life. I love them dearly – and their perception is so great that they know that – they really do, for I have not had a sting for years now and they are so quiet and sleepy with me, as though they know that I am their friend and would not hurt them.'

'That reminds me – I have a little gift for you.'

He stood in the middle of the barnyard, searching his pockets, grinning at the bright expectation which came leaping, as always, into Lavinia's eyes.

'Here we are . . . I saw it today in Chichester and was obliged to purchase it for you, having spied the nature of its title.'

Out of his coat pocket he drew a small slim leather bound book, the size of a prayer book. Mystified, she took it from him and opened the cover. The title page read:

THE HISTORI OF BEES

. . . . .

written out of experience
by
Charles Butler Mgd.
printed in OXFORD by Wmm Turner
for de Author 1623

'Oh Jess,' she whispered, staring down at the little volume in her hands as though it were all the treasure of Arabie. She had heard of this book. Indeed, it had become the bible for bee keepers of fifty or a hundred years ago. She bent her head and turned one page after another. He watched, charmed by the curve of her neck and the soft golden fall of shining ringlets on either side of her face. It took so little to please her.

He looked over her head towards the house, roof tiles

gleaming after recent rain. 'Look at her,' he said to it. 'Look at a completely innocent woman. What is there in her that you must seek to hurt?' Lavinia looked up with bright eyes and took his arm, pushing him forward towards the terrace door.

'Come in with me, Jess. I just can't wait now to settle down beside the fire and begin to read my Bee book.'

She almost skipped beside him, eager to explore all that was familiar to her and much that might be new.

Fresh storm clouds came sailing in low off the sea and the first fat rain drops sent them hurrying into the shelter of the open door. Jess put his hand under Lavinia's elbow as she tripped on the threshold.

'Come now, madam. There is no cause to break your ankle in order to get to your reading. There is plenty of time ahead of you.'

Indeed there was, she thought ruefully. There was too much time. It still hung heavily upon her in spite of her duties with Lawrence. She enjoyed her flower arranging and her apiary. She loved every moment with the little yellow-haired boy who would one day look so like his mother. She counted the minutes with fresh eagerness and anxiety each day to the moment when she could visit the paddock and make sure that her beloved Midas was still in perfect health. She could think of no time in her life when she had been happier than the periods she spent with Jess, the most desirous of husbands. In spite of such a roll of delights, there were those things which reduced her natural happiness into a constant uncertainty. Lavenham and its secrets: Amy and her unflinching rejection.

A wave of laughter greeted Jess as he pushed open the door of the private bar at the back of the Swan. The room was crowded, the air stale with tobacco haze. He passed through the crush towards the fire, bowing to Thomas Chatfield and raising a hand in welcome to one of the Chaldecotts.

John Freeland was sitting beside the hearth in close conversation with his companion. His head was bent forward as he listened with his usual courtesy to the other's words, but he looked up as Jess approached and there was the old familiar flash of pleasure and affection that the sight of Jess always promoted in him. The years had been kinder to John than they had been to Jess for he still wore a look of youthful expectation, almost of that same innocence that Jess found so endearing and exasperating in Lavinia.

'Sar shan, Bor,' John said, teasing Jess as only he was permitted to do.

If others were unwise enough to make disparaging reference to Jess' Romani roots they were treated to cold dismissal and – what was sometimes disastrous – a withdrawal of the Bayless patronage. Jess smiled at John and slapped the upheld palm of his hand in greeting.

'We were hoping that you'd be in at this time. May I present Master Pusey Brooke, presently Collector of Customs, Portsmouth.'

The man turned and stood, holding out his hand. His eyes were keen, searching Jess' face from beneath one long expanse of bushing eyebrow. His peruke was neat but yellowed at the front with tobacco stain. His head was level with Jess' chin.

'Good day to ye, Sir.' Master Brooke's voice was surprisingly deep in so compact a body.

Jess nodded at him and took the proffered hand in a hard grip. 'A pleasure to make your acquaintance, Master Brooke,' he said, smiling down into the piercing inspection with all the charm of a clear conscience. 'Master Carr, here in Chichester, has spoken to me often of you.'

Pusey Brooke returned the smile and placed his broad behind back on the hearth seat from whence he had risen. Jess joined him.

'What villainy do you and Carr pursue?' the Collector said, waving to the pot boy to fetch a tankard for Jess.

Jess leaned against the panelled back of the long settle and stretched his silk-hosed legs out towards the burning logs. He searched in his coat pockets for pipe and tobacco pouch, patting them until he found what he sought in an inner hiding place. He took his time lighting up, the better to review the presence of Master Brooke and John's eagerness to introduce them. There was a light in John Freeland's eye that was not unfamiliar to Jess. He began to suspect his brother-in-law of doubtful intentions. He proceeded with characteristic caution.

'Well, let us consider,' he finally said between puffs. 'Sometimes we meet to discuss the price of a particular piece of horse flesh. Then again, there are times when I have to see the Collector over some special shipment I may be expecting. Bayless' owns two vessels, as no doubt you know, sir, seeing that they sometimes moor off Portsea Roads and Spithead. Most of our cargoes are valuable consignments from the Indies and require a deal of paper work that is a constant headache to provide. Now and again we meet by the way, as you and I have done now. Then we mull over old times. I suppose you might call them the bad old days when John Carr was as guilty of free trading over there in Kent as I was of doing the same thing a bit nearer home.'

He grinned at Pusey Brooke, seeing the surprise on the man's face. 'Ha . . . you didn't know that Master Carr had run with the Owlers then. Set a thief . . .'

Pusey Brooke slapped his thigh and a great roll of laughter rumbled out of him. He laughed until the tears ran down his cheeks into the runnels on either side of his small ears. John and Jess grinned at each other and waited for the noise to subside.

'Oh, that was first class,' Brooke gasped, wiping his cheeks with a large red kerchief. 'Forgive me, sir, I beg you – but in one fell swoop you have played me well and trumped my ace like a veteran. Now I will be obliged to make you an offer without the delightful foreplay of keeping you in suspense. You were quite correct, of course, Master Freeland.' He stuffed the kerchief back into his pocket and reached for his tankard. 'He warned me, Master Bayless, that I would need to run like a rigger in order to stay ahead of you in any business venture . . . which is one of the reasons I am come to sound you out now.'

Jess took a brimming tankard from the pot boy and put it to his lips, content to wait upon an explanation.

John sat forward. 'Master Brooke would have attended you in your offices, Jess, but I suggested that you might prefer to become acquainted of his proposals in the more informal atmosphere of the Swan – initially, at least.'

Jess raised a quizzical eyebrow.

'I am sent by the Board of Customs to discover as informally as possible at this stage, the direction of your feelings were you to be offered the appointment of Collector for Chichester. Master Carr retires shortly, owing to his increasing ill health and your name has been put forward by several interested parties, as a possible successor.'

The smile broadened across his rubicund face. 'You see, dear sir, why your remark delighted me so. It appealed, I must admit, to my sense of humour – to the marvellous balance of nature; nay more. To the truly astounding twists of Fate which create such perfect patterns of our lives. I had no idea, you see, that Master Carr had been so employed before his conscience led him to the service of His Majesty. I was naturally well informed about the profitable indiscretions of your own youth though. What excellent symmetry my Lord's proposal assumes.'

Jess was no less amused, though startled into silence by Collector Brooke's assignment. It was not unusual in these hard times for known smugglers to be offered employment as riding officers and searchers for the pay was regular, even if it was less than the occasional spoils of night running. There was also a certain pleasing respectability attached to the position. From the Treasury's point of view, converts from the criminal classes often made the most thorough and implacable defenders of the Law. It would appear that this was their line of thinking in considering the now highly respectable Jess Bayless for the vacating post, since the source of his wealth was common knowledge and the fact that he had never been caught and convicted actually gave him an extra mystique and respect. He smiled across the tankard at Pusey Brooke, liking the man and his directness and lack of guile.

'There is an element of humour in it,' he agreed mildly and John subconsciously relaxed the grip he had on his clay pipe. 'Will you leave the offer with me, sir, so that I may weigh it up from all angles before committing myself to either an affirmative or otherwise?'

'My God,' he thought later, sitting behind the mess of deeds and papers on his desk and trying to sort out the possibilities in his mind. 'What sport it would be: the most hallowed Collector – Bayless of Chichester – one time leader of the Apuldram Blacks and presently runner of some of the most costly treasures to be landed illicitly on English shores.'

Trew entered the room and began to gather up the papers piled up around his master.

'Would you sign here, please sir . . . and Mistress Hall wishes to renew her mortgage on Cherry Tree Cottage so I'll leave the assignment with you. You've finished with the Stavely account books, haven't you, Sir?'

His voice droned on in its nervous way as the clerk gathered up the mess of a day's work and withdrew to put them all into tidy piles on the shelves in the outer office. He was like an old goodwife, doing his best to adhere to Jess' instructions that he, Trew, was to ensure that order was kept throughout Bayless' and that Master Jess Bayless in particular, was not to be permitted to dwell in a mountain of paper work.

The mantle clock chimed its reminder of the passing day. Jess rose stiffly and stretched. There was a slight sense of discomfort and heaviness across his chest and he took several deep breaths to relieve the feeling. However much profit there was in sitting in an office and signing his name on countless documents, nothing could compensate him for the loss of his freedom – for the open air and the vastness and comfort of owning nothing and thereby being truly the master of himself and his surroundings.

He rode Olivas home, sharing the road – as he did each dawn – with market waggons and huge transport carts which rumbled and swayed over the muddy roads from Itchenor and Birdham. More and more vessels were dropping their cargoes into lighters at the harbour mouth these days, for silting was becoming a serious problem and recently it was only during the spring tides that it was possible for the merchantmen to creep in as far as Dell Quay. The harbour traffic had doubled with the lighters scuttling across the water like black beetles, offloading at Cockbush and Itchenor, Birdham and Bosham.

He rode slowly, thinking of the offer that had been made to him that day. His chest ached and he frowned, aware of a certain shortness of breath. Twenty-nine and becoming short-winded. What kind of life is it when all the money in the world is not enough if your body decries the sour air of ill ventilated and odour ridden buildings. There was never bad air to be inhaled in a bender. Autumn was giving way to winter and the rightful place for a Bayless was out on the road with a westward turning face. Not skulking within brick walls among unwashed gorgios. The choice had been his own, though. He was accumulating great wealth for his descendants and it was too late to consider what he might have done had life given him a second try . . . To be without Lavinia? To have built his house on other ground? To have stayed among his people and taken on the leadership of his Clan so that all of them might benefit from his gifts and wisdom.

He was in pensive mood that evening, far away from Lavenham and the problems it wove about itself. Lavinia, seeing his abstraction, wisely muted her chatter. He looked pale and almost haggard and kept rubbing his chest and taking deep breaths.

'Just a touch of indigestion,' he said shortly, in answer to her question. 'Maybe a draught of Amy's peppermint water will ease it.'

By the time she returned to his side with a hot mug of the fiery liquid, he had made up his mind to refuse the Collectorship of Chichester.

The Watcher closed his eyes and concentrated the fullness of the Force upon the figure in the highback chair. It was regrettable, for they were an attractive couple and he had become fond of Jess Bayless. It was that very pride in sharing the blood of this man of achievement that made it necessary to terminate the line at this point. His control was not so strong over the woman for she was not of the blood and he could only reach her during the nine months of her pregnancies. She was proving too strong for him then also; her desire for procreation too great to break. The children were protected by their own Force – but Jess Bayless was beginning to age. He had lost his Power and was becoming vulnerable. It was the right time to cut the lifeline, before more seeds were sewn to thicken the skein of the Bayless line.

He honed himself into one supreme effort and released his Power.

★　　★　　★

'Ugh.'

Lavinia, coming into the parlour, saw Jess double up in his chair, cradling his body with crossed arms. She hurried to his side, putting the hot draught down on a table and rubbing his back as he gasped, head on his knees.

'Quick, take a sip of this, dearest.'

Hands on his shoulders, lifting him back into his chair. The hot sweet pungence of the liquid against his lips, scouring his throat and the upper tracts of his stomach.

The pain . . . the pain was excruciating. It entered his body and seeped downwards through his arms and torso, right into the upper muscles of his thighs. Hands rubbed his shoulders and he felt the blood pounding in his head, through the channels of his body like a river in spate; furious . . . uncontrolled . . .

There was a singing in his ears.

'Better now, my darling?' Lavinia's white face floated in front of him and he smiled up at it and tried to raise his hand to stroke her cheek but his arm felt as though it were encased in lead.

'A . . . little, I think . . .'

It was easing. More of the soothing liquid against his lips. He swallowed gratefully and with difficulty, but slowly the room ceased gyrating and slid back into focus.

Lavinia knelt beside the chair, holding his head with one hand and guiding the cup of peppermint water to his lips with the other.

'You look as though you have seen a ghost,' he said to her.

She did not return his weak jest.

'I thought for one moment that I had.' Her eyes suddenly filled with tears which spilled over and coursed down her ashen cheeks.

'I'm all right, Linnie,' he said. It was easier now to put his hand up to wipe her tears away. He felt better every minute, just weak and shaken by the passage of the pain. 'It was just severe indigestion . . . really, dearest girl . . . Please don't weep. I promise that it was just a passing disorder. Too much venison with John this luncheon, I'll be bound. Give me a few moments to get my breath back and I'll be as fit as ever.'

★　　　★　　　★

The Watcher groaned and struck himself in an agony of failure. The strength was not enough any more. It was fading; a sob shook him, bowing the great shoulders. Rest now and try again. And then again – and again.

It was odd, Jess thought, waking from deep sleep in the darkest part of the night. In the midst of that searing pain, when he had suddenly thought that life was being wrested from him, he had been aware of someone else besides Lavinia in the parlour with them. It had not been Amy, nor Polly . . . certainly not anyone familiar to him. And yet there *was* an element of deep familiarity there. Impressed upon his memory was the blood red imprint of a figure. A tall, bulky figure with no features, just that dread feeling of intense familiarity. It was a fantasy, of course. He knew no one of that size and there was no stranger in the house. He sank back into dreamless sleep, the brief image burned into his subconscious.

PART THREE

Violet and Lawrence

Chapter One

Jess went straight to the Swan after spending the morning at Dell Quay in the Shipping Office. The Golden Dawn was expected in on the morning tide and would moor off Cockbush. The weather was fair and misty, so that there would be little problem in landing the delicate cargo of Indian silks and brocades without mishap.

'Ho there, Bayless – just the man I want to see . . .'

He turned towards the speaker who sat within a small group occupied in demolishing some well-cooked pheasant. Jess approached and bowed.

'Good day to you, Your Grace,' he said.

The Duke of Richmond took a large mouthful of meat and potato off the end of his fork.

'Come and join us, Bayless. Boy . . . a pot of Swan's Best for Master Bayless . . . at the double.'

Jess settled himself at the refectory table, nodding to those who raised their heads to greet him.

'Chaldecott you know. Me Lord Vere, Freeman of this City, Tom Stanyford, Will Pescod. Gentlemen – Master Jess Bayless.'

The Duke treated the little group to a contented beam and turned immediately to Jess.

'It's been more than a twelvemonth since I visited Lavenham,' he said. His voice was pleasantly pitched though blurred with a permanent nasal blockage. He was possessed of an abundantly good nature, with a sharp sense of humour that was not always well timed. He was rarely in Chichester these days, having recently been created Master of the Horse to King George, but his heart was firmly attached to Goodwood and the Charlton Hunt – and especially to the improvement of his stables. With this last in mind, he had become a regular, if infrequent visitor to Lavenham.

'Thought you might like to come and take a look at our new hunter, Bayless.' His eyes twinkled above shining cheeks like rosy apples. 'The finest piece of horse flesh I've seen for many a year. Presented this past week by me Lord Bolton. The first prize hunter from his stable since Bay Bolton was put down. Come on out to Goodwood this afternoon and take a look at him, if you will. I'd appreciate your opinion.'

Of course, Jess was on his way up the road to Goodwood before another hour had passed. They rode together, sparring amicably over the pros and cons of the hunting field until, clattering into the untidy sprawl of ancient stabling, they had handed their mounts over to running stable lads and wandered across the sludgy yard into the main stable block.

'This is to be the next renovation,' the Duke said, waving his crop round him. 'We're building a new wing to the main house now, as you can see. Hope to create a novel shaped place when it is finally completed but next year the new stable block is to be started and, when finished, should be one of the best designs in the country.'

Bolton Red was in his stall being rubbed down. He was a young horse, no more than five years old. Jess examined his teeth and quickly sensed the nervousness in the creature. He ran his hands lightly over the fine head and majestic neck, gentling with sensitive fingers until he felt the muscles relax and Bolton Red's ears began to prick out a jumpy welcome. He was indeed a beautiful animal.

'My congratulations. You have a rare jewel here, Your Grace', he said warmly.

The Duke's eyes twinkled. 'Better, wouldn't you say, than your Midas, Bayless?'

Jess made a face and shook his head firmly. 'Sorry, sir, but I wouldn't agree there. Midas is finer, both in stature and temperament, than any horse I know – even after looking over Bolton Red here.'

'But just look at those hind quarters, man. Look at the

strength there, the great rope muscles. Think of the speed he can go with hind quarters like that . . . and the shoulders. Feel there – and there, Bayless. Oh, he's an absolute winner, this one and I'd wager him against any horse after seeing him at exercise yesterday and this morning.'

Jess grinned at him. 'Well, Your Grace, if it weren't for my Midas, I'd agree and put my money where my mouth is alongside you at that.'

The Duke laughed and rubbed the top of his thigh. 'My word, I feel tormented that my racing days are past. If it were not for this confounded leg injury, I'd be up on that mount now, showing you how much faster he is than that horse of yours.'

He paused in mid-sentence and looked at Jess thoughtfully. 'What say you, Bayless. Will you accept my challenge and run your horse against mine for a prize?'

'I most certainly will, Sir,' Jess said, feeling the heart leap in his chest. 'Any time you wish and over any ground agreed by us both. I'd welcome it, Your Grace, for I know the worth of that horse of mine – and a couple of other yearlings in my stable also.'

Richmond slapped Jess on the back, clearly delighted with such excellent sport. 'Come on into the stable office and let us drink to that,' he said happily.

Lawrence sat in the arms of his tree, watching the house. From where he crouched, knees up under his chin between two bulbous branches, he had an uninterrupted view of the south and west fronts. From this vantage point he could watch the changing moods of the place and sense when it gathered itself up into one of its manifestations. The windows seemed empty, save for the reflections of light from the creek which glinted and slid over the lead lights, creating an impression of movement within the casements. There was no watcher behind their blind eyes this day but the pulse was present; the latent heartbeat of its restless soul. A spider crept along the branch towards his hand. It had a tiny body and long, double-jointed legs which spread out round the oaken bark with neat, fastidious movements. He gathered his energy into a small ball of

231

pure strength – and flamed it as it approached him. There was a flash of light – orange, tinged with something metallic . . . lethal. The spider simply disappeared with the suggestion of a sizzle. A small scorch mark scarred the branch. Lawrence stroked it with a forefinger. It was quite hot.

'Never,' Dada had told him, 'never flame anything unless you have to. You have a gift which is given to few folks. If you are like me, it will fade as you grow up but I just don't know how it will be with either of you. Maybe it will stay with you both.' He had looked at the two of them; Violet leaning against his knee and Lawrence lying on his stomach by his feet. He had their total attention for once, for it was the first time that the Power had been openly discussed and both children were fascinated by their father's admission that he, too, had been able to flame things in his youth.

The Power, however, was just about the only fun in the boredom of Lawrence's babyhood. He enjoyed flaming things and he knew that Violet did too. Why shouldn't they? No one else would ever know, for no one else seemed to have the same gift. Aunt Amy did not, that was certain, and it was as well that she did not. Polly had no idea of its existence and once, when he had tried to explain it to her, she had pinched his cheek and told him what a clever boy he was to have such a vivid imagination.

Amy appeared in the terrace doorway. Lawrence shrank back into the foliage of the oak tree and watched her. Tall and straight-backed, she stood with her face lifted as though she was smelling the air. Maybe she was because, when the house filled its rooms with the stink of horse sweat, it made Aunt Amy rant and rave and sometimes brought on one of her 'turns'. Maybe they had told her that she and Violet were being sent away.

As he watched her the light seemed to shift on the rosy walls of the house. A dark shadow passed over the sun and extinguished the diamond points of light in the upper windows. The climbing creeper closed its leaves, wilting against the warm bricks. A hot wind swept through the trees, rattling the branches and he clung to the trunk and steeled his mind to deflect the coming assault.

Nothing happened.

He saw Amy open her eyes and look about her, disillusion turning her face from a strange expectant beauty into the ugliness of sullen defeat. She limped out across the terrace, dragging her leg painfully.

Twenty yards from the oak tree she saw him. Their eyes met, hatred glaring between them, stopping his pulse with the depth of their venom. Something small and young shrivelled inside him. 'I wish I dared . . . I just wish I dared . . .'

'Lawrence, get down from that tree this instant and come in.'

'Why is it,' he wondered dolefully, 'that Aunt Amy's voice always has that carping tone when she speaks to me?' There was shrillness there, born of constant irritation which was seldom deserved. He swung his leg over the moist branch, clung to the bowl of the tree and slid carefully to the ground.

'Why is it that you seem bent on giving yourself more coughs and colds than the rest of us put together?'

She grabbed him by the collar of his cord jacket and hustled him into the house, scolding and shaking him roughly as she shooed him upstairs to change his stained shirt and breeches. Her eyes were red rimmed and their colour like flat stones at the edge of a winter sea.

Women. 'There are too many women in this house,' he thought gloomily as he stomped up to his chamber. Dada was in Chichester all day, so that invariably left him to the mercies of Aunt Amy and Violet. Thank goodness for dear old Polly, though. She was a secret supporter when the others weren't looking.

He'd been whipped more than once for creeping off to the saltpans to see the cousins. He'd been whipped even harder for leaving the paddock gate open and letting all the horses out. That was last year when four of the foals had died. Violet said that he had done it – but he had not. The foals were young and he enjoyed watching their antics in the paddock. He wouldn't hurt anything that Dada loved, in any case.

He was not allowed to go fishing because they said he came home wetter than the fish. What *was* he allowed to do? Now he must also be punished just for sitting up in his favorite tree and doing no harm to anyone.

He sat on the bed and unlaced his breeches with bite-lip concentration – proud to be wearing them at last and mercifully rid of the girlish frocks and bonnets of babyhood. There was a clean pair of brown fustians on his chair and he climbed slowly into them, relieved to see that they had button fronts. The lacings still gave him trouble to tie so that they did not gape in the front. He blushed anew at the recent memory of Violet's pointing finger and whoops of laughter when he had looked down to see his breeches gaping shamefully and everything popping out. She was lucky to be a girl . . . that she was not made the way boys were – and she was nearly two years older than he was, anyway. *Women.*

He clattered down the stairs, his nose telling him that Polly had the broth on the hob.

'C'mon, Jukel,' he said to the lurcher pup who sat beneath the hall table waiting for him. She came out wriggling and wagging and pressing herself against his legs as they went through to the kitchen. They were all seated already – waiting for him. Amy and Violet, Polly, Manfri and Rueb . . . sitting at the scrubbed table with Amy at the far end, dishing out the broth into wooden bowls. Violet shot him a sly look as he slid into his place on the form beside her. Jukel crept under the table close to his feet and settled down in a commanding position between the children. She rested her long nose on her paws, eyes swivelling for food droppings.

Quickfare at midday was always a swift and silent business. Manfri and Rueb bolted their broth, dipping Polly's crusty bread into the thick liquid to cool it faster. They would demolish half a loaf each, wiping the bowl clean with the last twist and then be up and away to their work with little more than a touch of a forelock. Sitting with the women for quickfare was tedious because Amy and Polly took their time and the children must chew every mouthful thirty-six times before swallowing it. He wished he were Manfri or Rueb who could gobble and suck at their food and make all sorts of splendid noises without earning a scolding.

'Why,' he asked the room in general, 'can't I eat my food like the men do and leave the table when they leave it?'

'Because you're still just a little nipper,' Polly said, looking at him with a certain sympathy. 'Still, you won't be for long,

234

will you? There's your new baby coming soon – and mine too. Soon you'll be the second oldest.'

Polly and Manfri had wed the previous year and Jess had built a cot onto the end of the dutch barn for them. It had a good-sized room downstairs and two chambers above. They considered themselves lucky. Some labourers had to walk for two or three miles between home and work.

'When does Mama's baby come?' Lawrence asked Amy. She frowned at him and the full line of her mouth became a narrow purse.

'That's no business of yours. Nothing in this world is certain. It'll come when it's ready. Little boys should not discuss such things.'

'I hope it's a brother,' he muttered, munching his bread and stirring the bowl with a finger so that the particles of meat swilled about his dipping crust.

'Well, it won't be,' Violet said flatly. She was always quiet at the dining table. You could tell quite a lot about people from the way they attacked their food. She liked to gauge the moods of the family. They were quite easy to manage as long as you knew about their moods. Throwing flat statements at Lawrence was a regular dinner time game for her. He was so easy to rouse.

She smiled innocently at him, seeing the two red spots on his cheeks which betrayed his mounting irritation.

'I say it will be, then.' He jutted his chin at her. 'We've enough women in this house as it is. I don't want another one.'

'Well, we certainly don't want another spoilt little brat like you, Lawrence Bayless.' Violet made a face at him and he jerked an elbow into her ribs with a stab that rocked her backwards on the wooden form.

'That's quite enough.' Amy leaned across the table and dealt Lawrence a hard whack across his knuckles with her soup ladle. 'One more word out of you, sir, and you spend the rest of the day in your room.'

Violet lowered her head over her food but Lawrence could feel her watching him out of the corner of her eye. Well, she wouldn't catch him out this time. He ate quietly, cursing his lack of years and the indisputable fact that his nose was still so close to the top of the table. Violet's taunting pulsed between them and he felt her jeers, daring him to look at her. 'Oh, no . . . I shan't fall into that trap again.'

He had glared back at her one day, looking right into her eyes for just a second, to show her that he was nearly as strong as she was, even if he was smaller – and his platter of meat and potatoes had shot out from under his spoon, skittering across the table and knocking Rueb's dish onto the floor with it.

There had been a terrible fuss with all the mess of food and gravy spattered over the table and floor. He had gone to bed hungry that day, his small rump throbbing from the beating he had received.

It would not be as bad as this when Mama was in charge, he comforted himself. Mama and Dadrus loved him, even if Aunt Amy and Violet didn't. He thanked providence for Mama and Dadrus. Mama had an infinite supply of love and sympathy in which he could immerse himself when things became too tense downstairs. She was obliged to spend all her time up in her chamber nowadays, for the baby was imminent and she was not allowed to exert herself. He enjoyed sitting on a footstool beside her chair, saying his numbers and going through the tortuous business of reading from the texts she laid before him. He wasn't nearly as swift with his reading as Violet was, but he was still only just past his fifth birthday. By the time he was seven, like Violet, he would be sure to be reading even better than she could.

Dada was a comfort in another – but equally important – way. He would never interfere with Amy's discipline unless even he felt that her hand was heavier than the crime deserved. All the same, she was careful to chide Lawrence only in the mildest terms when Jess was within earshot – so that life was not too difficult when he was at home. It was when he was out of the house that trouble seemed to dog Lawrence's footsteps. Then it was as though he could do nothing right.

There was another side of Aunt Amy which frightened him even more than her contempt for him. Aunt Amy hated Mama even more than she did Lawrence. 'Maybe that is why there is so much ill feeling between Violet and me,' he had thought more than once.

There was no one area that he could pin down to explain their controlled animosity. Certainly Mama did her best to make light of the situation when she could, but you could see that it upset her and sometimes her sense of injustice over some slight or disagreement would spill over into her treatment of Violet. It gave him a great deal of comfort when Mama delivered a sharp slap to Violet when Aunt Amy had been the cause of the irritation. It went some distance towards making up for the continual ill treatment he received at the Aunt's hands. The blows would fall and it was as well that neither of his parents supervised his dressing, for his body was never without the bruises of Aunt Amy's rages – and tears were all too often the only comfort he took to bed with him.

It would not be like that for long now, he thought with secret gladness. Did they know what was in store for them yet?

He finished his food with unusual meekness, sitting straight-backed and eating without a single sound or dribble.

The children finished their food and sat quietly, waiting for permission to leave the table.

'Away with you then,' Amy said at last. She stood up and Polly began to collect the bowls. Violet would wipe them and put them away on the dresser and then settle down with her mother to mend sheets. The kitchen was very much their domain.

Lawrence tugged on his outdoor boots and went out into the misty yard, leaving the kitchen door swinging open behind him.

Chapter Two

Jess tapped his teeth with the stem of his pipe. He had not been long back from Goodwood and a comfortable languor, born of good tobacco and a tankard or two of small ales with His Grace made him long for the feel of the wind roaring in his ears and Olivas' smooth stride beneath his rump.

That and the overpowering feeling that he must ride while he considered the importance of the wager he had just accepted.

The two men stood just inside the door respectfully, holding their hats. He could feel their anxiety, even at this range. The quality of the rooms in his new chambers was impressive enough to deter the most determined of would-be borrowers, he knew.

'Well, Gentlemen . . . What may I do for you?'

The elder took a step forward and hesitated, awed by the expanse of rich turkey carpet between him and the formidable figure behind the desk.

'I'm Henry Clifton, Sir – and this'ns my brother, Samuel. We farm a smallholding over to Westbourne, be the name of Priors Gate.'

Clifton cleared his throat and took a deep breath.

'That means he's going to launch into a lengthy diatribe that will take half the afternoon to unravel,' Jess thought with an inward sigh, giving the man his most understanding smile.

'Well, it's like this, sir. Me and Samuel have been farming this land all our lives and our father before us . . .'

'Progress. What an excellent word.' Jess arranged himself into a listening stance and let his thoughts roam. 'In one decade I have progressed from a gypsy with no learning and no future into Jess Bayless: landowner, ship owner, merchant banker and owner of the Lavenham stud. Dordi dordi . . . That's progress. Then there is the excitement of all the progress going on in this country. In half a lifetime progress has spread all the way through the farming community from the big land owners and now we're getting the small fry interested too. Now they all want to borrow money to buy the mechanized tools that will ease their burden in the field and give them that most blessed of benefits – Time. Time to cultivate the soil better; time to till faster. Time to sew and to reap and to produce better quality grain.'

Most of his clients were small farmers . . . and they were all jostling to buy iron ploughs to replace their less durable oak ones. They all wanted seed drills too, eager to abandon the centuries of broadcast sowing.

His mind probed the chain of thought, while his mouth smiled its encouragement and his head nodded sagely over the farmer's unheard words. A whole new breed was emerging in this exciting atmosphere of the Age of Invention. Young men like Polly's brother, James Ayles. Now there was a lad with a future. He had just made funds available to Jim Ayles, whose inventiveness was outstanding. The loan would enable him to open a whitesmith's foundry outside South Gate during the next few months and then who knew what astounding innovations would emerge from his fertile brain. His energy and enthusiasm had even fired Jess' imagination after he had examined Jim's thick folder of designs for farm implements and household tools. They had not only raised the bushy Bayless eyebrows into his peruke but had quickly persuaded Jess to invest his own money in the young man's ideas.

Cheese presses, metal milk churns, a splendid dung knife with a serrated blade and double handle. Two men could cut twenty cartloads of dung in an eight hour day with that tool. Almost twice as much as is presently cut with the normal choppers . . . And one item that would gladden Amy's heart. An amazing cooking hearth of caste iron in which the coals burned in a cupboard and the skillets were laid on its red hot top. We must have one of those for Lavenham. Progress. What vigour and excitement there was in the word.

'. . . and having the two punches, we'd be able to turn over the soil in half the time, sir – and that'd bring forward the sowing and harvesting too, d'you see?'

'Yes, Mr Clifton, I most assuredly do see. I shall be quite happy to advance you the necessary funds against suitable securities . . .'

Another day almost over. Bayless' had had a good year – but then, they had never really looked back since the first loan that Jess had arranged with his first profits from the 'Blacks'. Now he could afford to pick and choose and that applied to his interests with the Blacks also.

Where free trading was concerned, he had little or nothing to do with the ordinary, run-of-the-mill consignments these days. There were plenty of murderous scoundrels willing to risk their necks for a few barrels of brandy. The secret compartments in the 'Grace' and 'Golden Dawn' were now very sophisticated with watertight linings and special Chinese locks on them. For these days he was only interested in importing precious goods from India and China – fine silks and carpets and ornaments and jewelry. Hand picked merchandise for hand picked clients. It was a monumentally profitable business.

Smuggling became the occupation of ruffians and cut throats. The highways and countryside abounded with charlatans and murderers and no one was safe on the roads any more. The 'Blacks' had always avoided violence where possible and after Tover had had his hand cut off in a fight, Sarey persuaded him to give up his leadership of the gang and they all went their separate ways.

The Clan also became fragmented. Piramis died in the West country during their winter wandering of 1735 and the rest of the Clan broke up and moved away from the area leaving Vasher alone at the Salterns. Naffie and Saiforella would have been the natural heirs, but they were long gone and living in the New Forest near Lyndhurst.

Jess had been obliged to take on the salt pans, since the alternative was to see them taken over by a stranger who would not have that special knowledge of the liquor and crystals that the Baylesses had. The pans were lying idle for the first time in nearly a century. It had been in Jess' mind to make them over to Rueb when he married – but Rueb was surprisingly resistant to the idea. He was quite content at Lavenham and that was where he intended staying.

Old Sarey Bayless went to live with Naffie and Saiforella. Now and then they all appeared without warning and made up their benders in the woods and spent a week, a month – or a day, quietly clearing out the acres of filthy smelling saltbeds. It was done as an act of respect to those Baylesses who had laboured there for the whole of their lives.

There were still some Baylesses in the area besides the Lavenham family. Fedor and Jack both had important jobs, from Jess' point of view. They had taken to the sea and now looked after the 'special' consignments on the 'Grace' and the 'Golden Dawn'. Piramis' youngest daughter had married James Ayles – and of course his sister Polly had wed her Manfri.

Jess was always at his desk by eight o'clock in the morning and his staff would have preceded him by at least an hour. Ships' business occupied the early hours of each day and twice a week Jess visited the little wooden office on the shore at Dell Quay where a clerk dealt with the business of the Bayless vessels. There was a move afoot at the suggestion of the present landlord, William Hamilton, to build up a new quay so that ships could anchor alongside the jetty, rather than in mid-stream. Colonel Hamilton proposed granting building leases to a few of the merchants who used the Quay on a regular basis and Jess had been the first to submit an application.

John Freeland handled all Jess' legal work and, through this, had established himself in a most lucrative practice. He had done particularly well with the difficult litigation and family feelings surrounding the Smyth Estates after Hannah Smyth had died – with the result that her heirs, the Hamiltons and the Bartelotts were still on good terms and the lands were at last in process of being amicably reassigned between the two sisters.

Afternoons at Bayless' were filled with loans business and he finally rode home to Apuldram with the last of the waggon traffic. Sometimes he cleared the tedium of his day from

241

aching muscles by letting his mount go as soon as he had passed through the crumbling south gate. It was good to blow the dust of the town from lungs and clothing by giving his horse its head and, lying low in the saddle with his chin grazing the mane, let the hard ground of Apuldram Common flash by beneath its hooves.

The sun was declining into Old Park woods by the time he clattered into the yard and slipped off his horse's back.

'Manfri . . .' he shouted as Rueb came forward to lead the animal away. Manfri poked his head out of the saddle room door.

'In 'ere, Bor,' he called. 'See'en what Blacksmith've made us. Come an' take a look.'

'Later, Bor . . . later. Where's Midas?'

'Just brought 'em inside so he's in 'is stall.'

They went across to the great double doors of the barn and strolled down the centre aisle between the stalls, drinking in the bland sweetness of freshly dried grain and fodder. One half of the Barn was stacked with baled straw right up to the grain loft, the other half boxed off into stalls for the mares and their young. In the past twelve months Jess had added a new wing to each end of the barn. The west wing, closest to the creek, now housed a new saddle room and Manfri and Polly's quarters. In the east wing was the special stabling for the three stallions.

Jess and Manfri leaned on a heavy wooden bar across the open end of Midas' stall, watching him nosing his hay bag. He was over sixteen hands now – half a hand prouder than Olivas and he shone with health and grooming like a freshly-minted coin. His tail and mane gleamed like snow in the half light, pure, creamy white. He turned his head to acknowledge their presence and, seeing that Lavinia was not with them, returned to the important business of eating. Jess put a hand to his shining rump. The coat felt slightly oily to the touch.

'Good. You're rubbing in that linseed oil I brought back.'

Manfri nodded. 'Boilen' it like you said, till it thins and then rubben' it in with a clean cloth before groomen'. It's doen' a power of good, too. Just look at the sheen on 'im . . . fair makes your eyes ache.'

He spoke softly, pride in his voice. Jess grinned at him.

'We're going to race him, Manfri,' he said.

It was the most exciting thing that had happened since the Lavenham stables had come into being and, should Midas win, would put them firmly on the map, for the Duke had casually mentioned that one of the judges at the Finish at Charlton would be that most eminent of masters of the horse, François Robichon de la Guerinière. Monsieur de la Guerinière was visiting Goodwood at the moment and had already expressed great interest in the Lavenham Stud. He managed the Royal stables and Riding School at Versailles and came to England several times each year, on the lookout for English bloodstock. There was no question of Midas not being equal to any of the Duke of Bolton's horses. Certainly the old Richmond favorite hunter, Bay Bolton, had been an exceptionally fine stallion but had had to be put down in 1729 after a fall. There had been little of outstanding merit in the Goodwood stables since then – until a few days ago.

It was frustrating to know little or nothing of Bolton Red's form but Midas was in peak condition, ridden daily – and with his exercise increased and his corn doubled, there would be no holding him.

There was no question of who should ride him.

'I'll exercise him these next three mornings,' Jess said. 'You give him another run in the afternoons. We'll beat the bounds of the Parish which should not take longer than an hour, but there are three streams to be forded and the Donnington wood will be a good obstacle course – and Chatfield's hedges for jumps. It's fair exercise but we need some hill work too. Come with me tomorrow and we'll pace the course between Charlton and Halnaker.'

He left a delighted Manfri and made his way to the house, his mind filled with the Saturday wager and all its connotations. The three lurchers bounded across the hall from their vigil before the hearth and Lavinia's hand bell sounded from up in her chamber, its fluting tinkle chiming her welcome. He went up the stairs, taking them two at a time. She was sitting in her comfy chair beside a coal fire, a red rug across her knees.

'How frail she looks,' he thought with a jolt. Her shining hair was neatly rolled into bunched ringlets on either side of her face. She wore a loose manteau of pale blue camlet which accentuated the violet shadows under her eyes. Her forehead was hot under his lips.

'Oh, you do look jaunty,' she said happily enough, seeing the vigour in his face. 'Have you had a good day, dearest? You look as though nice things have been happening . . .'

It was always such pleasure to come home to Lavinia for she was instantly aware of whatever mood he was in and matched her own to it. Now she sat forward, folding her embroidery as he leant against the mantelpiece and began to tell her about his encounter with the Duke and his excitement over Midas' chances against Bolton Red. It was an exceptional chance for him to advertise the qualities of the Lavenham stock, he told her. At worst they would lose the race, but as long as Midas gave the other horse a good run for his money, the name of Bayless would still be made in the equestrian world . . . and if Midas beat Bolton Red – well, de la Guerinière would certainly consider breeding from Midas, which would open up the French stockyards to him.

'So many dreams, my Jess,' she thought, listening to the excitement in his voice. '. . . and yet you have the facility for making them happen just as you dream them.'

The colts in the paddock at the moment were the proof of that dream, after continuous disappointment and a high mortality rate until 1734. Now there were three yearlings out there with qualities akin to Midas, although he was still the undisputed prize of them all.

She looked at Jess' animated face, seeing the surging life in the sparkling eyes and wishing joy to all those bounding hopes which were lighting up his normally calm, saturnine features. It was foolish to think of a man of his age in terms of beauty but there was still no single word that could better describe the arresting effect of those ever changing grey eyes in a face so strong and tender.

Feeling the depth of her regard, he paused in mid-sentence and stooped down to kiss her soundly.

'What a selfish monster I am to be so full of my own pursuits as to forget the most important person in the world. Tell me how you feel today, Chika . . . and where is that scamp of a son of mine, eh?'

She leaned her head against him. 'All is well with me, Jess, don't worry . . . though the babe weighs too heavily for comfort. My valise is packed and the baby's clothing and cradle are ready for the trip over to Fishbourne next week. Now there is little to do but to wait and hope that the journey there will have been worth our separation, dearest Jess. Lawrence has been here with me for most of the afternoon. His reading is really very good for his age – and Jess, he is already almost better than I am with his numbers.'

Jess tugged at the bell rope. 'Let's have some tea,' he said. 'And afterwards Polly can open the flood gates and send up the children. Maybe they will stop their bickering long enough to tell us what they have been doing with their time also. Since you are so determined to take Lawrence to Fishbourne with you, they may decide that they miss each other's company and get along better when he returns. In any case, they will not be irritating each other for much longer.'

There were only four days in which to prepare Midas for the race. Manfri applied every scrap of his expertise to his charge; knocking up a special mixed feed which would give him the greatest energy and the least wind; docking his mane and tail up to the coccyx as some of the foreign gentry were doing with their steeple chasers now. Although this slightly impaired Midas' elemental beauty, it gave him a clean cut look of great power that would leave the experts breathless. After the morning and evening exercise, Manfri went over every inch of him, feeling with his boney sensitive fingers for any little cuts or bruises or pulled tendons in hocks and fetlocks. After Jess' early morning runs, once he was satisfied that Midas was sound, he gave him a small haybag and fresh water and then set about grooming him as he ate. The morning rub down took the longest, for it not only included the removal of mud and dust from his coat, but also the picking out of soil from hoof and shoes. There was never anything gentle about Manfri's ministrations and, if Rueb did not put the same energy into his grooming, he soon had his ears boxed for his laziness. It required a steady movement with firm pressure on the brushes without banging them down onto the horse's coat. When the whole horse shone like a captive sun, Manfri pummelled the fore and hind quarters with a straw wisp to help build up the muscles and tone up the skin. Finally he rubbed a small quantity of the boiled linseed oil into coat and hooves, swabbed out ears and round his sheath and, after a final going over with his brushes, stood back almost unwillingly to survey his hour's labour with a critical eye.

The children appeared at the stable door and hung over the top of the half gate, watching Manfri at his exertions. He could feel their presence as he worked and grinned under his arm at them without breaking the movement.

'Rueb's getten' your little foal rope bridled this mornen',' he said to Violet and smiled to himself as her face lit up. She had a much greater interest in the Stud than did young Lawrence, he knew. Still, the boy was only a bitti raklo and not long breeched. At five years old, the Baylesses had all been little men with responsibilities towards the Clan. Gorgio children were kept in the nursery far too long. 'Shan't be that way with Polly's and my chavis.'

'Can I come and help Rueb, Manfri?' Violet sounded anxious and he nodded without looking at her, knowing that she needed to be with the foal from the start if it was to recognize her as its mistress.

'When you've finished helpen' your Mama, come out to the paddock and we'll have the slip on 'em in no time. You'll be needen' to handle that slip each day after that – till 'e gets used to you, see? Then, when 'e's weaned, we halter break 'im till 'e's full grown. Be that time, you'll be ready to ride 'im yourself, won't ye? Near grown you'll be too, be then.'

'What about me?' Lawrence asked, more from habit than any real inclination to have his own horse.

'We'll 'ave ter see about you, young Bor . . . won't we? You'm only a nipper now, but one day you'll be as tall as yer Dad and maybe as fine set in the saddle as him, too. You must come to the stables more often, like Violet does, see? Then you'll soon know whether you'm got the feelen' for the animals. Violet here . . . she's got it. You can tell – and so can the grais.'

Lawrence swung on the door without further comment. He was more than a little scared of these large and unpredictable creatures. He knew that Violet had no such fears. He glanced up at her and she returned the look. No. She said in his head. You won't go near the Stud ever. Remember that. Keep away from it.

He let go of the stable door and trailed away across the yard, kicking stones out of his path as he went. Upstairs in the main bedchamber, Lavinia watched him from her window.

'Poor little boy,' she thought. 'He looks so disconsolate. What has Violet been saying to him this time?' She turned away, anger flooding through her.

'Now calm yourself. Doctor Sanden said that you were not to get distressed, not to permit yourself to cross swords with Amy. Think of the baby . . .'

She settled herself back into her arm chair and drew the blanket over her knees with a sigh.

'What an unbelievable relief it will be when Amy and Violet are gone. It will all be so very much worth the present aggravation when Violet and Amy are settled and Lavenham belongs just to Jess and the children and me.'

The thought lifted her depression and she leaned back and let her imagination roam over the delightful prospect of Lavenham without her sister-in-law. Maybe all the other problems in the house would disappear with those two also . . .

Chapter Three

Lavinia paced her chamber, made restless by the fresh currents scourging the house. It was, in a few short hours, as though the whole focus of Amy's resentment was building up into a violent crescendo and the tension in her was becoming almost unbearable.

It was all to do with the decision to build Salterns Cottage, of course. She had known that there would be scenes and was doing her best to steel herself against the worst that Amy could do to her. All the same, it made her sigh with relief each time she thought of Lavenham without Amy and Violet. It had taken six years of humiliations, pleadings, and tears before Jess finally and unexpectedly gave in and agreed to remove Amy and Violet to a cottage of their own. Her relationship with the child was not too difficult for Violet was intelligent and affectionate by nature but clearly torn in two by loyalty to her mother in spite of a grudging regard for Lavinia. No – Violet's main problem had long been her attitude towards poor Lawrence. She could be such a cruel tease sometimes. The little boy was certainly suffering from her jibes almost as badly as his mother did from the effects of hatred in the house and even Jess eventually agreed that Lawrence would benefit in every way if separated from Violet.

On a winter's evening when frost rimed the bare trees fringing the house, Jess came stamping into the kitchen, unwinding the scarf from around his head. As he opened the door Amy's voice cut across him like a whiplash. 'Keep out of here, you simpering whore. Keep out, I say, or I shall cut your sweet little face so that he'll never look at you again.'

'What the hell's going on,' he said furiously.

Lavinia was standing near the hall door with a basket of nuts in her arms. She looked terrified and turned to Jess with such desperate fear that his exasperation and weariness cracked. Amy was standing beside the kitchen table, a carving knife raised in her hand. Her teeth were clenched under lips drawn back in a rictus of rage. He strode forward, snatched the knife from her and hit her hard across the face. She scarcely flinched but stood before him, slowly dragging her eyes from Lavinia and fixing him with a look that softened into doglike devotion. She stood proudly before him, wearing the deepening weal of his hand across the side of her face like a crimson flag of defiance.

'Don't ever do that again, do you hear?' he shouted at her, enraged by the blatent love in her face and weakened by the guilt of hitting a crippled woman with such force. 'Never let me hear words like that from your mouth – *never*. And as for threatening Lavinia in that fashion, I've had enough of it, Amy – and so have we all. If I ever have cause for complaint again you'll be sent packing, d'you hear?'

Up went her chin, as it had done all the years he had known her. She held his eyes with hers for an instant and then left the kitchen.

She had continued to resist Lavinia's use of the kitchen after that but with sulky passivity. They all noticed that her limp was becoming more pronounced though – and that the fits increased after that scene. It had happened soon after Lavinia had announced this latest pregnancy.

Lavinia began to feel unwell almost at once and double vision, constant sickness and fits of fever marked every stage of her confinement thereafter. She sensed Jess' growing unease, though he would not be questioned. All the same, she knew that he was worrying about Amy and when he had arrived in the kitchen in time to hear the tone of the insults thrown at Lavinia, it must have been the last straw. The following evening he returned looking serious but resolved.

That was the moment when the decision was made to move Amy and Violet before the violence erupted into a really serious situation.

There was also the indisputable fact that Lawrence was developing a tendency to cling to his mother – a soft streak which clearly worried Jess, who did not seem to appreciate the feeling of loss a small boy often has when a new baby is to be introduced into his household. Lavinia might have insisted on him spending more time in Violet's company in normal circumstances, but she had a feeling that he sensed the fear and dread in which she lived – and in some way was trying to comfort her. It was ridiculous, of course, for how could a little boy, not yet six years old, lessen the flashes of terror she felt all round her, lurking in the shadows and watching her . . . waiting. And how could he know anything of those voices which trailed their supplications and curses through her head at night?

The kitchen was quiet at dawn, after breakfast had been cleared away. It was then, after Rueb had taken himself off to the yard and Polly and Manfri were about their duties, that Jess had told them.

'Don't rush off,' he said to Amy with something of the old gentleness in his voice. Amy sat down again obediently. She didn't look at him but stared down at her hands as she had done for a long time now whenever engaged in direct conversation. 'Pen, look at me,' he said.

Violet was still sitting at the end of the table. Jess appeared to have forgotten that she was there for he ignored her. She looked at their faces, the brother and sister – her parents. They had been so alike in their youth, Manfri often told her. Now the different aspects of their lives had eroded the similarity. The height was there and the dark colouring and high cheek bones – even the olive skin, but where Jess was like marble hewn into perfect sculpture, the sap had run dry in Amy and it was as though she had fossilised into a living cadaver. She looked infinitely older than her thirty years. Her skin had dried upon the bones of her face, stretched into a bitter mask which turned the echo of past beauty into a sallow death's head whose only animation was in the rictus of epilepsy or the increasingly frightening rages when all reason abandoned her.

It frightened Violet when her mother became maddened,

250

for the violence in her was more than a child could cope with. At other times, Amy posed no problems for she permitted her to be her extra hands and even showed a grudging appreciation.

'Pen, look at me,' Jess said again and Amy, recognizing that special tone in his voice which had been reserved for her – and her alone a long long time ago, looked obediently into Jess' warm grey eyes and allowed herself the luxury of drowning in the affection she found there.

And then he told them. 'I have bought some land from Walter Bartelott at the corner of our lane,' he said with a gentleness in his tone. 'I am going to build there a well-appointed cot for you and Violet. You will be as close as possible to Lavenham – only five minutes walk from here – but it will be your very own home, just for the two of you and you shall choose your own furniture and have a maid to live in with you and a garden boy also, if you wish.' His voice had gone on and on with a tinge of anxiety coming and going and his eyes rejecting the look of blank shock on Amy's face.

'With Lavinia's new baby arriving soon it won't be long before we run out of rooms here, Chika, as you can appreciate . . . We only have the three chambers upstairs and I do not plan to make any house extensions at this time. Maybe we will in the future if Lavinia has more children but Doctor Sanden advises against this, as you know . . .'

'Dada,' Violet cut in.

Jess dragged his eyes away from Amy and turned to her in surprise. He had forgotten that Violet was with them. She had not moved since he had begun to speak.

'Dada, don't do that to Mama, please. You know how she feels about this house – about being with you. Please don't hurt her, Dada.'

The tears came then, and he leaned across the table and drew her to him, cradling her against his shoulder.

'I have to find you somewhere else to live . . . you know that, Chavi. The situation has been becoming more difficult between us all and is fast getting out of hand now. With the new child to think of, I must plan ahead for all of us, must I not? It will be some months before the cottage is ready for you, of course. In the meantime, Aunt Lavinia will be going to

Fishbourne with Lawrence in a few day's time and then you and Mama will keep me company until they return. It will be like old times, won't it?' He looked over Violet's head at Amy, a desperate pleading in him. She stared back at him and gradually the life came back into her. She laid her long hands flat on the scrubbed boards of the table top and watched as they curled themselves into tight fists.

'Old times,' she said and her voice was as dry and grating as metal against stone. 'Old times, you say. Yes, brother . . . you wanted much of me in those old times.'

Suddenly she threw her head back and laughed and there was no music in the sound. She dragged herself up onto her feet and came round the table to stand over him. 'Will you be wanting me again, brother? With your little simpering rawni gone from your bed? Will you want to lie with me out there in the hall beside the fire . . . just like old times? Will you want to take me and pump your seed into me with all the rotten lust of your greedy soul – just like old times?'

She spat at him and the gobbet caught him on the forehead and began to slide slowly down his temple.

The tremor was in her. Violet wriggled free of Jess' fierce grip and put her arms round Amy's waist. 'Come and sit down, Mama . . . don't fret, come and sit down and take some deep breaths . . .'

Amy shook her off with a hard cutting stroke that sent her skittering across the room into an empty butter churn. Jess raised his elbows above his head as Amy lunged at him, arms like scimitars.

She fell like a stone, jerking and arching as she went.

Sighing, he stooped and picked her up. 'Go and fetch Polly,' he said to Violet.

She shook her head, picking herself up and hastening over to him.

'I can look after her. She might hit Polly's stomach and hurt the baby. I can look after her.'

She couldn't look at Jess – couldn't call him Dada. He stood at the end of the bed as she settled her mother under the covers, tenderly wiped the perspiration from the threshing head, turning it gently onto one side as Doctor Sanden had shown her.

She felt Jess kiss the top of her head and then heard his retreating feet upon the boards as he left the chamber. She didn't look up. If she had, she might have flamed him. Her own father. A human being. She might so easily have given in to the terrible rising bubble of hurt and bewilderment which even now threatened to engulf her.

Dada didn't want them any more.

It was, in the depth of her small being, a kind of death.

It was a bitter joke that, before this pregnancy, Lavinia had almost forgotten the ordeal she had suffered preceding the birth of Lawrence. Time blunts the edges of memory, so they say – and certainly she had given little thought to the formless things that had seeped into her very soul and threatened her sanity. The years between had been filled with many fulfilments, despite the anger and underlying viciousness so often striking deep into the heart of the house. There had been three miscarriages but they had all been very early in pregnancy and her natural good health and the busy active life she led with Jess at Lavenham ensured a quick return to full strength.

After Lawrence arrived and she was once more in full health, she fell into a pleasing daily routine which took her out of the house and away from Amy's contemptuous regard. She rode Midas each morning after feeding and attending to Lawrence's toilet. Once he was tucked into his cradle and comfortably resting she left him in Polly's care and rode Midas out, sometimes across the common to take morning coffee with her mother in Fishbourne and at others, away across the Manhood flat lands, through gorse and woodland, flying – wrapped up in the rhythm of thundering hooves and pumping lungs. A rapport was established between them which was even greater than that between Jess and Olivas. Midas had not allowed anyone but Lavinia to ride him since she and Manfri had broken him in. He expressed his devotion to her by standing against the paddock gate at first light, whinnying and snorting as loudly as he could until she opened her chamber window to call her greetings to him. He would nod his head up and down and then wheel away, to canter round and round the field, as though to dissipate some of the pure emotion he felt for his mistress. Since her condition stopped her riding, he had allowed Manfri and Jess to exercise him but she still held court at her window and sometimes Manfri brought him over to the terrace so that she could talk to him.

There was no miscarriage with this pregnancy. Lavinia was young and healthy and the underlying relief of knowing that she would be with her mother during the actual confinement did much to ease her mind. There was, however, a great deal of time to spare, for Doctor Sanden had been most insistent that she did as little walking as possible in the latter months and was to stay in her chamber if there was the slightest ill humour in the weather. As a result, the large, airy bed chamber became the four walls of her existence and there was time – and plenty of it – to brood over her situation and the house and all its repellent shadows and odours and influences. She began to wonder whether it was Amy or the house itself which threatened her. Was it trying to stamp out new Bayless blood? Maybe children had some abrasive effect upon the place . . . Certainly Violet and Lawrence appeared to be unusually mature children for their ages, and each possessed a singular preference for their own company. Violet could be such a good child, quiet and attentive at her lessons and never rude to her elders . . . unlike young Lawrence who was often loud and argumentative in the manner of most little boys of strong will. She was certainly Amy's mainstay for she helped her mother most industriously and seemed to have a swiftly calming effect on her when she was having one of her 'turns'.

Or maybe the whole brooding, threatening atmosphere surrounding Lavenham emanated from Amy, after all. There had been few manifestations there outside the feelings of her own instincts. Mama thought that Lavenham was a delightful house and so, she knew, did her brother, John. The Baylesses seemed to shy away from it and Manfri had been heard to mutter about 'Mullos' being its guardians – but that was gypsy talk. Taking stock of the alien influences in the house, she began to realize that Violet worried her almost as much as Amy did.

Violet was, at seven years old, already a strikingly beautiful child with an excess of restless energy about her that made life quite tiring in her company at times. She was, like her mother, going to be unusually tall. Already her fine-boned young body had a leggy grace which brought to mind the foals gambolling in the paddock. She was wilful and moody, full of affection one minute and sulks the next. Recently she had taken to watching Lavinia with the same constance that had embarrassed her so strongly before Lawrence's arrival. It was too foolish, she chided herself, to get distressed by those grey eyes of Violet's . . . and she was probably imagining all this watchfulness. Having children brought on the strangest notions . . .

'Lawrence, it really is bad manners to stare at people,' she said sharply to him the afternoon before the race. 'Why must you keep doing it? What is it that you are looking at?' For now it seemed that her own son had caught the wretched habit also.

Lawrence looked away, colour flooding his round cheeks.

'I'm sorry, Mama. It's just that you look so nice in that shawl. I was thinking that I am very glad that *you* are my Mama.' And not Amy, he might have added. The unsaid words hung between the three of them. Violet gave him a look of such adult withering contempt that Lavinia winced for him.

'That's a nice thing to say, darling. Thank you for your gallantry,' she said hurriedly, trying to sweep away the animosity which seemed to surround the two children, for there was something about its intensity which had no place in such youthful minds.

'Give me your slates, both of you. I shall write down some words and I want you, Violet, to tell me what they mean and you, Lawrence, to copy my writing of them. Let's not waste any more time. I'm a little weary today and would like to have our lesson finished by four o'clock and not delayed as it was yesterday. Let us see whether you can be really good and finish by the time the hour glass runs out.'

Obediently the two heads bent to their work as she handed back their slates and writing chalks.

Her thoughts slid back to the child within her. 'Be dark and handsome like Jess,' she pleaded with it.

Lawrence was so very much a Freeland and she had to search for evidence of his father in him. There was little of the Romani there except for the high bridged Bayless nose. He had his father's dogged determination though, which was no bad thing since life under the same roof as Amy had been one long battle since he was old enough to register the imbalance of her moods.

A hardness in her stomach began to make her feel breathless and she shifted constantly in her chair. There was a slight but· tiresome ache in the small of her back and she pulled herself to her feet and began to pace to relieve her discomfort. Really, she wondered, maybe it would be better if I were to go to mother's before Jess' race. Then if the child were to begin coming before he was expected, at least Mama and her staff would see to it that all was prepared.

She suddenly distrusted Lavenham. Even Polly and Manfri and Rueb might be somewhere else and Amy was too strange to rely on at all, these days. The small ache became a worry until something distracted her.

The children sat huddled over their work on either side of the card table in the west window, the chalk slipping and squeaking in their hands. From the far side of the room she stared at them, for it seemed from where she stood that shadows crowded about each child – and yet they sat in bright sunlight. She blinked, for there was a dull red reflection in the room. It faded and she moved back towards the children, suddenly filled with a shivering foreboding.

'I must get away from here,' she thought in panic. 'I will tell Jess as soon as he comes home and we will despatch Rueb to warn Mama. I must go.'

Leaving the children at their studies, she opened the chamber door and went out into the gallery, to stretch her legs and keep moving to ease the ache in her back. She leaned against the bannisters and stared down into the hall, always aware of that night soon after her marriage when the sensation of horse down there in the darkness had turned the centre of the house into a place she preferred to avoid ever after.

Amy was standing close to the long table. She stood quite still, as though listening and Lavinia, seeing the closed eyes, wondered whether she might be about to have a turn. In the act of calling to Violet she paused, suddenly aware of Amy's stance. She had an expression so weird upon her face that it sent new shivers along Lavinia's spine. She was standing almost bent at the knees, her shuttered face filled with an ecstasy so intimate that Lavinia backed away, flushing to the roots of her golden head. She returned to her chamber and closed the door very quietly and leaned against it, disturbed and strangely revolted.

It looked as though Amy was communing very physically with some private deity.

Jess returned home with the fading day and, hastening up to the chamber, bent to kiss her, the tiredness of a tedious day made better by the sight of her.

'Jess, I want to go to Fishbourne tomorrow,' she said urgently, taking his hands and pulling at them as she had done when first they had become betrothed.

He was startled – his mind filled with the coming race the following morning. 'What is the trouble?' he asked anxiously. 'Do you feel close to your time? The child is not due for another two or three weeks, you told me.'

'I know, I know. I don't care when it is due, Jess. I just feel that I must leave here as soon as possible. I am very heavy, dearest, and I ache all over, so it is quite possible that things are about to begin. Whether they are or not, I have the strongest feeling that Lawrence and I should take the carriage in the morning.'

He soothed her, seeing her agitation. 'I shall dispatch Rueb at first light to warn Mistress Freeland of your arrival and then he and Polly and Amy can pack you and Lawrence into the carriage as soon as you have had breakfast and you'll be nicely settled in with her by the time I return from Charlton. How does that sound to you?'

Her relief was touching. Really, she looked as though a puff of wind would blow her away. He was well aware of the nightmares which crowded her sleep – just as they had done before. It filled him with a deep foreboding which he was careful to hide from her. There were not going to be any more children after this one, he thought grimly. Nothing is worth the agony of unease and fear which besets the poor girl every time a child is on the way. That it had connections with the Place, he had no doubt but why, and to what ends, he could not fathom out, though God knew, he had pondered over the situation time after time as he felt her shivering beside him in the darkness.

He sat with Lavinia until she drifted off to sleep, aided by one of Amy's sleeping draughts, and then went down to the stables to inspect Midas.

The evening was dank with a biting wind ripping across the flat fields to buffet against the Trundle's long straggling ridge of the South Downs. Manfri and Rueb were hard at work, Manfri as usual buffing Midas's coat. He grunted at Jess without pausing to turn round. Rueb was bent over with a hoof between his knees, patiently oiling the shining yellow bone.

'Thought he'd gone lame on my way home,' Manfri said. 'Picked up a flint in 'is shoe there but it hasn't split the skin. Put some Solomon Seal on it an' it should be good as new be the mornen' . . . How's Mistress Linnie?'

'Resting now, Bor, but I want you, Rueb, to go over to Fishbourne at crack of dawn and warn them that she is on her way over after breakfast. It looks as though the child may be closer to its arrival than we had thought.' Rueb nodded and took himself off to clean out the carriage for the morning ride. Manfri shook his head over Jess' stern, worried face. Polly had not had any trouble of that sort. She was close to her time now too, but as fit and cheery as she always was. Poor little Lavinia must be shorter of stamina than she had seemed.

'I wonder if Rueb is caring for my poor bees properly,' Lavinia thought, searching for a sleep which still eluded her. 'If he hasn't cleaned out the floors properly and noted the amount of dead drones or pupae, we'll be in trouble with the combes by June . . . It is no good. I must go . . . I must leave here *now*.'

Trying to think of anything other than the overwhelming desire to run from this place was becoming impossible . . . Her concentration wavered the harder she struggled, as an old and bitter fear fluttered in the pit of her stomach, close to the small life about to start its journey into the world. There was absolutely no reason for the feeling, apart from dim memories of the last lying in.

She lay on her back with her eyes closed, scolding herself and doing her best to push aside the shadows that gathered in the room beyond her eyelids . . . watching and waiting –

willing her to slide down that dark tunnel from which she had clawed her way back into the light last time.

Last time? She pulled herself up in the bed, tearing at the covers as she remembered the noise and the voices, the screaming and crackle of flames and the terrifying horse stench, the acceptance of death.

Violet was sitting on a stool beside the bed. The unexpected sight made Lavinia draw in her breath sharply. She had not heard the child come into the room. Violet's eyes widened with alarm as Lavinia jerked away from her. They had been fixed upon her with such intensity that her aunt's sudden movement startled her quite as much as she had Lavinia. She patted her arm timidly.

'Are you all right, Aunt?'

Lavinia stared wildly at her, suddenly terrified by those calm grey eyes. 'Where is your mother? Why are you here . . .?'

'Dada asked me just to come and see that you were comfortable. Would you like another pillow, Aunt? Dada says you are going over to Fishbourne in the morning.'

Her great grey eyes regarded Lavinia gently, almost with sorrow. 'I shall miss you . . . It would have been so nice to help with the baby coming, now that I am older.'

There was a wistfulness in her voice which made Lavinia pat her hand affectionately. 'We won't be gone for long,' she said. 'You will be over to visit, of course, won't you?'

Violet seemed to have an odd red halo all round her. Her face came and went, the concerned eyes at once huge and distorted and then diminishing into pinpoints of black light.

Amy stood in the centre of the hall, pressing herself against the refectory table. It was going to work this time – she could feel a vast gathering of forces in the shimmering air around her. She breathed in deeply, raising her face as though to the warmth of the spring sunshine outside.

'Go to it,' she said to the house. 'I have surely weakened her for you this time. Now it is up to you.'

It had been fascinating watching the very slight but accumulative daily reaction of the tiny doses of powdered Monk's

Hood crowns. She had been careful about the quantities so that there would be absolutely no evidence in Lavinia's reaction to regular dosing. Such quantities would never produce death, only debility. It was most encouraging to note the extreme slowness of her inevitable decline, however. The pleasure it gave was all the greater, knowing that, if Lavinia succumbed, she and Violet would not be leaving Lavenham as they had planned. It made her laugh aloud now and then, when she thought of all their efforts to part her from Jess.

'Oh no, my fine lady,' she said aloud. 'It won't be long.'

She heard Jess' feet clattering into the kitchen from the yard and sighed, turning away from the hall into the parlour. She stood behind the door and listened to his feet stamping up the stairs and into the chamber above, trying to tread softly without success.

'Not long, Bor . . . Not long now.'

Lavinia was in a deep sleep. Jess lay in the big bed beside her, watching by the light of a single candle, the even rise and fall of her chest and the lines of fear draining slowly away from her face.

Chapter Four

'Hold 'em still there, Bor. Acha 'doi, Midas . . .'

Manfri gentled Midas' nervous prancing till he stopped backing and bowing among the grooms and onlookers and allowed Manfri to tighten his girths for the third time. Jess sat easily in the saddle, stroking the horse's neck. He could feel Midas' excitement heightened by his own. The sleeping potion of mandrake and wild mint that Amy had infused for Lavinia had lulled her into a deeper sleep than she had enjoyed for weeks and she had still been in heavy slumber when he had left the house. Still, she would be awake by now and already preparing for the transfer to the reassuring comfort of Mistress Freeland's house. He shut his concern for Lavinia into the deepest recesses of his mind and concentrated on what was before him.

The race was to be run over a circular course, starting at the Richmond's hunting lodge at Charlton and taking in East Dean, Selhurst Park, Halnaker House, Goodwood and finally back to Charlton. The nine miles would have taken about an hour had the course been on the flat and across open land, but the Duke had chosen a hazardous run through woodland and park, up the shoulder of steep downland hills and across hedged fields. It had been agreed that they race soon after dawn, riding into a brightening morning which would ensure that the winner was past the finishing post before midday.

Jess and Manfri had ridden the course, setting the mare, Gilda, and Midas an easy pace with no pressure. It had been a wise move.

Charlton is situated beneath the rolling curve of the downs amid open woodland. To the south of the hamlet, the three estates of Goodwood, Halnaker and Selhurst spread across hundreds of acres of cleared park and arable land, fringed with oakwoods and steeply banked streams. The going from Charlton to East Dean would be fast, but as they veered south through Selhurst Park, the beech trees crowded up and closed in. Between Selhurst and Halnaker they had struggled through dense undergrowth until luck unexpectedly lent a hand. Spirals of woodsmoke led them to a charcoal burner's fireside. The three soot blackened men had been Romanies and Jess and Manfri had tethered the horses and settled down over a shared pipe for half an hour and had been well rewarded for the time spent there. The yoggers had drawn a rough map of the woods through which Jess must ride, marking hidden deer paths and the least hazardous ford across two streams. With certain landmarks that would be easy for them to identify and the promise of patrins – Romani markings – at different places along the route, they had finally continued on their way well pleased.

They followed the yoggers' instructions along open ridings, beneath holly-choked ridings and forded the streams from conveniently shallow banks. The red roofs of Halnaker peeked through the trees as they cantered across the Park, skirting the approach sweep as they went.

'Looks like the countess spends more on her person than she do on 'er country seat,' Manfri observed as they left the crumbling old mansion on their left and stretched out over flat fields towards the rising ground of the Richmond Estate . . . By the time they passed behind Goodwood House and cut across open forest towards the last hill and the Finish, both horses and riders were feeling the distance.

'Two hours and forty-eight minutes,' Jess had reckoned from his pocket watch. 'That's excluding the time spent with the yoggers. As long as the rain keeps off, I think we can knock nearly an hour off that.'

Now, sitting comfortably astride his dancing horse, he sniffed the cold morning air, testing its texture and the scents drifting on it. The breeze came lightly from the west, dry and fragrant. The Duke's horse appeared amid the thin scatter of onlookers, led out of the spacious stable block by a groom and surrounded by a gaggle of stable lads. The jockey was already mounted, dressed in a bright emerald green silk shirt with a yellow fox appliqued on his back and white kersey breeches. It would not be difficult to keep him in sight.

As the silver slashed dawn sky lightened, the Ducal party arrived. Eighteen or twenty gentlemen accompanying His Grace and Monsieur de la Guerinière and Jess smiled grimly and bowed as the Duke raised his hand in welcome as they approached.

'We appear to be all present and correct, Bayless, and most anxious for the start, if you are,' he said cheerfully, rubbing the top of his thigh as he limped across the road to where Jess waited with Manfri and a small gathering of town supporters. Jess inclined his head to the little Frenchman as they were introduced, noting the way the great Riding Master ran his eyes over Midas with obvious approval.

'We're ready at your convenience, Your Grace,' Jess said, grinning down at the stocky figure in its tye wig and yellow hacking jacket. There was little between their ages but the Duke's florid colouring and double chin gave him the illusion of age. He was a natural countryman, loving the rolling Sussex Downs and sprawling forests. His term of office as Mayor of Chichester had been a resounding success and Jess had been delighted to note the sparkle of humour and life that he brought to the appointment.

'Y'know, Bayless, if my damned leg had not precluded my riding today, I'd have had the greatest pleasure in trouncing you and your animal with Bolton Red. However, Harry Steele's the best horseman on the estate and knows the land like the back of his hand, so you won't get lost if you follow him! You'll certainly have a hard task to leave him behind, I can promise you that. The best of luck to you, all the same.'

He turned away and Manfri led Midas across to the starting post at the Lodge entrance. Someone had strung a cord across the road and the two horses moved up until their breastbones nudged it.

The onlookers crowded back onto the verges of the dirt track and the Duke pulled a brightly coloured silk kerchief from his cuff and held it above his head.

'*Silence*. I would have you know, before witnesses, the rules governing this wager.'

His voice bellowed out over the waiting crowd, bringing the buzz of conversation to a halt in mid sentence.

'This race is to be staked against the painting of the winning horse by Master Wooten; the account to be settled by the loser. The horses are to run from Charlton to East Dean, through Selhurst Forest to Halnaker House where Her Grace, the Countess of Derby has a large party watching the contest to ensure that no corners are cut. Up to Goodwood from Halnaker and then over the hills and back to Charlton for the Finish. There will be marshalls posted at the two houses but the way in between is up to the contestants. The first mounted horse past the Winning Post wins the race. The light is strong enough now, I think. What say you, Master Bayless?'

Jess nodded, concentrating on holding the dancing Midas on a tight rein.

Bolton Red stood quietly against the starting line, shaking the first of the day's flies from his ears.

There was a moment's silence while Jess murmured to Midas under his breath, gradually easing him back up to the Start. The moment his nose touched the rope, the silk kerchief flashed downwards and the rope was dropped.

The two horses rocketted away and were quickly lost from view in a cloud of dusty earth. The onlookers sighed with the excellence of such a clean start and settled themselves down on the grass with their backs to the stable walls, to share a hunk of bread and flask of ale while they waited and speculated and laid bets among themselves as to the outcome.

Lavinia woke slowly, drifting upwards through a miasma of weariness, like a leaf on the surface of turgid water. She opened her eyes and stared at the flowered chintz lining of the four poster bed frame above her. Fat pink and red roses nestled among layers of multi-green leaves . . . tiny buds peeping from amongst them. It was a relief to wake when sleep was so dogged with dark visions and racked by such ungovernable terrors. The chintz bed curtains always glowed at her with such comfortable reassurance. They reminded her of little Lawrence's pink cheeks and full mouth.

Her stomach hardened and the ache that had reached even through the black wall of sleep drove a knee hard into her back, forcing a yelp from her unprepared lungs.

The sound brought her fully awake and she rolled over in the bed and put her feet to the floor. The curtains were still closed but bright light filtered through them, casting a peaceful greenish shade over the whole room. She moved to the window on the Channel side of the chamber and pulled back the heavy curtains. Golden sunlight flooded in, washing over her. She stood in its comforting warmth, feeling it soothing away her tension as she waited for the next hardening.

The garden below her looked serene and well-tended. Three fat woolly sheep grazed the grass round the house these days and did a better and friendlier job than the geese had done. She caught sight of Violet, wrapped in a red woollen shawl, crouched down beside a spread of herb beds, painstakingly weeding round the new shoots. She was going to be a tall girl – difficult, moody but still a striking-looking child with her straight strong features and warm olive skin – and those huge eyes which missed nothing. She had her mother's willowy build but Jess' air of quiet authority which made her seem older than her seven years.

Staring down at the child through the closed casement, Lavinia noticed an odd hazing between her and the window. She put out her hand to rub away the condensation with which the warmth of the room had pearled the glass. Under her hand the leaded pane remained cloudy as though steam was trapped within the very glass itself. She stared at it behind her hand for it was moving, curling and thickening as though a sea fog gathered outside. But there was no fog. Something infinite and opaque was between her and the window.

She shrank back as Violet's distant figure was blotted out in swirling mists – *inside* the casement – and yet the chamber was bright and clear, lit by the sunshine streaming in from the other end of the room. Lavinia backed away until the bed gave her support and she sat down on it, eyes glued to the milky haze at the west window. Her stomach hardened and she

265

crossed her arms over it, cradling the unborn child as something stirred within the mist, reaching out.

An appalling stench pervaded the air suddenly. A moment before, the room had been fresh with the faint scent of the lavender and rose leaves which sat in open bowls on each of the clothing chests. Now, between one drawn breath and the next, the purulent stench of horse manure and rancid flesh made her start up and run for her wash bowl, gagging at the disgusting odour which filled her lungs. Through the gathering mists she groped for the bell rope and tugged again and again, in a frenzy of fright, sobbing under her breath as the drumming of hooves behind her drowned the thunder of her own frantic heartbeats.

'Polly, come quick . . . Oh Polly, Polly . . .'

Jess was content to let Bolton Red set the pace and they settled into a steady loping canter, traversing the curving hill that fell away beneath their hooves, down to a winding stream far below. East Dean was behind them already and now they were heading south-east over the hump of the downs into the unkempt swathe of Selhurst forest. Ahead was the Richmond Mill up on Halnaker Hill and three cart tracks fanned out from that point to meet Stane Street and the highway traffic between Chichester and London.

Jess eased Midas into an effortless rhythm which he thought they might be able to keep up indefinitely. These hills were the only snag, for they were so steep that there was no point in trying to take them at speed. Midas leant against the reins, aching to be let go on the downhill leg but on this first part of the course and the last one between Goodwood and Charlton they would need all the restraint they could muster between them. The steepness of the hills was acute and already he was blowing, short-winded.

A hedge stretched out before them and Midas gathered himself joyously and took it with Jess tucked against his neck. They were down and streaking across scrub land towards the next incline before Bolton Red's hooves struck the ground behind them. Now the going was all up hill. Midas pounded over the short turf and Jess could feel the great reservoir of his strength as the hooves struck the earth with a crisp, unbroken thud. The light was improving all the time and the sun would be up before they were through the tangled undergrowth that almost obliterated the track. Jess began to ease back imperceptibly, letting Bolton Red pass him further up the slope. He allowed fifty yards to widen between them and watched the chestnut's rump slithering and sliding down a steep bank as the track curved left towards the green lift of Halnaker Hill. He let the chestnut disappear out of sight and then cut swiftly into the barely noticeable entrance of an overgrown ride that the yoggers had described the previous day. The going was rough.

Undergrowth tore at Midas' shining shoulders and the springy branches of young beeches whipped Jess' face. But the ride was there and his sharp eyes could pick out the growth of new saplings and bramble where, in years gone past, the charcoal men had cut timber in their slow progress through the woods. The question was: how much time – if any – would this short cut save him?

The cart track up to the windmill formed a wide sweep to the east before Bolton Red hit the path that led down towards Halnaker House. He and Manfri had made a rough estimate that it added over a mile to that leg of the course. The yoggers' map showed that this riding led onto a series of old deer trails that sharp Romani eyes would have no difficulty in following through to Halnaker Park. Then there was a flat open stretch across the front of the mansion where the marshalls would be waiting to check his passing.

He let Midas make his own pace but the horse sensed Jess' urgency and needed little encouragement to keep up a broken trot, with Jess ducking and cursing the whiplash of brambles and branches all round them. They slithered down steep slopes into thick carpets of dead leaves; clambered up banks of loose earth, thick with daffodils just past their blooming. Overhead the first haze of green growth softened the cave-like silence of the hollow woods, magnifying the song of nesting birds. At one point Midas nearly unseated Jess as a hog rose under his sliding hooves and crashed away from them squealing in alarm. They thrust their way through the corrugations of the forest floor and came onto a beaten track that wound away from them into pale stands of trees. They picked up more speed here and Jess was content to lie along Midas' back and let him have his head for he would go no further than his instincts allowed him.

They burst out suddenly into sunshine and Midas laid back his ears with a long snore in his nostrils, gathered himself under Jess – and streaked towards the distant house.

'Why can't I go and watch "Neeley" unloading?'

Lawrence's full lips set in a pout like two raw sausages and he scowled darkly at Amy, hoping that she would be too busy shortly to check that he intended creeping off to Dell Quay, whatever she had to say.

She cut short his hopes. 'As far as I am concerned, you can go where you please – that's if you are not going to your gran's with your mother,' she said curtly, peering into the iron pot that hung over the cooking fire, filled with water for upstairs. Small silver bubbles were just beginning to rise up in a necklace round the rim. 'Take your chalks and slate and do some copying from that book your Mama uses with you. You'd best stay in your room until the carriage is ready to take you both over to Fishbourne.'

He turned away from her and picked up the slate and the little tin of chalks from their place on the kitchen dresser.

'I'll be up to see that you are doing as you're told.' Amy's parting shot floated up the stairs behind him.

'I'd like to flame her,' he thought and sucked in his breath at such wickedness. He hesitated outside his parent's chamber door. The oak panelling was stout but he could hear the murmur of voices within.

He knocked softly. He could hear Polly's voice. Poor Mama was a captive there in her chamber and would be forced to listen to all the tittle tattle of Birdham and Itchenor. Foolish hen cackle, Dadrus called Polly's gossip. He knocked again, fisting his small knuckles to beat on the door. It opened and Polly stuck her head out.

'Well, young Master, what's to do?'

'Please, I want to see my Mama.'

She shook her head. 'Not now, dear. Your Mama is getten'

dressed. You can see her later when she's ready to ride in the carriage.'

He straightened his back and stuck his chin out at her stubbornly. '. . . but I *wish* to see her . . . I always sit with her in the mornings. I haven't seen her for a long, long time . . . I want to see Mama . . .'

He raised his voice, trying to peer past her into the room but Polly's burgeoning bulk filled the doorway.

Behind her he heard his mother's voice. 'Let him come in just for a minute. Just to say good morning . . .'

He dived under Polly's muscular arm and ran joyously across the room to the partially-curtained bed and climbed up one of the end posts as he always did in the mornings. She was half-dressed and came over to give him a kiss, running her fingers through his golden curls.

'Oh Mama,' he said happily, 'I'm so glad to see you this morning. You were indisposed yesterday so they wouldn't let me say goodnight to you. I went with Uncle John to see Gran yesterday afternoon and she can't walk at all. She has two sticks with silver knobs from the Indies. She told me so. Mama, do you know what Unc . . .'

Hands scooped him up and deposited him firmly on the carpet. 'Now don't you go crawlen' all over your Mama's clean gowns,' Polly said crossly. 'Violet, love – give me that stomacher with the blue rosettes on it.'

In his delight he had not noticed Violet – but there she was, curled up against the carved bed post close to Lavinia's large travelling valise. He glared at her as she obediently handed over the folded garment from the pile on the bed. He pushed past her and pressed up close to Lavinia who smiled at him lovingly and patted his cheek. All colour had left her, leaving her the face of a weary, red-eyed stranger but the warm mother smell was the same and he snuggled against her, letting her put her arms round him. She felt very hot and yet she shivered now and then.

'I missed you, Mama. I wanted to tell you yesterday about my visit to Fishbourne with Uncle John – but they wouldn't let me see you to say goodnight. Why are we going to Gran this week? Is the new baby coming now? Is it going to be born like the foals, Mama? Is it in a bag like they are?'

Her face seemed to tremble and suddenly set stiffly and she gripped his hand so hard that her nails dug into his soft flesh. He opened his mouth to protest – and saw that her eyes were closed.

'That's enough, young man. Can't you see your poor Mama is not too well today? Away with ye – there's a good boy.'

Polly prized his hand loose from his mother's grip and shooed him out of the room. He backed off obediently, staring at his mother's rigid figure. She looked so tender; like a young girl not long out of the schoolroom herself. How could anyone inflict such suffering on her?

There was a small crowd gathered on the terrace in front of Halnaker House. Someone saw Jess and a thin cheer went up. Hands waved excitedly and the whole group moved as though a wind had gone through it. He urged Midas forward, seeing no other rider in the vicinity but keeping his eyes focused directly in front of him. Now he was off the grass, scattering a pack of house dogs that came tearing out of the open front door to leap, snapping at the horse's heels as they cantered across the gravelled forecourt of the old house. Out of the corner of his eye he spied movement among the trees on the other side of the park and as Bolton Red came hurtling down the Mill path a long way behind him, he snatched his hat from his head and doffed it as he passed Lady Derby, sending up a scatter of loose gravel as he went. Then Halnaker was behind him and they were heading swiftly and easily down the drive, between stands of black cypresses. Far behind him he heard shouts of encouragement and knew that Steele and Bolton Red, followed by a motley straggle of mounted supporters were thundering down the drive and closing the one advantage he would be able to take from them. He gave Midas a sharp thwack with the flat of his hand and the golden horse stretched under his knees, surging forward as Jess turned him off the pitted drive and across the park again, scattering sheep as they went. This was the flattest part of the course, with only the gentlest of inclines as they skirted the lower slopes of the downland range. At this point, most of the woods had long been cleared all the way up the hillside, for the soil was rich and the Duke an enthusiastic experimental farmer. Fifty acre fields stretched from Halnaker through Goodwood and along the valleys between the hills as far as Petersfield. It was prime country and ground over which Midas had trained all his life. He dipped his head and streamed away, the wind beneath his docked tail.

They were ready. The carriage crunched and rumbled across the gravel to the front door and Rueb leapt down from the buckboard seat and looped the reins into a wall ring. He opened the door in readiness for his two passengers and leaned inside to give the leather-padded seats a final wipe with his sleeve.

'Hey, Rueben, will you take the boxes down now,' Polly called from the upper gallery. He went up awkwardly, wiping his hands on either side of his breeches. He had never been in Jess' bed chamber before – never been in any Kenner bed chamber and his embarrassment was intense.

Lavinia was sitting in her chair dressed in her best blue travelling cloak. He noticed the moist pallor making the skin of her oval face shine damply.

'Mornen' Miss Linnie.' He touched his finger to his forehead and bobbed his head shyly as she smiled her greeting. The cradle and boxes looked as though she would be gone for a while, he thought uneasily. 'Can't blame the poor rawni either for this is a terrible house. You c'n feel the waiting . . . the watching . . . the angry mullos gathering.' He hefted the largest box up onto his shoulder and lost no time in taking it down to the carriage.

'I'll just see that young Lawrence is ready, M'm,' Polly said to Lavinia. She hesitated and put a hand shyly on Lavinia's shoulder.

'We'll miss you, Manfri and I, M'm,' she said. 'The house is kind of gloomy when you are out of it. I know that sounds silly – and I expect it is at that, but I shall be a lot happier, myself, when you are back with us.'

They regarded each other with the affection that had grown

easily between them in the six years that they had been mistress and maid. Lavinia patted Polly's hand.

'I won't be gone long, Poll. I hope very much to be back here by the time you start your own confinement and then I shall spoil you in the way that you have always cared for me. By then, we shall have a house full of children to keep us busy and there won't be time to think of mullos and things . . .'

Polly knew – without ever having seen or heard any of the things with which the house taunted Lavinia – of the indefinable menace which pervaded the whole atmosphere of the house. Had she been gypsy, Lavinia thought, she would probably have been even more conscious of the shadows and odours and unexplained sounds which had followed her down the years. Rueb heard them. She had watched the solidness of his craggy face turn furtive and uneasy as he came up into the bed chamber. Manfri knew also for he had referred to the unpleasant atmosphere more than once.

It wasn't simply the disordered imaginings of an overanxious mind. They all knew.

Lavinia stood up and began to pace. 'Quickly, quickly . . . Why is Rueb so long?'

'Is Lawrence ready?' she asked breathlessly as Polly came back into the room.

Polly patted her arm. 'Don't 'e fret, Miss Linnie. Master Lawrence is so keen to get to his Gran's that he's already downstairs and sitten' in the carriage since it came to the door.'

Lavinia resumed her pacing while Polly tied down the last of the bags and lumbered heavily to her feet with a deep sigh.

'Oh Polly, aren't I selfish,' Lavinia said, suddenly aware that Polly's own time was only four weeks away. The girl grinned at her, brushing her apron straight.

' 'Cause you aren't, M'm. You're a dear lady an' the best young mistress a girl ever had. Won't be the same here without you singen' around the place and cheeren' us all up.'

There was a suggestion of moisture in her eyes and she blinked it away as Rueb clumped through the door for the last bags.

'That's all, mistress?' She nodded.

Polly followed Rueb out of the room and her voice echoed up the stairs, calling to Lawrence.

Lavinia stood in the middle of the room. It was a cold day but quite bright. The mist had gone from the place and might never have been . . . 'Oh, God . . . how I wish we lived somewhere else. That I might never need to come back to this terrible house.' She straightened her back, trying to clear the fright from her mind. She looked about the pretty room with its chintz curtains and bowls of pot pourri on gleaming tables. It was the essence of home, of her life with Jess – and yet the urge to run from the place and put it behind her was over-powering. There was something very wrong.

Even as the thought occurred to her, she felt the familiar dread of pounding vibrations closing in on her. The neat colourful room slowly drained itself of colour and familiarity and she was standing among strangers in a coldly pulsing wilderness. The room wavered and trembled beneath her feet and then it was there, curling about her in noxious waves that brought the bile up into her throat. The stench of the horse . . .

She could hear her heart thudding – or was it the thunder of hooves down a thousand years? The light was changing, a faint glow of orange seeping into the shadows – and with it came the beginnings of the heat.

She moved. She forced her leaden limbs to carry her out of that place and away from the thing that stretched out to take her, to stamp upon her and grind the child within her to pulp. She ran headlong out of the door, unaware of anything but the hideous odour reaching out of that following presence.

She ran – and then there was nothing beneath her feet and only the impact of blows upon her body. The pain was almost welcome when it came for it was, at least something finite, onto which she could hang. She ground her teeth into the reality of agony and allowed her body to drift away.

Violet squeezed out a cloth dipped in warm lavender water and wiped Lavinia's face. It was important not to show her alarm so she made herself as small as possible in her corner beside the bed and willed the whole process to come to a conclusion soon.

Lavinia fretted in the big bed, sometimes aware of her surroundings – and at others, away in some fevered world of her own which seemed to fill her with a fear so formidable that

273

it set the two women shaking their heads. Polly's shock had been so great when Lavinia had suddenly come screaming out of the upper chamber and fallen headlong down the stairs, that she had had to sit down on the bottom stair while Rueb carried the poor mistress back up to her bed. He was long gone now, racing Glimmer across the common to fetch Doctor Sanden and then on up to Charlton to get the message to Manfri and Jess. Who are we to take care of the poor young thing? A pregnant woman and a lame epileptic. Thank the Lord for little Violet's calm obedience.

Lavinia's eyes opened, the blue, unfocused gaze like dull stars in her flushed face. Polly watched as Violet wiped the moisture from her aunt's forehead and then held her hand tightly as another pain worked its way through her. The contractions had been going very strongly for nearly two hours and Lavinia looked too exhausted for many more. Where *was* Doctor Sanden?

'Stay with 'r, dear. I'll be back in a few moments,' Polly said to Violet and beckoned Amy out of the chamber into the gallery.

'Mistress, we've got to fetch Mistress Whittle. Rueb be gone and I can't run quick enough in my state. Will you go up to New Barn and get one of the Lawrences to go for her?'

Amy nodded and drifted away.

'Quickly, Mistress, please,' Polly called after her.

Violet sat beside Lavinia with her damp cloth on the hot forehead.

She watched the next pain begin. With the onset of the contraction Lavinia's eyes rolled upward and she floated away into her other place. She threshed the upper part of her body as though trying to free herself from something.

Without warning, Violet felt the Power heat through her. It was different . . . engulfing her in a great tidal wave of pure force. It was oddly uncertain of direction, and had an oily quality which threatened the deadliness of her own power but was somehow blind – without direction.

She sat very still, concentrating . . . trying to identify it and discovering that the lethal feeling hung over them all in the room like a swinging sword which might drop down on any one of them.

Lavinia cried out and Polly came swiftly back into the chamber, the worry turning her plain good humoured face into a stiff mask. 'Violet . . . I just can't trust yer Mama to get help for the mistress. She might have a turn on the way . . . Go quickly to New Barn and get someone to ride over for Mistress Whittle.'

Violet hesitated. She recognized the wisdom in Polly's words but she couldn't leave now. She must stay close to Lavinia to beat off the thing that was poised to strike. She hesitated, searching for words. Polly lunged forward, twitched her off her stool and pushed her towards the door.

'Don't just stand there . . . *run*.'

Violet ran.

By the time the entrance to Goodwood was in sight, Midas was blowing hard. There was an ache across Jess' shoulders that seemed to tear into him with every jarring movement. Midas took a hedge on the wrong foot, timing his jump awkwardly and throwing Jess upwards, nearly unseating him. He came down just short of the lip of the ditch on the far side of the hedge and sank to his knees. For a split second, horse and rider teetered on the edge of balance before Midas righted himself and scrambled onto the flat grass. They both became aware of the thunder of hooves behind them at the same moment. Midas laid his ears back and set off, pounding over the turf to try and shorten the curve of the approach drive to the main entrance.

They skirted the front of the sprawling old house, scarcely noticing the flutter of red kerchief which heralded his approach, for Bolton Red was behind him, the horse's breath rattling close to Midas's straining flank. As they veered away from the building and headed off through the north end of the Park, Bolton Red inched ahead. They rode close together now, the squeak of leather and snorting breaths intermingling with the jingle of bridles and stirrup irons and the winded encouragements of the riders. Midas stretched his neck to get the last inch out of himself. He was a hand shorter than Red but his wind sounded stronger and he was not labouring quite as hard as his opponent. Steele lay against his mount's damp neck, his bright green and yellow shirt spattered with mud and perspiration. The ground was rising steadily ahead of them and the smooth breast of St Rook's Hill reared up sharply, cresting over to their left and crowned with the ruined chapel of Saint Roc, some two hundred feet above them.

It was the same place and the same horror. The terror and confusion in her mind, the agony that was not her labour. She was tossed and whipped in the maelstrom and rain lashed across her body, stinging her face and dragging her hair back in rats' tails. The horse stench was bile in her throat and she could hear the frantic drumming of the creature's hooves, kicking and lashing against the broken pillar which imprisoned it.

No one would hear her cries for help . . . for the building was too remote in the heart of the woods, as was fitting. The roof timbers had fallen in without warning.

'Oh mother, forgive my sins and deliver me from this pain . . . What's the use? They have surely forsaken me. How did I offend?'

Movement tore through her, jerking her knees up as the breath was slammed out of her.

Lawrence sat in the window of his chamber, staring out over the fields towards Rymans. The room was on the wrong side of the house for him to be able to watch his beloved boats going up and down the creek. Maybe not for much longer though. Dadrus had told Mama just the other day that Salterns Cottage was to be completed before the winter, so that meant that Aunt Amy and Violet would really be gone from Lavenham in less than five months. Then he would have their chamber – and would be able to see every ship and lighter that plied up and down past the west front.

Amy would no longer be there to snap at every move he made and Violet – Violet would not be around every corner to taunt him, using the Power to tease him to prove that hers was stronger than his. Well, it might be at this moment but he was exercising himself – stretching the depth of his contact. When he was as old as Violet, he would be as strong as she was. She might have stronger Power to flame things but she had never had his birth nightmare.

She had been born in the waggon belonging to Piramis and Sarey. But he had lived with the memory of his journey into life for as long as he could remember. Nowadays it was not as frightening as it had been when he was a little boy. Now he even found it comforting in a certain way, since he had had plenty of time to mull it over in his mind. It had finally occurred to him that it could not hurt him and that he was alive and strong and had survived the horror of it without scarring. It suddenly came to him that this unknown child was embarking upon the same journey at this moment. 'I wonder if it will remember too . . .'

Sitting in his favorite spot in the window, he could see right across the fields. The turret of Rymans and the little wooden bell tower on Saint Mary's church roof rose distantly out of a misty line of trees. The land was quite flat and open and it was possible to see any visitor to Lavenham from the moment he turned off Salterns Lane into the Lavenham drive. If he was not allowed to be with Mama, at least he would be the first to know when Dadrus and Manfri returned, so that he could race down and tell them that Mama had fallen head over heels all the way down the stairs, from the very top to the very bottom. She had banged her head and her tum and now her baby was coming. He fidgeted, feeling the ululations of her growing distress begin to seep into his veins.

Blood pounded in Jess' head. Progress was slow as the horses struggled up the almost vertical incline. A hare loped away from them and disappeared into a mess of gorse. The horses rattled and blew, their tired legs trembling and slipping on the slope.

Bolton Red was half a length ahead. Jess scarcely heard Steele's husky urgings, saving his own breath and gentling Midas with his knees. The going had slackened to a snail's pace. As the ever-distant rim of the hill cut across Jess' vision, Midas saw it too and seemed to generate an extra burst of energy and was suddenly pressing up close to Bolton Red – and then they were cresting the hill and feeling the swift scour of March wind cutting them and the sun on their faces.

Jess' hat tilted and lifted, scooped off his head by a mischievous gust that carried it, bowling into the air and away from them along the hill top. Then they were racing downwards, towards the distant stream at the base of the hill, winding its uncaring way across their path before disappearing into trees on their right. The incline steepened and Jess sat well back in the saddle to correct Midas' balance as they slithered and bumped, parallel with Bolton Red. Without warning, the chestnut faltered and in a moment was down, body twisting and kicking as momentum continued to carry him on past his rider who had leapt clear. Jess glanced over his shoulder as he drew away from the flailing horse and, seeing Steele pick himself up, gave the rest of his attention to getting himself and Midas safely down into the narrow valley below them.

He felt as though they had been riding all day but the sun was just clearing the trees across to the right. The tension in both of them eased without the sight of the other horse forever ahead of them and Midas slowed to a walking pace, picking his way daintily over grassy hummocks and hidden rabbit burrows. It took another ten minutes to reach the floor of the little valley. The brook was shallow here but steep-sided and altogether too wide to jump. Jess rode down to the edge of the bank and then, realizing that it was too steep to slither down, roved along the south side until they found a place where it had crumbled away into the water. As they went down its loose side and splashed across to the flatter northern bank, they heard the chestnut coming down behind them. Jess didn't risk a look until they were across the stream and tackling the rising ground beyond. Steele was hard on their heels, miraculously little time lost from his fall, and urging the mud-spattered horse down the hill in a clever zigzagging movement.

Jess drove his heels into Midas' heaving sides. By following the stream along the floor of the valley he reasoned that he would not have to climb back up the hill until it took a sharp turn away from the direction of Charlton. By that time they had made a gradual ascent and there only remained a light gradient before the crest of the last ridge came into view. Bolton Red was climbing out of the stream as Midas reached the top of the hill. Below, a line of foothills broke to left and right – fringed by the inevitable straggle of woodland. The ground dropped sharply and slid into undulations of winter corn which lapped the scatter of buildings and stabling that was the Finish.

Jess straightened his aching shoulders. He seemed to have got his second wind for the ache in them was happily less. Midas sensed the nearness of the stables and strained forward. They plummeted downwards off the bare hillside, traversing sharply. Midas' exhaustion showed in his stiffening muscle movements and heaving lungs but at no point did he slacken his pace. He loped and slithered, blowing flatly, sweat creaming round the edges of the saddle leathers and dropping in frothy bubbles from his bit. Pebbles waterfalled across their path and Jess looked up to see Bolton Red on the hill above them, plunging downwards with Steele lashing the horse's flanks with his whip.

'Not long now, my kushti grai (good horse),' he muttered to Midas, patting the heaving sides. 'There they are, the Charlton stables . . . Just keep our lead the way it is, Bor. There's a good clean stall for you and a rub down and a good drink down there . . . so keep going, Bor . . . just keep going.'

Sunshine warmed the earth, stirring the juices in the growing things. Midas seemed to get the scent of his promised hay bag and his ears sent signals, pricking and pivoting and they followed the cleft between two corn fields. Bolton Red snorted down the slope behind them, total weariness in the dull beat of his hooves against the hillside. The ground opened out ahead and a path led between a long tythe barn and the main stable block. Jess dug in his heels as he sensed the chestnut narrowing the gap between them. Midas plodded on, ignoring commands.

'Get on, damn you.' Jess dug heels in viciously, the sharp edges of his riding boots cutting the tightly stretched skin across Midas' ribs. He snorted with shock. He had never had a hand lifted in anger against him and the sudden pain in his ribs sent the adrenalin pumping through him. Head down, he dragged himself together and broke into a ragged canter, spurred on further by the sound of Bolton Red's whistling breath not ten yards behind him.

They passed a blur of colour and thundered onwards before Jess' mind registered that it had been the finishing line – he released the iron vice of his knee grip and brought the reins sharply against his chest. Midas checked and slowed, his movements becoming lumpy.

Jess took several deep breaths to get his pumping heart back to a more comfortable beat and then turned Midas and walked him quietly back towards the cheering crowd.

The light was brighter in the room, as though they had pulled back all the curtains. Voices murmured softly and hands moved her legs.

'The poor lady, she really has taken a bad fall,' Doctor Sanden's kindly voice said beside her.

She tried to smile her thanks at his red, comic face with its bushy clown's eyebrows but her body seemed to belong to someone else and nothing responded to her efforts.

'She always said that this house didn't like her having children.' Polly sounded tearful, as though she, too, was on the verge of breaking down.

'Every time she's with child there's some kind of tragedy. Oh, I'll never get that picture of her out of my mind, Doctor. She came screamen' out of this chamber as though all the devils in hell were at her heels and she just seemed to jump into the air instead of coming down the stairs . . . She rolled over and over – it's a miracle that more bones weren't broken – but her poor head . . .'

'Dear, loving Polly. Hang onto your baby. Don't let this hurt you as it has hurt me.'

Thunder in her head. Thunder without lightning. No – it was some part of her body bursting . . . in the head? The violent explosion raked her and she cried out, for the child was tearing itself from her and kicking, ramming its way out into the world. The shadows closed in on her. She saw the face of the Watcher emerging at last from the mists, to peer down at her agony.

It was strange, she thought, as the abyss rose up to claim her, all power spent. It was strange that there was an expression of infinite regret and even grief in the depth of his grey eyes.

The child, a girl, was born too small and bruised by Lavinia's fall, for survival. She died within minutes of her birth. Mistress Whittle wrapped a cloth hastily round the little body and handed it to Amy who stood by, mute and frozen. She put the bundle into the crib and returned to where Mistress Whittle peered over the little doctor's shoulder.

'Bleeding's stopping,' she said, relieved.

He straightened his back and drew the covers over Lavinia's legs, felt her pulse and put his head down on the quiet mound of her chest. The two women stared at him as they watched him lift an eyelid – press his cheek to her mouth.

'I'm sorry,' he said, getting up off his knees and dusting his breeches. 'I'm afraid that fall was too much for her, poor lady. There is internal damage, both in her head and in her body. I'm afraid she is dead.'

Amy closed the door of her chamber and stood against it, feeling the smooth silken surface of the polished wood with her hands.

'My door . . . my chamber,' she said to herself with fierce joy, for now there would be no move to the cottage on the muddy highway. Now Jess would need her again, just as he had needed her when first this house was built.

She gripped her arms tightly across her chest and hugged herself until her ribs hurt.

'Amy will care for you, my Kushti Chal . . . Amy is all you need. Take your women in the taverns and the fields, Bor, but Amy is here to see to everything for you . . .'

A laugh bubbled up in her throat and she sank down onto the floor as her body began its puppet jerking. She lay on her back and the laughter tore up from the pleasure in her heart, melding with the spasms. She stared at the ceiling, seeing the reflection there of that other still face across the upper gallery and she spat at it with all the venom of the victor and allowed the seizure to take her into oblivion.

The Watcher turned from the bed, engulfed in an anguish of sadness. How beautiful she had been in life. There was no guilt in her, no sin as there was in him – and yet he had had to erase her for she would have produced evil had she been permitted to live. He observed Amy, thrashing and twisting alone in her chamber and withdrew, locked in the revulsion of recognition of that same triumph in his own soul.

Violet stood outside the door of Lawrence's chamber. She opened it softly and peeped in. He was sitting curled up in the window seat, staring out at the sprawl of bare trees that hid the entrance to the drive.

'They're dead . . . both of them.' She spoke sharply, getting an empty kind of comfort from the flat statement – for pain was almost too good a punishment for him. He looked such a good little boy, sitting there with his golden curls shining in the fading light. How could such innocence compound the taking of life? Of his own mother's life?

'I know . . . I felt it all . . . it was like my dream but Mama was all right then. I felt something horrible reach out – and then she went, and the baby too . . .'

Violet inched in through the door and closed it behind her. She stood with her back against it, looking at him.

'We didn't want that baby . . . or her either – but at least I would not have done that to her. You disobeyed Dada, you know that?'

He turned his head then and the light made snail trails of the tears on his cheeks.

'I know you didn't want Mama or the new baby. You don't want any of us – except for Dadrus . . . You don't want me either – but you won't find me so easy to flame.'

The Power blossomed from him without warning, the force waves so strong that they were visible – like the petals of a great red poppy.

Violet recoiled, slammed hard against the door as the shock struck her. The shield went up round her but she could feel him draining her, bleeding her.

Pleasure erupted, pouring through her and turning the whole world golden again. She smiled at Lawrence and held out her hands to him.

'Oh, yes – I do, Lawrence . . . I didn't realize. I really do.'

Bibliography

A Duke and His Friends, Vol 1	The Earl of March
A History of Sussex	J.R. Armstrong
Bees and Mankind	J.B. Free
Encyclopedia of the Horse	E.H. Edwards
Gypsies, The Secret People	G.E.C. Webb
Handbook of English Costume in the 18th Century	C.W. & Phyllis Cunnington
Ill Gotten Gains	Mark Bullen
In the Life of a Romany Gypsy	Manfri Wood
Place names of Sussex, Vol 1	Mawer/Stenton
Records of Chichester	T.G. Willis
Something to Declare	Graham Smith
Smugglers & Revenue Officers in the Portsmouth Area in the 18th Century	Edward Carson (Portsmouth Papers.)
The Agricultural Revolution 1750–1880	Chambers/Mingay
The Birds of Sussex	Michael Shrubb
The English Yeoman	Mildred Campbell
The Feminine Monarchy	Dr C. Butler
The Gentleman's Magazine 1792	

Trends in 18th Century Smuggling   W. A. Cole

The History of Steeple-Chasing   Seth-Smith/Mortimer/
Lawrence

The Lost Gods of England   Brian Branston

The Universal British Directory   P. Barfoot/J. Wilkes